E. K. Miller

Reminiscences of Forty-Seven Years' Clerical Life in South Australia

E. K. Miller

Reminiscences of Forty-Seven Years' Clerical Life in South Australia

ISBN/EAN: 9783337313739

Printed in Europe, USA, Canada, Australia, Japan

Cover: Foto ©Andreas Hilbeck / pixelio.de

More available books at **www.hansebooks.com**

REMINISCENCES

OF

FORTY-SEVEN YEARS' CLERICAL LIFE

IN

SOUTH AUSTRALIA

BY THE

REV. E. K. MILLER.

*Twelve Years Incumbent of St. George's, Woodforde, and St. Martin's,
Campbelltown;
also,
Twenty-Nine Years Incumbent of St. Stephen's, Willunga, St. Philip
and St. James', Noarlunga, and St. Ann's, Aldinga.*

Adelaide:
A. H. ROBERTS, 131 King William Street.
1895.

𝔇𝔢𝔡𝔦𝔠𝔞𝔱𝔢𝔡

TO THE

MEMBERS OF THE CHURCH OF ENGLAND

IN

SOUTH AUSTRALIA,

BY THEIR HUMBLE SERVANT,

E. K. MILLER.

PREFACE.

THERE being, so far as I am aware, no concise account published of the early efforts to establish a branch of the Church of England in South Australia other than is contained in " Annals of the Diocese of Adelaide," published in 1852, long out of print, and Canon Whitington's " Life of Bishop Short" (to which this is designed as a companion volume), I have thought it well to give in connection with these Reminiscences a brief outline of those efforts, so far as my own observation and experience enable me.

The memoranda referring to my own work are given with the view of illustrating the actualities of mission-ary life. Work and incidents kindred to those herein recorded, fell to the lot of most of the pioneer clergy, and I regard mine as having been in nowise an exceptional experience.

I quite expect that some things I have recorded, quotations I have given, and opinions I have ex-pressed, will be adversely criticised. It is not within the limits of probability that all others will view all things spoken of precisely as I view them—and some may be displeased. Of course I should regret this; but the present position of the Church, and my sense of duty to the Church, appear to me to call for "great plainness of speech."

A principal object being to supply information to the younger clergy and others, I have given details concerning sundry matters well nigh forgotten, but which have had, and yet may have, an important bearing on the position of the Church in the colony; also drawing attention to certain dangers to which it has become exposed, and from which it has suffered, and is still suffering.

Bishop Short—who always spoke of himself as a "high churchman"—and his original coadjutors sought to establish a Church here on the principles of, and adopted the manner of service of, the National Church in England, and so long as those principles and manner of service were adhered to, the Church prospered; but directly they were in any material degree departed from, or thought so to be, suspicion became engendered and trouble ensued.

Having been compelled, in the first instance, to remove from Adelaide under medical advice, on account of my children's health, and ever since occupying country cures, I had no opportunity till after my retirement of becoming personally acquainted with the great divergence from the original principles and manner of service that obtains in some of our Churches. The result of such divergences I have endeavoured to point out; and if anything herein contained should have the effect of calling the attention of the members of the Church thereto, especially the clergy, and lead to the adoption of remedial measures, and the more thorough establishment of the Church in the colony, my object in penning these Reminiscences will have been accomplished.

E. K. MILLER.

KENSINGTON PARK, S.A.
APRIL 1895.

CONTENTS.

REMINISCENCES

OF

FORTY-SEVEN YEARS' CLERICAL LIFE

IN SOUTH AUSTRALIA.

—•—

CHAPTER I.

PRELIMINARY INCIDENTS.

IT having been suggested to me to jot down a few incidents connected with the earlier efforts to establish the services of the Church of England in South Australia, I have concluded to do so, and will commence by stating how I came to be connected with that important work.

While engaged as Sunday-school teacher and district visitor at St. Peter's, Walworth, near London, under the ministry of the Rev. J. Irons, and afterwards the Rev. G. Ainslie, I became deeply interested in the published reports of missionary work then going on, especially in the account by the Rev. John Williams of those labours in the South Seas which issued in his martyrdom, and conceived an ardent desire to engage in such work. My parents being dead, and having no friends who could aid me, I decided on engaging in tuition that I might have more opportunity

for study ; I had been for some time reading Latin and
Greek, under a private tutor, with a view to the ministry.
Further, deeming it desirable to become acquainted with
some definite school system, I entered the Training School
of the British and Foreign School Society in the Borough
Road, continuing there several months.   One day, during
a lecture by Mr. Saunders, one of the tutors, Mr. Dunn,
secretary to the Society, entered the room with another
gentleman who seemed to take much interest in what was
going on.   On their withdrawal, I was sent for, and
introduced to the late Earl Fitzwilliam.   His Lordship
inquired whether I was willing to go to Yorkshire, to fit
up and organise a school he was having built at Park
Gate, near Rotherham.   Of course I gladly consented, and
shortly after found myself an inmate of Wentworth
House, pending completion of the school and residence.
While there I became acquainted with the Rev. J. Upton,
chaplain to the Earl, and incumbent of Wentworth, who,
on learning my ultimate design, proved most kind and
helpful.

In a few weeks 1 took possession of my school and house,
which had been comfortably furnished for me, and soon
had a good attendance of children, in the discipline and
teaching of whom the Earl and members of his family took
the keenest interest, paying frequent visits.   Park Gate
being about midway between the churches of Rawmash
and Greasbro', I attached myself to the latter ; the
incumbent, the Rev. F. Hall, soon placing me in charge of
the Sunday-school, as superintendent, and getting me to
read lessons in the church, and act as district visitor.

Shortly after my arrival there, I had the especial good
fortune to become acquainted with the Rev. J. Aldred,
curate of Wath, who most kindly volunteered to give me

what assistance he could, allowing me to visit him every Saturday and helping me very much in my studies. The Rev. F. Hall also offered me a title for holy orders, wishing me to become his curate. I continued this teaching and studying about four years, my idea being, to obtain ordination, serve a short time at home, and then engage in missionary work.

While thus occupied, news arrived in England that there was but one clergyman in the newly-established colony of South Australia, and an appeal was made by the Society for the Propagation of the Gospel for clergymen willing to go there. This led the Rev. W. J. Woodcock and the Rev. Jas. Pollitt, formerly missionaries of the Church Missionary Society, but invalided home, and then holding small livings in Westmoreland, to offer their services, which, being accepted, they reached the colony early in 1846 to join the Rev. Jas. Farrell, colonial chaplain, whose predecessor and for a time coadjutor, the Rev. C. B. Howard, had died in 1843. Afterwards, Colonel Gawler, who had returned to England from the Governorship of South Australia, was anxious that a clergyman should be sent to the town of Gawler, just before established. For this service my early friend and companion, Mr. W. H. Coombs, volunteered, he having commenced reading for holy orders with the Rev. W. J. Woodcock, and being then at St. Bees' College; this offer being accepted, he was ordained deacon by the Bishop of London, arriving in Gawler at the end of 1846, of which place he is still incumbent. Shortly after reaching his cure, he wrote me to the effect that more clergy were urgently needed. The Rev. J. Pollitt, whom I had met just before his sailing, at a missionary meeting at Rotherham, had also urged me to at once enter the mission-field; therefore, when Mr. Coombs' letter arrived, I decided so to do, and wrote the Rev. E. Hawkins, secretary to the S.P.G., accordingly. A month or two after this correspondence commenced he wrote to say that through the liberality of Miss Burdet Coutts, funds for the establishment of a Bishopric in South Australia had been provided, and that the Rev. A. Short having been designated to the See, he had forwarded our correspondence to him. This was quickly followed by an invitation from Mr. Short to his vicarage at Ravensthorpe, in Northamptonshire, where I spent a few very pleasant days. It was arranged that I should be ordained at once by his cousin, the Bishop of St. Asaph, and sail with himself and four others then being selected. Subsequently—probably through a desire to commence episcopal functions soon after reaching his diocese—the Bishop wished me to defer ordination till after arrival at Adelaide, to which I reluctantly consented. The special work the Bishop wished me to undertake was, the organising and supervising church schools, combined with such clerical duty as might prove practicable. The Rev. T. P. Wilson was likewise engaged to open a collegiate or grammar school in conjunction with ministerial work, none of us then knowing anything as to the educational requirements or arrangements of South Australia. The Bishop also selected the Rev. M. B. Hale as his archdeacon, who afterwards became the first Bishop of Perth, the Rev. J. Bagshawe, the Rev. A. B. Burnett, and Mr. J. Fulford, a candidate like myself for holy orders. Opportunity offering for Mr. Bagshawe to go out as religious instructor in an emigrant ship, he was the first to leave, in the *Northumberland*, the Bishop and four others sailing in the *Derwent* in October, and arriving on December 28th, 1847. I, not being able to leave quite so soon, the Bishop arranged with his brother, Colonel Short, to select a ship and see me off, which he kindly undertook to do, and from that gentleman and his family I received every kindness and attention during the weeks I was in London prior to sailing. The S.P.C.K. also kindly made me a grant of sundry valuable works.

CHAPTER II.

EMBARKATION, AND BEATING DOWN CHANNEL.

ON reaching London I found Colonel Short had selected the *Enmore*, a barque of about 350 tons, for me as the earliest vessel for Port Adelaide. On visiting her, however, I found she had been built with a flush deck, and had had a poop added afterwards, so high and narrow that I felt sure it would be almost unusable, while there was only a lower stern cabin I could have. Not liking the ship or the accommodation offered, I succeeded in finding another, the *Hindoo*, a strong teak-built barque, about the same tonnage, which was to sail a week or two later. A comfortable stern cabin in the poop being offered, I engaged it, and commenced fitting up for a probable three months' voyage. Having completed all arrangements, including the trifling matter of taking to myself a wife, after many delays as to date of sailing, we joined the ship on November 23rd, 1847, and next morning hauled out of the London docks, being towed to Gravesend, where we anchored for the night, and to take in live stock. My wife being exceedingly timid as to gunpowder forming part of the cargo, we had inquired about it before taking passage, and were assured there was none on board except a little for ship's use if required, and this was strictly true then. When passing Deptford, however, a lugger hooked on alongside, from which a number of small casks, that I felt sure contained gun-

powder, were handed up and quickly stowed below; but it was too late then to ask questions, so I asked none, and my wife was not alarmed. At Gravesend another cabin passenger came on board in a somewhat peculiar fashion; being too much under the influence of liquor to get up the gangway ladder, he was hoisted in by a rope round his waist like a bale of goods, a poor augury for our comfort. Our party in the cabin then consisted of an elderly gentleman going out as merchant, who occupied the adjoining stern cabin; his nephew; the inebriate who had held, he said, a commission in the army; a medical student, who had failed to get his diploma, and was engaged as ship's doctor; the captain, chief mate and ourselves. Our captain was quite a young man, about 22, and this was his first command. He had, as chief mate on the previous voyage, brought the ship home from Batavia, where her former captain had died—and, being related to the owner, was appointed to succeed him. In the intermediate and steerage there were about sixty other passengers, including children. Among these, to my surprise, was a clergyman with a wife and eleven children, of whom the Bishop knew nothing.

Weighing anchor on the 25th, we soon got into what the sailors called " lumpy water," sea-sickness becoming the fashion, though I did not suffer. Passing the North Foreland, we met a vessel in tow of a steamer without a mast or spar left standing. Our captain, desirous of ascertaining the name of the unfortunate, steered close enough to read *Enmore* on her stern; and thankful were we at having escaped being among her passengers; she had evidently been dismasted somewhere down Channel, and was returning to London to refit. On reaching the Downs and discharging the pilot, we had to anchor, the wind being ahead. On Sunday I suggested to the captain that as a clergyman was on board, he should be asked to conduct divine service, rather than myself; this was done, he and his wife dining afterwards in the cabin. A fair wind springing up after three days, we weighed anchor with about a hundred other vessels that had collected, and a more interesting sight could scarcely be conceived than so many craft of all sorts and sizes making sail in the bright sunshine of a cold December morning. During the day they became considerably scattered; but at night the wind again drew ahead, and all were tacking—with so many in company this was rather risky. It happened fortunately to be moonlight; but this did not prevent our ship running into the main chains of another, which was plainly visible a mile off; I could only attribute this to gross carelessness. Being borne down considerably, the stranger's captain called out for our boats to be lowered, which was not done. Presently the vessels separated, our headsails and jibboom gone, the stranger's side much damaged and mainsail carried away. The wind freshening, and continuing contrary, we ran back to the Downs, where next morning we saw what we believed to be the vessel collided with at anchor, pumping vigorously. That the collision was the result of carelessness on our part was evidenced by a false name and destination being called out. On the stranger's captain asking—" What ship?" the reply was—" The *Sparrowhawk*, for Rio." A day or two after, we again weighed—but tacking every two hours between the French and English coasts soon became necessary; and nearly a week elapsed before we weathered Beachy Head. While this continual tacking lasted, we were frequently in danger of colliding with other vessels and especially with ships running up Channel with a fair wind. So often were we aroused during those long December nights by the fog-horn, bell-ringing, and speaking-trumpet, that I did not wholly undress. One night in particular, when off Beachy Head, a more than usual commotion, with the hoarse hailing of the trumpet—" Ship ahoy! Port your helm "—hurried me out. Passing through the cuddy, I met our inebriate friend in a state of terror, who exclaimed— "We are all lost! A big American liner is running us down." I stepped back to tell my wife to get ready to come on deck at once, and hurrying there myself found nearly all assembled watching a ship three times the size of ours bearing down close upon us under a cloud of sail. Providentially, however, she passed within a few yards without touching—our sails having been thrown aback, barely in time; had she struck, she must have gone over us, and probably none would have been saved unless by jumping on or clinging to the stranger, which some were preparing to do. Our captain declared that the other vessel neither heeded his hailing nor altered her course, probably a bad look-out being kept, for carelessness in these matters was something surprising. In those days the danger of collision was greatly enhanced by vessels not being allowed to carry lights, for fear they should be mistaken for shore lights by incoming ships; the system of side lights as now had not been thought of. Sometimes a case of turpentine, or other quickly inflammable matter, was kept ready to show a flash - light if needful, but our vessel had not one.

The danger was hardly past, when a scene of the utmost confusion, yet partaking of the ludicrous, ensued. The sails having been thrown aback, the ship rolled and pitched in the heavy sea in a most extraordinary manner, with the result that everything movable got capsized; tables, seats, the cabin stove, &c. broke from their fastenings, while crockery and small sundries performed all sorts of antics. What with the scarcely subdued terror of some, the crying of children, the shouting of orders, the hurrying about of the crew, and the clatter of blocks and ropes, a sort of Babel resulted, and it was some little time before anything like order and quietude were restored.

On December 4th we sighted the Isle of Wight, and toward evening, as a storm seemed coming on, bore up for St. Helen's Roads, intending to anchor till morning. When within about four miles, a severe squall assailed us, and we were quickly scudding before it under close-reefed topsails. After being driven back about one hundred miles, and there being no sign of the weather moderating, we put in to Dungeness Roads for shelter, and lay there with both anchors down from the 8th to the 12th, when we again weighed.

The hands being nearly all aloft, and the captain at the wheel, near which I happened to be standing, he said— "Just hold the wheel a minute." I held it, while he went forward. Not knowing the difference between the steering of a square-rigged ship and a sailing-boat, I kept the wheel steady, as if it had been a tiller, with the result that the sails just being loosed were blown aback, to the astonishment and danger of the men on the yards. The captain hurried up, saying he had forgotten leaving me at the wheel, and that I should have "met her," an expression I did not understand, but which I soon learned the meaning of—taking the wheel becoming a favorite recreation. The issue was, we had to wear, and passed so close to a stranded vessel that it seemed doubtful whether we might not get stranded too, so I got the credit of nearly

refreshed, and then started for a race back to the ship, two
or three hundred yards away. When they were about half-
way, the chief officer shouted through the trumpet—" Boat
ahoy ! shark under the stern."   Down went the pannikins,
out went the oars ; before the boat's head was well round,
again the trumpet hailed—" Two sharks under the stern ;"
and immediately followed by—" Three sharks under the
stern."   This was exciting.   Two of the swimmers held
on their way to the ship, while the boatswain swam to us
and was hoisted in somewhat paler than when he left ; and
we were not a little relieved to see the two others assisted
by willing hands up the ship's side.   Of course we were no
sooner on board and the boat triced up than a tempting bait
was thrown over; the shark party consisted of a dam and
two young ones.   My wife and I had retired to change
clothes, for there was not a dry garment in the boat, when
we saw mamma shark take the bait.   She was immediately hoisted up close past our windows, into which
she sent her tail ; fortunately they were wide open or they
would have been smashed.   On reaching the poop, over
our heads, she lashed the deck with her tail as if determined to split it, but an axe soon stopped that amusement.
Being dragged down to the main deck she was quickly
dispatched, and found to measure 16 feet in length, her
carcase furnishing an ample meal to the crew and steerage
people, who were glad of any change from the hard salt
beef and pork that formed their general diet.   One of the
calves, about three feet long, was also caught, and some
cutlets from it appeared on the cabin table, but none
seemed to relish them.   Long after the large shark had
been cut up, and partly eaten, its heart showed symptoms
of sensation, by shrinking when touched.

On January 30th, in lat. 1°27′ N., long. 14°56′ W., the early

morning showed a sail astern just above the horizon
Before noon she was up with us, but two or three miles
to the eastward, when to our surprise she shortened sail,
hauling up her mizen, then making the same rate as
ourselves. In an hour or so she made sail again, and
drew ahead. Again she shortened sail, reducing speed;
and this making and shortening sail, so that she kept
within two or three miles, continued till towards dusk,
when, being still to the eastward and ahead, she
suddenly altered her course, and, crossing our course,
went away to windward. We were sorely puzzled
to guess what this might mean. Certainly she was no
ordinary trader, making the best of her way to her
destination; nor was she likely to be a man - of - war
exercising her crew, for then she would have shown
her colours or replied to our signals. The captain and
officers could arrive at no other conclusion than that
she was a slaver, willing to do a little piracy if she
conveniently could; and certainly her keeping so carefully near us all day, and going off to windward,
apparently to gain a position from which she could run
down upon us, and send her boats to board during the
night, strongly favoured this supposition. At all events, it
was thought well to be prepared for any emergency, and I
believe there was not a man on board but was determined
to resist to the utmost the ship being taken and ourselves
probably maltreated or murdered by a gang of cut-throats
such as slavers' crews were then known mostly to be, while
the fate of our women would be dreadful to contemplate.
In the midst of our anxiety and preparation, however, the
element of fun again cropped up. On the stand of arms
in the cuddy, consisting of a dozen percussion muskets,
and some boarding-pikes, being handed out for clean-

ing, &c., it was discovered that though we had plenty of
gunpowder on board, there was not a single bullet, nor any
missile suitable for our one gun. The idea of having to
resist a possible piratical attack with blank powder was
the source of no little fun at the expense of our captain
and officers. However, most of the passengers had
fowling - pieces or pistols, with ammunition ; and the
carpenter and others were set to work to manufacture
missiles by cutting up lead, nails, &c., while weapons of
various kinds were improvised wherewith to maim or kill.
I need hardly say that all but the children kept watch
that night, mostly on deck, peering through the darkness
to windward. Some urged the captain to change the
course, so that if our suspicions were correct we might not
so easily be found. He replied—"No; it is my duty to go
as directly as possible to my port; and I will do so."
Drearily the hours went by till after midnight, when we
were startled by the look-out aloft shouting—"Sail on the
starboard bow." Exactly what we feared. " Look out
for boats," cried the captain, but the order was scarcely
needed, every eye being strained to penetrate the dimness, through which a vessel was presently discernible,
apparently making for us, and as she neared some fancied
they could make out boats also. However, instead of
coming close, she crossed our course some distance ahead,
and was just disappearing to the eastward when the look-
out again shouted—" Sail on the starboard bow." Our
anxiety was at once renewed, and this second approaching
craft was eagerly watched; but she did precisely as the
previous one, crossing a little way ahead of us, directly in
the track of her predecessor, soon becoming lost to view.
What either of these vessels were, of course we could not
know. From the suspicious behaviour of the one that had

been with us all day, however, it was surmised that she really must have been what we suspected, but that when she went off to windward one of our cruisers—several of which were in the neighbourhood engaged in suppressing the slave-trade—had fallen in with her, made her out, and was giving chase. Anyway, we were only too thankful to be rid of her, and spend the remainder of the night in peace.

On the 31st we were becalmed close to the equator. It was therefore put to the passengers whether they would object to the crew indulging in the fun usual on crossing the line. Anything to relieve monotony was gladly welcomed, and we agreed; so the hands went to work with a will, making up costumes, &c. Some time after dark a great flare was seen ahead from which, apparently, a trumpet hailed—" Ship ahoy ! What ship ? Where from ? Where bound ?" &c.; all which being duly answered, we were informed from Neptune's fiery car (a tar-barrel) that his majesty would visit us in the morning to receive the homage of new arrivals in his dominions. Accordingly great preparations were made for the reception of his marine highness, who shortly after breakfast appeared from somewhere over the bows, very elaborately got up, and was with much ceremony conducted to his throne on the forecastle. Having been duly acknowledged by those who had on previous occasions done obeisance, he commanded his lieutenant to bring all new arrivals before him. One by one the novices were led on deck, on reaching which they were instantly saluted by a bucket of water from aloft by way of washing off any dust adhering as the result of their travels, and that they might appear clean and decent in the presence of royalty. Conducted into the royal presence, each was catechised as to birth-place, age, occupation, object in entering his majesty's territories, destination, &c. On the replies—which I need hardly say were of the drollest—being deemed satisfactory, the initiation rites were ordered to be administered. These consisted of being seated between two officials on a spar, which formed one side of a large bath formed of a sail, and full of water. A very fussy lathering ensued by the royal barber, then a scrape with a formidable-looking razor of hoop-iron, half a yard long, with jagged teeth, the smooth edge, however, only being applied. When sufficiently scraped, the two officials, called bears, doused the shaved one backwards into the bath, leaving him to scramble out as best he might; I managed to grab the two attendants and drag them in with me, to the detriment of their uniforms and the amusement of the onlookers. The whole thing, in fact, was made the occasion for unlimited fun and merriment, the greatest good humour prevailing, except in the case of two or three steerage passengers, who had managed to make themselves obnoxious, and got rather more dousing than they liked. The day, however, being intensely hot, an unexpected dash of water, which was flying about everywhere, could hardly be deemed disagreeable. The affair wound up by music, singing and dancing in the evening, the passengers treating the crew to a little extra grog.

Nothing further occurred to break the monotony till we sighted Trinidad and the Martin Vaz rocks, on February 14th, except seeing a vessel or two, and a fracas between our inebriate passenger and another. The conduct of the former had become intensely annoying, and his having grossly insulted one of our cabin passengers, a stalwart young fellow, it was decided to administer a lesson on behaviour. As he was wont to swagger a good deal about his military antecedents and family connections, it was arranged to send him a formal challenge, and failing its acceptance, to treat him to a sound thrashing. He was, therefore, duly waited on, and requested to name a friend to arrange preliminaries for a duel. But he became suddenly unwell, and no friend appeared to confer with the other gentleman's friend. A couple of days passed during which the transgressor kept close in his cabin. Meanwhile pistols were brought on to the cuddy table, every now and then examined, cleaned, snapped, &c. ; arrangements being discussed, so near to the sick man's stateroom, that he could not fail to hear through the venetians all that went on. The part of the ship most suitable, the number of paces, and so forth were made frequent matters of discussion, probably not very soothing to the invalid's nerves. In event of his courage proving equal to the occasion, which was not at all expected, it was intended the weapons should be charged with blank cartridge, but his opponent's with a clot of blood. However, no friend came forward, and when the delinquent again ventured to appear, he was collared, dragged on the main deck, well bullied as a coward and blackguard, and got about as severe a caning as the most recreant schoolboy ever experienced, to the no small amusement and satisfaction of all hands, the only expressions of sympathy that reached his ears being—"Give it him," "Serves him jolly well right," and so forth. Sore as he must have been, and utterly crestfallen, for some time he behaved himself more decently, though the evil spirit of intemperance every now and then re-asserted its sway.

On the morning of the 22nd we signalled the ship *David Clark*, bound to Bombay. It being calm, and she but two or three miles off, some of us jokingly asked our captain to signal and invite her captain to dinner, and he did so. Somewhat to our surprise, he signalled back accepting ; so about three o'clock the *David Clark's* gig brought Captain Swan on board the *Hindoo*.   Delighted were we with the novel idea of inviting a friend to dine in mid-ocean, and pleased enough was he to find himself with a cheerful party, having no one on board his own ship but his crew and officers, with whom of course he could not be altogether free.   After a pleasant evening—his boat's crew having been duly entertained by our crew—Captain Swan departed, with the understanding that as many of our cabin folks as could were to dine with him next day, weather permitting. As the weather did permit, and the ships kept near each other, several of us dined on board the *David Clark*. Alternate visitings were kept up till Sunday, the 27th, when Captain Swan and some of his crew came on board to attend divine service, remaining to dine.   Our captain and a small party returned with him for tea, and to spend an hour or two.   Coming on deck about ten o'clock, we were surprised to find several vessels near at hand that had been brought up by a breeze we were only just beginning to feel.   As some of the new comers were close, indeed all around us, it became a question as to which was our ship ; we started for the nearest, and were not a little relieved on discerning a light at the gangway, and getting safely on board.   Next day the weather became cold and squally, and we lost sight of the ships in company.

On the 3rd March, lat. 35° 54' s., long. 3° 20' w., one of the seamen who had been ill for some time died, and we had opportunity of assisting at the solemn ceremony of a burial at sea.   The 6th brought us again into company with the *David Clark*, continuing, within signalling, and sometimes speaking distance till the 15th, the heavy sea precluding any other intercourse. Being then in the longitude of the Cape, and working down to 42 degrees south, we encountered heavy weather and high seas, but sustained no damage. The question had arisen as to the advisability of calling at the Cape for water, as we were running short; but it having been decided in the negative, for some three weeks we became limited to a pint a day for all purposes. On the evening of April 17th we sighted Kangaroo Island, entering Investigator's Straits the next morning. It fell calm, and we were in some danger from currents carrying us into shallow water, especially near Troubridge Shoal. On rounding it, we met a light northerly wind in Gulf St. Vincent. When tacking somewhere off Willunga, a small cutter, the *Midge*, from Port Adelaide, ran alongside, and her master threw a copy of the *Register* newspaper on board, dated April 19th. The captain naturally looked first at the shipping news, and created no small amusement by reading out—" There were reports current yesterday that the *Hindoo* had been lost on the west coast of Cornwall, but from all we can learn they have no foundation in fact. It is true she put back with loss of a topmast, but she left again about December 23rd, and was spoken in the Bay of Biscay." It was singular that we should be greeted with such a statement respecting our narrow escape from wreck just on the eve of our arrival. During the night of the 23rd we were off the lightship, but her light being mistaken for a fire on shore, we held on till daylight, when finding our mistake, we came in from the northward, causing the pilot on boarding us to inquire if we had been surveying. Sailing up the river, we were gratified at seeing a number of vessels, with a steamer, indicating a greater amount of settlement and trade than we had looked for. Nor were we less pleased at a boat meeting us with fresh provisions and vegetables, for owing to the extreme length of the voyage our stock of preserved meats, &c., had got very low, and shore bread was a grateful change from hard biscuits. On the 151st morning, therefore, from hauling out of London docks we stepped ashore at Port Adelaide, deeply thankful to the Overruler of All that He had brought us safely through so many and great dangers to the haven whither we would be.

The *Enmore* did not arrive till May 7th, having been 135 days from Plymouth. Her passengers complained of having a most miserable voyage. The poop had proved, as I anticipated, quite unusable for most of the time, while lack of suitable provisions, &c., furnished ground for legal proceedings against her captain; so my having decided against taking passage in her was another ground for thankfulness.

CHAPTER IV.

PORT ADELAIDE AND CITY.

VERY little indeed was known in London about South Australia in 1847, so that our first impressions on landing were of surprise and satisfaction. We expected to find a newly - settled pastoral country with a very scattered European population of about 25,000, and hardly any settled towns or villages. I had been shown a parcel of wheat from South Australia in the London docks, so knew agriculture had to some extent commenced, and that wheat could be spared for export; but we were quite unprepared for the bustle and activity Port Adelaide presented. There was a steamer, I think the *Havilah*, and a number of vessels, while the wharves were full of bullock-drays—a novelty to us—delivering copper ore from the Burra mine, then at the height of its productiveness. The buildings in the Port were numerous but of very varied construction. The better class were of weatherboard, or paling, many of cob, *i.e.*, earth mixed with straw, others of wattle and dab, as it was called; that is, posts placed at short intervals, plaited with tea-tree, the interstices filled with clay and whitewashed, nearly all roofs being of shingle. There was a weatherboard church built on piles, under and around which the tide often flowed, so that occasionally the congregation had to be fetched away in boats.

The only public conveyances to the city, about seven

miles distant, were spring-carts, drawn by two horses driven tandem, and carrying six or eight passengers. In one of these I took passage, and found we had to travel over a very rough road with a full load. Stopping at public-houses on the way, I was puzzled and amused at the variety of refreshments called for. One wanted a "nobbler," another a "spider," another "shandygaff," another a "cock-tail," &c.—to me an entirely new nomenclature. Reaching the city, I found Hindley-street —then the principal street—contained a few fair-sized shops and buildings; it was evidently the nucleus of a large town. Calling at Government House, where I was informed Bishop Short was staying, to report myself and deliver a packet of letters, I found his Lordship and Mrs. Short were away. I, therefore, proceeded to St. John's Church, where I found the Rev. W. J. Woodcock in a small brick parsonage, by whom I was warmly welcomed, having been expected some weeks previously. Next I waited on the Rev. James Farrell, incumbent of Trinity Church, residing in a weatherboard parsonage, which afterwards became the chapter-house, who also received me most kindly—these being the only clergymen then in Adelaide. Next day I waited on the Bishop, who said he was looking for me by the *Enmore*, his brother, Colonel Short, having written to say he had proposed engaging my passage by her. This accounted for no one meeting us when the *Hindoo* was reported. It appeared that on the arrival of the Bishop and his family a somewhat similar incident occurred. It being known he was on board the *Derwent*, when she arrived at the lightship, the few clergy with some laity took a boat with a view to go on board and welcome their diocesan. But unluckily the boat stranded on a mud-bank, and was obliged to remain there till the tide rose. Meanwhile, the harbour-master, Captain Lipson, had gone off in the custom-house boat to the ship, and invited the Bishop and Mrs. Short to take passage for the shore with him, which they did. On entering the river they of course had to pass the stranded boat-load of clergy and others, but Captain Lipson did not inform his Lordship as to who they were; so that on reaching the wharf the Bishop was a little surprised at there being no clergy or others to receive him; this of course was afterwards duly explained, and laughed over, notwithstanding its being somewhat annoying. Two or three days elapsed before my wife and I could leave the ship, as some of our luggage had been accidentally stowed in the hold, and till my wife's clothes-trunk was recovered she deemed herself scarcely presentable on shore. Mr. Woodcock having kindly procured for us very comfortable lodgings at Mr. Dodgson's, a large weatherboard house in Rundle-street, in due course we transferred ourselves and belongings thereto, till we could find and furnish a cottage, and began to look about us.

The city was laid out on a large scale, only a small portion being occupied by scattered tenements; Hindley-street and Rundle - street were the ones principally favoured by tradespeople. There were no pavements, but a few shops had slabs of slate laid before their doors; the said shops were mostly small; some of stone or brick, but many of paling or wattle and dab. Most of the streets had trees standing in them, and all were full of holes, furnishing mud in winter and dust in summer. These holes, where trees had been grubbed out, getting filled with water in winter, were really dangerous; planks were laid across, some in the more frequented thoroughfares; it was said that goats and sheep were often smothered in them, and I was also told a bullock or two had been. The greater number of buildings were in the northwest part of the city, as being nearest to the Port. Between King William-street and St. John's Church, commonly termed "St. John's in the wilderness," there were scarce any buildings. That church had been placed so as to accommodate the few settlers in that part of the town, also those along the foot of the hills, and at Unley, a township laid out just across the Park-lands. In winter it took considerable navigation to get from the vicinity of St. John's to the more inhabited part of the city after dusk. Often, after turning in various directions to avoid the holes of mud and water, the pedestrian, attracted perhaps by a light, would find himself about where he had started from, or on the Park-lands, a belt of land surrounding the city, and then a forest of dead trees. Victoria - square was a specially dangerous locality, there being but two or three narrow tracks across it, to diverge from which was almost certainly to get bogged. I found it expedient in winter to wear fishermen's boots, to wade through the sheets of water that frequently crossed the tracks; so that altogether to pedestrianise Adelaide then was considerably different to what it is now.

A bridge that had been erected over the river Torrens, the Frome-bridge, had been washed away the winter before our arrival. The only means of crossing, therefore, was by planks spiked on to the tops of low posts driven into the bed of the river, without any hand-rail, or by vehicle, usually the Irish jaunting-car; and as North Adelaide then had a number of residents, there was considerable intercourse. Water was supplied to both North and South Adelaide by carts filled from the river, consequently not free from impurities, rendering filters a necessity wherever they could be had. In hot weather, the river being low, and the water-carts sometimes leaking, by the time a load had been driven a mile or two, the consumer would receive part of a barrel of tepid fluid, by no means clear, which he would find advisable to let settle for a few hours before using, and for which he had to pay one shilling and sixpence or two shillings, according to distance. Now we sometimes see letters in the newspapers grumbling at the quantity or quality of the water supplied from the reservoirs; it would be well if some of the malcontents could be relegated to the earlier time and circumstances described. The wells that had been sunk about the city proved brackish. Wood was the only fuel, and though there was abundance of it close at hand, the labour of cutting up and carting caused its cost to be about one pound per ton, sometimes more. Rents, too, were high. I had to pay forty pounds a year for a house of four small rooms, so that wood, water, and rent helped to make living somewhat expensive. Meat, however, was very cheap; thousands of sheep being boiled down simply for the tallow, legs of mutton were often sold for sixpence each.

The first time I took my wife for a walk to explore the city, we saw some apples for sale. Not having tasted fresh fruit since leaving England we purchased some, and found they were sold by weight, receiving three, as weighing a pound, for which we had to pay a shilling; this settled the question of apple pies and puddings for a time. Anent the keeper of the said shop a good story is told, which I believe was true. He had a wooden leg and lived quite alone, though having relatives, who, as he was miserly, hoped to come in for something at his death. He died suddenly, but no will or money could be found; the business, however, was carried on by one of the family. After a while the wooden leg began to be considered a piece of lumber, and was condemned to be burnt. On breaking it with that intent, it was found to be hollow, and in the hollow were concealed bank-notes amounting to a considerable sum. Its proprietor must have had the bump of secretiveness well developed to have hit on such a hiding place for his treasure.

Though we found Adelaide had some roughs and inconveniences, those before us had found it very much more so. Illustrative of this, the following extract from a little work entitled—" Annals of the Diocese of Adelaide," by the Rev. W. Norris, M.A., Rector of Warblington, Hants, published in 1852, may be cited :—" In the early part of the year 1837, the late Sir John Jeffcott, Chief Justice, gave the following graphic account of the settlers of this incipient colony. 'On my arrival here, I found the Governor, His Excellency Captain Hindmarsh, R.N., Knight of the Hanoverian Order, &c., in a mud hut, which consisted of only two rooms, in which were stowed, besides himself, Mrs. Hindmarsh and her three daughters, young Hindmarsh, and a maid-servant. How they found room passes my comprehension. In the hut, I dined with His Excellency, in company with Captain Crozier, commander of H.M.S. *Victor*. We passed a very merry day, and had the pleasure of hearing the young ladies sing and accompany themselves on the guitar in the evening. The site of this incipient city (Adelaide) where I now write, in a tent be it said, is most beautiful, and looks quite like an English park. Nothing can be finer than the rich pastures spread over the land in all directions.' " Sir John was evidently describing the lands surrounding Adelaide, now largely built over, but which on our arrival were exceedingly beautiful and park-like; the ride from Adelaide to the foot of the hills through what was really an open evergreen forest, with but little underwood, was always a pleasure. Sundry spots had been marked out for townships, as Unley, Mitcham, Glen Osmond, Kensington, Magill, &c., but these were very scantily occupied; indeed one might ride a long way without being troubled with fences. Much of the land within a few miles of Adelaide was under cultivation, and many gardens were planted, some having got into bearing; vegetables and fruit, however, were very scarce and dear.

Taking it altogether, the place was much more advanced than we had expected to find it; and it was not easy to realise that we were pretty nearly at England's antipodes, so thoroughly English did many things appear—although of course there were some novelties, especially the evergreen character of the trees, which caused us to term it a place of perpetual spring.

CHAPTER V.

ORDINATION AND WORK IN ADELAIDE.

BISHOP SHORT being desirous of holding his first ordination on the anniversary of his own consecration, fixed St. Peter's Day, June 29th, 1848, for that event. The candidates were the Rev. W. H. Coombs, of Gawler, for priest's orders, with J. H. Fulford and myself for deacons' orders. The examining chaplain was Archdeacon Hale, afterwards Bishop of Perth. This being the first occasion of the kind in South Australia very considerable interest was manifested, and on the day of ordination Trinity Church, which the Bishop had adopted as his pro-cathedral, was densely crowded. The service was, to me at least, a peculiarly solemn one, for I felt that I was then and there being dedicated to what was to be my life's work, viz., to aid in establishing a branch of the Church of England, and an educational system in this newly founded province. After service, the Bishop, clergy, and sundry laity were invited to dine with Mr. F. S. Dutton, the occasion being made quite a fête—a very agreeable termination to a period of mental strain and anxiety.

I considered myself now fairly launched on my sphere of duty, viz., to conduct school, train teachers, and take such ministerial duty on Sundays as the Bishop might direct. The Rev. T. P. Wilson being in the like position, between us we held services as often as possible at Walkerville, Magill, the Sturt, Hindmarsh, Glenelg, and other places. Our list of clergy then consisted of the Bishop; Archdeacon Hale, stationed for a short time at Kensington and afterwards at St. John's; the Revs. J. Farrell, Trinity Church; W. J. Woodcock, St. John's, and afterwards Christ Church, North Adelaide; G. Newenham, Port Adelaide; J. Pollitt, Mount Barker; J. Bagshawe, Burra Burra; A. B. Burnett, Willunga; W. H. Coombs, Gawler; J. Fulford, Sturt; T. P. Wilson and myself, unattached; or, twelve, all told.

The Bishop having taken a house at Kensington, three and a half miles from Adelaide, arranged that all the clergy who could should meet there every three months, and many exceedingly pleasant meetings were held. They were always of a combined social, clerical, and business character, and marked by most thorough cordiality. The Bishop on one occasion thought well to give us a homily on smoking, he being a non - smoker. While he was speaking one gentleman in taking out his handkerchief drew out with it a stick of tobacco, which fell at the Bishop's feet, at which he laughed as heartily as any of us. These meetings, to which we all looked forward with pleasure, were never devoid of interest. Every one had experiences, or adventures, to relate—sometimes narrow escapes of being "bushed"—information to seek, suggestions to make, plans to propose, or difficulties to discuss. Among these was a proposition from the Government, through Mr. A. M. Mundy, colonial secretary, that, except the Bishop, all the clergy should be placed on the commission of the peace. It was thought by the Government that it would be of considerable public advantage, especially in the outlying districts, to have educated persons appointed to such positions. After carefully discussing this proposal, it was decided that it could not be agreed to. The first duty of a clergyman being to his Church, it was felt to be quite possible his occupying the position of magistrate as well would sometimes clash with that duty; that it would be difficult for a clergyman.in his magisterial position to decide against, perhaps fine or sentence, a member of his congregation, and afterwards visit him or his family in his pastoral capacity. Though it had been pointed out that holding the commission of the peace would add somewhat to the status of the clergy, we concluded that the possible injury to the Church would far more than counterbalance any advantage in this respect, therefore the proposed honour was respectfully declined. There being no elected Parliament, Governor Robe and his immediate successors had not the advantage the governments of the present day possess, viz., that any gentleman having taken active interest in securing another gentleman's return to Parliament is, *ipso facto*, deemed eligible, on recommendation of the M.P., for the commission of the peace, and dignified with a J.P. - ship accordingly.

One important matter that engaged attention was the selection of a hymn-book. Trinity and St. John's Churches had hymn-books, but there were none elsewhere. In the issue, it was decided that what was known as the " Mitre Hymn-book " should be adopted for the whole diocese, and it continued so for many years. Pending procuring a supply of these the Psalms at the end of the Prayer-book had to be used, and more often than otherwise the clergyman had to lead the singing; a tuning-fork and copy of a few well-known tunes being part of his ordinary Sunday equipment. I have still a little book of tunes, copied for me by Mrs. Short from the Union Tune-book, then the chief repertoire of music for nearly all places of worship. Sometimes a

zealous individual would relieve the clergyman by starting
a tune, but this was not invariably a success, the wrong
metre being now and then hit upon. On such occasions I
usually allowed my helper to go on till the collapse came,
then again give out the psalm and start the tune.

In connection with this matter, an awkward incident
occurred at Christ Church, North Adelaide. On its being
opened, someone had offered a large harmonium, to be
paid for afterwards. The offer was accepted; the time
for payment arrived, but not the wherewith. Notice was
accordingly given that the instrument would be removed
unless paid for within a certain time, and, it was returned
to the owner. The Sunday morning after its removal Mr.
Woodcock asked me to preach, that he might take the
prayers and explain the reason for there being no instrumental music; accordingly, he proceeded to the desk, and
I to the chancel. The Canticles and Glorias between the
Psalms having been read, in due course he gave out some
verses of a psalm, and having explained why the harmonium was missing, asked if some member of the
congregation would be kind enough to lead a tune. All
stood silent, no one venturing to raise his voice. After a
minute or two, the situation became embarrassing, on which
Mr. Woodcock evidently had not calculated; therefore he
looked round to me, nodding significantly. I fear I had
been too much amused to have noted either words or
measure; but I soon made them out, and started a well-
known tune, which was instantly taken up, and that by
many whose voices were seldom heard, so that for once we
had hearty congregational singing. The following Sunday
the harmonium was again in its place.

Anent the introduction of musical instruments into
churches, an amusing incident occurred not long before

my leaving England. On going to reside in Yorkshire, I of course attended the village church. The instrumental music there consisted of two or three violins, a bass viol, some flutes, &c. Accustomed as I had been to the organs of the London churches, this seemed strange. After awhile, therefore, as the incumbent wished me to become his curate, accepting my assistance in various ways, I got subscriptions enough to procure a small but good pipe organ, and soon had a choir trained for the ordinary parochial service. It so happened, however, that there was but one gentleman in the neighbourhood who could play the organ, and he kindly gave us the benefit of his services. A few months after we had got into working order, on arriving at the church one Sunday morning I found the violins, &c., in the gallery again ; the organist being away, it had been arranged for the instrumental music to be as aforetime. Having to read the lessons, I proceeded to the desk to do so, and on the first lesson being ended, the clerk from his desk below me—the pulpit being behind and above the reading-desk — gave out a hymn. It had been the somewhat odd custom before the organ arrived, to sing a hymn instead of reading the *Te Deum* between the lessons. But the musicians had been long out of practice; therefore on the hymn being announced, the violins scraped, the bass viol growled, the flutes tootled, in order to chord. On the first verse being read, the orchestra struck up, but at the second line came to a stop; they had the wrong metre. The clerk just below me, who, under the old *régime*, had been choir-master, shouted out "Common metre!" A turning of leaves, some whispering, another chording, and they started again, but again to stop. I think some had the wrong key. At that juncture the stillness was broken by a plaintive but very distinct

" Baa, baa," from the church porch ; one of a few sheep grazing in the churchyard had got sufficiently near to supply what might be regarded as an approximate key-note. This would appear to have been of value, for the performers again started and tumbled through the tune. Controlling the risibilities was difficult.

On another occasion the congregation of Christ Church had a very unpleasant experience. Mr. Woodcock being ill, on a certain Sunday I had to take the morning service alone. Shortly after commencing, a violent tornado occurred. A dense cloud of dust caused a lurid dimness, through which the lightning flashed incessantly, while thunder pealed. Rain came down in torrents, and the wind seemed likely to raze the building to its foundations, there being neither trees nor other buildings to break its force. It so happened, that there had been much dis-cussion as to the stability of the church. The walls, of limestone, some twenty-five feet high without buttresses, a high slate roof, the principals of which were only tied by iron rods, had been pronounced by many not likely to withstand any great strain. This idea seemed to receive a measure of confirmation by a well-known architect going out with his wife into the midst of the storm by the only leeward door, others quickly following his example. The thunder peals became supplemented by the large top of an inside wooden porch at the entrance to the nave flapping up and down, making a great noise. Altogether, there was quite sufficient to try the nerves of the nervous. Fearing a rush to the door, I kept on with the service, reading as loudly as possible that the organist and choir, who fortunately kept their places, might hear. While the *Te Deum* was being sung, a fussy old gentleman, one of the wardens, came to my side, saying—" You had better stop

the service, no one can hear." I replied—" I know that ;
go and sit still." From the first, I had noted that the wind
was on the angles of the building, which were of course
better able to resist its force than any other part. While
the storm was at its height, I observed that the lamps,
which were suspended by wires from the iron tie-rods of
the roof, were being considerably shaken, indicating that
the roof was undergoing a severe strain ; this could only
be seen by myself, the lamps being about level with my
eyes, and above the heads of the people. In half-an-hour or
so the force of the hurricane abated, and the service concluded with something like half the original congregation,
the others having departed, happily without anything
approaching to a stampede, which probably would have had
unfortunate results. The principals of the roof were afterwards found to have been slightly driven over on the leeward side, and some plaster was loosened ; had any fallen,
there would probably have been a rush out. This incident
settled all doubts as to the stability of the building. During
the storm, a large ship, the *Grecian*, was driven from her
anchorage off the Semaphore, becoming a total wreck.
Very considerable damage also occurred in Adelaide and
other parts of the colony.

The first building matter with which I became connected
was the erection of the schoolroom attached to St.
Andrew's Church, Walkerville. With the aid of Messrs.
G. W. Hawkes, W. Macdonald, J. Williams, J. Brinkworth,
and Mr. Lambeth, then government architect, as a committee, a good building was completed and fitted up, and
has continued in use ever since. A large class-room was
also added to the Pulteney-street school.

Unfortunately for myself, in a financial point of view,

but at the Bishop's earnest request, I consented to take charge of the boarding pupils of the Collegiate school. Mr. Wilson, the head-master, was unmarried, and it was judged advisable the boys should board with a married clergyman in Adelaide, so for above a year they were with me. Between my own school, these boarders and church services, my hands were rather full. The boarders were afterwards transferred to one of the masters of the Collegiate school. After about two years of this work, I began to feel it rather much. Governmental action in matters educational had rendered establishment of a Diocesan system impracticable, and Dr. Wyatt had been appointed inspector for all schools, aided from public funds. I, therefore, expressed a wish to the Bishop to be appointed to some cure, towards the close of 1851 becoming licensed to St. George's Woodforde, and Magill, about five miles from Adelaide. I continued, however, in charge of the school, riding to and fro daily for nearly a year, when an unfortunate misunderstanding with the trustees caused me to resign it altogether.

CHAPTER VI.

VACATION TRIP.

AT the end of December 1850, my school being closed for three weeks, I started for a holiday trip to the North, of course on horseback. Reaching Gawler, twenty-five miles from Adelaide, I spent two or three days with my friend the Rev. W. H. Coombs, who had managed to get a church and parsonage erected, and preached for him on the Sunday. The next day being intensely hot, I deferred starting onward till toward evening, reaching a small inn on the river Light, some twenty miles from Gawler, about 9 P.M.; here I could get no fodder for my horse, except hay made of native grass, while the water was brackish and too muddy to drink. Next morning breakfast consisted of chops from a sheep just killed and some English ale, which unusual dietary induced unpleasant symptoms before I had ridden much further. Passing through Auburn and Watervale, I reached Penwortham, where I found the Rev. J. Bagshawe, who had charge of the mission, residing with Mr. Robinson, a sheepfarmer. who received me with genuine bush hospitality. A room had been built here of wattle and dab to serve for day-school, Sunday-school and church, while at Clare, seven miles distant, service was held in the courthouse.

Wishing to visit the Burra copper mines, Mr. Bagshawe agreed to accompany me. Mr. Robinson kindly supplying me with a fresh horse, we crossed the arid plain of some thirty miles without water, the only waterhole that existed being so spoiled by sheep that the horses would not drink. In crossing this plain I for the first time saw the mirage to perfection, and certainly the illusion was very complete, most inviting sheets of water seeming to appear, but disappearing as we approached. The Burra was then a very busy and dusty place, full of people but with very indifferent accommodation in the way of dwellings. As a deep creek ran through the township, many miners had dug caves in its banks to live in, cutting apertures to the surface to serve as chimneys, which were only protected at top by a beer cask or a few pieces of wood driven into the ground, sometimes nothing—so that an unwary traveller along the bank after dusk was liable to make a sudden descent into someone's fire-place or frying-pan, and such things I was told did sometimes happen. We found the Rev. J. Pollitt, who was in charge of the mission, had just gone to Adelaide, so failed to see him. He had a large schoolroom to hold service in, and was materially aided by being made chaplain to the copper company. A letter, however, from Mr. Pollitt was handed to me. On his way to Adelaide, staying, as I had done, at Gawler parsonage, he heard that I had gone north, and intended visiting the Burra. He, therefore, wrote to ask me to remain and take his duties at the Burra on the following Sunday, as he would thereby be enabled to remain with his wife, then seriously ill at Glenelg. This was difficult, as I was due for duty at Walkerville church that Sunday morning, and the next morning my school was to re-open; while it would not be possible for me to make the one hundred miles from the Burra to Adelaide in less than two days with a single horse. After consultation with Mr. Bagshawe,

it was arranged that he should undertake Mr. Pollitt's
duties at the Burra, while I remained to take his duties
at Clare and Penwortham, whereby I should be twenty-
five miles nearer to Adelaide. Of course we expected Mr.
Pollitt would inform my wife and Archdeacon Hale—(the
Bishop being away)—that he had written me to take his
duties, and provide for mine. I also wrote my wife,
explaining the position, and directing my assistant to carry
on the school till my arrival, but there being only two
mails weekly, I knew my letter would not be delivered till
the Monday morning.

Returning to Penwortham, we visited most of the
settlers, and on Saturday I accompanied Mr. Bagshawe
part of the way to the Burra. On Sunday, after conducting morning service at Penwortham, and afternoon at
Clare, according to arrangement, dining at Mr. Gleeson's, I
started to reach Mr. Masters' station at Saddleworth, so as
to be twenty miles nearer Adelaide in the morning. The
road was merely a track, entirely without fences, and from
it other tracks, more or less defined, branched off, and one
of these I had to take to reach the station. In the dusk,
however, I rode past it, only becoming conscious of the
mistake when I had reached the river Gilbert. I retraced
the main track, but failed to find the branch one I wanted.
Coming upon a deserted hut I would have made a fire, but
not being a smoker, had no matches, for it became cold,
and I had only light clothing; then, too, I found the hut
was full of fleas. Shortly after midnight, I heard a dog
bark, and thinking it probable I was near the station,
rode towards the sound. Fortunately the barking continued,
and I shortly came to a flock of sheep, camped; the hutkeeper, roused by the dog, came out of his bunk to meet
me. They were Mr. Masters' sheep, and I asked the man

to show me to the house, but he very properly said he could not leave his flock. Pointing to a star, however, he told me the station was in a line with it a mile or two away ; so, guided by the star, I knocked Mr. Masters up about 3 A.M., not at all sorry to find myself and horse in comfortable quarters, and thankful my being " bushed " had been of so brief duration. They had sat up late expecting me, but supposed I had changed my plan, and would reach them for breakfast.

Being afraid of knocking up my horse, I decided to go only as far as Gawler on the Monday, and leave there at daylight on Tuesday, so as to be in Adelaide by school-time, therefore did not leave Mr. Masters' till the afternoon. Falling in with the mail conveyance from Clare, I kept company with it till we reached " Templer's," a well-known hostelry about ten miles from Gawler, the mail from the Burra arriving at the same time. As both vehicles were full of passengers, who had tea, I stabled my horse, and decided to wait till they had started—and they had some trouble in starting. In those days horses for the mail conveyances were not kept stabled and fed, ready for use, as now, but had to be turned into the scrub to feed, and brought in when wanted. These horses being very imperfectly broken in, sometimes not at all, starting was often a work of difficulty. Leaving shortly afterwards, I rode quietly through the heavily wooded scrub, which had been but partially cleared to form a road, for five or six miles, when I came upon a sad scene. The first of the conveyances had caught a stump, and upset ; the second, being too close, or the horses too wild, could not be pulled up in time, so capsized over the first. When I rode up, the passengers were lying about, many more or less injured, some severely so, and stretchers were just arriving from Gawler to carry in the wounded. What with the broken vehicles, and harness, injured passengers, frightened women and children, the scene was one to be remembered. Before I had time to dismount, and see if I could be of any use, Dr. Lewis of Gawler came up, and said he was very thankful to see me, as he understood I had been lost. I replied—" I certainly lost my way for several hours last night, but I don't know how you could have heard of it." "Oh," said he, "there has been great alarm about you, someone came from Adelaide yesterday to inquire for you." I knew at once what had happened—that Mr. Pollitt, having kept me back on account of his duties, had neglected to inquire about mine, and had not informed my wife or anyone else of the matter. As, however, the letter I wrote from the Burra would have been delivered that morning, I knew the alarm at home must be over. Dr. Lewis, however, urged my at once pushing on to Gawler, as arrangements to search for me were on *tapis*, and sufficient assistance to the wounded could be rendered by the uninjured passengers and others. I, therefore, made all haste to Gawler parsonage. Reaching it, and seeing no one about, I stabled and fed my horse. Entering the house I heard voices in Mr. Coombs' study, and was in the act of tapping at the door when it was opened from the other side by Mrs. Coombs, who started back, hardly able to believe that it was I myself, so decidedly had I been given up for lost. In the room were the police-trooper and others with Mr. Coombs arranging to start in search of my humble self the next morning. Of course the matter was soon explained ; at the same time, I felt deeply grateful and duly thankful to those preparing to take so much trouble on my behalf.

It turned out that Mr. Pollitt went through Adelaide to Glenelg without informing anyone that he had written to keep me back, and held service on the Sunday in Mr. Wigley's drawing - room. Meanwhile, my wife was naturally surprised at my non-appearance on the Friday or Saturday; knowing, however, that I had duty at Walkerville church on Sunday morning, she thought my horse might have knocked up, and that I would return by Walkerville, taking the service on my way home. When, however, a messenger arrived to say that the congregation had met, and there had been no service owing to my absence, she became seriously alarmed. Sending for my assistant, Mr. Pepper, she directed him to hire a trap and drive at once to Gawler. There he was informed I had left a fortnight previously, in the evening, and had not since been heard of. Forthwith a messenger was despatched by Mr. Coombs to "Templer's," it being known I intended calling *en route* to the river Light. But the people there said they were sure no clergyman had gone northward during the last fortnight; Mr. Pollitt had gone south. but no other clergyman had called. The fact being, I had called, and taken tea, but they did not suspect I was a clergyman, as I had adopted a black necktie for bush travelling instead of the ordinary white one. When, therefore, the messenger returned to Gawler with the news that no clergyman had passed "Templer's," at the time named, it was concluded I had mistaken the track, and turned off into a vast extent of waterless scrub called the Pine Forest, and that as a fortnight had elapsed, there would be but little chance of my being found alive, others having lost themselves and perished there. This version of the matter being given on my assistant's return to Adelaide the same night, not a little consternation ensued, loss of life in the bush being by no means uncommon, and it was not till the letter delivery took place next morning that the

minds of my wife and others were relieved. Duly arriving
on the Tuesday morning, my first vacation trip in South
Australia ended. Of course Mr. Pollitt got a merited
reprimand from Archdeacon Hale for his thoughtlessness
in the matter.

A much more unpleasant incident had occurred not long
before to a party of clergy on a missionary journey to the
North. Driving in a spring-cart, then the most usual vehicle,
they alighted on arriving at a water-hole to allow their
horse to drink, it being hot weather, and led him to the
edge of the water. Attempting to go further in, he got to
where the water suddenly deepened, and slid forward,
completely losing his foothold. The reins were ineffectual
to hold him back, and the vehicle pressing him forward,
he presently plunged in, trap and all, and disappeared, the
hole being of considerable depth. We may imagine the
dismay of the travellers at helplessly witnessing the dis-
appearance of their horse, trap, and belongings. However,
there was nothing for it but to trudge through the heat to
the nearest station, and relate their misfortune. The next
day suitable appliances being procured, the drowned horse
and vehicle were recovered; and after the luggage, &c.,
had been dried, with a fresh horse they pursued their
journey. That water-hole became known afterwards as
" Parson's Folly "—but why, it is hard to say, for they
could not have known that the hole, like many others,
deepened so suddenly. In sundry instances persons
bathing in such holes, and not being able to swim, have
been drowned.

On another occasion, when Dean Farrell, Archdeacon
Woodcock and myself were crossing the Gawler river at
the ford, in a spring-cart, the Dean driving tandem, the
leader suddenly turned round in the middle of the stream,

nearly capsizing us, and I had to jump into some two feet of
water to lead him to the opposite side. But such incidents
were common. On reaching the parsonage, too, a difficulty
arose about firewood ; so Archdeacon Woodcock and
myself set to work to crosscut some logs, the former
jocularly protesting that it was altogether *infra dig.* to set
a dignitary of the Church to cut up firewood.

CHAPTER VII.

MY FIRST CURE.

ON my taking charge of St. George's Woodforde, and the district of Magill, there was but one unfinished church, although, strange to say, it had been consecrated soon after the Bishop's arrival; of course there was neither house nor endowment. About eighty sittings were let at ten shillings each per annum. This low rate, perhaps, had been fixed to induce the more people to take sittings, and so enable a larger amount to be claimed from the Government than otherwise might be. By an Act of Council of August 3rd, 1847, entitled " An Act for Promoting the Christian Religion," it was directed that from fifty pounds to one hundred and fifty pounds should be granted from the revenue toward building a place of worship, or minister's residence, with from fifty pounds to two hundred pounds annually toward a minister's maintenance, proportionately to the number of sittings let; twenty acres of land could also be granted for glebe purposes. This Act had been passed for three years only, and was availed of by most religious bodies. The Independents, however, and a few others, declined to accept aid from the State, and organised so strong an opposition, that on the three years expiring, the Act was not renewed. Therefore, all aid from Government toward public worship ceased, and the various religious bodies were left entirely to their own resources.

Having, however, come to the colony for the express purpose of helping to found a branch of the Church in it, and expecting to find but little accomplished on that behalf, it was clearly my duty to hold my ground by all possible means; then, too, there were two years yet to run of the guarantee of one hundred pounds per annum from the Bishop or S.P.G. funds. Prior to leaving England, the Bishop had asked if I could " endure hardness ;" I was now about to experience it.

In order to maintain my position after resigning Pulteney-street school, I decided to take pupils, which rendered it necessary to rent a larger house, and I had to expend a good deal on it to accommodate boarders. This I could only manage by mortgaging some land I had purchased; this I was unable to redeem, and consequently lost. I soon obtained sufficient pupils, in connection with the little the church afforded, to support my family. Seeing, therefore, that the way was so far opened, I proceeded with the endeavour to definitely found the church in the district.

The first matters that engaged attention were, of course, completing the church and establishing a Sunday-school. As I had always to lead the singing, I strove to obtain an harmonium, and succeeded, through the kindness of our synodsman, Mr. R. B. Lucas, who was visiting England, in obtaining one of Alexandre's then largest instruments at wholesale price. Next, of course, came the training of a choir, and this was followed by the laying out and planting the churchyard, &c. These things occupied fully three years, but meanwhile the people were getting gathered, and the church income increasing.

In 1853 I was called one Sunday afternoon to visit a young man who was not expected to survive the effects of an accident. He had noticed a flight of ducks settle on the

river Torrens near his home. Taking a gun, he put it at
half-cock' over a fence he had to cross. Placing his foot
on the bottom rail he sprang over, and as he did so the
weapon discharged its contents into his throat; the knot of
his tie broke its force to some extent, but the front of the
windpipe was destroyed, and most of the shots dropped on
to the lungs. It appeared there was a splinter on the rail
on which he had placed his foot, and his weight bore it
down sufficiently to catch and raise the hammer of the
gun; his springing over released the hammer and the discharge took place. He ultimately recovered, the shots
being coughed up, but the escape was almost miraculous.
During my visits, I made some remarks about youths'
indulging in shooting on Sundays, which was becoming
very common, to the neglect of public worship. The
excuse was, distance, in that instance of over three miles.
There being a good many residents in the locality and no
place of worship, I said that if they could find a place to
meet in I would endeavour to arrange so as to supply a
service once on a Sunday, my then services being morning
and afternoon at St. George's. Shortly afterwards a gentleman I did not know met me in Adelaide and asked me if
I had made such a promise. On my replying in the
affirmative, he offered the use of his drawing-room, and it
was arranged that I should call and see if it would be
suitable. In a few days I found myself at the residence
of Mr. Clark at Paradise, on the Torrens. His drawing-
room, I felt, would scarcely be the place to be opened to all
comers, being full of furniture and ornaments; moreover,
the house had to be reached through a large garden, then
full of fruit. In the garden, however, there was a weather-
board building with canvas top which I suggested might
be temporarily used till it should be seen whether a

congregation could be got together. This being decided on,
willing hands soon had it fitted up with seats, and in a few
Sundays an afternoon congregation of from thirty to forty
persons attended ; the service at St. George's I had changed
from afternoon to evening. A strong desire being manifested for the continuance of these services, a movement
was initiated for obtaining a site for a church. In 1855
the gift of two acres in a very suitable position was
obtained, and a small cob building erected thereon to
serve as schoolroom and church, constituting the only
place of worship or schoolroom in the district. In 1857 we
managed to get the nave of a small church erected, which
was opened under the designation of St. Martin's, Campbelltown, and this became well attended, the original building
being used for Sunday and day school—the latter for some
years under the charge of Mr. and Mrs Doke. Hence, the
sad accident that befel the youth resulted in definitely
establishing both church and school in that locality. My
principal coadjutors in this work were, Messrs. Clark, J.
Hancock, H. Mildred, E. M. Bagot, C. Wills, and H. E.
Downer, of whom all but the two last have passed away.
Of course the wives of those named, and other ladies, did
a very large share of the work involved in bringing these
undertakings to a successful issue.

In 1855 the late Mr. R. Beetson offered to give five acres
of land near St. George's Church for a glebe. It was of
course advisable that this should be held by the same
trustees as the church. But for some months the trust-
deed of the church could not be found. At length two
deeds were discovered, a second having been executed in
consequence of a serious flaw in the first. At the time the
land for the church had been given, it was under mortgage,

and the mortgagee had not consented or signed the conveyance, hence a second conveyance was executed. But, lo! this second deed was also pronounced invalid by the late Mr. Charles Fenn, who was acting gratuitously in the matter. It had been drawn up under the " Act for Promoting the Christian Religion," which specified that in the case of all churches and ministers' residences aided under its provisions there should be not less than three or more than five trustees. This deed, however, contained the name of the Lord Bishop as well as the names of the five trustees appointed under the first deed ; hence, professing to be drawn in accordance with the Act, and containing what was an infringement of its provisions, it was declared valueless. Consequently a third deed was prepared, including the land for the church and the five-acre glebe. Of course all this caused considerable delay, during which Mr. Beetson changed his mind, desiring to withdraw from his promise—and not a little pressure had to be exercised to induce him to sign the conveyance, which he ultimately did.

In 1859 we succeeded in getting six rooms of a parsonage erected on this glebe, when I surrendered my highly-rented house and dismissed my pupils. Having two years previously secured an endowment of forty pounds per annum to St. George's, I thought 1 might cease teaching and give myself wholly to the ministry. In this, however, I acted too precipitately, and after about a year had to resume tuition. Indeed, during that year I took the work of the late Mr. C. May, second master of St. Peter's Collegiate School, in consequence of his some months' illness.

Toward the end of 1860 I commenced a Sunday evening service at Payneham, in the house of Mr. Cornish, sen.

That was soon transferred to the schoolroom of Mrs. Cornish, where we had an average attendance of from thirty to forty. After about two years, as the tendency was to increase, and I received an address with thirty signatures thanking me for commencing services there and soliciting their continuance, we began to talk about a church, and the late Mr. Bakewell, though a Congregationalist, was kind enough to offer a very suitable site. Just as this occurred, however, opportunity offered for my exchanging to Willunga, which on the score of health I felt bound to avail myself of. For some time the long continued strain of clerical and educational duties had been causing frequent attacks of indisposition and nervous debility, for which the medical advice always was, less mental and sedentary work, and plenty of horse exercise. When, therefore, the Willunga cure was becoming vacant, the Bishop recommended my exchanging to it, which I was thankful to do though it involved interruption of work I was anxious to complete, and the severance of many pleasant connexions. The only assistance I had had during my occupancy of the cure was from Mr. A. Treuer, who for about two years resided with me as general assistant and German tutor.

After expiration of the one hundred pounds a year guarantee, at the end of 1852, I received no grants from synodal or other church funds toward income, the rules disqualifying me in consequence of my taking pupils; while above fifty pounds I had been compelled to expend on the parsonage was not recouped. The general issue, however, of these twelve years' work was, that the church had become so far established in the district that my successors have not had to pupilise. The Payneham congregation, I am sorry to say, became broken up, as my successor did not continue the services. Though, in this, as in other cases, I had commenced services without any stipulation as to payment, the few people attending handed me fourteen pounds odd as the result of fees and offertories during the two years the services continued, and would soon have done more.

The only liability on the district when I left was one hundred pounds on the church at Campbelltown, for which those zealous friends, Messrs. E. M. Bagot, J. Hancock, H. E. Downer, and one or two others had made themselves personally responsible, and this became liquidated about a year afterwards.

In order to show the actualities of pioneering work, I append a statement (see Appendix A) of all receipts during the first ten years I occupied the cure, as rendered to Bishop Short; the accounts for the last two years I omitted to copy before leaving.

CHAPTER VIII.

SUNDRY INCIDENTS.

DURING the twelve years I was at Magill, not only had many difficulties to be encountered and overcome, but various and sometimes odd incidents occurred. I found an individual acting as clerk who deemed it his duty to lead the responses in a rather loud tone—but, was apt to make mistakes. At the Good Friday morning service after my arrival, I had given out the number of the first of the proper Psalms, and allowing a little time for people to find it, slowly read the first verse. My clerk, however, had failed to find it, and no one else attempted to usurp his customary taking the lead. Thinking it a good opportunity for administering a quiet rebuke, as there were but few persons present, I waited. A minute or two's silence ensued, while he was hurriedly turning the leaves of his prayer-book. Presently he broke forth, double-forte—" I stick fast in the deep mire," and as suddenly stopped, commencing to turn his leaves again amid renewed silence. He had stumbled on the first psalm for the evening service. After such a declaration of his bemuddlement, I thought it useless to wait, and proceeded to read the psalm alone, others being too timid to respond. The effect may be judged—books or handkerchiefs hiding faces, especially among some boarding-school young ladies. The following Sunday I suggested to my clerk that as there were again proper Psalms he had better look them out beforehand, and not stick in the " mire."

As further illustration of the close connection sometimes

made to exist between the solemn and the ridiculous I may mention the following. A valued friend, who had helped me much on sundry occasions, though a staunch dissenter, having died, I attended his funeral. Finding myself approaching a chapel burial-ground, I was curious as to the form of service I was to hear, and not a little pleased to find it to be the Church service, with addition of a hymn and short address in the chapel. On arrival at the grave, the Church service was continued; but when those solemn words occurred—"We commit his body to the ground, earth to earth, ashes to ashes," the minister unfortunately adopted very emphatic aspirates, "hearth to hearth, hashes to hashes"—it was difficult to repress one's annoyance. On being asked afterwards to permit the Noble Grand of a lodge to read their form of service at a grave after the Church service, I replied—"Yes, provided you don't murder the Queen's English." The said official afterwards said he did not wonder at my stipulation, for a former Noble Grand of his lodge, when reading the customary form in the lodge-room before proceeding to a funeral, solemnly pronounced the words "reverential awe," "reverenti-al a we"—not to the edification of the brethren.

The discovery of gold in Victoria causing the exodus of nearly all our male population, was the cause of no little loss and inconvenience to the clergy, none of whom, however, abandoned their cures. Business was brought nearly to a standstill for a long time, most shops in Adelaide being closed, and having notices up to the effect that their proprietors proposed returning in so many weeks or months. Hence, supplies were difficult to obtain, and many things had to be done by the people themselves which ordinarily were done for them. For instance, it was often exceedingly difficult to get a load of firewood brought. In such a difficulty I called on Judge Gwynne one morning to purchase or beg a dead tree in his paddock, near to my house. I found his honor acting groom, busily cleaning his horse to proceed to town. Inviting me to join him at breakfast, he readily gave me the tree, and wished he could send some one to cut it up for me. Chatting over matters, I suggested that the legal as well as the clerical profession ought to serve society on the voluntary principle. My host, however, couldn't at all see the equity of the proposal, on the contrary he frankly admitted that clients' contributions to their legal advisers were often very involuntary. Procuring a crosscut saw, maul and wedges, I got the tree down, and in due time cut up ; nor did I find myself any the worse for an hour's exercise of this kind before breakfast. As the house I was renting had no well, water had to be brought from a creek about a quarter of a mile away. No water-cart being available, I had a hogshead fitted with an iron axle at each end, on which a rod was fastened, and rolling it to the creek filled and dragged it home. A like difficulty occurred in regard to hay. Needing a winter's supply for my horse, and unable to rely on getting it as wanted, I and a neighbour arranged to buy a few acres of standing crop and get it cut and stacked, having previously engaged a returned digger to do the work. But unfortunately, just as the crop was ready, he became ill, and could not do it. There was but one resource—do it ourselves. Accordingly, forks, scythes, &c., were purchased, and from five in the morning till dark, for a week or two, every hour I could spare from teaching or other duties was employed in the hay-field. Of course the first handling of the scythe was attended by a good deal of blundering and fun ; the point, for instance, would keep sticking in the ground, till we discovered that it required to be bent up a little before using. Then, too, there were the arm-aches and back-aches that so unwonted an exercise induced. However, we got the hay down and safely stacked, and it was well we persevered, for fodder went up to famine price owing to the demand for shipment to Melbourne. Then, too, if a boot or shoe showed a fracture, or sole threatened to leave its upper, no professional gentleman was to be had, you must repair the damage yourself, or allow the article to drift into an unusable condition, and buy at a fabulous price some imported substitute, often flimsy and unsuitable. Consequently, the shoemaker's awl and other appliances became necessary additions to one's stock of tools. An incident arising out of this was amusing. The Bishop being at the time in London was asked as to the correctness of a report that had reached there, viz. that some of his clergy were reduced to such straits that they were obliged to take to shoemaking in order to live. His Lordship knew nothing of the matter, but surmised the truth, and replied accordingly. Calling at Beaumont a week or two after his return, I found him with tool-chest open busily mending his mangle. He mentioned the rumour he had heard, and asked if I knew any foundation for it. I told him that I and one or two others of his clergy had been compelled to do a little cobbling, to prevent our children's shoes from becoming useless, but nothing further, suggesting that it would be about equally correct to describe him as an episcopal mangle manufacturer as to term us shoemakers. Evidently, some one who knew of our purchasing tools had jumped to the conclusion that we were going into business as clerical cordwainers, and written home accordingly.

The most disagreeable thing I found to be, occasionally having to kill one's own sheep or steer. I always had the greatest repugnance to taking life, and would never, if I could avoid it, kill a chicken. Having to kill larger creatures came at first as a great trial ; however, it had to be done. Whenever possible, I got two or three neighbours to assist me in such matters, paying for their help out of the results ; when this could not be managed, the pickle tub got filled. The same when a horse had to be broken in ; a rough rider might sometimes be got for a week or so, but afterwards " do it yourself " was the order of the day.

As for matters domestic, servants were sometimes obtainable, sometimes not ; sometimes very efficient, oftener with everything to learn. Anecdotes of their oddities furnished frequent matter of amusement among ladies. One we had, a spinster of some forty years, a daughter of Erin, was told to watch some tarts that had been put in the oven. Hearing nothing, in due time my wife went to see after them, when she found Biddy sitting on the ground in front of the oven, with its door wide open, intently watching said tarts and wondering when they would be done. Another, on being told to make some melted butter for use with vegetables, literally did so, putting a quantity of butter into a saucepan, melting it, and so serving it up. Another, being told by my wife to wash the buggy cover, calico, popped the black water-proof rug into the boiling water instead, utterly spoiling it. As a natural consequence of this position of things, the mistress of a household had often very heavy duties to discharge. Cows had to be milked, butter made, bread baked, and all other ordinary duties attended to, which with a young family rising round called for incessant toil. My own children numbered ten,

five of whom died in infancy. Yet, though thus over-
taxed, the clergyman's wife was looked to to take a leading
part in, or superintend, the Sunday-school, especially, as
in my case, if the clergyman were precluded by other
duties from attending. Mrs. Miller acted in this capacity
nearly thirty years. She was also expected to pay frequent
visits, preside at sewing-meetings, organise or work for
bazaars, arrange for tea-meetings, &c. Hence, it will be
seen that neither the early clergy nor their wives were
blessed with sinecures. In towns the pressure was not
quite so severe.

I was accustomed to conduct school from 9 A.M. till
3.30 daily and then start on parochial visitation. One
afternoon, the mare I was riding fell, and I sustained a
broken collar-bone, with sundry bruisings. This, however,
did not prevent attention to scholastic or other duties.
Not very long after, I had the misfortune to lose this mare,
my only means of conveyance. Coming in with other
horses from a paddock, she was found with a broken leg,
and had to be shot. For a week or two I had to
pedestrianise. Attending a sale with the view of purchasing
another horse, I met Mr. Price Maurice, a squatter, and
one of my parishioners. On my saying I was horse-
hunting, he replied—" Pray don't trouble yourself; surely
some of us can find you another horse;" therefore, I did
not further trouble myself. In a week or two Mr. Maurice
sent word that a mob of horses had arrived from his
Pekina station for market, and that he had selected a
filly he thought would suit me. Taking an assistant, I
forthwith proceeded to his yard, and found a beautiful
chestnut two-year-old awaiting me, the offspring of Mr.
Maurice's racing mare, Kitten, and the Hon. J. Baker's
steeplechaser, Forlorn Hope. I need not say I was delighted

with such a present and specially thankful for the spirit which dictated it. She did my work for above twenty years, producing three colts and a filly, which have kept me fully supplied ever since. Mr. H. E. Downer also presented my wife with a young horse; so that the fifteen pounds I paid for the filly I bought shortly after arrival out of a Sydney mob constituted my only purchase money for horses during forty-seven years, and I now have three left.

The following incident illustrates the mischief too often wrought by works of fiction, or travels and adventures concocted by writers who have no actual knowledge of what they write about, and who perhaps have never quitted their native land.

A youth who had been educated at Christ's Hospital, London, came out to join his father, a brother clergyman and valued friend of mine. A position in the Government survey department was obtained for him, as his training fitted him specially for it. His father residing at a distance, it was arranged that he should live with me. Unfortunately, he had read a good deal of romance about bush life in Australia, and imagined it full of stirring incidents and adventures. The routine of office work, therefore, proved so thoroughly distasteful, and opposed to his preconceived ideas of Australian life, that he could not be prevailed upon to continue it. In the issue, a position on a station had to be obtained for him. It was not long before he found the ordinary duties of a cattle-station, the rough accommodation, and often rougher associates, with the almost unvarying dietary of mutton, damper, and tea, anything but romantic. Being sent to Adelaide once or twice with cattle, we found him evidently disappointed,

though he would not confess it.   After awhile he quitted
the cattle-station and engaged himself on a sheep-station.
Rarely writing to his friends, his whereabouts could only
be known by the reports of others, till he was suddenly lost
sight of; I learned that he had quitted the sheep-station,
but could not hear of him elsewhere. Had he reached any
other of the stations near I should have heard of it, having
special opportunities for doing so and instituting inquiries.
Months passed by without a clue, when the newspapers
announced the finding of a body in the bush about twenty-
five miles from the station my young friend last quitted.
The report stated that the unfortunate one was past
all recognition, having apparently been dead some months,
but that a watch, pocket-book and some small articles
found on the body had been forwarded to the Adelaide
police-station.   Fearing the issue, I called to examine the
sad relics, and at once felt that the watch had belonged to
the lost youth, it having the maker's name and number
on its face. I took it to my watchmaker, Mr. Perryman.
His books showed he had cleaned it in my name at the
time I fitted out the youth for his bush career.   This,
together with a damaged cheque for wages in the pocket-
book, completed his identification ; he had perished in the
bush, a miserable ending to a life full of promise. The
watch, which was in a sad state, the bereaved father had
repaired and insisted on my retaining as a memento of his
unfortunate son, and I still have it in use.

Being early one morning in Magill, I was called to
a cottage inhabited by an Irish couple, living as I afterwards discovered in cohabitation. I found several women
in great excitement, and a little girl about six years old
just dead. I was informed that the man who rented the

cottage had killed her, and gone away towards Adelaide.
I at once sent for the nearest doctor, and requested a
friend who was going to business in Adelaide to inform
the police, forwarding a description of the person accused.
The doctor soon arrived, and as there was a severe con-
tusion at the back of the child's neck, after turning the
head about he declared the neck was broken. It appeared
that the man and woman had been drinking and quarrelling over-night, and as he was apt during or after a quarrel
to vent his spite on the child (the issue of a former
cohabitation) the mother sent it out of the house in the
morning till the man should have departed. Passing,
however, near where the child was sitting, it would seem
he must have struck her with the handle of the bullock-
whip he carried ; the blow falling across the nape of the
neck, she at once fell, and quickly died.   In due time the
police arrived, and the man having been arrested, the
ordinary course of inquest, &c., was entered on. Doubting
the doctor's statement as to the neck being broken, I
suggested the desirability of a *post-mortem* examination
before giving his evidence. He, however, was very positive,
saying he distinctly heard the bones "crick" as he turned
the head about, and that a *post-mortem* was quite unnecessary.   His evidence was given accordingly at the inquest,
and afterwards in the police court. A few days after I had
interred the child, a police inspector arrived with a request
from the authorities that I would permit exhumation of
the body in order to have a *post-mortem*, the medical
evidence not being deemed satisfactory.   Disinterment,
therefore, took place, the examination being made by the
same doctor in the church porch, in the presence of
sundry officials and myself.   Instead, however, of the neck
being broken, there was found extravasation of blood at

the base of the brain, no other cause of death being discoverable.

At the trial, Judge Crawford presided ; Sir James Hurtle Fisher was engaged for the defence, and Sir Richard Hanson (afterwards judge) acted as Crown prosecutor. Preliminary evidence having being taken, the doctor was called on. Previously, he had worked himself up into a state of nervous excitement, partly as a result of the mistake he had made, and partly lest, through his evidence, the prisoner should be hung ; therefore, on entering the witness-box he was just in a condition to get confused After admitting his error in at first deposing to the neck being broken, and stating that the *post-mortem* showed extravasation of blood at base of the brain to be the only cause of death, and that such extravasation was possibly caused by a blow from the bullock-whip, cross-examination by Sir J. H. Fisher began. The mother having said the child had been sick the evening before its death, all sorts of suggestions were made to lead the doctor to admit some other possible cause of death than that he had deposed to. In this Sir James called as an opposing witness my esteemed friend Dr. Wm. Gosse, whom I then met for the first time. After nearly two hours' badgering, during which the doctor became more and more nervous, Sir James suddenly asked—"How long after death does the blood continue in a fluid state ?" The doctor scarcely knew, but said—" Some little time." "You saw this child very shortly after death, do you think the blood was then completely set ?" The doctor thought that it " might not have been." " In trying to ascertain if the neck was broken, you said you gave the head more than one sharp twist. Now, since you so strongly twisted the head that you heard the bones " crick," though the neck was not

broken, don't you think—the blood not being quite set—
that the wrench you gave might possibly have ruptured
a vessel, and allowed blood to escape?"   "It is not impossible," said the doctor. Sir James sat down with a very
self-satisfied air. Silence ensued. Presently Sir Richard
Hanson rose, and in his quiet deliberate style said—"Well,
doctor, after what you have just told my learned friend,
viz., that it is not impossible you yourself ruptured a
vessel by twisting the child's head about shortly after
death, possibly so causing an extravasation of blood, what
then, in your opinion as a medical man, was the cause of
death?" The doctor then seemed to wake up to the
awkwardness of the position he had been led into, and
addressing the judge, said—"Your honour must allow me
to go back a little." The judge replied—"As it is near
lunch time, the court will adjourn till two o'clock;" thus
kindly giving the unlucky one time to collect his scattered
senses. As we were passing out of the court, Sir James
Fisher, who rarely allowed opportunity for a joke to pass
unimproved, said to the police inspector—"You must not
lose sight of the doctor; if the prisoner gets acquitted, he
will have to be arrested, for if the prisoner did not kill the
child it is clear the doctor did." Sir James affected not to
see the doctor close by, and who I fear did not much enjoy
that day's lunch. On the court re-assembling, the doctor
was again unmercifully catechised—his mistakes being
made the most of by the lawyers on both sides. Of course
he had to confess to his error, and fall back on what every
one saw to have been the cause of death, viz., extravasation
of blood at the base of the brain resulting from a severe
blow, such as a back-handed stroke from the handle of the
bullock-whip might have given. In summing up, the judge
animadverted very strongly on the unreliable character

of the medical evidence, and he could scarcely be blamed for doing so. In the issue, the man was convicted, and sentenced to two years' hard labour for manslaughter, which he richly deserved.

The introduction of lay-readers has been of immense advantage to the Church, enabling services to be held in many places where it would have been simply impossible for clergymen to act, owing to their small number. But even this has its difficulties. There are not wanting those who desire to obtain the Bishop's license, and act as lay-readers, in order to gratify vanity, or attain the status it may be thought to confer, or some other reason than the simple desire to do a measure of good. Then, too, sometimes persons who cannot be deemed quite suitable offer themselves, and if not accepted are apt to become irritated, perhaps inimical. Such a case occurred to myself. On my declining proffers of service repeatedly urged, the individual took offence. Presently unpleasant rumours *re* matters financial got into circulation, such as were calculated to seriously impair my influence amongst my parishioners. On these being traced home, I requested the Bishop to institute an inquiry, and their originator was asked, by his Lordship's direction, to put his statements in writing, according to the rules of Synod, that they might be fully gone into. This, acting under legal advice, he declined to do ; therefore, as the Synod was powerless, the Bishop instructed me to go to his solicitor, and act under his advice. I did so, and an action for defamation was commenced. Owing to some legal technicality the trial got postponed from one session to another, but when it did come on I obtained a verdict for forty shillings, not having claimed vindictive damages, but only sufficient to clear myself and throw all costs on the other side. This illustrates the necessity for Synod being able to protect the clergy without legal proceedings being resorted to.

Returning late one Friday night from a church-building committee meeting at Campbelltown, I was told I had been three times sent for to Dr. Wark's. Reaching there about midnight, I found the house apparently closed for the night, though there was a light in an upper room, and I could see the doctor asleep on a couch in the surgery. Not liking to disturb him, I returned home. Going early next morning, I was surprised and shocked to find Mrs. Wark and a newly-born infant dead, and four other children ill from what was then termed Boulogne sore throat, since known as diphtheria, and of which Mrs. Wark had died. The doctor being completely unnerved by the affliction that had so suddenly befallen, asked me to undertake the arrangements for his wife and child's interment the next day, which of course I did, sending notes to numerous friends, it being too late to advertise. On the arrival of Drs. Woodforde and Gosse, who had attended Mrs. Wark, they wished me to take charge of the four remaining patients, and use the prescribed remedies, which I gladly did, having the assistance of Miss Malpas, a neighbour, who was most assiduous throughout. During the day a little boy about four years old died, and when the undertaker brought Mrs. Wark's coffin in the evening I ordered another for him. Feeling that a girl about nine years old would scarcely survive the night, I ascertained that a coffin could also be furnished for her if necessary, being anxious not to have two funerals. As I feared, so it fell out, for she died, and at daylight I sent orders for a third coffin to come out with the hearse ; the infant had been placed in its mother's coffin. When, therefore, the friends assembled to follow, as they thought, Mrs. Wark's remains to the grave, there was no little astonishment and consternation at three coffins being brought out and placed in the hearse. The Rev. T. Q. Stow, on arrival, inquired if the disease was infectious, seeming to hesitate at entering the house. He had married the doctor and his wife, and it was wished that he should conduct a service in the house after the Presbyterian custom. I told him I had been in the house from the previous morning without any ill effects, and that he had better go in and do what was required, I accompanying him. On reaching the church, the undertaker whispered to me that the grave was not long enough for the two children's coffins to be placed on the mother's in one length, as I had directed. I told him to set the grave-digger to work, and I would keep the people in the church till he should enter the porch and raise his hat. Therefore, after the ordinary service in the church, which was crowded, I commenced an address on the circumstances that had brought us together. Having abundant scope, there was no difficulty in keeping the people's attention engaged, and many eyes were moist. I was not sorry, however, when the arranged signal appeared, for it was not easy to command one's own feelings in such a case, especially as only on the previous Sunday evening I had spent a pleasant hour or so with the doctor and his family, three of whom, with one since born, were then lying dead before us. Asking Mr. Stow to join me in leading the procession we arrived at the grave, and solemnly committed at one service four bodies to its silent keeping. It was an occasion to be remembered, and produced a deep impression upon many. The doctor, utterly broken down, was at once taken away by some friends. Returning to the house, I found another child almost beyond hope, and resolved that if he continued till morning I would send him and the others to the sea-side, out of the contaminated atmosphere.   He and a little girl continued ; so procuring a close carriage, I sent them all away to the sea beach ; and I have little doubt the change mainly contributed to the sick ones' recovery.

A few days afterwards, my wife, who had taken my place in the doctor's house while I was away at the funeral, and three church services, being there indeed all day, was attacked with the same complaint; then two of my children, and the servant. No one being procurable to undertake the nursing, for the people had become thoroughly scared, I had everything to do for a while, and was mercifully preserved and enabled to do it, never experiencing any of the dangerous symptoms, neither did Miss Malpas, who so ably assisted.   Luckily, I was at the time without pupils. Dr. Wark being away, Dr. Taylor, of Kensington, attended my wife, but from the numerous cases on hand he could not visit often.   The treatment then was, touching the throat with caustic, or brushing the throat with a solution of it, and for some months I always carried a caustic pencil and some solution to use in cases occurring in my ordinary visitations.

Dr. Wark's was the first case in which this disease was definitely recognised as having entered the colony, though my own opinion was that it had existed for some time, but had been regarded as virulent croup.   In a short time about a dozen deaths occurred in my district, whereas the usual mortality was but three or four per annum.

CHAPTER IX.

WILLUNGA, NOARLUNGA, AND ALDINGA.

THE districts of Noarlunga, twenty miles, and of Willunga, thirty miles south of Adelaide, were united as one of the first country cures established by Bishop Short on his arrival. Visits to those districts had occasionally been paid by the Rev. Jas. Farrell, W. J. Woodcock, and W. H. Coombs, but nothing could be done to establish services, for want of clergymen. The Bishop placed these districts in charge of the Rev. A. B. Burnett—who had accompanied him from England—and who proceeded to the then very small township of Willunga, which, having reference to Port Elliot and Yankalilla, was deemed the most central position, and pitched a tent there. In this he lived for some time, till he found accommodation in the house of one of the settlers. Sunday services were commenced in the large room of the public-house at Noarlunga and at Willunga in a house. Advantage was taken of grants from the Government; one hundred and fifty pounds each being obtained toward erecting churches at Noarlunga and Willunga, and one hundred and fifty pounds toward erection of a parsonage at Willunga, where a grant of twenty acres for a glebe was also obtained ; to this twenty other adjoining acres were added, at the upset price of one pound per acre. These grants, with grants from the Bishop's fund, together with subscriptions from the settlers, enabled the foundation of the Church to be laid in these districts. Mr. Burnett held charge of the cure for seven years, and then returned to England. Out of his own means he had done much toward erecting the parsonage, planting the garden, &c., though he had been unable to complete it or the churches. He was succeeded by the Rev. T. R. Neville, who for seven years held the incumbency, during which time no advance appears to have been made. On his resigning, I became licensed to it.

On removing to Willunga in February 1863, I found that the church had been built about a mile west of the township, while the parsonage was quite a mile to the south of it, with a somewhat difficult road owing to hills. One result of this misplacing of buildings had been the erection, not only of a Roman Catholic church in the centre of the township, but four Methodist chapels, to which a Christian Disciples' chapel was afterwards added. Had the church buildings been better placed, some of these would certainly not have been built, to the waste of means, and fostering of schism.

The parsonage, which had never been thoroughly finished, was in a sadly dilapidated condition, nothing having been done to it since Mr. Burnett's leaving, and nearly one hundred pounds had to be expended at once to make it decently habitable and repair fences. It was on the glebe, at the base of a range of high hills, behind which an almost uninhabited scrub extended for many miles. The house being thatched, was often in danger from bush fires, which sometimes continued for days together to threaten it with destruction, live embers being brought over by the wind from the trees burning on the heights just behind. While the fires lasted, we had to keep watch all night, with vessels of water ready round the roof, which

at one part was level with the ground, the house having
been built into the side of a hill. Had the grass near at
hand ignited, nothing could have saved the house; our
efforts were, therefore, always directed to beating or burning the fire back at a distance. Then, too, our only water
was from a well, a good deal below the house, so that
drawing and fetching up water for a fire would have been
all but impossible. A good many years elapsed before we
could get the thatch replaced by a slate roof, after which
we felt in less danger.

The means of access being difficult, in fact unsafe for
vehicles, three acres from an adjacent property were
purchased at a cost of seventy pounds and added to the
glebe shortly after my arrival in order to obtain a better
road, so making it in all forty-three acres; and the whole
was re-fenced.

Homestead matters having been thus far completed,
attention was directed to the churches. Willunga church
was renovated, plastered, and painted. A large harmonium
was also secured at the cost of sixty pounds, and we had
the advantage of an excellent organist in the late Mr. H.
R. Pounsett, whose services, with members of his family
as choir, were gratuitously rendered.

Not long after these things were completed, the congregation became too large for the accommodation provided, and meetings were held to consider the best means
for adding thereto. It being deemed inadvisable to enlarge
the church, which had been very badly built, on a small
scale, it was decided to erect a new one, when division
at once arose as to its position. By far the greater number
of worshippers came from the township, or northward and
eastward of it, and these wished a new building to be

erected in the township, or close to it. The donor of the two acres, which formed the cemetery and site of the existing church, contended that he had a right to have the services continued on that site, that to discontinue holding them there would be a breach of covenant, and urged the erection of the proposed new church on the site he had given, and some, but quite a minority, supported this idea. In the issue, a building committee was appoint d, and it was arranged that its members when canvassing for subscriptions should endeavour to ascertain from subscribers their opinions on the matter, and duly report them.

While this was going on, an advertisement cut out of the newspaper was posted to me inviting the residents of Aldinga, some three miles west of Willunga church, to attend a public meeting to consider the advisability of erecting a church at Aldinga, and this was accompanied by a note specially requesting my attendance at said meeting. This was a surprise, as but two or three families from Aldinga attended the Willunga church, and it was thought there were but few church people there ; I knew comparatively little of Aldinga at the time. However, I complied with the request, went to the meeting, and found about twenty settlers assembled, evidently very earnest in regard to the object for which they had met. The principal thing they required me for was, to know whether, if they built a church, service could be provided for in it. As I had then but two services on Sundays, one at Willunga in the morning, and one at Noarlunga in the afternoon—which had been the arrangement from the establishment of the church in the district—I was able to say, that were a church erected in Aldinga I would undertake to supply an evening service every Sunday, pending some better arrangement, though it would involve more travelling, making about twenty-three miles round. This seemed to satisfy, and resolutions were passed to forthwith commence operations. A committee consisting of Mr. R. Palmer (chairman), Messrs. W. Bowering, A. Coles, W. Hilton, J. Ellis, and myself (as secretary) was appointed, and toward one hundred and fifty pounds at once promised. A committee of ladies was afterwards formed, consisting of the wives of the foregoing with some others, and to their energy and perseverance the success of the undertaking was largely due.

On my reporting to the Willunga church building committee what had transpired, and expressing the opinion that in all probability a church would be ere long erected at Aldinga, they decided to suspend operations, and await the issue. One plea for building a new Willunga church on the site of the old one had been, that it would convenience the church members in Aldinga; so that were they to provide a church for themselves, this plea would be done away; besides, it would be impolitic to undertake two such buildings at once, and Aldinga had already got the lead.

A few months after, the foundation-stone of St. Ann's Church, Aldinga, was laid by Mrs. Short, an acre of land having been presented by the South Australian Company. It being resolved not to incur debt, the work was only carried on as funds came in till about five hundred pounds had been expended on walls, roof, floors, and doors. The wish was then expressed that the building should be at once utilised, and service commenced, with temporary seats. This I objected to, and suggested that as but about two hundred and fifty pounds were required to complete and fit up the church, the six trustees should be asked to advance forty pounds each as a loan, and that the half of all income from seat-rents should be devoted to reduction of the debt till its extinguishment. This was agreed to, and the money advanced without interest; and on the building (it was only the nave) having been completed, it was opened for service by the late Dean Farrell, the Bishop being at the time in England. Hence, from where there were supposed to be hardly any members of the church, a congregation of from fifty to sixty attended, and above seventy sittings were let. In about four years from its commencement the entire cost, seven hundred and eighty-five pounds, was defrayed without any aid from Synod or other church funds, and the church consecrated. Mrs. Short presented it with a handsome communion service as the final requisite; a Sunday-school was also, of course, established.

As the services were only in the evening, the sacrament of the Lord's Supper had to be administered in the evening. It being desirable to alter this, and give an occasional morning service, I concluded to obtain the assistance of a lay-reader once a month for Willunga, to allow me to be at Aldinga in the morning for administering Holy Communion. On this proposal being submitted to the Willunga vestry, quite a storm arose. Some were a little jealous on account of Aldinga succeeding in what most Willunga folk had pronounced an impossibility; while others contended that, as a morning service had always been held at Willunga, they ought not to be deprived in any degree of it. I explained, that if they would procure lamps I would hold an evening service at Willunga on the Sundays when I should be at Aldinga in the morning. But it was all no use. A resolution was passed that service at Willunga should be continued as it always had been, and no alteration permitted. Allowing a little time for the excitement to

subside, I obtained the assistance of Mr. R. Bosworth, of
Noarlunga, to act as lay-reader, who kindly undertook to
ride over and conduct morning service at Willunga once a
month ; and procuring some lamps, I proceeded to carry out
my plans, regardless of the vestry's decision. Of course
this raised a fresh commotion ; some, on arriving at the
church and finding a lay-reader officiating, turned back
and went home. For a while, indignation at the vestry's
decision being ignored ran high ; but having subsequently
proceeded in getting Dr. R. G. Jay, Mr. A. Coles, and Mr.
Malpas to act as lay-readers, we were able to start morning
and evening services every Sunday both at Aldinga and
Willunga, and these have been carried on ever since.
Thus, five services became established where but two had
previously existed, myself taking three and lay-readers two.
After a while this met with general approval ; I believe no
one now would wish to see it altered ; and since my retirement the arrangement has been continued.

The immediate requirements connected with the parsonage, Willunga church, and Aldinga church having been
completed, Noarlunga church came in for attention. This
had been named the "Church of St. Philip and St.
James ;" it was said the designation was chosen because
two gentlemen having those as Christian names took an
active part in its erection. This church had been left
unplastered, unpainted, and without chancel or vestry,
though having a too large tower ; consequently the interior
was cheerless and unattractive. Its position, too, a quarter
of a mile from the township, on a steep hill, while somewhat picturesque, was by no means conducive to good
attendance on wet or very hot Sundays, and was made a

frequent excuse for absence by old folks and weakly ones.
All things considered, a large congregation from a small
population could hardly under such circumstances be
looked for.

A committee having been formed, consisting of Messrs.
G. Yates, Thos. Dungey, J. Mudge, C. and W. Holly, and
one or two others. they went to work with a will. The
slates of the roof, which had been so put on that they
rattled with every breeze, were stripped off and relaid
more securely. A chancel and vestry were added, and the
whole plastered, painted, and made more meet for divine
worship. A bell was also procured and hung in the
tower. The total outlay was about two hundred and fifty
pounds, of which part remained as debt for a year or two.
The churchyard, also, was laid out and planted, but unfortunately a number of goats kept by near residents ate off
the trees, the fences not being close enough to exclude
them.

Not long after the completion of the buildings mentioned
—but fortunately not till the debts connected with them
had been discharged — the exodus to the newly opened
agricultural areas commenced. In the earlier years it had
been thought that the cultivable land in the colony was of
very limited extent, and mostly near Adelaide ; Mount
Barker, twenty-five miles to the east, and Willunga, thirty
miles to the south, were the principal agricultural districts
at a distance from the city. Hence it came about that
much of the other land was let on long leases, generally
twenty-one years, for grazing purposes ; runs for cattle and
sheep containing hundreds of square miles being held by
squatters, often at very low rental. In the course of time,
however, it was discovered that on some of these runs

there was land suitable for cultivation; therefore, on the leases terminating, many were resumed by the Government, laid out as farms, often of a square mile each, and offered on easy terms to settlers. Consequently, the farmers in the old agricultural districts, who generally had to pay high rents, ten shillings or more per acre, were attracted to these new lands, or sent their sons to settle on them. To such an extent did this go, that in two or three years the districts of Willunga, &c., lost more than half their population. When I removed to there in 1863, it might be said in general terms that every 80-acre section supported a family, more or less directly. When I left, there were three or four sections to a family, sometimes more. This altered condition of things, of course, largely affected the churches, and it was seen that the only way of giving anything like permanence to what had been effected would be to increase their endowments. I had found the Willunga church endowed to the extent of two hundred pounds, and Noarlunga to four hundred pounds, on which ten per cent. was being paid by the attorneys of the S.P.G., or sixty pounds per annum. With a view to inducing congregations to give increased stability to the Church, the attorneys in 1873 offered to make a grant of seventy pounds as a supplement to thirty pounds raised to secure an endowment of one hundred pounds, on which, again, they liberally offered to guarantee ten per cent. for ten years. This handsome offer came most opportunely. We needed three hundred pounds to raise the Willunga endowment to the maximum of five hundred pounds. Some subscriptions were obtained, I think about sixteen pounds, and the balance required was borrowed by my people from the bank, I undertaking to repay it from the proceeds of the additional endowment. By these means the endowment of this church to the permitted limit was secured. The Aldinga congregation, having but just before cleared their building debt, could not take up the matter, neither did the Noarlunga folk. Before my leaving, however, means were obtained to complete the endowment of both these churches, so that a total of fifteen hundred pounds was attained for the united cure, though no longer at ten per cent., but only six, owing to the altered rate of interest. The original idea was, to provide a fifty pounds endowment for each church, but it is now thirty pounds, and may become less.

It was not till 1884 that the long-talked-of project of building a new church in the township of Willunga assumed a definite shape. A very eligible site having been obtained, a building-committee was formed, and three hundred pounds handed over to them from a committee of ladies who had been for a long time working to obtain that amount. These gentlemen, none of whom had had any previous experience in church building, took the matter entirely into their own hands, without in any way consulting me, acting indeed in avowed opposition to my advice. They were desirous of getting a church erected to seat about two hundred persons for five or six hundred pounds, which I deemed impossible. An architect was engaged, who produced what they considered a very pretty plan, the carrying out of which, however, involved over twelve hundred pounds, leaving a debt of nearly six hundred pounds, the interest on which, and its reduction, necessitated, and still necessitate, continual effort. Of this amount, three hundred pounds remained when I left. So badly, too, was the work done, that the roof admitted water in several places before the building was opened for service, and has continued to do so ever since; there were also sundry other defects, the results of inexperience and mismanagement. But, notwithstanding these things, it was a great matter to have the church services transferred to the township, where they could be better availed of than formerly; and the attendance materially increased. The original church, being in the cemetery, was, just before I left, partially prepared to become a mortuary chapel, for which it is well adapted. With the exception of church schools, these districts are now, therefore, sufficiently supplied with buildings, the first desideratum in establishing a church anywhere.

During 1890 my health gave way somewhat seriously, and the continuance of Sunday duty, travelling twenty-three miles and conducting three services, became all but impossible—often during the third service my voice quite failed, especially in hot weather. Some time previously I had sought to exchange my cure for one of smaller area and wished to get appointed to some church suburban to Adelaide, but younger men were always preferred. Then, too, rheumatic pains in old injuries became increasingly troublesome. At different times I had broken both wrists, dislocated an ankle, contracted a large hernia, and hydrocele, results of horse accidents and much riding. For eighteen years 1 had done the duty of this large district entirely on horseback, and when injuries rendered riding impossible, the Noarlunga friends presented me with a buggy, by which I was enabled to continue duty eleven years longer, till a complete break-down threatening, I felt compelled to apply for superannuation. My wife, too, had not long before broken a leg, and through slipping on the hill-side previously, dislocated the opposite ankle, besides otherwise being unwell. Hence, at over seventy years of age, we had both become incapable of much more active duty.

During the twenty-nine years I had held the Willunga cure, I only missed Sunday duty on about a dozen occasions, from accident or illness. When my wrists were broken, for a few weeks on each occasion my wife drove me the Sunday's round, and I managed the services with an arm in splints. No cessation of duty for a holiday fell to my lot, for had it been possible to temporarily provide for my duties, I was at no time able to afford the indulgence.

During my occupancy of the cure I experienced many acts of kindness. I had not been long there when a new saddle and bridle were presented me, with sundry smaller matters, as half a ton of flour, &c. On trying to establish one of my sons on a farm, neighbours would offer, on finishing their ploughing, to bring a team to help. Once, no less than seven teams, mostly with double-furrowed ploughs, assembled to finish a forty-acre paddock, it was like a ploughing match. The year preceding my retirement, a stack of about ten tons of hay was put up for me, supplying fodder for the season. Hence, in quitting the district where I had laboured so long, I felt I was quitting many to whom I had become sincerely attached. Of course I had encountered a few cantankerous ones, whom nothing would please nor concession mollify, but one can afford to disregard such when there is kindly feeling on the part of the majority, and this I had the satisfaction of experiencing throughout. My application for superannuation having been kindly granted by the Bishop and standing committee of Synod, and a purse of sovereigns presented on Christmas eve by a few friends, in January 1892 I removed from the district, thankful for the prospect of rest after forty-three and a half years' uninterrupted work, dating from the issue of Bishop Short's first license.

As in the case of the Magill cure, I append a statement of moneys received for church purposes during the twenty-nine years of my incumbency at Willunga, to furnish some idea of the work done in material matters and the remuneration accorded.   (See Appendix B.)

CHAPTER X.

SUNDRY INCIDENTS.

THE routine duties of a country cure are seldom marked by incidents worth noting; a few things, however, I may mention. On taking charge of the Willunga district, I found it had been customary to hold public races at Noarlunga on Good Fridays. Hence, on giving notice for divine service on the afternoon of my first Good Friday there, I was told it would be perfectly useless attempting to hold service; that all had been accustomed to regard the day as a holiday simply, and probably some of those who usually attended, but took part in the races, would take offence. Disregarding this, the service was held, with very few present, races going on at the same time about a mile off. It was, however, the last Good Friday on which races were held there. The incongruity, I suppose, presented itself so strongly to the minds of those having the management thereof, that they fixed another day for their sports, and subsequent Good Fridays saw the church moderately well attended.

Conducting the burial service, in some cases, is apt to become a serious difficulty with ministers. The only instance in which I felt compelled to vary from the usual custom occurred at Noarlunga. Being telegraphed for one morning to inter a person I had met and spoken to the previous evening, and who then appeared to be in his usual health, I rode over, wondering what could have occurred.

Arriving at his house, I found it to have been a case of suicide. An inquest had been held, and the verdict said there was nothing to show the state of mind of the deceased. Sundry particulars, however, were told me. It appeared when I had met the unfortunate the previous evening, he had been giving his pet dog away; some other things he had also given away. Shortly after retiring for the night, he had summoned his housekeeper to give him some water, when she noticed a medicine bottle, glass, &c., on a chair by his bedside. She gave him the water, and retired. In a little while she was again called, and more water wanted; he then told her not to be alarmed at anything she might hear. Becoming uneasy, she inquired if he had been taking anything; he refused to satisfy her—but said his troubles would soon be over. She went to call a neighbour, who, however, would not go till he had called another neighbour—and by the time they reached the house tetanic convulsions had set in, and all was soon over. Being a medical man, he had evidently asked for water that the poison, strychnine, might the more quickly act, though it was remarkable he had not chosen some less painful agent. The rash act was the result of continual inebriety. As he had displayed the most perfect rationality up to the last, it was not possible to cloak the matter under the plea of insanity; therefore, I had to decide either on no burial service at all, or a modified one. I told those acting to bring the body to the churchyard, where a grave was ready, and I would consider what to do. Deeming it better there should be some service, for the sake of others, rather than none, I met the procession at the gate, and instead of leading into the church, as usual, proceeded at once to the grave, only reading the preliminary sentences. Obviously, I could not say it had

" pleased Almighty God to take to himself the soul of our brother here departed." Therefore, on the body being lowered, instead of proceeding with the ordinary service, I gave a short address to those assembled—mostly the deceased's boon companions—closing with an extemporaneous prayer and benediction. This seemed to give satisfaction, and was, as I think, preferable to compliance with the old law directing that a suicide should be buried in unconsecrated ground, or at the cross-roads, and have a stake driven through his body. In such sad cases, I regard it as of more importance to endeavour to influence or console the living than, so to speak, excommunicate the dead. I reported to the Bishop the course I had pursued, and he approved it; being, however, a little put out at first by my accidentally saying, I felt I had been guilty, to some minds, of a grave irregularity, and he thought I was punning; quite a mistake.

Among the various ways in which a country clergyman is required to assist his parishioners, the making of a will often crops up. Many persons defer attending to this important duty till they feel themselves on the eve of departure, and then, when distant from legal advice, the clergyman, or some other friend, is called on; I have frequently had to act in emergencies such as this. Unfortunately, it sometimes happens that wills so informally and hurriedly made furnish food for litigation; but only in one instance did this happen in regard to a will with which I had to do, and the circumstances were so peculiar that I am tempted to narrate them.

Being telegraphed for while attending Synod to a gentleman said to be dying, I hurried to his residence, arriving in the evening. I found that a medical consultation had pronounced that the patient had but a few days, or perhaps hours, to live. On entering his room, I found him propped up in bed, and with his wife's assistance trying to make a will. The first thing he said was—" Oh ! I am so glad you are come; I want you to help me settle my affairs." I knew nothing else was likely to be attended to till these were off his mind, and accordingly began to note down his wishes; as this could only be done at intervals owing to his often swooning, it was morning before I got all his views from him. There being, so far as I could judge, many thousand pounds' worth of property involved, and two trusteeships to be provided for, I felt doubtful as to my ability to make a will including so much without risking its being open to litigation afterwards. I, therefore, told the relatives that it would be advisable to send for legal assistance as soon as the telegraph should be open, and they decided to send for a gentleman with whom the testator had previously done some business. In case, however, indications of departure should appear before the solicitor could arrive, or a proper will be prepared, I proceeded to draw up a will in order to its being signed if needful. Certain property bequeathed to a married daughter had to be put in trust so that it should not be liable for her husband's debts, and that in event of her dying without issue, it should revert to other members of the testator's family. This I expressed in the clearest terms I could ; and by the time the solicitor arrived, had completed the will, so far as I knew how.

The relatives thinking it best not to let the testator know that legal assistance had been procured till the will should be ready for signature, the lawyer and I retired to complete the matter, he reading my will, and dictating to me, as clerk, the proper formula. The bequest to the daughter before mentioned, however, was left exactly as I had expressed it ; I, therefore, concluded I had effectually secured the property to her. When the document was ready, we waited on the testator, who was much annoyed at not having been informed of a lawyer being sent for, remarking that he should not have sent for the gentleman who had acted. However, he signed the will, and in a day or two died.

Soon after probate had been obtained, a claim was made on the daughter's trustees for debt of, if I remember rightly, one thousand pounds, contracted by her husband before marriage. This I regarded as futile, deeming the property bequeathed to her quite secure from any such claim. But I was wrong. On the matter being argued out in the law courts, it was held, that though the property could not be sold to defray the debt, there was nothing in the will to preclude the income arising from it being hypothecated for that purpose. To completely secure the benefit of the bequest to her. " without power of anticipating the income arising therefrom," or words to that effect, should have been inserted. Of this I was not aware when I made the will, and my legal friend did not correct the omission. Consequently, as the will before the court was drawn by a professional man, and had to be interpreted according to the strict rules of law, the decision was given in favour of the claimant, and the income from the property became forfeited to discharge the debt. It only remains to add, that the legal gentleman who came to my assistance was partner to the claimant.

On another occasion I got into the awkward position of having to take a leading part in a law-suit. The chairman of the District Council solicited my assistance to bring about, if possible, an amicable adjustment of a dispute about a watercourse, which had been subject of litigation, and promised to become so again. With a view to promote peace, and prevent further waste of public funds, I consented to see the party concerned, a widow, and advise a pacific settlement. On calling to see her, and stating my object, she promptly referred me to her solicitor. I declined having anything to do with law or lawyers in the matter, urging that differences among neighbours should be settled in a neighbourly way. I offered if she would state her view of the affair, to put it before the District Council, who, the chairman assured me, were willing and anxious to do all they could to satisfy her requirements. After much talking and persuasion she consented, and what she said she wanted was, briefly, to have the water from a certain spring on the opposite side of the road in front of her house conducted into her garden, for irrigation purposes, and the flood waters from a large gully beyond the road kept out of the garden. Should these two matters be accomplished she promised that all litigation should cease.

Having had no previous knowledge of the affair, I had next to ascertain the possibility of the requirements specified being complied with. Examination of the locality showed that the cottage, built of cob, and garden, were as nearly as possible in the centre of the watershed of the large gully referred to; therefore, as it seemed to me, a man who had deliberately so placed his house could hardly expect the expenditure of considerable public funds to protect his property from the risks natural to its position. With respect to the spring water required, and which already was conducted by an iron pipe the council had placed across the road into the garden, I was credibly informed that the natural course of that spring had been away from the garden, but that when the woman's husband built the cottage, he cut a channel to conduct the water from the spring on to his ground in order to mix the cob for building it. Having regard to these facts, I was led to wonder how it had happened that two or three cases in the local court had been decided against the council. But still, as my object was to prevent further litigation, I wished to discover a way to comply with what was required, notwithstanding its seeming unreasonableness. The main difficulty was, preventing storm waters from the gully flooding the place, which, as things then were, was impossible. The only way I could see was, for the District Council to purchase an opposite vacant allotment, and cut a sufficient drain through it to carry the water across the road clear of the complainant's property. On suggesting this to the council, they decided to do it, though it involved an expenditure of about one hundred and twenty pounds, it being thought better to incur that expense than be continually liable to claims for damages. On this being done, it was hoped the trouble was at an end. We were mistaken. A fresh action for five hundred pounds damages was shortly after commenced, the old lady complaining that the supply of spring water was not satisfactory, it being hot weather and the spring nearly dry, and that she did not believe the storm waters would be kept off by the means adopted. I then discovered that the place had become mortgaged to her solicitor, probably for costs, and she was only nominally plaintiff. The idea of five hundred pounds being alleged as damages in regard to a two-roomed cottage of cob and about half-an-acre of ground, the lot not worth one hundred pounds (it was subsequently sold for seventy), was simply preposterous. Two actions in the local court for small amounts having been successful, it was apparently intended to further deplete the ratepayers by way of costs in the Supreme Court. Having by that time become fully acquainted with the circumstances, and feeling convinced that no valid case could be established against the District Council, I consented to assist in their defence in conjunction with their solicitors, Messrs. W. and T. Pope, and the late Mr. Rupert Ingleby, who was engaged as counsel.

Just before the trial came on, I fortunately discovered a mistake that had been made by some of the witnesses in previous trials, and which accounted for the decisions that had been arrived at. They had imagined that the term " watercourse " applied alike to the natural course of the water from the spring and the course or watershed of the storm waters from the gully. Hence, while the District Council alleged that the natural flow of water from the spring, or its watercourse, was originally away from the plaintiff's land, it was deposed by some that the watercourse had always been through that land, meaning that the course of the flood waters, from the gully, or its watershed, had always so been. Of course I had to explain the distinction of the terms watershed and watercourse, or the mistake would have been repeated.

After all other witnesses had been examined, I was about to get into the box to state what I had done in the matter, when Mr. Ingleby said I need not unless I wished, as the case was quite complete without any evidence I could give. As he seemed very decided on this, and I had no wish to appear, though I thought I might have strengthened the council's case, I deferred to his opinion. The Chief Justice summed up very decidedly in favour of the council, and the jury retired. On their returning into court, everyone was astonished at the verdict being for the plaintiff, with five pounds damages—no one more so than her own counsel, Mr. Charles Mann, who hid his face in his hands and indulged in a hearty laugh. Afterwards I asked one of the jurors by what process of reasoning they had arrived at such a verdict, against the weight of evidence and the judge's ruling. He replied—" It was because we thought it would be very hard to throw the costs of such an action on the poor old woman." Of course a new trial was at once moved for, which resulted in a non-suit. As she had no means of paying the council's costs they had to pay their own, and her cottage was sold to pay hers. So ended a litigation that had lasted three or four years; but the ghost was laid.

Another instance occurred in the case of a sheep-farmer who had been long confined to his bed through illness, and whom I frequently therefore visited. Contention had arisen between him and another sheep-farmer who held adjacent land; it was a case of trespass. A summons having been issued, and the sick man being unable to attend the court at Willunga, and having no one to represent him, he begged of me to engage a lawyer, if one should be at the court, and instruct him as to the facts. This I consented to do, conditionally on being in the first place allowed to see the other party and endeavour to obtain a settlement. He agreed. I at once waited on his opponent, and endeavoured to get him to come to terms, and abandon litigation. But he proved quite impracticable, and would listen to nothing; he had gone to law, and law he would have. So I begged of him not to blame me if he should lose his case, as I fully believed he would; and he did.

One thing in connection with this matter was amusing.

It was customary after the court for the magistrates and lawyers to dine together at the neighbouring hotel. On that occasion I dined with them. In the course of conversation, some one remarked to the solicitor I had engaged, concerning the case—" But, Mr. So-and-so, you argued quite differently at Morphett Vale court at such a time in a similar case, at least the cases appeared just alike." " Ah !" said he, " but then I was on the other side."

In a small country township there are usually but few sources of amusement for young people, youths and young men in particular, while their homes are not always made attractive. Consequently, they are apt to be led to frequent the public-house, not so much perhaps in the first instance for the sake of drink, as for the satisfaction of meeting others and gossiping away their evenings ; while they cannot be there without spending some money in drink, acquiring probably the habit of or love for it. Then, too, they are led to engage in this game or that, as cards, dice, bagatelle, &c., while publicans naturally try to make their establishments as attractive as possible. Institutes, reading-rooms, church and chapel agencies there may be, but there will always be some whom such agencies do not attract. I, therefore, regard a recreation ground as an almost necessary attachment to every village or township, certainly as an important adjunct to the moral and physical training of the young, acting, as it always does, as a counterpoise to the attractions of the public-house. Hence it was that I proposed the purchase of and had the satisfaction of assisting to secure, eight acres as recreation ground for the township of Willunga. At a total cost of about two hundred and forty pounds this was purchased, fenced, and planted. The state-school adjoins it on one side, and an agricultural hall, which I presume will become also an institute, has been added on the other. The ground is available for all purposes, and open as a public resort at all hours and at all seasons, becoming quite an evening resort for the young. Of course opposition had to be encountered, in fact we had to assert our title in court, while the idea of " collecting money for a playground," as it was put, called forth much ridicule, especially on the part of some publicans. However, those by whose efforts it was obtained have no reason to regret those efforts, and 1 think none of the inhabitants would now be willing to forego the advantages it confers. Since I left, I hear the inhabitants of Aldinga have secured a similar benefit for their district. The residents in Noarlunga have always had sufficient unoccupied ground adjoining the township to answer the same purpose.

In the hills adjacent to Willunga is a valuable vein of slate, the outcrop extending for miles. I have been given to understand this is the principal, if not the only, bed of good roofing slate as yet discovered in Australasia. The distance from Adelaide, thirty miles, and further from the Port, has so far prevented the quarries opened being profitably worked, carriage by wagon costing from fifteen to twenty shillings per ton; to which, for export, wharfage, freight, &c., have to be added. During fine weather shipment from the jetty at Port Willunga, an open roadstead seven miles from the quarries, is possible; but vessels cannot lie there safely, while boating slate off is risky and expensive. I have often known cargoes of, say, one hundred tons, to be months in getting shipped from there. The result is, that slate from Europe and America is cheaper in the other colonies than that from Willunga. A recent builders' price-list in Melbourne quoted Willunga slate at seventeen pounds per thousand, and English and American at twelve pounds per thousand, these being brought as dead - weight to stiffen ships at a nominal freight; I have been told at from ten to twenty shillings per ton.

Thinking it unfortunate that so valuable a deposit, calculated to furnish employment to many should lie to a large extent unavailed of, I took steps by calling public meetings, getting a committee appointed, petitions signed, &c., to bring the matter before Parliament in order, if possible, to obtain railway facilities for cheapening the cost of transit for slate and other produce from the district. These efforts were so far successful that a select committee was appointed by the House of Assembly to inquire into the matter. After exhaustive evidence had been taken, they reported so strongly in favour of the scheme, that the Government, of which Sir John Bray was Premier, included it in their programme, as set forth in the Governor's speech at the opening of Parliament. At the second reading of the Bill, however, a former member for the district moved an amendment in favour of an impracticable route in order that the line might pass through or close to property in which he was largely interested. This being carried by a small majority, the matter became shelved for a fresh survey. A change of government soon after resulted in the matter being allowed to lapse as the result of political intrigue. The estimated cost, too, would seem to have been exaggerated; the assistant engineer-in-chief saying in his evidence that the line as proposed was " provided with every luxury," *i.e.*, in the way of elaborate station buildings, half-a-dozen turn-tables, and other costly items ; whereas the least expensive arrangements, consistent with safety, were only required to get produce conveyed at a cheaper rate, so that labour might be more extensively employed and natural advantages availed of.

1 have no doubt that railway facilities will eventually be granted; and when the district shall be brought into connection with the railway system of the colony, a largely increased output from the quarries will result, and a market be opened not only with other colonies, but by the Murray with the vast interior.   The late Mr. T. Goode, of Goolwa, informed me he could dispose of any quantity of slate up the river.

CHAPTER XI.

YANKALILLA AND MYPONGA.

AT the time I took charge of the Willunga cure, the Yankalilla cure, about twenty-five miles south of Willunga, became vacant. There being but two small churches in that district, viz., Christ Church, Yankalilla, and St. Paul's, Hay Flat, and neither house for a minister, nor endowment, it was impossible for a minister to be supported in so thinly-peopled a locality. Consequently, it became placed on the list of missionary districts, under charge of the Rev. B. T. Craig (afterwards Dr. Craig), whose special work it was to hold services as often as possible in places where there were no resident clergy. As I was the nearest clergyman to Yankalilla, it fell to my lot to in some degree look after the vacant district, and I had often to visit it for occasional duty, meetings, &c. There were in it some very earnest church workers, by whom Dr. Craig and myself were always welcomed, and who exerted themselves assiduously to get the place into a position to maintain a clergyman. The Sunday services were kept going between Dr. Craig's and my visits by several Lay-readers, among whom Messrs. C. W. Scott, J. Heathcote, and Mather may be specially mentioned; Mr. and Mrs. Hibbert also did good service in various ways. This position of things lasted about six years; and as the people were content to pay seat-rents and continue their offertories at every service, a fund was created with a view to endowment, which in 1868 was effected. The presentation of a piece of land and small house for a parsonage by Mr. C. W. Scott in 1872 completed the objects aimed at, viz., the making a small permanent provision for maintaining the Church's services in the district. I was exceedingly thankful when the Bishop was able in 1868 to appoint a clergyman to Yankalilla, as visiting it entailed much extra work on me—every journey being at least fifty miles through sandy scrub, for there were no made roads—the remuneration being nil.

While conducting a confirmation class at Aldinga church in 1868, a bullock-driver entered, whip in hand, to inquire whether I could baptise some children at Myponga, a place I had been accustomed to pass through on the way to Yankalilla, and about twelve miles from Willunga. I undertook to go if the children could be brought to one place; and wished it to be a place where service could be held, and that others besides the parents might be invited to attend. Shortly afterwards my inquirer rode up to the parsonage in a very different guise: he was in fact an illustration of what then was often the case, viz., a well educated person engaged in what some would deem the meanest, and certainly the most laborious, kind of employment. It was no uncommon thing to fall in with a well-read classic, or university man acting as shepherd, hutkeeper, or boundary-rider, in the roughest bush costume, and living in the roughest fashion. My visitor having informed me that arrangements had been made in accordance with my suggestion, I named the next moonlight evening for the service, as I should have about a dozen miles' return journey. Reaching the place at the time appointed, I found some thirty persons gathered together in a cottage. The ordinary evening service was gone through, and several children baptised. Afterwards, while writing down the children's names for registration, I overheard the people saying to each other—" This is the first church service ever held in Myponga ;" " I have not heard the church service for about twenty years," and so on. When I had finished writing, as the people still hung about, I asked if any of them wished for the services of the Church ; the reply was—" Yes, we would like them, but didn't think any clergyman would come to us, we are so poor and scattered." I replied—" You asked me to come and baptise your children, and I am here. You shall not have occasion again to say no clergyman will come to you, for if you will meet me this night month, I will meet you." This they gladly promised to do, and a monthly service became established.

The room in which we met proving too small, the use of a building that had been erected for a school and chapel, but which I was told was only occasionally used by local preachers, was obtained by some of the people. The day-school had been closed two or three years previously, so that there was really, as I was informed, neither Sunday nor day school, and only irregular Sunday services. For our use, it was needful to renovate the building in question, and willing hands soon accomplished this. It was plastered and ceiled, forms and lamps were provided ; a total of about twenty pounds being expended. Here the week-night services became attended by about fifty people. I also succeeded in obtaining the services of Mr. and Mrs. Doke, who had been teachers in my former cure, to re-establish the day-school, and they soon got from thirty to forty children together, becoming licensed by the Government. No Sunday - school was attempted, as the Bible Christians re-opened one, and more frequently used the chapel for Sunday services. Things went on very quietly till I received a note from Mr. W. Nosworthy, dated February 2nd, 1871, which ran as follows :—" Resolution of Quarterly Meeting of the Yankalilla Circuit. Resolved— ' That this meeting recommend the trustees of the Myponga chapel not to grant any further facilities to any parties for conducting religious services in the above place of worship.' (Signed) JOSHUA FOSTER, chairman." Till this arrived, the people had been under the impression that the building they erected, with the idea that it should be a Union chapel, was open to the use of any Protestant body. The Bible Christians, however, had managed to obtain the title to the land, and decided that Church services should not be conducted there, even at times when the building was not used by themselves or others— a somewhat unfortunate illustration of " Bible " Christianity. This prohibiting the continuance of Church services was quickly followed by a notice to the day-school teachers that they would be no longer allowed to conduct school there, though having a fireplace, desks, &c., it had manifestly been intended for both school and chapel.

This proceeding roused the ire of the people not a little, finding they were refused the use of the building they had nearly all assisted to erect for themselves and their children. They proved, however, equal to the occasion. Procuring the use of an empty cottage, the slab partition was taken down, and it was quickly in a condition to serve for school and worship, the lamps, forms, &c., being transferred to it, not however, without protest from the chapel trustees, who tried to claim them. Mr. Doke then as Lay-reader, commenced regular Sunday services, and a Sunday-school was established. Mr. C. Forbes also gave an acre of land in a very suitable position as site for a school-room-church and teacher's residence, and steps were taken for at once erecting the latter, as being the more urgently needed.

Shortly after I had commenced monthly services at Myponga, the Rev. C. W. Morse, was appointed to the cure of Yankalilla. I therefore suggested to the Myponga folk to inquire of Mr. Morse, whom I did not then know, whether he would undertake a monthly week-night service for them also, which would result in their having a fortnightly service. This they acted on, and he held such services for a while, but then withdrew. His ostensible ground for withdrawal was, that as I had established an offertory to defray current expenses, lighting, &c., and while it was being taken read some of the offertory sentences from the communion service, and suggested that he should do the same, he could not conscientiously use any part of the communion service in connection with the evening service. But I had merely suggested this, and it was in no sense obligatory. As, however, the services had become fortnightly, thinking it well that nothing like recession should occur, I decided to continue them so myself, as nearly as possible, with an occasional Sunday morning service for holy communion after the church was built.

In 1875 the foundation-stone of the church was laid by the Rev. J. Pollitt, and a good stone building erected, to accommodate about one hundred people ; it was also used for the day-school, till the Government erected a public school half-a-mile away, when of course the church-school had to be given up. The cost of the church and teacher's residence was about six hundred and twenty-five pounds cash, besides labour and material given. The church was opened by Archdeacon Marryat, afterwards Dean.

An amusing incident occurred in starting this building.

I had marked out the ground, having to act in this, as in
other cases, as architect and general director, when delay
occurred in excavating the foundations.   At length a
bevy of young women determined to get the ground ready
for the concrete; so on a certain morning they met on the
site, armed with picks and shovels, and began digging
away in right earnest.   This was too much for their
sweethearts and others, who soon joined the fair toilers,
and during the day accomplished what we had been waiting for.

Some time after the church had been got into use, the
old chapel we had at first used, and been expelled from,
became unusable; the Bible Christians, therefore, decided
to take it down and build another.   As this would take
time, I was applied to to allow them the use of the church
on Sunday evenings, it being then used only for service
in the morning and Sunday-school in the afternoon.   I
assented to the request, but stipulated that female
preachers should not act therein.   This proved an un-
palatable restriction, and the church was not availed of.

On Bishop Kennion's arrival, after visiting these districts, he wished me to resign charge of the Myponga
church and district, that it might be attached to the
Yankalilla cure, as nearer.   At the time, I was under
pressure for seventy-five pounds, resulting from my having
become personally responsible on account of that church;
I therefore consented to resign if relieved of that responsibility.   This was duly arranged for; and after about
fifteen years' struggle to establish the Church there, it
became transferred to other hands.   I have, however, the
satisfaction of knowing that services have since been
maintained there, and that something is done toward
raising an income for its minister.

During my visits to this district, I fell in with an old sergeant of the Grenadier Guards who had been through the whole of the Peninsular war under Wellington, and in most of the great battles, Salamanca, Badajos, &c., escaping unscathed. On being asked if he ever felt anxious when going into action, he replied—" Oh ! no. We only thought of how many Frenchmen we could pot, and what plunder we should get." The only occasion, he said, when he felt any qualm was at Waterloo. He woke on the morning of the second day with so strong an impression that he would be killed or wounded that day that he wrote a letter to his friends and put it in his knapsack, telling some of his comrades that, should he be killed, to see it forwarded. The fight had not long begun when a musket ball went through his hat, just grazing his head. As he was kneeling in the front rank of one of the squares, a charge of French Cuirassiers came down upon it, and the sword of one of them gliding down our friend's musket, cut his hand ; " I was not sorry," he said, " to see him tumble off his horse the next minute, as my rear rank man had shot him." Binding up his hand, he kept his place, till he received three more wounds, and was carried to the rear, thought to be dying. One ball, in the thigh, could not be extracted, and he carried it to the grave with him. He was two years in hospital, and of course duly pensioned. This was one of those instances of prescience often so remarkable.

About the same time that week-night services were commenced at Myponga, I commenced similar services at the Lower Meadows, about six miles east of Willunga. These were held at the house of Mr. Barns, with an attendance of from twenty to thirty persons. At the time of the exodus to the areas, however, nearly all the residents, including Mr. Barns, left the district, and the few remaining being Romanists, the services had to be given up.

These outside services, as I may term them, with continuous visiting, of course involved much riding, often one hundred miles a week; for two or three years I was the only clergyman south of Adelaide, and then the duties were specially heavy, occasional duties requiring attention from O'Halloran Hill to Yankalilla, nearly forty miles.

CHAPTER XII.

CHURCH ORGANISATION.

THE first organised attempt towards the establishment of Church services in South Australia was made during the ministry of the Revs. C. B. Howard and James Farrell, when a " Church Society " was formed. That society, we find from the report presented at its first general meeting on March 15th, 1841, was constituted as follows :—

President :

His Excellency Lieutenant-Colonel Gawler, K.H.

Vice-Presidents :

His Honor Chas. Cooper, Judge of the Supreme Court.
Rev. C. B. Howard, M.A., Colonial Chaplain.

Committee :

W. Bartley, Esq.	B. A. Kent, Esq., M.D.
Henry Colton, Esq.	C. B. Newenham, Esq.
Rev. Jas. Farrell	R. F. Newland, Esq.
W. P. Fleming, Esq.	Hon. W. Smillie
Hon. Capt. Frome, R.E.	Hon. C. Sturt
Osmond Gilles, Esq.	R. R. Torrens, Esq.
E. B. Gleeson, Esq.	H. Walters, Esq.
H. Jickling, Esq.	W. Wyatt, Esq.

Treasurer :	*Secretary :*
George Hall, Esq.	A. D. Gell, Esq.

Among other matters, that report contains the following :—

To their brethren of other denominations they make grateful acknowledgment for the promptness with which they have offered to the clergymen of the Church of England the use of their places of worship for the establishment of weekly services in such places as Messrs. Howard and Farrell cannot attend on the Lord's day.

Through the kindness of the Wesleyan Methodists and the Society of Friends, the Rev. J. Farrell has been enabled to hold a Wednesday evening lecture at North Adelaide, and through similar kindness on the part of the Congregationalists, the Rev. C. B. Howard will be enabled to commence a Thursday evening service at Hindmarsh immediately.

As no other reports of this society are to be found till 1847, it would seem that its operations were brought to a stand-still, or nearly so, after the death of the Rev. C. B. Howard, in 1843. On the arrival of the Revs. W. J. Woodcock and Jas. Pollitt, early in 1846, the society was resuscitated and a general meeting was held in Trinity Church school-room on October 5th, 1847. By then, however, news had reached the colony of the Constitution of the Diocese of Adelaide, and the appointment of Dr. Short as its first Bishop—consequently it was decided to elect his Lordship president, while His Excellency Lieutenant-Governor Robe was made patron. A committee was again formed, including most of the original committee and some other leading colonists. The amount raised during the preceding year is stated at three hundred and sixty - seven pounds twelve shillings and eleven pence, most of which was voted in aid of erecting churches at the Sturt, Blakiston, Gawler, and Magill. When Bishop Short arrived, therefore, on December 28th, 1847, he found himself officially connected with the ociety, and threw himself heartily into its work.

As might be expected, on his Lordship's arrival considerable enthusiasm was engendered. In Canon Whitington's "Life of Bishop Short" we find it recorded, that the Legislative Council awarded a cordial vote of thanks to the Baroness Burdett Coutts for her munificence in founding the Diocese, and directed that the resolution should be handsomely engrossed and forwarded to England. The first *Government Gazette* for 1848 published the following official recognition of his Lordship's appointment :—

Colonial Secretary's Office, Adelaide,
January 5th, 1848.

The Queen having been graciously pleased to erect into a separate See and Diocese so much of the Bishopric of Australia as is included within the limits of the Province of South Australia and Western Australia, and to appoint thereto the Reverend Augustus Short, D.D., under the style and title of "The Lord Bishop of Adelaide," His Excellency the Lieutenant-Governor has directed the publication of Her Majesty's letters-patent to that effect, together with the notarial attestation of his Lordship's consecration for general information.

By His Excellency's command,
A. M. MUNDY, Colonial Secretary.

The documents referred to were duly subjoined in full to this announcement.

This formal declaration of the Bishop's appointment and status evoked, so far as I can ascertain, no criticism or opposition of any kind; he was welcomed by all.

On the withdrawal of the Government grant to churches in 1851, further effort on the part of members of the Church became necessary, if she was to maintain her position in the colony. The Bishop, therefore, addressed the following letter to the committee of the Church Society,

which, so far, had been regarded as in a certain sense
the Executive of the Church :—

September 2nd, 1851.

Gentlemen—The recent vote of the Legislative Assembly, whereby
all aid from the State in disseminating the doctrine and moral laws
of our adorable Redeemer has been cut off, and, so far, His Kingdom
upon earth no longer publicly recognised, compels me to address you
earnestly and affectionately with reference to the future support of
your clergy, and the extension of the means of grace to the members
of our Church, who are scattered through the province, and continually arriving in considerable numbers. It appears to me that
the time has arrived when every earnest - minded Christian in
communion with our Church is imperatively called on to contribute
to his power, yea, and beyond his power, for the furtherance of the
Gospel, so far as it depends on the Ministry of the Word ; and to
exert his influence in order to raise a General Diocesan Fund for the
support of clergy, both parochial and missionary. The moral
degradation of a people deprived of the ordinances of the Gospel is
certain and progressive. Nor can we expect any other result than
the spiritual deterioration of the people of this colony if the means of
grace are not supplied in proportion to their increasing numbers.
Let it be remembered that the next generation will not enjoy the
privileges we have possessed in our fatherland, and in the bosom of
our Church, while experience forbids us to hope that a population
deprived of the public worship of Almighty God can preserve that
sense of His Providence and government of the world which is
essential to its well-being, and the observance of the Eternal Laws
of Truth and Righteousness. Under these circumstances, I would
urge the appointment of a committee of five *Lay* members of the
Society to consult upon the best means of developing the resources
of our communion for the support of its Ministers ; and to report
upon the best mode of enlisting the sympathies of the great body of
the Lay members of the Church in this most Christian and necessary
work. Among other plans which have occurred to me are: First—
The assembling together in Adelaide of one or two Lay Members,
being communicants, from each congregation, to act as a *pro-tempore*
convention in furtherance of the above object. Secondly—The
appointment of two Laymen to act as Stewards of the Diocesan
Fund to be raised ; and of a Treasurer. Thirdly—That the

endeavour should be made to obtain *not less* than one shilling per quarter over and above their local contributions from every one who frequents the worship of our church for a Diocesan Fund for the support of the ministry; to be collected and paid over by *local* Stewards appointed for this purpose by each congregation. I have only to add, that I shall be ready to contribute all the aid in my power towards the proper support of a zealous and efficient Ministry.

I remain, gentlemen,

Your faithful Friend and Brother,

AUGUSTUS ADELAIDE.

This letter having been considered by the committee, they fully concurred in the Bishop's suggestion, and the necessary steps were taken to obtain the assistance of the Laity, most congregations electing representatives. The first conference was held on the Feast of the Epiphany, January 6th, 1852, being constituted as follows:—

CHURCHES.	CLERGY.	LAY REPRESENTATIVES.
Trinity, Adelaide	Dean Farrell	Judge Cooper Capt. Butler Mr. W. Roberts
St. John's, Adelaide	Rev. T. P. Wilson	Capt. Freeling Mr. G. W. Hawkes ,, G. A. Branthwaite
Christ Church, North Adelaide	Rev. W. J. Woodcock	Major Campbell Mr. Macdermott ,, Wicksteed
St. Paul's, Port Adelaide	Rev. E. Bayfield	Dr. Duncan
St. Andrew's, Walkerville	Rev. F. Platts	Mr. Macdonald
All Saints, Hindmarsh	Rev. W. Wood	Dr. Hammond
St. Matthew's, Kensington	Rev. J. Watson	—

CHURCHES.	CLERGY.	LAY REPRESENTA- TIVES.
St. George's, Wood- forde	Rev. E. K. Miller ...	Mr. Silke
Christ Church, O'Hal- loran Hill ...	Rev. J. W. Schoales	Major O'Halloran
St. Mary's, Sturt ...	Rev. J. W. Schoales	—
St. James', Blakiston	Rev. J. Fulford	Mr. J. Smith
St. George's, Gawler...	Rev. W. H. Coombs	Mr. P. Butler
St. Stephen's, Wil- lunga	Rev. A. B. Burnett	Mr. T. S. Kell
Clare and Penwortham	Rev. J. C. Bagshaw	—
Burra Burra ...	Rev. J. Pollitt ...	—
St. Thomas', Port Lin- coln	Archdeacon Hale ...	Mr. O. K. Richardson

The Clergy and Lay Delegates met at Trinity Church.
After service and holy communion, with a sermon by the
Bishop on " Outward pressure—inward strength," ad-
journment was made to the school-room. The position of
the Church in the colony as then viewed can hardly be
better stated than in the words of the first resolution
adopted by the Conference, which was as follows:—

Whereas, the Church of England in South Australia receives no
aid from the Local Government by grants of land or money; but is
dependent solely on the voluntary contributions of its members for
the support of its ministry; the maintenance of Missions to the
Aborigines and other Heathen, and for the building of churches,
parsonages, and schools—in which its doctrine and discipline may be
taught: And whereas, for the edification of its members, and
" provoking to love " and the above-mentioned " good works " it is
desirable that they should be brought into closer fellowship by
Parochial organisation, and the " assembling of themselves together "
periodically: We, the Bishop, Clergy, and Laity in conference
assembled, have agreed to recommend the following plans and
suggestions to the several congregations of this colony.

And whereas, this Diocesan Church is part and parcel of the

United Church of England and Ireland, by law established in the United Kingdom ; and, therefore, subject to the general Ecclesiastical Laws enforcing the Supremacy of the Crown, the use of the Book of Common Prayer, the Authorised Version of the Holy Scriptures, and subscription to the Thirty-nine Articles : We, the Bishop, Clergy, and Laity, being under the obligations thus implied, and being earnestly desirous to maintain inviolate that unity and fellowship in the Church of our Fathers, do declare that we hold it to be incompetent for any Diocesan Assembly, or Synod of the Clergy, or Convention of Lay Representatives, held in pursuance of these recommendations, to "treat, debate, consider, consult, or agree upon" any alteration in those Formularies and Principles, except it be initiated by the direct authority of the Crown obtained in that behalf : "Under this limitation, with the view of promoting the closer fellowship as well as efficiency of this Diocesan Church, we have resolved to recommend that an Assembly consisting of the Bishop, Chapter of Clergy, and Convention of Lay Representatives be convened periodically, composed as herinafter specified, and to be called the Diocesan Assembly."

The Conference then proceeded to frame, suggestively, a series of Resolutions defining the Constitution of the proposed Diocesan Assembly ; providing for the election of Representatives, Meetings of the Assembly, Mode of Deliberation, Manner of Voting, Committees, Finance, Pastoral Aid, Endowment, Building, Mission, and Educational Funds, Trust Deeds, Ecclesiastical Tribunal, and other matters, concluding with a Memorial to the Queen soliciting Her Majesty's sanction to their proceedings. That Memorial was as follows :—

To Her Most Gracious Majesty Victoria, by the Grace of God Queen of the United Kingdom of Great Britain and Ireland, Defender of the Faith.

The Memorial of the undersigned Bishop, Clergy, and Laity of that part of the Diocese of Adelaide comprised within the Province of South Australia in Conference assembled :

Humbly showeth :

That the Church of England in this Diocese not being by Law established, and the Clergy not enjoying Corporate Rights as in England, much expense and inconvenience arise in the conveyance of Ecclesiastical Property to Trustees. That changes in the office of Trustee are very frequent in a newly settled colony. That Church-wardens are elected annually by the Minister and Congregation. That the Churchwardens so appointed have no *legal* right to perform the duties usually appertaining to that ancient and popular office ; the Church and Church Property being Vested in Trustees, who may remove to a distance from the Church, or even depart out of the colony.

That the body of English Ecclesiastical Law has not yet been adapted to the wants and necessities of the Church in the colonies. That the jurisdiction of the Bishop over the clergy is left without any prescribed form of Process ; that he is not armed with legal authority to deprive of temporalities a Clergyman duly convicted of teaching contrary to the doctrine of the Church of England, or of immoral conduct. That there is no prescribed form or mode of Appeal to the Metropolitan, or of giving effect to the sentence of his court.

That the periodical meeting of the Bishop, Clergy, and Laity in Diocesan Assemblies is as yet unauthorised by the supreme authority of the Crown.

That your Memorialists are persuaded much good is likely to arise from such Assemblies when conducted according to prescribed rules, and with powers properly defined.

Your Memorialists, therefore, humbly pray that your gracious Majesty may be pleased to sanction such Diocesan Meetings of the Bishop, Clergy, and Laity ; and to empower them to make and give such effect to Rules and Regulations as may be deemed expedient for the better government of the Church in this colony, and as may be consistent with the Doctrine and Discipline of the Church of England and the lawful Supremacy of the Crown.

In 1853 the Bishop decided to visit England in order to ascertain the true position of the Church in the colony in relation to the Church and Government in England—

and also the result of the Memorial to the Queen. At first
it was thought the sanction of Parliament was needed to
enable colonial churches to organise assemblies or conventions to manage their own affairs, and the Archbishop of Canterbury (Sumner) introduced a Bill into the
House of Lords with the view of empowering them so to
do; but this Bill did not pass. Bishop Short then consulted
some of the most eminent ecclesiastical lawyers on the
matter. These were — Sir Richard Bethell (Solicitor-
General), Sir Fitzroy Kelly, Sir Joseph Napier, and Mr. A. J.
Stephens—who were unanimously of opinion that imperial
legislation was not necessary to enable colonial churches
to arrrange for their own self-government. In the issue,
the draft of a Constitution for the Diocese that had been
adopted as suggested by the Conference held in Adelaide
on June 6th, 1852, was placed in the hands of Mr. A. J.
Stephens, who, therefrom, proceeded to draw up a complete
Constitution for the Diocese. As his elaborate printed
opinion on this important matter may be of interest to
many members of the Church, I have thought well to give
some extracts therefrom bearing on the principal points
that had to be considered.

EXTRACTS FROM THE OPINION OF ARCHIBALD JOHN STEPHENS, ESQ.,
BARRISTER-AT-LAW, PUBLISHED DECEMBER 5TH, 1854.

I have finally settled the Draft Constitutions for the Diocese of
Adelaide; and am of opinion that Imperial Legislation is not
requisite to enable the Bishop of Adelaide to carry out what I have
recommended, his episcopal powers being sufficient for the purpose.

I am also of opinion, as at present advised, that Imperial Legislation is not required for the United Church of England and Ireland in
the Diocese of Adelaide, except it be in respect of an efficient
appellate tribunal.

In compliance with the desire of the Lord Bishop of Adelaide, I proceed to give an exposition of the laws ecclesiastical relative to Diocesan Synods under four heads—

1. The Construction of Stat. 25 Hen. VIII. c. 19, ss. 1 and 2.
2. The Persons who may be summoned to a Diocesan Synod.
3. The Powers of Diocesan Synods in Promulgating Constitutions.
4. The Powers of the Diocesan Synods in exercising Jurisdictions.

1. The Construction of Stat. 25 Hen. VIII. c. 19, ss. 1 and 2.

As the first section of the Stat. 25 Hen. VIII c. 19, recites the Submission of the Clergy at length, and then proceeds to enact " according to the said submission," it is evident that the enactment cannot be extended further than the Submission strictly and properly requires. That Submission is strictly confined to the attempting, alleging, or putting in use, enacting, promulgating, or executing of Canons and Constitutions " *in the convocation.*" It is, therefore, to Canons and Constitutions made or promulgated *in the Convocation* that the enactment in this respect is strictly applicable ; and to these it is limited, in the enacting part, by the words " in their Convocations in time coming." The premise, moreover, at the end of the second section, is expressly limited to acts done by authority of the *Convocation*—thus evincing the intention of the Legislature to deal with that Assembly alone.

Convocation is a term which has a meaning ascertained and defined by the English law—viz., an Ecclesiastical Assembly of a *Province*, or of more than one Province, in which the Bishops and Dignitaries are present in person, and the Chapters and Clergy by their Proctors ; and the term has never been applied to a mere Diocesan Synod.

Bishop Stillingfleet (1 Eccles. Cases, 255) says—" Convocation, properly so called, is an occasional assembly, for such purposes as the King shall direct them when they meet. And this was the true foundation on which the Statute 25 Hen. VIII. was built." And to the same effect, Sir E. Coke says (4 Inst. 323) that the word " Convocation " is derived *à convocando*, because it is called together by the King's writ.

Synods, properly so called, were held in England from the earliest times. " Convocation " was originally an assembly for purposes not

"Synodal." It was an invention of Edward I. (1 Blackstone, Comm. 279) for taxing the clergy for civil purposes ; and for several ages after its institution "Synods" continued to discharge those functions which were purely Synodal. But by degrees, this assembly of ecclesiastics, called "Convocation," though originally intended for a purely civil purpose, assumed the power of acting synodically ; and Synods, properly so called, were laid aside. In the time of Henry VIII. both functions were thus united in the same assembly. . . . . . This synodical character of Convocation is also acknowledged by Archbishop Wake, who says that the King, "as his writ shows, has it now in his own breast whether he will let them act at all *as a Church Synod.*"

The legality of Diocesan Synods is recognised by Stat. 28 Hen. VIII. c. 10, s. 4 (an Act for Extinguishing the Authority of the Bishop of Rome).

Diocesan Synods were held from the earliest ages down to and after the time of the Reformation by the exclusive authority of the Bishop ; and no authority has been produced in which the *writ*, the *assent*, or the *licence* of the Crown was ever thought requisite for the summoning or holding of Diocesan Synods. . . . . If, indeed, a *licence* from the Crown to a Bishop to convene his Diocesan Synod had been produced, it would go far to prove that a licence was necessary ; but nothing of this kind has yet been produced ; whereas there are a multitude of cases in which Bishops held Diocesan Synods without either licence or compulsion by the Crown. . . . Diocesan Synods are likewise recognised in the 68th Canon of 1634. The Archbishop of Canterbury, in a recent charge, stated there is "nothing [which] prevents any number of clergy, or any society of clergy, or *the clergy of any diocese*, from assembling together and consulting for the common good." . . . . It appears, therefore, that Diocesan Synods are not subject in law, and have not been subjected, in fact, to the restraints of Stat. 25 Hen. VIII. c. 19.

2. The Bishop of Adelaide desires further to know, whether, and how far, the laity are admissible.

The assembly recorded in the Acts of the Apostles, ch. xv., has been regarded as affording a pattern for Ecclesiastical Councils. The parts respectively acted by the clergy and laity in this assembly should be carefully observed. 1. The deputies of Antioch "go up to Jerusalem unto the *Apostles and Elders* about this question." 2. "They were received *of the Church and* of the Apostles and Elders." 3. "*The Apostles and Elders came together for to consider of this matter.*" That the question of doctrine was, then, considered *in the first instance* by the clergy apart from the laity is acknowledged by the chief writers of the Calvinists themselves. 4. *After* the matter had been thus *considered of* by the Apostles and Elders, there was then *another* assembly, of which we have the result in v. 22. "Then it pleased the Apostles and Elders *with the whole Church* to send chosen men," &c. "And they wrote letters by them after this manner:—The Apostles and Elders and *Brethren* send greeting," &c. Thus it is evident that the question of doctrine was first considered in the assembly of the clergy; and their decision being adopted by the laity, it went forth in the name of all. . . . Such is the precedent recorded in Holy Scripture for adjusting the respective parts of clergy and laity in doctrinal decisions.

In the first four General Councils, the Christian Emperors, either in person, or by their deputies and some of their lay councillors, were present, and took part in the proceedings; and the Roman Senate sat in these Councils: thus, as far as precedent is concerned, the question is settled; there was a lay element in all those Synods whose example and authority remain as acknowledged precedents and rules to all later ages.

The object and effect of the Emperors' presence was thus stated in Matthews *v.* Burdett (2 Salk., 412)—"In the Primitive Church the laity were present at all Synods. When the empire became Christian, no Canon was made without the Emperor's consent. The Emperor's consent included that of the people, he having in himself the whole legislative power." The right of the civil powers to take part in General Councils has continued to be acknowledged in the Church to modern times: at the Council of Constance and others of the later (so-called) general councils, the Princes of Europe were represented by their "ambassadors" and "oratores," who might be, and generally were, laymen. . . . In England, the presence of the laity in Provincial Synods prevailed from the earliest ages. . . . In the Synod of Cloveshoe (A.D. 747) Ethelbald, King of Mercia, was present, with thirty-three princes and aldermen—"*ducibus;*" and the record says, that the Canons passed by the

Council were then and there translated into Anglo-Saxon—as appears to have always been done before the Norman Conquest—that the country gentlemen might know what it was to which their assent was required.

In like manner Burn says (1 Eccles. Law, 398)—" In the ancient Episcopal Synods the Bishops were wont to summon divers creditable persons out of every parish to give information of and to attest the disorders of clergy and people. These were called *Testes Synodales*; and were in after-times a kind of impanelled jury, consisting of two, three, or more persons in every parish, who were upon oath, to present all heretics and other irregular persons. And these in time became standing officers in several places, especially in great cities, and from hence were called *Synod's men*, and by corruption Sidesmen. . . . Gibson states . . . that they subsequently obtained a further character—' to represent the people at the Bishop's Synods.' "

For the presence of the laity for consultation in Diocesan Synods, we have the authority of St. Cyprian (Epist. xiv., about the year 255), who writes to his Presbyters and Deacons—" From the beginning of my episcopacy I resolved to do nothing of my own private judgment, without your advice *and the concurrence of the people*; but when, by the grace of God, I shall have come to you, we will consult together of the things which either have been, or are to be done, as becomes our respective stations."

With respect to this admission of the laity to consultation, it must be remembered what the question is which I have to consider. The question for Churchmen is *not* whether the laity had a right to be consulted by St. Cyprian (for instance) about everything that he did ; the question is, whether St. Cyprian had a right thus to consult the laity, and to lay down the rule for himself that he would consult them ? The Bishop of Adelaide, in the exercise of his judgment, and as the result of his experience of his Diocese, is of opinion that the principle which St. Cyprian adopted in the infancy of the African Church is the best adapted to the infant state of the Diocese of Adelaide. I have to consider, not whether the Bishop of Adelaide be bound to adopt that principle ; but whether it be lawful for him to adopt it—whether there be any law of the land, or any Canon of the Church, to restrain him from adopting it. And I am of opinion that consultation by the Bishop with the laity of his

Diocese, or with persons elected to represent them, is not against any ecclesiastical or legal principle.

I am aware that the admission of the laity to deliberate in a Diocesan Synod on a question of any alleged error in doctrine may possibly experience objection ; but so far as these objections can be urged with reason, they are met in the Chapter of the Constitution on Diocesan Synods. It is there proposed, that the clergy must first consider a question of doctrine by themselves ; it will then have to be considered by the clergy and laity together, in order to becoming the act of the whole—but it cannot be considered by the laity apart. These provisions are in accordance with the precedent of the Council at Jerusalem in Acts xv.

So true, as respects his own Diocese, is the opinion of the Bishop of Adelaide in his Pastoral Address of January, 1852 — That the laity should be directly represented in the Convocation ; and that this would be, like the rest of the Reformation, a return to the usage of the Apostolic Church.

3. The powers of Diocesan Synods in promulgating Constitutions.

Diocesan Synods are the assemblies of the Bishop and his Presbyters, to enforce and put in execution Canons made by General Councils, or National and Provincial Synods, and to consult and agree on rules of discipline for themselves. . . . No instance, perhaps, can be shown of a new Canon (properly so-called) having been enacted in a Diocesan Synod : *their* Canons are invariably a re-publication or adjustment of Canons previously enacted by a higher authority. And no authority has been produced to show that for this the licence or consent of the Crown was ever necessary in England. It is evident there could have been no object in requiring it. . . . It must, however, be borne in remembrance that the power of Diocesan Synods is limited to such matters as they are competent to deal with, and cannot affect legal rights without a temporal sanction. . . . It is also necessary to observe that a Diocesan Synod cannot in any way bind or limit a higher jurisdiction ; and, therefore, it cannot deal with the question of appeals. . . . The Bishop and Diocesan Synod may constitute rural deaneries, and may define the powers and duties of rural deans, provided nothing be done contrary to the laws ecclesiastical.

The publishing of Canons in Diocesan Synods appears to have originated in this way—The Canons of Provincial Councils were legally binding on every Diocese represented at the Provincial Council by the presence of its Bishop; but in the enforcement of these Canons great difficulty was experienced. The duty of enforcing these Canons devolved on the Bishop of each Diocese, but some Bishops did not enforce them because it was impracticable to do so, without the concurrence of their clergy and people; in fact, where a Bishop was anxious to enforce them, he was often liable to resistance on the part of the clergy and people until he had obtained their concurrence. To remedy these inconveniences, a custom grew up, that each Bishop on returning to his Diocese should read the Canons of the Provincial Council to his clergy and people, and ask their assent; and this was often commanded in the Provincial Council. . . . By this means the clergy and people were informed of those Canons . . . And by their consent thus formally given resistance was obviated and obedience secured.

The nature of the authority of Diocesan Synods in promulgating Canons, as compared with the authority of Provincial Synods enables us to account for the fact of Diocesan Synods having fallen into disuse subsequent to the Reformation. Diocesan Synods had been useful chiefly in supplying the weakness of Provincial Synods, and accomplishing by consensual compact what central authority, though armed with legal power, was not able to effect. As great public powers became developed and effective, such subsidiary supports ceased to be resorted to. The Reformation in England developed a national power, which at once enforced and restrained the Canons of the Church by the laws of the land; and Diocesan Synods then fell into disuse — not because they were prohibited by law, but because the increasing strength of a centralised power rendered them unnecessary. But the experience of the Church in all ages points to Diocesan Synods as most useful in the infancy of churches, while yet unsupported and unregulated by public and general law.

No mere imposition of laws by a superior authority, however powerful in a legal point of view that authority may be, can supply the wants of the Church in the colonies, or accomplish the objects of the Bishop of Adelaide. Those objects can be accomplished only by institutions which secure the effective co-operation and the voluntary obedience of the colonists themselves. This was the object of Diocesan Synods in ages past; this was the source of their efficacy and strength ; this is the thing needed by the Church in the colonies.

In dealing with these subjects, the cardinal difference between the church system at home and in the colonies should never be lost sight of. The parochial system was not the original system of the Church. It commenced in the sixth century, and was perfected in the tenth, or even later. The original system of the Church was purely Diocesan, and knew of no lesser subdivisions. Each system grew out of, and was adapted to, the necessities of its age. . . . That system has as yet no legal existence, and scarcely any actual existence in the colonies. The Diocesan system is there in operation. Institution and induction, with all their consequences—the " parish church" with all the duties, the rights, the obligations, the limitations which it involves both in respect of Clergy and Laity—are all as yet wanting in the colonies. A colonial Diocese is more like the Diocese of Cyprian or Firmilian than a Diocese in England. Hence a great portion of our Canons and ecclesiastical laws are wholly inapplicable to the Church in the colonies. . . But, the habits, the feelings, the recollections, of the colonists, all turn to a speedy change to the parochial system as the great necessity of the Church in the colonies.

The practical conclusion to which these observations lead is plain. As repects the promulgating of constitutions, Diocesan Synods were *once* essential in England ; they have completed their purpose, and were then no longer resorted to. Diocesan Synods are *now* essential in the colonies; and there they will accomplish their purpose also.

I am, therefore, of opinion that no valid objection can be raised against the Bishop of Adelaide consulting the clergy and the laity—or the clergy and the representatives of the laity, of the Diocese of Adelaide ; and presenting for their acceptance Constitutions in accordance with the Canons of the laws ecclesiastical of the United Church of England and Ireland.

I am, therefore, of opinion that the provisions in the Constitutions for assisting the Bishop of Adelaide in the exercise of his episcopal jurisdiction may be lawfully used.

4. Powers of Diocesan Synods in Exercising Jurisdiction.

The Diocesan Synod was a court without formality. . . . The use of Diocesan Synods arose from an unlimited jurisdiction in

Bishops, which they were unwilling or unable to exercise without the support of their clergy. This was evidently, as has previously been shown, St. Cyprian's object in his Diocesan Synods. . . . A colonial Bishop has jurisdiction by his Patent : it ought, therefore, to be exercised in Synods. It is a mistake to say a colonial Bishop has no court ; his Synod is his proper court. And he may invite laymen there to assist him in the exercise of his jurisdiction.

I am, therefore, of opinion that the provisions in the Constitution for assisting the Bishop of Adelaide in the exercise of his episcopal jurisdiction may lawfully be used.

If the Bishop of Adelaide approve of the proposed Diocesan Constitutions, I recommend his Lordship to hold a Synod at the Cathedral Church of Adelaide, in order to present them to the clergy and laity for their acceptance. The Bishop should cite to that Synod all the clergy of his diocese, and invite so many of the laity as his Lordship in the exercise of his discretion may deem expedient.

The Constitutions and my Opinion thereon should then be read to the clergy and laity, and if they approve of the Constitutions, they should respectively signify their assent thereto under their hands and seals. The Diocesan Synod ought to be then dissolved, and a new Synod convened in accordance with the Constitutions.

(Signed) A. J. STEPHENS.

On the Bishop's return to Adelaide, the steps indicated by Mr. Stephens were taken, the first meeting to consider the Constitution being held on January 16th, 1855, when there were present nineteen clergy and twenty-seven laity. The matter having been referred to all the vestries, and the Constitution accepted by them, the first Synod was held on April 29th, 1856; and from then the Synod has met shortly after Easter in each year.

This colony having been the first portion of Her Majesty's dominions to cast off all governmental connection with the Church, the State neither exercising control over it nor aiding in its support, it fell to the lot of

Bishop Short not alone to definitely establish the Church in the colony, but also to inaugurate what cannot be regarded otherwise than as an entirely new departure, so far as the Church of England was concerned, though it was, after all, but a return to the position and practice of the Primitive Church. The successful accomplishment of this great work is a lasting testimony to the administrative skill and energy of the Bishop; and the fact that other dioceses quickly followed the example set, sufficiently shows the importance to the Church at large of what it was his high privilege to initiate, viz., a complete organisation of the Church apart from State control. His Lordship was permitted to see his labours in this behalf crowned by the establishment of a "General Synod," representing all the dioceses of Australasia, and to attend the earlier meetings thereof. That the work he laid the foundation of is likely to endure, may be fairly inferred from the fact that the Synodal Constitution as he introduced it has worked with little or no friction for forty years, and that but few amendments have been suggested, indeed none affecting its fundamental principles.

Besides this great work, there became established an Endowment Fund, a Clergy Widow and Orphan Fund, and a Clergy Superannuation Fund; of which last I have been compelled to avail myself, the leisure resulting enabling me to pen these "Reminiscences."

Of course, in constituting a branch of the Church in the colony, Bishop Short contemplated the eventual erection of a cathedral. Shortly after his nomination to the See, and while still in England, he was informed that a site for a cathedral had been reserved in the centre of Adelaide, and was led to make inquiries about it. As a result of those inquiries, he received a letter from the Colonial Office in London, enclosing one from Colonel Gawler, formerly Governor, and saying that the Colonel's letter was "very satisfactory, as setting the question quite at rest." The Colonel's letter was as follows :—

United Service Club, July 23rd, 1847.

My dear Sir—A journey to Brighton and return to London last night on my way to Derby prevented your letter of the 20th—which followed me—coming to hand until this morning.

In reference to the question you propose in it, I would say, that when I arrived in South Australia I found several portions of land marked off in the Government maps for specific public purposes by the Surveyor-General, Col. Light, under the order, I presume, of my predecessors, Governor Hindmarsh and Mr. Fisher. *The centre of Victoria-square for a cathedral was one of them.*

When I heard of Miss Coutts's liberality to South Australia, I wrote to Governor Robe *to call his attention* to this fact, as it might have escaped his notice, and my testimony might be important to him.   Very sincerely yours,

GEORGE GAWLER.[*]

Gordon Gardiner, Esq., Downing-street.

As a result of this communication, soon after reaching Adelaide, the Bishop made further inquiry, and found, as Colonel Gawler had said, that an acre in the centre of Victoria-square was marked in the plan of the city as the site for a cathedral, and had a sketch of a church on it, and that plan must have been drawn several years previously. His Letters-Patent constituting him the official representative of the Church of England in South Australia, his Lordship took the necessary steps to obtain a title to the said acre, and a land-grant was accordingly issued in March 1848, conveying it to the Bishop on behalf of the

[*] NOTE—For this letter I am indebted to Canon Whitington's " Life of Bishop Short."

Church, four stones being placed at the corners by the Government to mark the spot. The validity of this land-grant, however, was not long afterwards called in question. It was contended that all land within the city boundaries belonged to the Corporation, and that the Governor had no more power to alienate a portion of one of the squares than one of the streets. The other religious bodies, too, raised a great commotion, insisting that the Church of England ought not to have a degree of precedence accorded by having a site in the centre of the city conveyed to it. Altogether a large amount of excitement and opposition became engendered. The Bishop, regarding himself but as a trustee for the Church, did not feel at liberty to surrender the title on his own responsibility, and consulted the Synod, then in course of being established. By advice of some of its legal members, it was decided to allow the validity of the title to be tested in the Supreme Court; and as the corner-stones had been removed by the Corporation, an action for trespass was instituted by the Bishop, and tried in June 1855. In the issue, the land-grant was declared invalid, and the idea of a cathedral in the centre of Victoria-square had to be given up.

Unfortunately, this incident has frequently been made matter for animadversion by those inimical to the Church, it being alleged or implied that her representatives attempted surreptitiously to acquire an advantage over other religious bodies. But the facts of the case are entirely against such allegations. The only clergyman in the colony at the time the plan of the city was drawn up was the Rev. C. B. Howard, and it is in the highest degree improbable that he would have interfered in such a matter, especially as an acre had been presented for Trinity Church, in the north-west of the city, by Mr.

Grenfel. Colonel Gawler, and doubtless Colonel Robe, imagined the acre they found marked on the plan of the city as for a cathedral had been so marked by Colonel Light at the instance of an earlier Government; but this was not sustained at the trial. Sir G. Kingston deposed that, as surveyor under Colonel Light, he had laid out most of the city, and that in the plan he drew there was no reserve for a cathedral; also, that Colonel Light told him he had no power to make reserves for religious purposes. That plan had been lost—believed to have been burnt shortly after the first sale of lands. On another plan being made by Mr. Thomas, an acre in the centre of Victoria-square became marked as for a cathedral, and a sketch of one was made thereon; but under what circumstances or authority this was done did not transpire. As for the Bishop, he had no reason to doubt the information he had received from Colonel Gawler, sustained by the then plan of the city, nor could he surmise that in issuing the land-grant Colonel Robe and his executive were acting *ultra vires*.

The result has been, that Bishop Short, having obtained some funds, chose the present site for his cathedral, in North Adelaide, and a few years before his retirement had the satisfaction of erecting a portion thereof and worshipping therein. He also built St. Barnabas' College, adjacent to it, for the education and training of clergy. His successor, Dr. Kennion, was very earnest and assiduous in his endeavours to complete this work, but insufficiency of funds, and his translation to the See of Bath and Wells, have caused it to be still unfinished.

CHAPTER XIII.

SYDNEY MINUTES.

IN September 1850, Bishop Short sailed for Sydney to meet the Metropolitan and four other Australasian Bishops in Conference. The result was, the formulating of what became known as the "Sydney Minutes," which on their publication encountered quite a storm of opposition from the members of the Church in South Australia. The objects contemplated by the Conference were stated by their Lordships as follows :—

MINUTES OF PROCEEDINGS OF A MEETING OF THE METROPOLITAN AND SUFFRAGAN BISHOPS OF THE PROVINCE OF AUSTRALASIA HELD AT SYDNEY FROM OCTOBER 1ST TO NOVEMBER 1ST, A.D. 1850.

REPORT.

The Metropolitan and Bishops of the Province of Australasia having by the good Providence of God been permitted to assemble themselves together in the Metropolitan City of Sydney, on the 1st day of October, in the Year of Our Lord 1850, and having consulted together on such matters as concern the progress of true Religion, and the welfare of the Church in the said Province, and in the several Dioceses thereof, did agree to the decisions and opinions contained in the following Report :—

We, the undersigned Metropolitan and Bishops of the Province of Australasia, in consequence of doubts existing how far we are inhibited by the Queen's Supremacy from exercising the powers of an Ecclesiastical Synod, resolve not to exercise such powers on the present occasion. But we desire to consult together upon the various difficulties in which we are at present placed by the doubtful application to the Church in this Province of the Ecclesiastical Laws which are now in force in England ; and to suggest such measures as may seem to be most suitable for removing our present embarrassments ; to consider such questions as affect the progress of true religion, and the preservation of Ecclesiastical order in the several Dioceses of the Province ; and finally, in reliance on Divine Providence, to adopt plans for the propagation of the Gospel among the heathen races of Australasia and the adjacent islands of the Western Pacific.

We request the Right Reverend the Lord Bishop of Newcastle to act as our Secretary, and to embody our resolutions in a Report, to be transmitted to the Archbishops and Bishops of the United Church of England and Ireland.

W. G. SYDNEY.
G. A. NEW ZEALAND.
F. R. TASMANIA.
AUGUSTUS ADELAIDE.
C. MELBOURNE.
W. NEWCASTLE.

Their Lordships then proceeded to pass a series of resolutions expressing their opinions and decisions on the undermentioned subjects, viz. :

The applicability of the Canons of 1603-4 to the requirements of the Church in the colonies—The advisability of establishing Provincial and Diocesan Synods of Clergy only, with Provincial and Diocesan Conventions including Clergy and Laity—The Subdivision of Dioceses—Consecration of Bishops — Church Membership — Discipline of Clergy and Laity—Status of Clergy—Liturgy—Holy Baptism—Education—and Missions.

In regard to certain of their Lordships' " decisions and opinions" strong disapprobation was expressed ; first at the annual meeting of the Church Society on the 8th January, 1851, and at a special meeting on the 28th, when a very large number of the more prominent Lay member of the Church attended, the Hon. John Morphett presiding.

The principal matters objected to were those referred to in the following " Minutes ":—

We are of opinion that the Constitutions and Canons . . . . of A.D. 1603 . . . . are generally binding upon ourselves and the clergy of our respective Dioceses. Where they cannot be literally complied with, in consequence of the altered state of circumstances since the enactment of the Canons, we are of opinion that they must be as far as possible complied with in substance. We concur also in thinking that a revisal and fresh adaptation of the Canons to suit the present condition of the Church is much to be desired so soon as it can be lawfully undertaken by persons possessing due authority in that behalf.

We consider it to be most desirable in the present state of the Church of England in our Dioceses that candidates for holy orders should devote themselves to the service of the Church in that willing spirit which would induce them to place themselves at the disposal of their Bishop for some definite term of years, and leave to him the responsibility of appointing and changing their stations during such period.

Inasmuch as it is directed by the 99th Canon that no person shall marry within the degrees prohibited by the Laws of God and expressed in a table set forth by authority in the year of Our Lord God 1563, we are of opinion that any clergyman of the Province who shall solemnise matrimony between persons so related, will be acting in violation of the law of the Church. . . . . We are further of opinion that persons so marrying within the prohibited degrees are liable to be repelled from the Holy Communion until they have repented and be reformed. We are of opinion that ministers of the Church of England ought not to solemnise marriage between persons neither of whom is of our own communion, except in cases where the marriage cannot without extreme difficulty be solemnised in any other way.

We are of opinion that the general principle of Colonial legislation, by which the equality of all religious denominations is recognised, releases the clergy of the Church of England in these colonies from the obligation to perform religious services for persons who are not members of our own Church.

As Bishops engaged in the charge of extensive Dioceses are debarred from frequent opportunities of conference, we do not presume to think that we can inform or guide the judgment of the Church at large; but at a time when the minds of pious and thoughtful men are in perplexity, we cannot remain altogether silent, nor refrain from stating what we believe to be the just interpretation of the Creed, Liturgy, and Articles of the Church of England respecting the Regeneration of Infants in Holy Baptism.

We believe Regeneration to be the work of God in the Sacrament of Baptism, by which infants baptised by water in the name of the Father, Son, and Holy Ghost die unto sin, and rise again unto righteousness, and are made members of Christ, children of God, and inheritors of the Kingdom of Heaven.

We believe this regeneration to be the particular grace prayed for and expected, and thankfully acknowledged to have been received in the baptismal service.

We believe that it is the doctrine of our Church that all infants do by baptism receive this grace of regeneration.

The above comprise the views of five of the Bishops concerning baptism, the Bishop of Melbourne preferring to state his views separately as follow :—

Regeneration is that operation of the Spirit of God upon the heart which produces a death unto sin, and a new birth unto righteousness. By regeneration we are made members of Christ, children of God, and inheritors of the Kingdom of Heaven.

Baptism is the sacrament of regeneration which is the particular grace prayed for, expected, and thankfully acknowledged to have been received in the baptismal service.

The work of regeneration is wrought in all, whether they be adults or infants, who receive baptism rightly (Art. 27) but in none others (Art. 25).

The Church in her office for the baptism of infants, and in that for the baptism of adults, uses the language of faith and hope, and is not to be understood as declaring positively a fact which it cannot certainly know, viz., that every baptised infant, or every baptised adult is regenerate.

Repentance and faith are required of those who come to be baptised, but the Church is silent as to the fitness or unfitness of an infant, who is incapable of repentance and faith, for receiving regeneration in baptism.

Parents are nowhere mentioned in the Article, or in the baptismal service ; but infants are baptised because they promise repentance and faith by their sureties.

There were some additional paragraphs in the statements of the Bishop of Melbourne, and in those of the other Bishops on this subject, but these quoted contain the gist of what was objected to.

Before the public meeting proceeded to the consideration of the "Minutes," the Bishop's registrar, Mr. W. Bartley, obtained permission to read a letter from his Lordship, written with the view of throwing oil on the troubled waters.   It was as follows :—

Claremont, 21st January, 1851.

My dear Mr. Bartley—To you as a layman, I wish to address a few words of explanation respecting the Minutes of Conference at Sydney, which appear to me, from remarks I have both heard and read, to have been much misunderstood. . . . .   When I left Port Adelaide for Sydney, I was perfectly ignorant of the topics I should be called on to consider. I was summoned by the Metropolitan Bishop to meet my brethren, and I obeyed the summons.   The proposed meeting was known to the Archbishop of Canterbury, and it was called for by the Legislation touching the Colonial Church in the Imperial Parliament.   On this head, the leading principles which guided our deliberations were : First—Unity with the United Church of England and Ireland in doctrine, worship, and the Canon of Scripture.   Second—The lawful supremacy of the Queen.   Third —The due representation of the Clergy in Synods.   Fourth—The representation of the Laity in Convention and their co-operation in making ecclesiastical regulations concerning the temporal matters of the Church. And if in the last particular we were guided by the *existing* constitution of the Church of England rather than that of the American Episcopal Church, I express my own opinion, and that of some at least of my brethren, when I say that we shall willingly see the Clergy and Laity represented in Diocesan and Provincial Conventions, as is now done in the *latter* Church. It is from want of Conventions so framed that the isolated action of the Episcopalian portion of the Church of this Province is now, perhaps, without conference, discussion, or mutual explanation, to be impeded by the lay portion of it. This is badly contrived in comparison with the American system ; but as the canons and decisions of the Clergy of England in their convocation are not binding on the *laity* without their *consent*, given by the Queen's Majesty and by Parliament, so the voice of the laity must be listened to with becoming respect in the Colonial Churches.

It has been said that the introduction of the topic on baptism was unnecessary and gratuitous. I am guiltless of this introduction, beyond being able to give a reason for the faith that is in me when asked. I have never entertained the thought of narrowing the communion of the Church, nor am I aware of any such desire or intention on the part of my right reverend brethren. My rule is that of Gamaliel—" If this counsel or this work be of men, it will come to nought ; and if it be of God, ye cannot overthrow it !" So long as any clergyman subscribes and keeps the three Articles of the 36th Canon, I shall not study to force upon him that construction (on a point which, though important, is not I suppose essential to salvation), which I deem to be the plain, literal, and grammatical sense of the Liturgy ; but I am ready to allow that same freedom of judgment which I claim to myself.

I observe offence has been taken with regard to the Minutes concerning marriage and burial as if they were offensively aimed at Dissenters. The one was intended to guard against clandestine marriages and bigamy, which in the vast interior of New South Wales are likely to take place if the clergy were to marry indiscriminately persons of whom they knew nothing. In regard to the burial service, the Minute was adopted in consequence of the letter of a pious clergyman, certainly not of Tractarian views, whose conscience was sorely burdened by having been compelled (as he thought) to read the beautiful language of our service over

the remains of "notorious ill-livers," dying "*hardened in sin.*"
The Bishops resolved to claim for the Clergy the same liberty as is
enjoyed by the Ministers of every denomination. We asserted,
therefore, the absence of any *legal* obligation (which exists in
England) compelling every parish minister to bury the dead of that
parish. I am persuaded that every religious dissenter will own that
the laxity of discipline exhibited by our Church in the indiscriminate
use of that office has been one of their main objections to the
Establishment in England.

I have nothing more to add, but trust that both I and my Right
Reverend Brethren will strive always to have consciences void of
offence both towards God and towards men ; resting assured that He
in His own good providence will take care of His own truth and His
own Church.

I remain, faithfully yours,

AUGUSTUS ADELAIDE.

The meeting, which had been opened by prayer by the
Rev Jas. Farrell, Dean of Adelaide, then proceeded to the
consideration of the " Minutes." The general tone of the
discussion may be gathered from the subjoined extract
from the speech of Mr. Macdermott, who, in moving the
first resolution, said—

Having carefully considered the Sydney Minutes propounded to
the Australian Church as decisions and opinions, with a view to
discover their real character and object, I confess I have encountered
some difficulty. I don't see the great doctrine of the atonement,
or, indeed, any of the fundamental doctrines of our Church insisted
on. But I do see a dogma put forth in a most formal and gratuitous
manner on the subject of Baptismal Regeneration, apparently because it is the great symbol of Tractarianism, and therefore doubly
offensive to a large majority of our Church. By the promulgation
of this manifesto the Australian Bishops have set authority at
defiance, virtually spurning the Queen's supremacy and condemning
the decision of the Privy Council in the case of Gorham against
Exeter (in which our Primate, the Archbishop of Canterbury, concurred), who have left this question, as our reformers did, an open

one. And I am forced to the conclusion that the Minutes were less intended to edify and promote the spiritual interests of the Australian Church than to serve the purposes of the Tractarian party in England, and with a view of procuring Imperial legislation in ecclesiastical matters prejudicial to freedom of conscience in these colonies. By these Minutes the Australian prelates have, to a great extent, identified themselves with the Bishop of Exeter, who would, indeed, narrow the terms of communion with the Church within infinitely small limits, having already subjected the Archbishop of Canterbury to a kind of excommunication by branding His Grace as a heretic and schismatic on account of his sanctioning the judgment of the Privy Council. He has refused to receive testimonials in his Diocese because they were countersigned by His Grace, and refused to licence clergymen because they held Mr. Gorham's views on Baptismal Regeneration. . . . We are not schismatics, we are the supporters of order and legitimate authority. It appears to be contemplated by the Minutes "that candidates for Holy Orders should devote themselves to the service of the Church in that willing spirit which would induce them to place themselves at the disposal of their Bishop for some definite term of years, and leave to him the responsibility of appointing and changing their station during that period." And, also, that a portion of the clergy should be licensed by the Bishop to temporary charges, who would, of course, be also for a term of years, at the disposal and under the entire control of their Lordships. Now, the systematic training of a number of young men under strict rules of discipline and obedience for a number of years as Novices and Deacons, who would ultimately absorb all the offices of the Ministry, and whose prospects in life shall be wholly dependent on the Bishop, appears well calculated to destroy the independence of the Clergy, and to inflict deep wounds upon the Church. Those men must obviously adopt the views of their chief, be he a Gorham or an Exeter, or abandon their prospects in the Church ; and the system seems open to some of the strongest objections urged against the Order of the Jesuits. . . . Tractarianism I believe to be a system of theology having for its object to unprotestantize the Church of England, to introduce Popish ceremonies, to exalt the priesthood, to substitute the Prayer-book and traditions for the Bible, to introduce the Popish doctrines of transubstantiation, purgatory, confession, penance, absolution, &c., &c. The following is an extract from a letter addressed by the Rev. Mr. Dodsworth (who is reported to have since joined the Church of Rome) to Dr. Pusey, dated May 1850, and is very characteristic :—" You have been of the foremost to lead us on to a higher appreciation of that Church system of which Sacramental Grace is the very life and soul. Both by principle and example you have been the most earnest to maintain Catholic principles. By your constant and common practice of administering the Sacrament of Penance ; by encouraging everywhere, if not enjoining, auricular confession, and giving special priestly absolution ; by teaching the Propitiatory Sacrifice of the Holy Eucharist as applicatory to the Sacrifice on the Cross and adoration of Christ, *e.g.*, to His five wounds, by adopting language most powerfully expressive of an incorporation into Christ, *e.g.*, our being inebriated by the blood of our Lord ; by advocating counsels of perfection, and seeking to restore with more or less fulness the Conventual or Monastic life. I say, by the teaching and practice of which this enumeration is a sufficient type and indication, you have done much to revive amongst us the system which may be pre-eminently called Sacramental."—Letter pp. 16, 17. God forbid that I should lay such heavy charges against a large body of men who regard with favour only portions of this system. Among Tractarians there are many shades of opinion. But numbers having once entered on this downward course, often wandering for a time in the devious paths of tradition, and finding no rest for the soles of their feet, are finally driven to seek shelter in the Church of Rome. . . . The Australian Bishops can hardly complain when we follow the example of disobedience they have set before us by solemnly rejecting and repudiating *in toto* their unauthorised Minutes as *null* and of no effect. I have to propose therefore— That this meeting has heard with regret and alarm that the Australian Bishops at their recent Conference, held at Sydney, have attempted to narrow the terms of Communion with and admission into the Ministry of our Church by their formal, gratuitous, and unnecessary dogmatical declaration on the subject of Baptismal Regeneration ; thereby disturbing the peace and harmony which have hitherto prevailed among its members in this Diocese.

This was seconded by G. S. Walters, Esq.

Sir J. H. Fisher moved and Dr. Wyatt seconded—

That as Members of the Protestant Church of England in South Australia, and desirous to pay proper deference and respect to the Lord Bishop of the Diocese, we totally and absolutely repudiate any assumption of ecclesiastical authority by the Church in this Province, and solemnly protest against any attempt on their part to exercise the same.

F. S. Dutton, Esq., moved and Mr. Burr seconded—

That one of the evident objects of the unauthorised Conference of the Bishops at Sydney being to obtain an extension of power dangerous to the peace of the community, this Meeting deems it necessary to express its opinion that it is highly inexpedient that any extension of ecclesiastical power should be permitted, or that authority should be given to establish courts with any secular jurisdiction for so-called spiritual purposes.

J. Baker, Esq., moved and Mr. J. A. Adams seconded—

That the Clergy of the Church of England in this Province be respectfully invited to meet and express publicly their opinion on the ecclesiastical character and authority of the Minutes and Proceedings of the Bishops at Sydney.

Capt. Bagot moved and Capt. Hart seconded—

That, apprehensive that the recognised standards of the Church might be perilled by their unauthorised construction, and by the innovations of the Tractarian and Anti - Protestant part of the Church, it is necessary that measures be taken to guard against the spread of dangerous error in the doctrines of the Protestant Church in this Province, and to maintain those doctrines in their purity.

Capt. H. Watts moved, and Abraham Scott, Esq., seconded—

That the following gentlemen be a Standing Committee to re-

present the Laity, and watch over their interests generally, and to
call meetings of the Laity when and as often as they may deem
necessary, and to replace their number when reduced to five :--
Mr. Macdermott, Capt. Hart, Dr. Wyatt, Mr. J. H. Fisher, Capt.
Bagot, Mr. F. S. Dutton, Mr. J. Baker.

G. S. Kingston, Esq., moved and Capt. Duff seconded—

That a copy of the foregoing Resolutions be forwarded by the
Chairman to the Lord Bishop of Adelaide, and to His Grace the
Archbishop of Canterbury, our Primate, with an earnest supplica-
tion that His Grace will use his authority to protect the Church in
South Australia from any Episcopal interference with its doctrines
and discipline, which has not previously received the direct sanction
of His Grace and Her Majesty the Queen as the Supreme Head of
the Church.

These resolutions were unanimously and enthusiastically
carried, and in due course forwarded to the Bishop and the
Archbishop of Canterbury. The speeches of their movers
and seconders strongly emphasised the sentiments embodied in Mr. Macdermott's speech. His Honor Judge
Cooper moved an amendment on the first resolution, saying " it was with the form in which the Resolution was
put rather than the principle it contained that he disagreed," and moved :—

That this meeting has heard with alarm that at a meeting of the
Metropolitan and Suffragan Bishops of the Province of Australasia,
recently held in Sydney, a plan has been devised for the government
of the Church of England in Australasia, wherein no provision is
made for appeal from the decisions of the Provincial Synods to Her
Majesty in Privy Council. That a petition be prepared for presentation to Her Majesty the Queen respectfully praying Her
Majesty that she will be graciously pleased not to assent to any
measure for establishing a general system of Church government
in the Province of Australasia, in accordance with the " Minutes "

of the Right Reverend Bishops thereof, until Her Majesty's faithful subjects, members of the Church of England in South Australia, have had an opportunity of considering the same. That a committee be appointed for preparing such petition.

This was seconded by Mr. Newland and supported by Sir R. R. Torrens, but negatived by a large majority. On receiving the Resolutions, the Bishop wrote to the chairman as follows:—

Adelaide, January 31st, 1851.

Dear Mr. Morphett—I beg to acknowledge receipt of the Resolutions passed at a meeting held on the 28th in Pulteney-street schoolroom, which reached me this day ; and I take the opportunity of making a few observations, which I request you to make public, and transmit, together with the Resolutions, to His Grace the Archbishop of Canterbury.

1. The attempt "to narrow the terms of communion and admission into the Ministry" alleged against the Bishops in the first Resolution, is negatived by the language of the Minute itself on Holy Baptism ; which states that they " do not presume to think that they can inform or guide the judgment of the whole Church " in this matter, and, secondly, by incorporating in the same Minute the statement of the Bishop of Melbourne, which appears to favour another construction of the Baptismal services ; thereby indicating liberty of judgment on this subject.

2. The institution of duly elected Conventions of the Laity, suggested in the Minutes, sitting simultaneously with Synods of the Clergy, under authority of the Queen as Supreme Head of the Church, negatives the attempt on the part of the Bishops to "assume ecclesiastical authority, and obtain an extension of power," alleged in the 2nd and 3rd Resolutions. With such Conventions and Synods sitting, either simultaneously or conjointly, it would be morally impossible.

3. Any disloyal wish to repudiate or restrict the lawful supremacy of the Queen is negatived by Minute No. 2, affirming the Canons of A.D. 1603 to be binding on the Bishops and Clergy of the Australasian Dioceses. The first Article of the 36th Canon expressly affirms

the Queen's supremacy ; and it is further secured by subscription to the Thirty-nine Articles, in the declaration to which it is set forth.

Lastly : With respect to Tractarian and Anti-Protestant views. Having witnessed the beginning, rise, progress, and eventual tendency of that party in the Church, I have no hesitation in saying, that, with their doctrinal statements on sin after baptism ; the mystical presence in the sacred elements, and propitiatory efficacy of the Lord's Supper as a sacrifice ; the virtue of penance ; meritoriousness of works ; the exaltation of the Virgin Mary ; the invocation of the saints—set forth in one of the Tracts for the Times ; reserve in preaching the doctrine of the Cross ; the assumption of the priesthood and apostolical succession being necessary to give validity to the sacraments as means of grace ; Romanising books of devotion, and lives of the English saints ; the setting up of outward forms and disused ceremonials ; insubordination to the civil power as supreme "in all cases and over all persons ;" the putting a non-natural sense upon the Articles and Liturgy ; the disingenuousness and want of moral honesty in many of the disciples ; with all these things, and possibly many more if brought to my recollection, I neither have, nor have had, any sympathy whatever. I recorded my vote in Convocation at Oxford against Mr. Ward and his book, entitled the "Ideal of a Church ;" and I am fully prepared, with God's grace, to stand by the scriptural principles of our Reformed Protestant Church, both as to discipline and doctrine, in their plain, ordinary, moderate, and general acceptation, as understood before the late Romanising movement ; and in which, for twenty years of parochial ministration, I ever held them, previous to my consecration as Bishop of Adelaide. I rejoice to witness a godly jealousy among the laity for the purity of the faith won for us at the Reformation ; and would conclude with the prayer that we all—Bishops, Clergy, and Laity—may be guided into all truth, and kept from any zeal which is not after knowledge.

I remain, dear Mr. Morphett,
Yours faithfully,
AUGUSTUS ADELAIDE.

The Clergy having met at the instance of the Bishop to consider the matter, reported to his Lordship as follows :—

To the Right Reverend the Lord Bishop of Adelaide.

Chapter-House, Adelaide, February 5th, 1851.

My Lord—We, the clergy of the Diocese of Adelaide, having deliberated, at your Lordship's suggestion, upon the " Minutes of Proceedings at a meeting of the Metropolitan and Suffragan Bishops of Australasia, held in Sydney in October last," have now the honor of submitting, for your Lordship's consideration, our views and opinions thereon, as embodied in the following propositions.

Though unfortunately under the necessity of differing from your Lordship on many points, we trust our manner of doing so will be deemed unexceptionable. We are persuaded that we only do justice to the Chief Pastors of the Australasian Churches by giving them credit for a sincere and earnest desire to advance the interests of true religion in their respective Dioceses. As Presbyters and Deacons of the Church of England, we must claim to be considered no less desirous of securing the attainment of the great ends of the Church's institution.

It was not thought necessary to remark upon those matters contained in the " Minutes " which are determined by the Rubrics ; referred to the decision of the Ordinary ; or, judging from the general usage in the mother country, left to the discretion of each individual clergyman.

Any attempt to enforce a *rigid* uniformity in minor or trivial matters would, it is to be feared, not only fail in its object, but would tend to engender strife and evil surmisings.

The Church needs rest. May its Chief Pastors be endued with the spirit of wisdom, power, love, and of a sound mind; and may we all —Clergy and Laity—be divinely enabled to maintain the faith " in unity of spirit, in the bond of peace, and in righteousness of life."

PROPOSITIONS ABOVE REFERRED TO.

1. That our proceedings be made public.
2. That we proceed to the consideration of the " Minutes " *seriatim* ; omitting, however, all discussion upon the question of Baptismal Regeneration, except to affirm the propriety or otherwise of its introduction into the " Minutes."
3. That we regard the meeting of the Bishops respectively of Sydney, Tasmania, New Zealand, Adelaide, Newcastle, and Mel-

bourne, simply as a voluntary assembling of the Chief Pastors of the Australasian Dioceses to confer upon matters affecting the interest of the Church.

4. That while we approve mainly of the objects on which the Bishops proposed to consult—as specified in Section 1.—we cannot refrain from expressing our regret that, as they had not conferred with their respective clergy before their meeting, they should have forwarded their "Minutes" to England, with a view, it is presumed, to Imperial Legislation, without previously submitting them to the Clergy and Laity of their respective Dioceses.

Future Synods and Conventions.

5. That adverting to chap. iii., "On Future Synods and Conventions," we are of opinion that it would be preferable for the Clergy and Laity to meet in *one* Assembly or Convention, consisting of every licensed Presbyter having cure of souls, and one or more laymen, chosen by and out of the members of each congregation, in full communion, and presided over by the Bishop of the Diocese.

Subdivision of Dioceses and Nomination of Bishops.

6. That the right and power of Her Most Gracious Majesty to subdivide the Australasian Dioceses and to nominate Bishops thereto has hitherto been wisely and beneficially exercised, and ought for the present to be retained intact ; and that, should a period arrive when it should be deemed expedient that Her Majesty should relinquish the right of nominating to Colonial Sees, we are of opinion that, according to ancient usage, such right of nomination should be vested in the Clergy of the Diocese over which the Bishop is to preside.

Church Membership.

Minute.—On a discussion of the phrase " duly baptised," it was understood that the word "duly" was intended to be explained by the words following, viz., " with water, in the name of the Father, Son, and Holy Ghost," and *not* to refer to the person baptising.

Discipline—Clergy.

7. That as the Australasian Bishops " disclaim " the right, power, or wish " to suspend or revoke, at their own discretion, the licences of clergymen," we are of opinion that the licences to incumbencies

should, as far as possible, be in the same form of words as those issued in England, and not revocable "at pleasure."

8. That it is desirable that there should be a power of depriving clergy convicted of immorality or heresy of their incumbencies.

Status of Clergy.

9. That we view with some degree of fear and disapprobation, the desire of the Australasian Bishops to licence clergymen to charges of a " temporary nature," and the wish expressed by them that candidates for Holy Orders " should place themselves " entirely " at the disposal of their Bishop for some definite term of years, and leave to him the responsibility of appointing and changing their station during such period "—as we believe such a policy, if general, would, under present circumstances, be injurious to the maintenance of mental independence, doctrinal purity, and pastoral fidelity among the junior clergy, and would be inimical to their domestic comfort and general usefulness.

10. That it is of the utmost importance to the respectability, influence, and efficiency of the clerical body in this Diocese to keep up, as far as possible, the standard of secular and theological learning for candidates for Holy Orders, which is required by the Bishops at home.

11. That, under present circumstances, it is not desirable to admit to the Diaconate, for the service of the Church in this Diocese, persons whose previous position in the colony would materially impair their influence.

12. That, for the due preservation of order and harmony, it is desirable that no Deacon or Catechist should be introduced into any district under the care of a Presbyter, but on the nomination of such Presbyter, to whom the said Deacon or Catechist should be subordinate.

Liturgy.

Marriage of persons neither of whom belong to the Church.

13. That whereas up to a recent period no marriages of Dissenters in England were legal unless celebrated according to the rites and ceremonies of the Established Church, and whereas at the present time the majority of Dissenting marriages are so celebrated in the mother country, we are of opinion that no Australasian clergyman ought to refuse to marry any parties who may apply to him, though they be not members of our communion.

Ministering to Dissenters.

14. That while we are relieved from any *legal* "obligation" . . "to perform religious services for persons who are not members of our Church," yet, to guard against any misconception, we desire to express our readiness to afford our ministerial offices, as far as in us lies, to any who may desire or need them.

Minute.—We deem it inexpedient to express an opinion on some points touched upon in chap vii., as we believe these points must be left, to a certain extent, to the discretion of the officiating minister. We feel bound, however, to remark, that in Section IX., letter *d*, no mention is made of marriages to be solemnised on certificate from the Registrar's office; but we cannot suppose that it is intended by such omission to condemn the solemnisation of such marriages by Ministers of our Church.

We desire also to express the difficulty we are under of understanding what is meant by the advice of the Bishops to repel from the Holy Communion persons who have married within the prohibited degrees "until they have *repented* and be *reformed.*"

Holy Baptism.

15. That the introduction by the Australasian Bishops of the question of Holy Baptism into their "Minutes" was uncalled for and injudicious; that the construction put by them upon the "Creed, Articles, and Liturgy," with respect to this subject, would, if imposed, be tantamount to a new article of faith; and that the dogmatical determination of a question which has ever been practically considered *an open one, virtually* narrows the terms of communion with our Church.

Education.

16. That, whilst desirous of seeing a school established in connection with every church in this colony, we shall be prepared to regard favourably any system of education in which the Bible shall be the basis of the instruction given.

Missions.

17. That we hail with great satisfaction the establishment of the Australasian Board of Missions in connection with our Church, with a view to the conversion of the aboriginal inhabitants of Australasia, and the Isles of the Western Pacific, and we earnestly hope and

pray that such measures may be adopted and carried out by its members as may be crowned with the Divine blessing.

> JAMES FARRELL, Dean of Adelaide and Incumbent of Trinity.
>
> WILLIAM JOHN WOODCOCK, Canon of Adelaide and Incumbent of Christ Church.
>
> THEODORE PERCIVAL WILSON, Canon of Adelaide and Incumbent of St. John's.
>
> JAMES POLLITT, Curate of Kooringa, and Chaplain to the Patent Copper Company, Burra Burra.
>
> W. H. COOMBS, Incumbent of St. George's, Gawler.
>
> JOHN CHARLES BAGSHAWE, Incumbent of St. Mark's, Penwortham.
>
> ARTHUR B. BURNETT, Incumbent of St. Stephen's, Willunga.
>
> JOHN WATSON, Incumbent of St. Matthew's, Kensington.
>
> JOHN W. SCHOALES, Officiating Minister, Magill.
>
> JOHN FULFORD, Deacon, St. Mary's, Sturt, and Christ Church, O'Halloran Hill.
>
> E. K. MILLER, Deacon, Head Master of Pulteney-street School, and Assistant Minister of Christ Church, North Adelaide.

To these resolutions the Bishop replied as follows :—

Claremont, February 6th, 1851.

My dear Mr. Farrell—I return for publication the resolutions and opinions arrived at by the Clergy on the Minutes of the Conference at Sydney, which on my return I submitted for their consideration. They appear to me to be characterised by a calm and serious spirit, which, under the circumstances of excitement lately prevailing, is peculiarly gratifying. Should Her Gracious Majesty, as Supreme Head of the Church of England, authorise the Clergy and Laity of the Australasian Dioceses to frame their own ecclesiastical polity, subject to her approval, and should it be deemed advisable to depart on any point from the existing constitution of the English Church, I trust that the pattern of other reformed

Protestant and Episcopal Churches will be followed, and the relations of the Bishops, Clergy, and Laity, as set forth in the Scriptures, carefully preserved.

I remain, yours very truly,
AUGUSTUS ADELAIDE.

Thus terminated the first unpleasant incident in connection with the establishment of the Church in South Australia. Like all such incidents, it left a residuum of doubt and loss of confidence in the minds of many, and furnished ground for abundance of adverse comment. In the excitement that then prevailed in England, consequent on the Bishop of Exeter refusing to institute the Rev. Mr. Gorham to a living in his Diocese because that gentleman's views on Baptismal Regeneration did not accord with his own, and the Privy Council having decided against the Bishop's action, it was most unfortunate the Australasian Bishops should have promulgated a formal declaration adverse to the Council's decision. Certainly the sending the " Minutes " to England, apparently to influence impending legislation, without consulting either Clergy or Laity, was injudicious. This, however, is only an illustration of what often happens, viz., that the very best of men err in judgment, and so fail in effecting the good ends they have in view.

CHAPTER XIV.

EDUCATION.

ON Bishop Short's arrival, he found that considerable interest had been manifested in matters educational, and some important steps taken. In the preceding August an Act had been passed by the Legislative Council providing that any school established by any person, and having not less than twenty pupils, might be granted from the revenue one pound per annum for each child attending, up to forty, and one pound extra for each of such children as were instructed in the "higher branches;" but no teacher to receive above one hundred pounds per annum. This Act made no provision for buildings. The recommendation of the parents of twenty children and a magistrate qualified any one setting up as teacher to claim the subsidy. A proprietary or grammar school had been established about a year previously, conducted in the school-room attached to Trinity Church, while a large school-room was being erected in Pulteney-street as a public school, both originating with members of the Church of England. On my landing I found that the Rev. T. P. Wilson, M.A., who had come out with the Bishop with a view to starting a collegiate school, had been placed in charge of the proprietary school, and the Bishop was desirous I should be appointed to the public school, and make it a normal school for the Diocese. A difficulty, however, arose between the trustees of the building and the Bishop concerning the Church Catechism, which his Lordship wished to be included in the school curriculum. Though built primarily as a Church school. its promoters desired that it should be open to all denominations. The trustees feared that the introduction of the Catechism would cause some not to send their children to it who otherwise might do so. So strongly did the Bishop feel on the matter that he spoke of placing me in a cure and having nothing to do with the school. On his consulting me, I pointed out that as it was provided the Scriptures should be read and taught daily in the school, as a Church school, whatever religious teaching was given would of course be in accordance with Church principles; therefore, whether those principles were taught directly from Scripture, or through the medium of the Catechism— which would be taught in the Sunday-school—was not, in my view, of vital moment; that dissenters availing themselves of the school for their children would do so with full knowledge of the nature of the religious instruction given, therefore could have no possible ground for complaint; while it would be better both for such children and the school that they should not be excluded by any hard and fast rule as to the form of words in which religious teaching was to be conveyed. In the issue, his Lordship waived the point; the school was placed in my charge, and I proceeded with its fitting up and furnishing, a good supply of material having been brought out by the Bishop, granted by the Society for Promoting Christian Knowledge. It was opened on May 29th, 1848. When about one hundred children had been admitted, I applied to the trustees for an assistant; this was refused on the ground that there was a debt on the building they wished to liquidate. Hence I was compelled to conduct the school monitorially, as indeed I had done almost from the beginning. At length I obtained the services of Mr. W. Pepper, who proved a most valuable assistant. He afterwards organised a good school at North Adelaide, and leaving for Victoria, was long head master of a Government school there. A succession of persons coming in for training, and acting as assistants, resulted in the school becoming sufficiently supplied; the late Mr. and Mrs. L. S. Burton, of Gawler, were among these.

In the report of the S.P.C.K for 1850, the following notice of it from Bishop Short appeared:—"The Pulteney-street School continues to flourish under Mr. Miller; the addition of a class-room has made the building still more complete. Since the school was opened in May last four hundred children have been admitted." Also, later— "On Wednesday last the half-yearly examination of the Pulteney-street School, under the Rev. E. K. Miller and Mr. Pepper, was conducted by the Archdeacon, with Rev. T. P. Wilson, in my presence. This may be considered a first-rate national training-school, on the model of which others may be formed, and over which, hereafter, I trust Mr. Miller will exercise the office of inspector." In the Society's report for 1851, a further report on educational matters from his Lordship's pen also appears—"In educational matters I am happy to report progress. At Gawler and Hindmarsh day-schools in connection with the Church have been opened with great success. . . . Though we do not compel the children to learn the Catechism, yet only in one single instance, in North Adelaide, has exemption been claimed. . . . I am happy to say that we have not only many competent masters, but, under the care of the Rev. E. K. Miller, as many can be efficiently trained as there will be openings for."

The subjoined letter from one who had been a Baptist Missionary may be taken as indicating the feelings of dissenters in regard to the religious teaching of the school :—

Adelaide, January 7th, 1851.

Rev. and dear Sir—Being under the necessity of removing my son from your school, I feel it my duty to express to you my heartfelt thanks for your kind and efficient attention to his education, and for the Christian sympathy and kindness which you have showed to him during a severe illness.

We cannot on this occasion avoid expressing our high satisfaction at the uniform impartiality hitherto shown to children whose parents are of different religious denominations. Charles has left you, but his heart will long remain with you and the pleasing associations connected with Pulteney-street School. May you, dear Sir, be long spared to be a blessing to both children and adults in South Australia. I beg of you to present our thanks to the trustees and all friends connected with the institution.

I am, Rev. and dear Sir,

Yours respectfully,

Rev. E. K. Miller.   JOHN CANHAM.

During the same period the Collegiate School was succeeding well. Towards its establishment the Society for Promoting Christian Knowledge had made the munificent grant of two thousand pounds. Writing to the Society for the Propagation of the Gospel, in 1849, the Bishop said—" I found the College Grammar School established, but hoped to incorporate it with the College. The proprietors seem very willing; if so, we shall have a good establishment together." The incorporation having been accomplished, and thirty acres of land secured a short distance from the city, contributions began to come in; largely through the energetic efforts of Mr. G. W. Hawkes, secretary to the Governor—to whom this institution, as indeed the Church generally, is much indebted. Captain W. Allen gave a first donation of seven hundred pounds, and afterwards another of two thousand; Mr. J. Ellis also gave three hundred pounds; so that the building fund soon amounted to four thousand five hundred pounds. The first stone was laid by the Bishop on May 24th, 1849, in the presence of the Governor (Sir. H. F. Young), the clergy, and a large number of the leading colonists. Writing to the S.P.C.K. of that event, the Bishop said—"Nothing could have passed off better than the ceremony. It has excited the liveliest interest, and given the Church of England the entire lead in the education of the colony." The *South Australian* newspaper the next day said—"Every one was much pleased with the ceremony and the addresses of the Governor and Bishop."

Early in 1850 the school-room had been so far completed that the pupils were transferred from the school-room of Trinity Church to their new location. The school prospered well under the Rev. T. P. Wilson, M.A., and Mr. C. May, till, as the result of an unfortunate misunderstanding, the former resigned charge of it, becoming incumbent of St. John's, Adelaide; and shortly after leaving for England.

In 1850, I was elected to the cure of St. George's Woodforde, and Magill, about five miles from Adelaide. For about a year afterwards I continued in charge of the Pulteney-street School, riding to and fro daily. Having then resigned, I commenced school on my own account at Magill, and soon had a sufficiency of pupils from the best families. Not long after resigning, the Rev. W. J. Woodcock, on behalf of the trustees, applied to me to resume charge of the school, which had become disorganised; but I felt compelled to decline. The Bishop, too, on Mr Wilson's resigning the Collegiate School, was very urgent that I should take charge of it till a fresh master could be procured from England, and subsequently wished me to take the position of second or third master permanently; both these requests I felt obliged to decline, at which, I am sorry to say, his Lordship was much annoyed. The position of *pro tem.* head master was afterwards accepted by the Rev. E. Jenkins, who held it till the arrival of the Rev. G. H. Farr, M.A. (now Archdeacon), under whom, with Mr. C. May and the Rev. F. Williams, M.A. (since head master), the school attained a high degree of efficiency.

In 1852, a new Education Act was passed, which provided for establishing a Board of Education, with power to aid school buildings and teachers' stipends; also providing for inspection. As this had been for some time in contemplation, and a Government inspector was to be appointed, the Bishop's plan of organising an educational system for the Diocese on Church principles, and my becoming inspector, had to be given up. Conversing with Sir Henry Young, then Governor, on the matter, I suggested that in the condition of many of the schools, conducted by inexperienced and untrained teachers, it would be desirable the proposed inspector should be able to act on occasion as organising master also, and assist in introducing some definite plan of teaching. His Excellency thought, however, that as different methods of instruction existed, it would be undesirable to appoint an inspector who had a predilection for any particular plan or system; but that a perfectly impartial person should be appointed, who could report as to the results of different systems;

he also thought it would be very inadvisable to have all schools conducted on the same plan or model, as the different powers and talents of the teachers might become cramped and hampered, and competition precluded. In the issue, as it was deemed inexpedient to appoint as inspector any minister of religion, Dr. Wyatt received the appointment. It is curious to notice how diametrically opposite were the views of Sir Henry Young and his government to the governmental views of the present day. Now, we have not only a rigid uniformity enforced in the conduct of all public schools, but, if the statements of many of the teachers are to be credited, an absolutely despotic rule, which cramps their energies and abilities, abolishes all discretionary power, and leaves no room for competition. So far as appears, the schoolmaster is now by no means the master of his school, but simply an instrument compelled to carry out another's will.

After the Act of 1852 had been in operation for a few years, dissatisfaction sprang up in regard to it. A Select Committee of the Legislature pronounced very strongly against a large expenditure from revenue being continued for what were stated to be very meagre results. It becoming clear that fresh legislation on the subject would be undertaken, while sundry newspaper writers were urging the adoption of a purely secular system, I thought it well to try and induce a preliminary discussion of the matter in the public press. With this view I drew up the subjoined propositions—somewhat crude, perhaps—to form the basis of such discussion, and these were published in the *Register* of April 5th, 1856 :—

PROPOSITIONS OR SUGGESTIONS ON PUBLIC EDUCATION.

1. The education of children naturally devolves on their parents.

2. Parents frequently do not recognise, or have not the opportunity of satisfactorily discharging this duty.

3. A large number of children are consequently not educated, or very imperfectly so.

4. Civil governments and religious bodies have, jointly or otherwise, endeavoured to supply the deficiencies hereby occasioned.

5. The leading object of such endeavours should be—the inducing parents to educate their children ; the placing the means of education within the reach of all ; and the providing education for such as could not otherwise be educated.

6. Where freedom of opinion prevails, as in England, the civil powers have experienced much difficulty in aiding education from the differing religious tenets of those to be educated, and the fact that up to a recent period the only important efforts to promote education had been made by the various religious bodies.

7. Religious principle being the foundation of virtue and morality, its inculcation cannot safely be omitted in any scheme of general education.

8. A Government desiring to promote education should commence by stating the character and extent of the religious teaching it deems essential.

9. Since no rule can well be framed to meet, in this respect, the views of all, the one adopted should be such as may accord with the general principles of the greatest possible number ; power being reserved to treat extreme or exceptional cases on their own merits.

10. Such a rule might at least require, for instance, that schools be opened and closed by the teachers reading a portion of the Psalms or Proverbs, and the Lord's Prayer ; and that the children be instructed in the "Selections for Scripture Reading," published by the British and Foreign School Society, or some such work. Devotional habits would thereby be cultivated, and as much Scriptural knowledge and religious principle imparted, without special doctrinal instruction, as would serve for the foundation of that training which seeks to produce a virtuous and moral life.

11. The control and application of sums voted by the Legislature for educational purposes might be advantageously vested in a Standing Committee of Council on Education, who should report to the Governor in Council.

12. Aid should be tendered towards the erection of school-rooms,

teachers' residences, stipends, and school materials, in such proportion as may be determined on by the dispensing body or committee.

13. District Councils or Municipal authorities should have power given to levy rates for the erection and support of schools, or itinerating teachers, in such parts or districts or towns as may appear to need them—such rates to be supplemented, where required, by grants from the general revenue.

14. Religious or other societies desirous of establishing schools on special principles, should be eligible to aid from public funds, on conceding to the Government the right of inspection, and on the general education afforded by such schools being reported as satisfactory.

15. Parents wilfully neglecting to educate their children, thereby inflicting injury on those children, and on society, should be subject to a penalty.

16. To secure efficient organisation and supervision, there should be a superintendent of public schools and an assistant; one of whom, at least, should be competent to act as either inspector or organising master. These, with the aid, perhaps, of a board of experienced teachers, might recommend the granting of licences, superintend the training of candidate-teachers, suggest the best method of organising schools and communicating instruction, and so inspect schools as to report accurately on the character and extent of the instruction they afford.

17. In the absence of a normal school, certain of the best existing schools might be specially licensed as training-schools, the teachers thereof being allowed a gratuity for each candidate-teacher successfully trained.

18. Periodical meetings of teachers should be encouraged for the discussion of or hearing lectures on educational matters.

19. A teachers' library should be established, containing two copies of every important work on education; one copy to be for circulation and one retained for reference. Specimens of lesson-books, apparatus, &c., should be added.

20. Four rooms should be erected on the site and to form part of the future normal school; two to be offices for the superintendent and inspectors, one for the teachers' library and reading-room, and one to be fitted up as a theatre for lectures, meetings, &c.

21. All details of school arrangement, as holidays, hours of tuition, &c., should be left to the local managers of schools; the Government merely ascertaining whether the schools it aids are efficiently conducted, and assisting, if otherwise. to render them efficient.

22. If material changes be decided on, they should be executed gradually. Where necessary, aid on the present plan might be continued till the inhabitants or local authorities take steps to provide a suitable school and teacher.

These were followed by a series of letters in support, three of which the *Register* published, but declined the fourth on the ground that it " might lead to controversy;" I append it, with the editorial notice, as it afterwards appeared in the *South Australian Times :*

The subject of education is one on which there may be differences of opinion, but none so great, we should suppose, as to justify a public journalist during these slack times in closing his columns against the discussion of any plan in furtherance of what every one admits to be so desirable. But the *Register* is not of this mind, and we have, therefore, to publish a letter from the Rev. E. K. Miller on the subject, which that paper has rejected. We have given Mr. Miller's letter a very careful perusal, and we are quite at a loss to understand on what ground the refusal to insert it was based.— *Times.*

EDUCATION.

To the Editor of the *Times.*

Sir—Some three months since, at the suggestion of a friend interested in the promotion of education, I undertook to originate, if possible, an amicable discussion on the leading difficulties connected with that subject. With this view, I forwarded letters to the *Register* newspaper, dated 31st March, 2nd April, 5th June, and 7th July respectively. These were duly published, but without calling forth the discussion I had anticipated.

In pursuance of my plan, I forwarded to the *Register*, on the 26th ultimo, the communication now submitted for your consideration.

On sending, fourteen days after, to inquire if it would be published, I was surprised by its being returned, with the message that it was deemed unsuitable for publication, as it " might lead to controversy."

I do not desire to comment on what appears to me a very novel reason for seeking to suppress the stating of opinions on a particular subject : but I at once appeal to your kindness and candour to afford space for the letter rejected by the *Register* ; and such further remarks as may be necessary in endeavouring to indicate the course most advisable for advancing education in this colony.

I trust you will oblige by granting this, though the views advanced may not, in all respects, agree with your own. Otherwise, the conclusion must inevitably be drawn, that South Australia is so thoroughly press-ridden that expression can be given to no ideas which editorial wisdom disapproves.

Yours truly,

Woodforde, August 13th, 1856. E. K. Miller.

To the Editor of the *Register.*

In my last communication I endeavoured to show that the inculcation of religious principle could not be " safely omitted in any scheme of general education."

This being granted, it follows, that whoever is desirous of promoting education, must see that provision is made for the inculcation of such principle. In the case of a Government aiding education, attention to this point is especially necessary, since the advancement of moral rectitude, and the prevention of vice and crime, will be among its more prominent objects.

In attempting to secure these, it will require to consult the views of all whose efforts it desires to aid or induce. So long as those views do not embody principles which would militate against the good order or moral well-being of the community, they should form no ground for the Government withholding aid, or otherwise discouraging educational effort on the part of those who may entertain them.

While prepared to aid education among all classes of its subjects, and to encourage persons of every shade of opinion to exert themselves in this behalf, a Government might, with great propriety, as largely contributing to the extension of education, and as conservator of the public weal, indicate the "character and extent of the religious teaching it deems essential" for laying the "foundation of that training, which seeks to produce a virtuous and moral life."

It might, for instance, affirm, as a general principle, that, in schools it aids, the Holy Scriptures, or extracts therefrom, should be read and taught daily. It might likewise recommend that schools be opened and closed with prayer, singing, or reading the Scriptures ; that in schools attended by children whose parents belong to various religious bodies, no Catechism, or formulary, peculiar to any denomination should be used during the usual hours of school instruction : also, that teachers urge on their pupils the duty of attending the Sabbath-school, or place of worship, their parents may prefer.

Though a Government would be fully justified in affirming such a principle, and in making such recommendations, and though the great majority of school managers should willingly assent thereto, were adhesion to them made imperative, some might find themselves precluded from participating in that assistance which should be within the reach of all, since the funds which supply it are contributed by all.

In the case of a Roman Catholic or Jewish school such principles would hardly apply : yet. since an educated Jew or Roman Catholic will be a more valuable member of society than an uneducated one, it would not be politic, and certainly not just. for the Government to withhold from him those means for obtaining education which are freely granted to others.

Where Roman Catholics, Jews, or other religionists are numerous, and desire to establish schools, in which their children may be daily gathered and taught the principles themselves believe, aid from the Government, if sought, should be accorded, so long as the schools be well attended and efficiently conducted.

Hence, however, comprehensive the principles or rules the Government may seem fit to adopt, with the view of securing the moral training of the young in day-schools, provision for exceptional cases will be needed : otherwise, injustice will be done. ignorance fostered, or parties called on to sacrifice principles they, perhaps, conscientiously deem of the first importance.

Supposing certain general principles to be affirmed, if not made imperative, and, consequently, to some extent exclusive, it will be necessary to leave their adoption to the local managers of schools. As, in the majority of cases, the principles indicated, or similar ones, would probably be adopted, the Government might direct its inspectors to ascertain whether the principles are faithfully carried out; *and with what apparent effect.* But, in doing this, instances may occur where the managers of schools would object to any inquiry into the religious or moral education afforded in their schools. In such cases, the inspectors might be instructed to report on the state of the school as to general instruction, and to procure a certificate from the managers to the effect that the moral and religious culture of the pupils are duly cared for.

If it be objected that the adoption of such principles as are here laid down might lead to competition among the different religious bodies, I reply, that the Government would not, of course, in any case, grant aid till satisfied that the establishment or maintenance of a school in a given locality was really required. This being shown—by, perhaps, a memorial of parents or subscribers—I conceive the Government would have no right to inquire into the motives of those who endeavour to supply the deficiency, and ask aid in so doing. Whatever those motives may be, so long as the parents for whose children the school is designed are satisfied with the principles on which it is to be conducted, the Government should not refuse its aid.

As to the matter of competition in itself considered, I confess to the opinion that a little wholesome competition would be infinitely preferable to the general apathy and indifference so frequently lamented in the reports of the chief inspector as now prevailing.

I much fear, however, that when every available agency shall have been brought to bear, South Australia will not prove surcharged with schools. Usually, the difficulty is to prevail on parents, from any motive, to exert themselves in the matter. It would be interesting to see a few facts and figures adduced, whereby the probability of an opposite state of things arising could be fairly demonstrated.

If a government deem the promotion of morality and virtue, based upon religious principles, a necessary part of education, it should ascertain that—at least where its aid is claimed—provision is made for the inculcation thereof.

Principles or rules designed to further this end should be such as
the greatest possible number could assent to.

Provision should be made for promoting education among those
who may conscientiously object to the principles and rules framed
for and acceptable to the majority.

To promote education among all, the agency of all, so far as
possible, must be brought to bear.

Yours, &c.,

Woodforde, July 26th, 1856.   E. K. MILLER.

To the Editor of the Times.

Sir—Having watched with pleasure the increasing interest
attached to this question—all important to a young community—I
must trespass once more on your columns, with a view of suggesting
a few points for the consideration of those who seem disposed to
unchristianise our schools, so far as it is possible to do so ; and to
substitute for the divine teaching of the Gospel, and the pure
precepts it supplies, a heartless system of morality, such as might be
educed from the writings of Plato or other heathen authors.

All, seemingly, admit that "*moral culture*" is what the State
has specially to secure in connection with education ; and, yet,
because there are differences of opinion among adult Christians
on doctrinal matters, it is seriously proposed to banish from our
schools what a Christian government must ever regard as the basis
of its laws and the safeguard of its power—viz., the *Bible*. Those
who, calling themselves Christians, propound this unchristian, this
atheistic course, seek to justify it by saying that to the ministers of
religion alone pertains the duty of inculcating moral and religious
truths. But, if so, and if the inculcation of such truth be essential
to the well-being of the community, it is clearly incumbent on the
State to see that ministers are provided for the performance of
that duty: but this the government of South Australia is forbidden
to do. While, therefore, on the one hand, the government is made
to withhold all aid from ministers of religion as such, it is urged on
the other hand, to commit the whole care of the moral and religious
training of the rising generation to those ministers. The question
therefore naturally arises, "have ministers the power and opportunity (for I cannot doubt their will) to discharge satisfactorily the
additional duty thus sought to be imposed on them ?" I venture to

affirm, without fear of contradiction, *they have not*. An illustration will perhaps make this clear. In Gawler there are six ministers of various denominations ; five of these, as I am credibly informed, are obliged to engage in tuition, in order to eke out a living. Nor is Gawler an exceptional case ; for many ministers in and around Adelaide, and elsewhere, are constrained to engage in scholastic duty, or quit their stations. Yet, while these facts are patent to all, it is coolly proposed to throw upon ministers thus engaged the whole moral and religious training of the young in their several localities, including even that elementary portion of such training usually committed to the teachers of day-schools. I know not how other ministers may be disposed to regard this proposition ; but in my own case I feel it to be utterly impracticable. In event, therefore, of the Government excluding the Bible, and the moral and religious training based on it, from the day schools, the high probability is that in very many instances no such instruction will be otherwise supplied.

But what induces the desire for this unsatisfactory state of things? Simply the wish, on the part of some, to dictate to others how they should educate their children. In these days of liberality, a number of parents, who wish for a school in which their children may be educated, are told that they must not presume to decide for themselves on what principles that school shall be conducted ; and, strange to say, this tyrannical interference and dictation is seriously sought by those who professedly advocate liberal principles ; to my mind such interference savours of the grossest illiberality, however speciously disguised.

The principles of the British and Foreign School Society (commonly spoken of as the Lancasterian System of Education), will, I am satisfied, be found acceptable to nineteen-twentieths of the parents in this colony. Those principles require that no catechism be used in the schools, that the children be diligently instructed in the Scriptures, and that the religious, and all other instruction, be carefully superintended by the managing committee of every school. In schools established on such principles, children are to be found of every religious persuasion ; and, so far as my observation has extended, without any difficulty being experienced as to the religious teaching. If this be the case in England, why should it not be here ? Local self-government is advocated in many matters ; why should persons who voluntarily combine for educational purposes be

held incompetent to judge for themselves in this particular? If the
Government would merely confine itself to tendering aid, and seeing
that such aid is judiciously applied, it might confer much benefit. If
it prescribe such conditions as shall check local effort, and preclude
those deeply interested from exerting themselves in the matter, it
will inflict great injury, and retard, instead of promoting, real
education.

Yours truly,
E. K. MILLER.

Woodforde, January 29th, 1857.

To the Editor of the Times.

Sir— Since, with a view of eliciting others' opinions, I advanced
the proposition that " Religious principle being the foundation
of virtue and morality, its inculcation cannot safely be omitted in
any scheme of general education," about fifty letters have appeared
in the public journals, affirming often with much able and unanswer-
able argument, the general principle involved in that proposition.
On first stating it, I anticipated a decided opposition on some defined
principle from the advocates of what is termed secular education ;
but, instead of this, all who have written upon the subject express
the opinion that elementary religious teaching should be given in our
public schools. Even the Register, having commenced with secular
education only, now " doubts not that a very large proportion of the
people of this colony would be favourable to the impartation, at the
expense of the State, of so much religious instruction to youth as is
usually given in schools ;" and thinks "that, if religious training is
to be given in national schools, it ought to be of a perfectly
unsectarian character, and, if so, there could be no reason why the
inspectors should not report upon this as upon any other branch of
scholastic training."

This so closely accords with my original propositions that, save in
one point, it may be regarded as identical with them. They
suggested that the rule as to religious teaching should be such as
would accord with the " general principles of the greatest possible
number : power being reserved to treat exceptional cases on their
own merits ;" —that "such Scriptural knowledge and religious
principle should be imparted, without special doctrinal instruction,
as would serve for the foundation of that training which seeks to

produce a virtuous and moral life ; and that the Government might direct its inspectors to ascertain whether the rules are faithfully carried out in this respect.

The only material point of difference is, as to " exceptional cases." Where a considerable number of persons are united in desiring to establish a school on principles which they cannot conscientiously forego (as in the case of our German fellow-colonists, some of whom are precluded from aid by the present Act), they should, I submit, be eligible to receive aid from the general funds without being required to violate principles so highly valued. These exceptional cases could not be numerous, nor should they be regarded as invalidating the general principle of unsectarian Scriptural instruction. In the great majority of instances, the school committees would probably be composed of members of different religious bodies ; and this alone would secure the unsectarian character of the schools. If, in addition, the teachers were made aware that any attempt at proselytising instead of instructing their pupils, would be followed by suspension or withdrawal of salary from the Government, there would be little danger of what some so much affect to fear—the transfer of children from one religious body to another, through the influence of the schoolmaster.

The question of permitting or excluding religious teaching from our schools having been for the past twelve months almost constantly before the public, and nearly all persons engaged in its discussion being of opinion that such teaching is a matter of the first importance and necessity, such opinion may, I think, be fairly taken as a sufficient indication of the public wish in this matter. The chief objection mooted has been the supposition (and it is merely supposition, without one fact adduced to support it), that religious teaching must endgender sectarian strife. But unfortunately for the propounders of this notion, every teacher who has written upon the subject, not only declares that religious teaching *can be*, but *is*, in nearly all schools given without any approach to sectarianism. The very able letter of Mr. Martin in the *Register* of the 3rd instant well illustrates this, and proves the fallacy of the theory that religious instruction and sectarianism are inseparable. If necessary, I could adduce a hundred instances of English schools illustrating the fact that no *practical* difficulty is experienced in communicating elementary religious truth. Hence, the assertion that religious.

teaching *must* produce religious strife is contradictory to the facts of the case.

As to another objection, that because State aid to religion is refused, aid to schools in which religion is taught should not be granted, it will be time enough to insist thereon where the "separate machinery" which is suggested for the religious and moral training of youth shall have been established, and no one can assert that it at present exists.

They who would advocate secular education here should remember that they cannot take the same ground as the advocates of secular education in England. Those who suggest that the English Parliament should establish secular schools, are also for "taking care at the same time that the clergyman shall do what, in fact, he has sworn to do, and what he is paid and put there to do." But the Parliament of South Australia could not do this; it could not insist on aid from clergymen, even were the clergy able to render it efficiently, which I contend they are not.

The fact that after a year's discussion in the public journals, the conclusion has been almost unanimously arrived at that Scripture teaching must form a part of any scheme of national education, is well worthy the consideration of those who are to determine respecting this matter. Several candidates for Legislative honours have expressed themselves in favour of secular education, but 'as they do not define the term, and suggest no adequate provision for the religious and moral training of youth, it may be doubted whether they have duly considered the subject in all its bearings, and are quite clear and decided in their views.

In Stow's "Moral Training" there are some passages so exceedingly appropriate to our present position as to this subject that I cannot forbear quoting them. He says—

"The welfare and stability of a State depends, not on the amount of its wealth, but on the degree of the moral worth of its inhabitants. With all wise legislators, therefore, the most important consideration is, how can the greatest amount of moral worth be attained and maintained; for, in proportion as the mass of people are moral and virtuous, so, in exact proportion, will they prove themselves good subjects and sound patriots.

"On close inspection it will be found that religion alone introduces good morals among the working classes ; and that in proporportion as the religion of Christ is diffused, so, in exact proportion, will the people be virtuous and happy.

" The wealth of an empire may increase, political privileges may be bestowed, the means of intellectual knowledge may be afforded, and the understandings of the whole mass of the people, in consequence, may be cultivated and improved ; but unless the *heart* is impressed, so as to prove a regulator within, and to form the man into virtuous habits, such political privileges, and this mighty power of improved intellect, will fail in giving security or happiness to any country ; on the contrary, insubordination, insecurity, and national profligacy must inevitably follow.

" Moral training is, or ought to be, the *primary* aim of all national education. There must be called into exercise the intellectual and physical, above all, the religious and moral faculties of our nature. Moral ends must be brought about by moral means ; unless means are taken to affect the heart by virtue of a thorough Bible training, unless the varied announcements of God's love to mankind, contained in that book, be made to bear upon the children, we are assured that the mind exercised on human science alone must fail in producing a moral people.

" As religion affects, in the most powerful degree, our moral conduct here, and happiness hereafter, it ought, therefore, to hold, not simply a prominent, but a pre-eminent place in every national system of education.

" If morality is to be promoted and widely established in our land, it must be by training up the young to pure religion, in other words to the plain and simple truths of the Bible.

" A complete system of education will alone thoroughly elevate a people, and that system, we again repeat, must be an intellectual system, not merely upon secular knowledge, but an intellectual Scriptural knowledge, and a practical training to moral habits in real life."

These opinions, of one of the most eminent and successful educators of our day, deserve serious consideration from all who would advocate the exclusion of religious teaching from our schools. Whatever plan may be ultimately adopted, we should unquestionably endeavour that the young men should make Scripture the habitual rule of moral conduct.

In conclusion, to quote the words of the Hon. J. Baker, " I know that great and many difficulties will attend the working of any system that may be set in operation, but I think the Lancasterian system less open to objection, and more likely to be generally useful than any other."

Yours truly,
E. K. MILLER.

Woodforde, March 9th, 1857.

Though the *Register* in the first instance pleaded hard for a purely secular system, it was gratifying to find it so far convinced of the inexpediency of that system, and of the public feeling in regard thereto, as to write in its leader of April 8th, 1857, as follows:—

We do not, however, aim to confound a vote for school education in which religion is comprised with grants-in-aid of chapel building and ecclesiastical stipends. There may be a connection, but the divergence is more remarkable by far than the correspondence, and we really should not fear sectarian ascendency even though religion was taught in the schools supported by the State. And we doubt not that a very large proportion of the people of this colony would be favourable to the impartation at the expense of the State of such religious instruction to youth as is usually given in schools. But all that the State supports the State should recognise. Whatever is taught by the national school-master during those hours for which he receives Government remuneration is, of course, taught by the State, and it would be better that the Government should be on a right understanding. It will not be decorous to establish schools at the expense of the State, the State pretending ignorance of a very large and important part of the school curriculum. If, therefore, the decision of the people [as gathered in the new Parliament should be favourable to religious teaching in national schools, we hope that this portion of the school duties may not be ignored by the inspector. His questions on this point would indeed tend to obviate that danger of sectarianism which is with many the chief objection to the introduction of religion, for it would be easy for the Board of Education to instruct the inspector not to put questions on controverted points, and as the children would have to prepare for an unsectarian examination, the teacher certainly could not chiefly instruct them in sectarianism. But to pay national school-masters out of the public funds and then leave them at perfect liberty to inculcate, apart from the check of inspection, whatever ecclesiastical tenets they thought fit, would be in effect to hand over the rising generation of each district to the sect therein predominant. Consequently we think that if religious teaching is to be given in national schools, it ought to be of a perfectly unsectarian character, and if so, there could be no reason why the inspector should not report upon this as upon any other branch of scholastic training.

After this newspaper correspondence closed, I forwarded to the Governor (Sir Richard MacDonnell) a series of suggestions for improvements in educational matters. One of those suggestions was, that corresponding classes of conveniently adjacent schools should be occasionally examined together, in order to induce a healthy competition, and some system of rewards adopted. This idea was taken up by Sir R. MacDonnell, and amplified into a general system of competitive examinations. Very few schools, however, were at that time in a position to enter the lists on the lines laid down. My own pupils had been dismissed three months previously to the first examination, owing to my removal of residence. One who had gone to St. Peter's College, and one who had gone to Mr. Young's school, successfully passed, both having been boarders with me for about three years.

The suggestions I forwarded were, of course, based on the assumption that Government would *continue to assist* the efforts of those who interested themselves in educational matters. The idea that the Government would arrogate to itself the *sole* right to educate, that it would seek to abolish all voluntary effort, and close the various excellent private and other schools that had been for years established, certainly never occurred to me, and I feel confident was not contemplated by many of those who were induced to pass the present Education Act. All that was really needed was, to compel parents to send their children to some school, such as they might prefer, and provide for the education of the comparatively few whose parents might be unable to pay school fees. That parents should be practically told, as they now are, that they have no right to choose teachers for their children, or in any way direct the education of their children, and be compelled to send them—certainly in all country districts—to schools they may not approve, or are, perhaps, wholly adverse to, the entire educational arrangements being reduced to a thoroughly despotic *régime* alike as regards parents, teachers, and scholars, this idea and state of things, if clearly set forth when the Act was under discussion, would have been scouted.

I do not know that the advocates of the present system ever ventured to allege, or could produce facts to show, that the educational appliances of the colony precedent to the passing of the Act were so deplorably insufficient and inefficient that it was imperatively necessary for the State to borrow nearly half a million of money for the erection of school-rooms, and incur an annual outlay of one hundred and fifty thousand pounds per annum in order to, so far as possible, abolish those appliances and introduce the existing state of things. Neither do I know, and I think it would be impossible to prove, that the proportion of our population who were educated here prior to the passing of the Act—and from among whom have been mainly drawn our professional men and legislators—are likely to compare very unfavourably with those who have been educated in

the existing State schools, notwithstanding the enormous
expense incurred on the latters' behalf.

When the Act began to be administered, I pointed out
to Mr. Neville Blyth, the then Minister of Education, the
injustice of attempting to close schools that had in many
instances cost the proprietors much expense to establish,
and that a large and constantly increasing governmental
department would ensue that would prove enormously
expensive and unsatisfactory—which has resulted. The
annual cost is far greater than the revenue ought to be
called upon to bear; one-third the amount judiciously
applied might be made to produce quite as good results
intellectually, and far better morally. As for free education, it was neither asked for nor desired by the majority
of parents.

Notwithstanding that I had originally considered my
life's work to be aiding in the establishment of the Church
and Church schools in South Australia, I concluded, after
consultation with the Bishop, and with his consent, to
offer myself to the Government for the office of school
inspector; this I did twice. Feeling, however, that my
being a clergyman would militate against success, I obtained testimonials and recommendations from the parents
of my pupils, and other leading colonists of different
denominations, of which the subjoined are specimens :—

Morialta, June 6th, 1857.

My dear Sir—Understanding that you are about to apply to be
appointed an inspector of schools, I have very much pleasure in
expressing my belief that you are well fitted for that office. During
the several years that you have been my near neighbour, I have had
opportunity of watching the progress made by boys at your school,
and have no hesitation in saying that it has been satisfactory. I

can speak positively of my own. The position taken by Richard at Eton, and his gratifying advancement there, prove that he was well grounded by you both in mathematics and classics ; and although I shall much regret the loss of your future services, I trust you will be successful in your application.

I remain, my dear Sir,
Yours very truly,
JOHN BAKER.

Norwood, July 21st, 1860.

My dear Sir—I have much pleasure in giving my testimony, at your request, to the entire satisfaction with which you conducted the education of two of my sons during the time they attended the school lately kept by you at Magill. The progress made by them in general knowledge gave me the highest opinion of your qualifications as a teacher.

I remain, my dear Sir,
Yours very truly,
B. T. FINNISS.

Adelaide, July 23rd, 1860.

Dear Sir—Of your general eligibility for the office of inspector of schools I cannot doubt ; and on ecclesiastical grounds I can see no objection, for you have never committed yourself to exclusive views, nor presented yourself in an illiberal aspect.

I am, dear Sir,
Yours truly,
THOS. QUINTON STOW.

Similar testimonials were given by Messrs. E. W. Andrews, Wm. Bakewell, J. Howard Clark, Chas. Fenn, Wm. Giles, J. B. Neales, Patrick Auld, R. W. Newland, Robt. Hawkes, W. Scott, and others, besides the Bishop and Clergy. The prejudice, however, against a clergyman occupying such a position proved too strong, and I was unsuccessful. But this was only in keeping with that clause in our Constitution which declares that—besides the judges—lunatics, convicted felons, and clergymen shall not be eligible for election as Members of Parliament. Dissenting ministers, however, on resigning their chapels, and local preachers, are deemed eligible for, and have filled, the positions of school inspectors, legislators, and ministers of the Crown ; while those who have some regard for their ordination vows are deprived, in these respects, of their civil rights. This position of things seems scarcely equitable, but so it is ; and since payment of members of Parliament has been introduced, more dissenting ministers than before become candidates for parliamentary honours. In the near future such may have to contest their seats with lady candidates, perchance of their own congregations, or lady local preachers, and possibly sustain defeat ; this the Clergy are at least spared.

CHAPTER XV.

ENDOWMENT.

THE subject of Endowment was first mooted in the Report of the Church Society for 1850; it is there briefly mentioned as an object to be aimed at, especially in the shape of providing parsonages and glebes, which may be regarded as a kind of endowment.

In 1856, the Standing Committee of Synod reported that they had endeavoured to carry out a recommendation of their sub-committee on Church Funds by arranging to grant a pound for every pound subscribed by a congregation toward permanent endowment up to one hundred pounds, so making two hundred pounds for investment; and on that amount the Attorneys of the S.P.G. had agreed to allow a rent-charge of twenty per cent., but this rate did not long continue. Of this I availed myself for St. George's, Woodforde, obtaining a few subscriptions and borrowing the balance of the one hundred pounds required to secure forty pounds per annum, repaying the loan from the income resulting.

In 1859, another system for the endowment of churches was agreed upon by the Attorneys of the S.P.G. and the Standing Committee of Synod. By this system it was arranged that so soon as a sum of not less than seventy-five pounds and not exceeding one hundred and fifty pounds should be raised by a congregation for endowment, it should be met by a grant of a like sum from the

Attorneys of the S.P.G. and by a further grant of two-thirds of such sum from the funds at the disposal of Synod ; also that on the total amount so obtained the said Attorneys would guarantee an annual interest of ten per cent. for ten years, and afterwards the current rate of interest. This system, however, not being availed of to the extent expected, in 1873 the Attorneys and Synod decided to make a grant of seventy pounds for every thirty raised by a congregation for endowment, and on each one hundred pounds so made up, to guarantee interest at ten per cent. for ten years. As the Willunga church needed three hundred pounds to complete its endowment up to the five hundred pounds limit, this offer was availed of for that church, and ninety pounds being paid in (borrowed as before) secured thirty pounds per annum additional for ten years.

In 1858, I believe it was, Dr. Wm. Brown, then one of my parishioners, was conversing with me respecting the Church's future, and the difficulty of maintaining services in sparsely peopled districts. Suddenly he said—" Why not do as private people do—purchase land at one pound per acre, upset price, let it at ten per cent. on cost, with right of purchase at an advance, and so gradually accumulate a fund from the interest of which provision for endowments might be made ?" I replied—" That might be easily done if capital to purchase could be found." The doctor thought subscriptions for such a purpose could be obtained, offering a handsome amount to start with. On this, we went into calculations, on the basis of leasing lands purchased for seven years, with right of purchase at from thirty to forty shillings per acre. From these it appeared tolerably clear that were it possible to raise, say, five thousand pounds as purchase money, at the expiration of seven years there would be a capital approximating to ten thousand pounds, the interest on which would be probably one thousand pounds per annum.

In subsequent conversations, it was suggested that nothing should be granted from the funds towards endowments for seven years, but all receipts added to capital. Also, to ensure this, it was further thought it would be advisable to constitute a society altogether apart from Synod. This was the original idea as sketched out between Dr. Brown and myself.

The doctor then proposed that I should submit the matter to the Bishop, with a view to some action being taken in regard thereto. I, however, preferred that he, as originating the idea, should lay it before his Lordship. Before this could be done, Dr. Brown had occasion to visit Port Lincoln. On board the steamer, he fell in with the late Mr. Nathaniel Oldham; knowing him to be much interested in Church matters, Dr. Brown mentioned the plan we had been discussing. Mr. Oldham thought it an admirable idea, but suggested that instead of waiting to obtain purchase money by subscriptions, the entire sum of five thousand pounds, or sufficient to make up five thousand pounds, should be obtained as a loan from London, which he, being a bank manager, thought might be done if interest thereon at five per cent. could be guaranteed, in addition to deposit of the deeds as land became purchased. In due course the matter was brought under the Bishop's notice by Mr. Oldham; his Lordship highly approved of the scheme, and a provisional committee was constituted to work it into shape, meeting with much encouragement in the way of obtaining subscriptions.

The first official notice of the projected Society was by the Bishop at the meeting of Synod on May 8th, 1860, when in his report on the state of the Diocese his Lordship said—

There is another source of expected revenue to be placed at the disposal of Synod, to which I cannot but look with pride and hope ; I mean the proceeds of the Church Endowment Society. Originating with some of the wealthier lay members of our Church, and sustained principally by their contributions, judgment, and credit, there is, I think, no reason to distrust the ultimate success of the scheme. I know not why it should interfere with local parochial endowment as inaugurated by Synod. It has only opened *new*, so to speak, auriferous ground ; and certainly does credit to the wise and generous impulses of its founders.

On June 11th, 1860, at a public meeting in White's Rooms the Church of England Endowment Society became formally inaugurated. Nothwithstanding very inclement weather, toward one thousand persons attended. The Governor, Sir Richard MacDonnell, presided, and on the platform were the Bishops of Sydney, Melbourne, and Adelaide, with his Honor Judge Cooper, Sir J. H. Fisher (President of the Legislative Council), G. C. Hawker, Esq. (Speaker of the House of Assembly), Major Warburton, Dr. Mayo, Dr. Wyatt, and a number of other leading members of the Church. The first resolution was moved by Judge Cooper, as follows :—

That the spiritual wants in various parts of this diocese of the members of the United Church of England and Ireland call loudly for a combined effort on the part of all to ameliorate the condition so much to be deplored.

This was seconded by Sir James Hurtle Fisher, who also submitted a statement of funds—being donations, subscriptions, and amounts guaranteed toward interest on loan, if obtained, for seven years. It appeared there were then one hundred and forty-one subscribers, ninety-four being members of the Society, whose annual subscriptions amounted to eight hundred and forty-five pounds, which for seven years would, with the donations, total six thousand two hundred and fifty-six pounds. The Bishop of Adelaide having spoken in support, the resolution was carried.

Sir R. R. Torrens then moved—

That the cause of religion, so far as the instrumentality of the Church of England is concerned, and the blessing which attends her ordinances when properly administered, demands that a due supply of able, devoted, and highly educated clergymen should, as far as possible, be secured.

This was seconded by Arthur Blyth, Esq., M.P., supported by the Bishop of Sydney, and carried.

F. S. Dutton, Esq., moved—

That the means hitherto applicable for the competent sustentation of clergy so qualified have been confessedly insufficient.

This Mr. Oldham having seconded, and the Bishop of Melbourne supported, was carried.

G. C. Hawker, Esq., moved—

That to facilitate the introduction as required of clergymen of high education and attainments, immediate steps be taken to place the stipends of the clergy on a scale suitable to their sacred calling, the greatness of their responsibilities, and the social position which they ought to occupy.

This was seconded by Chas. Fenn, Esq., supported by the Dean (the Rev. J. Farrell), and carried.

E. W. Andrews, Esq., moved—

That, having regard to the practicability which is imparted to such a design by the formation of the Church of England Endowment Society in this colony, that association is entitled to the cordial co-operation of the Church at large in this diocese, and has the hearty wishes of this meeting for its rapid progress and permanent establishment.

Seconded by Major Warburton, supported by Archdeacon Woodcock, and carried.

The Society having been thus publicly inaugurated, Rules and Regulations were in due course framed for carrying out its objects. As it was intended to be an entirely *lay* Society, twelve lay gentlemen were appointed as Directors, having, however, the Bishop for their president — the secretary being Mr. N. Oldham. The first set of Rules I have not been able to obtain a copy of. For about three years the Society continued to flourish, and in 1863 became incorporated. By then, however, some very material alterations had been introduced into its constitution ; and the Rules under which it was incorporated differed materially from those originally adopted.

In 1878, Dean Russell, as Administrator of the Diocese, in his Address to Synod drew attention to this fact, and among other things said—

According to the constitution then proposed (*i.e.*, at the public meeting), it was announced that the management of the Society was to be in a board of directors. . . . . That the appropriation of the income was to be under the control of Synod. . . . . The objects were to be the "placing of the stipends of the clergy on a footing which should be at once permanent, becoming, and liberal" . . . . and the "adding to the number of that body." It was provided that a general public meeting should be held each year on a given day in January, and that this meeting "the clergy should be invited to attend." The Society was not incorporated till 1863, but by that time the constitution of the Society had been materially altered, though it does not appear that either the Synod or the public had received any intimation that the original plan had been so greatly modified. In the altered constitution the control of the Synod over the appropriation of income was practically withdrawn. For though the distribution and application were still to be "in the discretion of the Diocesan Synod," that discretion was distrusted and disallowed by subsequent clauses. The Synod was to be "guided" in such distribution by "the recommendation of the president and board of directors." . . . . . The "recommendation" of the latter, when funds were paid over, was further to "govern the Synod in the application of the funds so paid over." I know nothing of the history of the private deliberations which led to these certainly not unimportant changes. The standing committee until recently were not aware that such changes had been made, for though the new rules and regulations of the Incorporated Society were printed in 1864 in an outward form closely resembling that of 1860, the one publication was naturally supposed to be a mere reproduction of the other. Even in this second document, however, it appears that the directors are still bound "to pay over" to the Synod the whole of each year's income which is applicable for distribution, to inform the Synod by way of "recommendation" of the intended mode of application; and to afford the clergy and lay representatives of the Church an opportunity of making known any objection that may occur to them, the provision for holding annual meetings having disappeared. In point of fact, the income though no doubt well administered, has never, as a whole, been paid over. . . . . . I am given to understand the capital is not less than twenty thousand pounds.

The clause "adding to the number of the clergy" was introduced, I well remember, at the instance of Bishop Short. He entertained very sanguine ideas as to the increase of land values; and, as he expressed it, thought the time *might* come when the Society would be "too rich," *i.e.,* have more funds than would be required for endowments, therefore urged the inclusion of a secondary object as a sort of safety valve ; this certainly was not contemplated by Dr. Brown or myself in the first instance, nor was it spoken of at the public meeting, as may be seen in the *Register's* report thereof.

The Society having been established independently of Synod, the Directors for some time rendered no information as to their doings to Synod. That it was deemed incongruous for a body having control of large Church funds not to in some way make public the state and application of those funds was evidenced by the Synod on May 7th, 1872, passing the following resolution :—

That in the opinion of this Synod an account should be annually laid before Synod by the Incorporated Church of England Endowment Society, and that this resolution be communicated to the Society.

In 1887, my attention was drawn to the small proportion of the Society's income that was being devoted to endowments. Two-thirds or three-fourths thereof was usually handed over to the Bishop for missionary purposes. Thus in 1885, out of eight hundred pounds income, six hundred pounds were paid to the Bishop, and but two hundred pounds towards endowment, so that practically the Society had become more a missionary than an endowment Society. To some extent this was brought about by a congregation being required to raise forty pounds towards an endowment of one hundred pounds, the Society making a grant of sixty pounds. But poor congregations, for whose benefit endowments were specially needed, could rarely raise two hundred pounds to secure an endowment of fifty pounds per annum for their minister, as was intended. On looking into the matter, I found that about six thousand pounds had been paid for the importation, instead of to securing the sustentation, of clergy. Hence I brought the matter before Synod, and moved for a select committee to confer with the directors. Opposition to this was at once raised, the directors strenuously opposing any inquiry as to their administration of the Society's funds. After considerable discussion, however, the Synod resolved—

That a committee be appointed to inquire into and report on the administration of the Church of England Endowment Society, and to consider what amendments, if any, are necessary to carry into effect the original principles on which such Society was founded, and whether any amendments in such principles are necessary and advisable; such committee to confer with the directors of the Society, and to report to the standing committee, who may request the Bishop to call a special meeting of Synod to consider such report.

The committee consisted of the Rev. Canon Green, Messrs. J. H. Cunningham, H. E. Downer, J. W. Castine, W. B. Webb, and myself, with Mr. A. Sturcke as secretary.

Very little inquiry sufficed to show that the Society had become "moribund"; there being no subscribers, and but few directors, who seldom met, the transaction of business apparently being left very much to the president and secretary. On the secretary being written to on behalf of the Synodal committee, the directors managed to meet, and seem to have been very much horrified, or terrified, at the idea of any investigation being made into their method of management; at all events they came to the conclusion that it would be injudicious on their part to meet, or afford any information to, the committee appointed by Synod. On this determination being communicated, the committee decided to fall back on the printed Rules and Regulations of the Society, which required that the directors should call a general meeting of subscribers on receiving a request to do so signed by a certain number of subscribers. As there were no subscribers, twenty-six gentlemen agreed to become such, paying a guinea each, and signing a request to the directors to call a general meeting. This, however, was also refused, a most improper and unconstitutional course; it only remained, therefore, for the committee to forward a report of the circumstances to Synod, and leave that body to deal with the matter. That report, as submitted to Synod in 1888, I append.

REPORT OF SPECIAL COMMITTEE ON THE INCORPORATED CHURCH OF ENGLAND ENDOWMENT SOCIETY.

The Committee beg respectfully to report that they have held several meetings, and had correspondence with the Directors of the Church of England Endowment Society, but with very unsatisfactory results.

In the first instance a letter was addressed to the Directors inviting them to meet the committee in order to confer as to the best means for securing the more effectual carrying out of the objects for which the Society was founded. In reply a letter was received conveying the following resolution :—

" The Board do not believe it would conduce towards the welfare of this Society to meet the gentlemen named by Synod, and therefore must most respectfully decline to do so. But will be happy to give the fullest consideration to any suggestion which the Lord Bishop, as President of Synod, may think desirable in the rules and operations of the Society."

Finding the Directors declined to meet them, the Committee decided, as it was understood there were few, if any, subscribers, to endeavour to procure some additional subscribers in order to resuscitate the Society, as was suggested in Synod and recommended by the Bishop. The names of twenty-six gentlemen having been obtained as new subscribers, they were forwarded, with their subscriptions, to the Directors.

To the very great surprise of the Committee, on February 15th, the subscriptions were returned, with a letter, from which the following is an extract :—

"We have received an opinion to the effect that the constitution of the Society is irregular, and that we are not in a position at present, to receive any further subscriptions ; consequently, we respectfully beg to return the amount forwarded, in all twenty-seven pounds six shillings."

The Committee feel it their duty to point out that the course pursued by the Directors in returning these subscriptions is in direct contravention of the printed Rules and Regulations of the Society. Rule 2 on page four states—"The object of the Society shall be " —"to raise money"—"By means of contributions of any amount." —"By means of annual subscriptions of any amount "—and "by means of annual subscriptions of one pound one shilling,"—" to be devoted to the general objects of the Society."

The Committee would also call attention to the fact that since the year 1872, the balance-sheets of this Society, as published in the Synodal Reports, do not show any subscriptions whatever as having been received ; while Rule No. 3 on page six of the printed Rules and Regulations, after specifying the various officers of the Society, expressly says that " every Director shall be a professing member of the United Church of England and Ireland and a subscriber of the annual sum of five pounds at least to the Interest Fund." Hence, as no such subscriptions appear to have been paid, it is doubtful if the gentlemen at present called Directors have any title to be so called, or to exercise the functions of Directors.

The attention of Standing Committee is called to the extraordinary circumstance of a body of gentlemen having control of large Church funds declining to meet, or afford any information to, a Committee appointed by Synod to confer with them, and refusing to receive subscriptions in aid of the Society for the promotion of the objects of which they have been appointed.

The unpleasant duty, therefore, devolves upon the Committee to report, that they have made every effort short of litigation to carry out the object for which they were appointed, but have been through-

out thwarted in their endeavours, and can now only leave the
matter in the hands of Synod to decide upon any further action,
coercive or otherwise.

(Signed)

E. K. Miller, Chairman.

Of course this report created no little surprise, and a
motion was promptly tabled to the effect that Synod
should direct the directors to receive the subscriptions
they had returned, and which were then in the hands of
the secretary of Synod. It being understood that the
directors had refused to meet the Synodal committee, or
call a meeting of subscribers, from fear of legal proceedings
resulting from irregularities in the management of the
Society's affairs; also, that they were anxious that the
Society should be reconstructed under a private Act of
Parliament, chiefly in order to secure their personal in-
demnity from the possible consequences of such irregularities, the Rev. Canon Green moved as an amendment that
the Synod agree to such Act of Parliament being obtained.
A long discussion resulted. As the rules and regulations
of the Society gave ample power for all such alterations
as were necessary being made at a general meeting of
subscribers, it was contended that the expense of obtaining an Act of Parliament ought not to be incurred. In
the issue, it was decided by a small majority that an Act
should be obtained, and the standing committee of Synod
was requested to confer with the directors of the Society
respecting it.

At the same time the Synod appointed another special
committee "to inquire into and report upon the dealings
and transactions of the Society." This committee consisted of Messrs. E. G. Blackmore, J. H. Thornley, G.
A. Connor, F. Halcomb, and J. C. B. Moncrieff. The

directors finding Synod determined to have an investigation of the Society's affairs, at last submitted their books and records for inspection by this committee, who devoted much time and attention thereto.

At the Synod of 1889, this second committee submitted their report, which showed that the capital of the Society by subscriptions and donations " up to 1867 amounted to eight thousand nine hundred and fifty-eight pounds eighteen shillings and six pence, *when all subscriptions ceased.*" This pretty nearly corresponded with the original estimate, though it was never intended that when the seven years on which the calculation was based expired, all subscriptions should cease. Out of the income resulting, it appeared that eight thousand two hundred and eighty-four pounds twelve shillings had been devoted to endowments and the building of parsonages ; four hundred and twenty-five pounds to the Theological Tutorship Fund ; and to "chaplains' stipends and passage-money for new clergymen, &c., six thousand three hundred and seven pounds two shillings." The average income from 1882 to 1887 was stated to have been five hundred and seventy-nine pounds nine shillings and eight pence, out of which one hundred pounds per annum (which had been the rate all along) was paid as secretary's salary—nearly twenty per cent. on the receipts—a very unwarrantable expenditure. The committee conclude their report by saying that " To place the Society on a sound financial footing, having regard to the present values of the several properties, we think it would be necessary to write down the capital as represented by mortgages and freeholds to eleven thousand pounds." Precisely how the twenty thousand pounds, reported to Dean Russell as the capital, diminished to eleven thousand pounds is not explained ; the shrinkage in value of land or securities one would think could hardly have amounted to so much as nine thousand pounds.

In the issue, after much discussion in Synod, and some important alterations in its passage through Parliament, an Act was obtained for re-establishing the Society, and absolving the directors from the consequences of their mismanagement. The principal defect of the Act, as I regard it, is in not giving subscribers an adequate share in the management by allowing them to elect directors. If there be less than thirty subscribers, they would not be allowed to choose a director at all ; while should there be five hundred subscribers they would only be allowed to elect one director out of the six who now constitute the board. My view was, that three directors should be elected by the Synod, and three by the subscribers ; but this was overruled.

In 1889, I succeeded further in getting the following resolution passed by Synod :—

That in the opinion of this Synod it is advisable to encourage the more general endowment of churches in poor districts by reducing the amount to be required from a congregation in order to obtain an endowment of one hundred pounds from forty pounds to twenty pounds.

The rule requiring forty pounds to be raised to secure an endowment of one hundred pounds, or two hundred pounds to secure the limit of five hundred pounds, had caused most of the poorer congregations not to attempt endowment; on the reduction, however, being made to twenty pounds, applications for endowments came in far in excess of the means for meeting them, precisely the position the founders of the Society had in view, viz., to get all, especially the poorer, churches endowed; the requirement of forty pounds toward each one hundred pounds had proved an effectual bar to this in many cases. The general issue is, that by means of the Synodal Endowment Fund, and grants from the Endowment Society, there is now a fair prospect of all churches becoming to some extent endowed—a most important matter in country districts.

Besides the endowments effected through the means of Synod and the Endowment Society, a few churches have been endowed by private individuals, as St. Saviour's, Glen Osmond, by the late Mr. Osmond Gilles, and St. John's, Morialta, by the late Hon. J. Baker, with, I believe, one or two others.

Bishop Kennion's attitude toward the Endowment Society was expressed in his Pastoral Address in 1889 thus :—

If I do not refer to the Church of England Endowment Society in more than a few words, it is not that my interest in re-invigorating the Society is less than your own, but it is because the report of standing committee will sufficiently bring it before your notice. I think all churchmen owe a debt of gratitude to the Rev. E. K. Miller for the vigour and persistency with which he has called the attention of Synod to the capabilities which this Society has, if popularised, for meeting some of our present wants. It is lamentable to hear it stated that our older cures are in greater need of support than our newer ones. I am told that in many cases effort would be made to increase the endowment of these if the regulations admitted of it. We may, therefore, look forward to new hopefulness being imparted by the new departure which we trust the Society will be shortly enabled to make.

I cannot conclude this subject without expressing my sincere thankfulness to Mr. H. E. Downer, M.P., for the able assistance he rendered in urging upon Synod the importance of reconstructing the Church of England Endowment Society. His legal acumen and eloquence contributed very largely to the success of the efforts made on that behalf by myself and others, conferring thereby an obligation on the Church at large.

CHAPTER XVI.

DISSENT.

ON arriving in Adelaide, I found dissent very decidedly in the ascendant. The colony had been founded on what were considered distinctly dissenting principles; that is to say, all bodies of religionists were to be regarded as on one level, there was to be no preference shown by the Government to one body more than another, nothing approaching to a State Church, or interference with religious teaching by the Government. A certain concession, however, to the National Church had been made by the Rev. C. B. Howard being brought out as Colonial Chaplain, who received a stipend from the Government, and which was continued to his successor. By the aid of the Society for the Propagation of the Gospel and sundry friends, Mr. Howard had been enabled to import a weather-board church, and managed, I believe with much of his own labour, to get it erected on the site of the present Trinity church. Afterwards a weather-board parsonage was erected beside it, which was subsequently used as a chapter-house for the first meetings of Synod, &c.

The dissenting ministers in Adelaide when I arrived were, the Rev. T. Q. Stow, the Rev. R. Haining, the Rev. J. Draper, and the Rev. G. Drummond. Between these and the few clergy very friendly intercourse obtained. As ministers were few and services many, owing to the people being scattered, it was often difficult to find time for sermon preparation, especially by those teaching. Conversing one day with the Revs. J. Draper and W. J. Woodcock on this topic, the former remarked—" Many people regard the parson pretty much as they do a bottle of porter; you only need to draw the cork, and out pops the porter ; so they think you have only to get the parson into the pulpit, and out pops the sermon."

The arrival of ministers belonging to other dissenting bodies, more clergy, and increasing population, caused the former friendly intercourse to become somewhat restricted. In fact the spirit of competition arose with the multiplication of agencies, sometimes degenerating into opposition, under the guise of zeal for winning souls to Christ. When debate arose as to the continuance of grants from the public revenue to religious bodies, Mr. Stow and his adherents took an active part in opposition, as also afterwards in excluding religious teaching from schools aided by public funds, and this increased the estrangement. Mr. Stow declared that he would rather the Bible were excluded from the schools than that any part of the public funds should be applied to sustain teaching he deemed erroneous, specially referring to Roman Catholic schools. By this extraordinary conjunction of an important religious body with the secularists, it was afterwards brought about that Scripture teaching became entirely banished from our public schools, the teachers of which are now not even required to be Christians. Practically, some are Romanists, others avowed freethinkers, whatever that may mean—a sorry result of the differences among Protestants ; because, whatever may be said to the contrary, a teacher's religious or non-religious predilections—it may be quite unconsciously to himself—will certainly have a measure of influence on those he teaches.

In a new country, where there is no State Church, nor governmental interference with religious matters, maintenance of the numerous sects that now exist is utterly unjustifiable, and inconsistent with the teachings of Scripture. Then, too, it engenders social as well as religious estrangements. Persons naturally feel a difficulty in entering into and maintaining a thoroughly cordial intercourse with others who differ so widely from them that they cannot bring themselves to unite in the worship of the Highest. The idea is very apt to exist in the mind, though perhaps almost unsuspected, that those who separate themselves from us in religious matters, entertain a sort of feeling that in some respect or other they are superior to us, more correct in doctrine it may be, or more pure in life. Or, perhaps we on our part conceive ourselves on some ground or another superior to those who separate themselves from us. Now, when such ideas are merely latent, to say nothing of their developing into active opposition, they must manifestly be preventive of a sincere social or religious cordiality; the idea of being in some way or other looked down upon by others, is naturally repugnant to us, and apt to beget feelings of a more or less resentful character. That this is the actual practical result is evidenced by the avoidance of each other on the part of the different religious teachers, and the respectful distance observed by the members of each body towards the members of other bodies; that the diversity of religious views and feelings is destructive of social intercourse, or greatly impedes it, is in fact too palpable to be denied. As for the professions of fraternal regard for each other customarily tendered by different religious conferences, they must be regarded as so much unmeaning formality where no attempt is made to really approximate or amalgamate. The Saviour said—"If any man will come after me let him deny himself and take up his cross and follow me." Few actively contentious ones are disposed to deny themselves the pleasure of contending, or to subordinate their own peculiar notions or proclivities to the promotion of the general interests of Christ's Church; yet self-denial is as important in such matters as in respect to undue indulgence in any other matters. Sometimes persons set themselves up as religious teachers without any authorisation, or special fitness, merely with a view to carry out some ideas or object of their own, leading their followers into a false position — often involving waste of means and injury to Christ's Church.

No doubt there are numbers who seek to become religious leaders simply from an earnest desire to do good, but many of whom have very little fitness for or power of effecting good from lack of education or other circumstances. Thus, the Cornish miner, when his mind is directed to religious matters, very often deems it his duty, or makes it a chief object of ambition, to become a local preacher. Remarking to a dissenter upon such a one, who could neither read nor write, but who was deemed a "powerful preacher"—he was a very noisy one—I was reminded that Christ told His disciples not to take thought as to what they should speak, for it should be given them by the Holy Ghost what they should speak. So preachers, said my friend, of the present day speak by the same divine influence—and he thought that human learning, though doubtless useful, was by no means essential to proclaiming the Gospel of Christ. I chanced to be one day travelling on a coach, the driver of which was an exceedingly zealous methodist, class-leader, &c. It beginning to rain, I took advantage of a stoppage to put on my

over-coat. The driver said—" I hope you'll 'scuse me, Sir,
but I never likes to see a minister with a great-coat on."
" Indeed ; why ? Are ministers less liable to take cold
than other people ?" " I don't know about that, Sir ; but
I know it ain't Scriptural; 'cause the Master said to them
as he was going to send to preach that they wasn't to take
two coats." Being called on to visit through his last
illness a school-master who had been an exceedingly zealous
local preacher, the conversation on one occasion turned on
lay readers, whom I then had difficulty in obtaining, and
local preachers, who were so readily obtainable. I happened
to remark that, from what I heard, I thought it would be
more advantageous to the congregations if some local
preachers were to read sermons occasionally, instead
of giving the people the benefit of their own extemporaneous effusions. " Lord bless you, Sir," said the old
gentleman, " they couldn't do it. They can get up and
spout away at something or other, but if you put 'em to
reading, they're beat ; some of them give me the belly-ache
when they try to read a chapter." The spread of education,
however, is fast doing away with this class of local
preachers, the noisy ranting of a few years ago being rarely
heard ; there is an undoubted levelling up of both hearers
and preachers.

On the occasion of a Sunday-school festival at one of my
churches, I thought well to invite the teachers and Sunday-
school children of two adjacent chapels. The invitation
was accepted, and the utmost harmony prevailed. Nearly
three hundred in all gathered ; the affair was held on
grounds I then occupied, and wholly provided for
by my people. Shortly after, however, at a chapel
anniversary in an adjacent district, I was attacked
by one of the reverend speakers as having sought to

allure the children of other denominations to the Church Sunday-school, an idea that never entered my head. I believe the gentleman had few co-thinkers, but the fact of such an attack being made effectually prevented a repetition of the offence. Too often, I fear, do the vituperative utterances of such as he contribute to the maintenance of the estrangements that exist between religious bodies, and that bitterness toward each other which so ill becomes the disciples of the Saviour to display.

Dissenting bodies, too, are often found as antagonistic to each other as to the Church—some affecting not a little superiority in regard to others. Thus, I have known Wesleyans look down disparagingly on Bible Christians, these again on the Primitive Methodists, while these last deem the Salvation Army people as by no means eligible for acting in their chapels. One of the ablest dissenting ministers I have known told me, that where several religious bodies existed in a small township, if contention arose in one of them, members of other bodies would sometimes watch it narrowly, or even foment it, in hope that a malcontent or two might break away and join their party.

The course most advisable to be adopted by the Church of England toward those unfortunately estranged from her, and from each other, many feel difficulty in determining, in fact it is one of those questions on which widely different opinions exist among the clergy and laity of the Church. Some deem it the Church's duty to stand wholly aloof from all not of her communion, to act as if they existed not. Others think they should be regarded as enemies of the Church, and denounced accordingly. Of late years, however, there has been a growing desire for some basis of union to be laid down which would admit of their becoming either united to the Church, or brought to co-operate with it. That *all* will be brought to accept precisely the same form of Church government and manner of worship is hardly to be looked for. Many devout believers have been brought up to, and prefer, modes of worship untrammelled, as they deem it, by forms; but there is no valid reason why such should continue divided into a host of sects instead of uniting in some way for non-formal public worship, and so diminishing the estrangements that exist, with the sinful waste of means resulting. There has been something like an acknowledgment of this being desirable by the formation some years back of the Evangelical Alliance, and latterly of the Ministerial Association. I do not know on what, if any, definite principle these bodies were established, but fear their cohesion and power for good will prove to be but as a rope of sand. Meanwhile, the attitude of the Church toward such bodies I think should be that of kindly regard, certainly not of asperity. I remember the first Roman Catholic Bishop of Adelaide, Dr. Murphy, remarking on this point—"I have known many flies attracted by sugar, but never saw one caught by vinegar."

I conceive that, without anything like forfeiture of principle, a Bishop and his coadjutors might *open communication* with the representatives of at least some of the leading dissenting bodies, expressing regret at the differences existing, and intimating their perfect willingness, or even wishfulness, to enter into such conference as might be calculated to diminish these differences, and induce greater concord. This idea I embodied in resolutions submitted to Synod on two or three occasions, but could not succeed in carrying them—though I quite fail to see that such course would be in any way derogatory to the Church or inconsistent with her imperative duty, viz., to *cultivate* as well as *follow* " peace with all men."

In order to test the sincerity of the desire for greater unity frequently expressed by dissenters, and if possible promote such unity, I addressed a letter to the representatives of certain bodies, which, with the replies as published in the *Register* of December 29th, 1890, and subsequent dates, I append.

RELIGIOUS UNITY.

To the Editor of the *Register*.

Sir—I should be glad if you could grant space for the accompanying correspondence on a matter of some importance to our community. Copies of the letter bearing my signature were sent to the Rev. H. T. Burgess, as President of the Wesleyan Conference, on August 19th ; to the Rev. T. Piper, as President of the Bible Christian Conference, on September 13th ; to the Rev. J. Lyall, for the Moderator of Presbytery, on September 13th ; to the Rev. Walter Jones, as Chairman of the Congregational Union, on September 14th ; to the Rev. Silas Mead, for the Chairman of the Baptist Union, on September 14th ; and to the Rev. Hugh Gilmore, for the President of the Primitive Methodist Conference, on September 19th. Copies were sent to the Revs. Lyall, Mead, and Gilmore for transmission, as I did not know the names of the gentlemen presiding over the bodies to which they belong. Three months having elapsed, and no copy being returned, I presume each reached its destination. I append the only replies received, and sincerely thank the Rev. H. T. Burgess for his kindly expressed sympathy with the object in view. I certainly had thought from the professions of a desire for unity frequently expressed by the different religious bodies, and their habit of sending fraternal greetings to each other, that anything like a definite proposal in regard to unity would have elicited at least an acknowledgment from all ; but I am mistaken ; Christianity and courtesy are not everywhere synonymous. I was glad, however, to observe from the report in the *Register* of the meeting of the Congregational Union on October

16th, that the Rev. F. Hastings read a paper on the " Union of the Evangelical Churches," and that the views he submitted met the approval of that body, a resolution being passed in accordance therewith. Also, on December 1st, he is reported to have read the same paper before the Ministerial Association with much acceptance. Whether, prior to writing his paper, Mr. Hastings had seen my letter forwarded to the Chairman of the Congregational Union a month previously I do not know, but as his paper, so far as reported, would seem to have been nearly identical with my letter, certainly advocating the same object, I think he must have done. In any case I congratulate him in having been more successful in inducing action by the Congregational Union than I was in inducing action by the Synod. It would doubtless further the object in view were he to publish his paper, that the general public might have the benefit of his views on points probably not referred to in my letter. It is quite time our community recognised the fact that, as Mr. West wrote in your journal some time back, " the pulpit costs more than it is worth." Also, that our senseless divisions are mainly responsible for its excessive cost, to say nothing of other evils. Thus, in Willunga, the Roman and English Churches have expended on buildings four thousand three hundred pounds, and the various chapels seven thousand and fifty pounds, contemplating further outlay ; while in the adjacent district thirteen chapels as against two churches is in greater disproportion. These facts speak for themselves, and would suggest that the local option principle might with advantage be brought to bear on this as well as on excess in other matters. Trusting the action of the Congregational Union, or the Ministerial Association, may result in diminishing what has become a crying evil, and brings no small discredit on the Christian profession,

I am, Sir, &c.,

Willunga, December 23rd.   E. K. MILLER.

Sir—At the last session of the Synod of the Church of England, held in Adelaide, I submitted the following resolution, which having been seconded by Mr. C. T. Hargrave, was withdrawn after a brief discussion :—" That in order to assist in diminishing the evils resulting from divisions among those religious bodies in this colony who professedly hold the same articles of the Christian faith, a select committee be appointed to communicate with the authorities or ministers of such bodies with the view of ascertaining whether the union of such bodies, or any of them, with each other might not be possible, and in cases where it may seem possible to endeavour to bring about such union." Some members of Synod thought the matter outside the province of Synod, it having been constitute l for managing the affairs of the Church of England only, without reference to other religious bodies. Others deemed the object contemplated by the resolution quite Utopian, considering the antagonism between the different religious bodies such as to render any attempt to induce them to unite in the worship of God utterly useless. In neither of those views do I concur. The Church of England in this province, as a branch of the National Church is, I conceive, fully warranted in endeavouring to grapple with, and in attempting to remedy, whatever has become a national evil in connection with religious matters, and I imagine few can regard the present multiplication of religious agencies and their excessive costliness otherwise than as a national evil, especially since it has resulted in the exclusion of Scriptural teaching from our public schools. Many who admit the desirability of Christian union advocate deferring any definite attempt to attain it to a "more convenient season." My own feeling is that the longer such effort is delayed, the more confirmed divisions will become, and proportionately more difficult to deal with. Before any further action so far as Synod is concerned, I wish, if possible, to ascertain whether any of the religious bodies referred to in the resolution would be willing to accept the mediation suggested, and co-operate in giving it effect. As presiding over one of the most important of those bodies, I therefore respectfully solicit the favour of your opinion as to whether any such action as the foregoing resolution contemplates would be likely to be useful in bringing into closer relationship bodies of believers now worshipping apart, though holding the same essential truths. In asking this, I wish it to be clearly understood that I in no way suggest, or aim at, their becoming, any of them, united to the Church of England, however desirable I may think such union to be. Simply on public, economic, and Christian grounds, I desire to see some line of action initiated whereby those now alienated from the Church of England and each other may become more united, and the manifold evils of existing divisions diminished. Admitting

Nonconformist bodies, by which I mean all not conforming to the principles of the Church of England, admitting these to be important factors in carrying out the work of Christ, it must be patent to all that a united nonconformity would be infinitely more potent for good than the disunion now existing. Of course action in the direction indicated might be taken by those bodies themselves, but I am not aware of its having been taken to any appreciable extent in this colony. I think it may be fairly assumed that mediation by an impartial body in no way connected with, or predisposed toward, any of those it is desired to amalgamate, would be the best calculated, under God's blessing, to weigh the *pros.* and *cons.* fairly and adjust differences. The Church of England, it seems to me, is a specially, if not the only, suitable body for this purpose if she could be induced to take the matter up, being in no way identified with other religious organisations. It may be objected that differences of opinion and practice obtain in the English Church as well as elsewhere ; but such differences do not involve the separations and waste of means that result from what is · commonly termed Protestant dissent. Of course difficulties of no slight importance would have to be dealt with : but if only a sincere desire for unity exists, a way will doubtless be found to minimise or neutralise those difficulties, if they cannot be wholly removed. [Should mediation by the Church of England be deemed inadvisable, or not obtainable through sufficient encouragement not being afforded, something akin to the Trade Boards of Conciliation might possibly be devised to check the preposterous waste of effort and of means that now goes on. The present divided condition of Christ's Church is professedly lamented by all, and enormously enhances the cost of Christian teaching to the community. How it may best be remedied, and who should attempt its remedy, are the crucial questions. After above forty years' ministerial experience in this colony, and much thought, I venture to suggest a course which I think may, if fairly carried out, prove remedial to some extent, and should be glad to obtain the views of others thereon, especially those to be affected by it. Hence, I would solicit the favour of your views, or of those you may think fit to submit the matter to.

As illustrative of the evils sought to be remedied, I subjoin a statement of the results of division in this district. In the township of Willunga and within a mile's radius there may be from three to four hundred inhabitants, including children. Provision for public worship among these has been made as follows :—

	SITTINGS.	COST.	
Roman Catholic Church ... about 200		...£750	
Manse ... ... ,,		... 700	
School ... ... ,,		... 300	
			—— £1,750
First English Church ... ,,	100	... 500	
Second do. ... ... ,,	200	1,200	
Manse ... ... ,,		... 850	
			—— 2,550
First Wesleyan Chapel ... ,,	100	... 250	
Second do. ... ... ,,	400	3,500	
Manse ... ... ,,		... 800	
			—— 4,550
Bible Christian Chapel ,,	150	... 750	
Manse .. ... ,,		... 650	
			—— 1,400
Primitive Methodist Chapel (sold for £60) ... ... ,,	100	... 400	
			—— 400
Christian Disciples Chapel ,,	200	... 700	
			—— 700

Total sittings, say 1,450   Cost £11,350

Besides this eleven thousand pounds odd in the township, which I feel sure is below the actual outlay, and perhaps half as much more as interest on debts, within a radius of ten miles from the township, and in a sparse population, thirteen other chapels have been built—five of which are in ruins—two churches, and one manse, and now the Salvation Army seeks to establish a " cause " and build " barracks."

This extravagant building expenditure, and consequent attenuation of means of support to the various agencies, is but a sample of what is done, or sought to be done, in most other localities, and loudly calls for some remedial measure, and an amalgamation of the various non. conforming bodies seems to me the only probable mode of cure. If only the different Methodist bodies could become united, as I believe is the case in Canada, it would be an immense gain.*

Trusting you will pardon my intruding on your patience at this length, for which the importance of the subject must be my excuse, and soliciting your kind consideration of the matter on behalf of our common Christianity,

Believe me to remain, yours faithfully,

August 19th.   E. K. MILLER.

The Rev. E. K. Miller.

My dear Sir—I must apologise for not having replied more promptly to your long and interesting communication of August 19th. The matter was too serious to be dealt with hastily, and my hands are just now overfull.

I have long regretted the waste and friction that is caused by the absence of union between the several sections of Christ's Church, and done what lay in my power to diminish it. Perhaps no minister in my own church has been so pronounced an advocate for Methodist union. You will readily understand, therefore, that I am prepared to sympathise with any judicious movement for bringing Christian people and their organisations closer together. If this is to be done to any considerable extent, the Church of England may appropriately lead the way. There are difficulties to be overcome, but the discussion of the subject will do something to remove them ; and, speaking personally, I hope you will persevere along the line your letter indicates. I am strongly of opinion that were such a motion as you quote to be passed by your Synod, it would have great possibilities of usefulness.

Yours faithfully,

September 9th.   H. T. BURGESS.

Baptist Church Vestry, September 25th.

My dear Mr. Miller—I have forwarded your letter to the Rev. W. E. Rice, of North Adelaide, President of our Baptist Association. He will, I doubt not, send you an official reply in due time.

Personally, I do not see any likelihood of the denominations

---

* This sentence was omitted in copies sent to non-Methodist bodies.

merging into one. It appears to me reasonable that the various Methodist denominations might without sacrifice of any principle unite. Still they do not. I think Presbyterians and Congregationalists might unite without compromising principle.

Lately an attempt was made to bring those believing in the immersion of the believer as the only revealed way of honouring Christ's example and precept into some organised union. It was a failure. . . . There must be great spiritual forces in the breasts of Christ's disciples constraining to a real fellowship of saints ere anything satisfactory can result.

Yours faithfully,

SILAS MEAD.

———

Way College, December 25th.

My dear Sir—Your letter *re* union of the various Churches has reached me in Victoria, where I am travelling for a few weeks.

I highly appreciate your desire for the lessening of the number of rival Churches in the towns and villages of South Australia, and would join you with all my heart in that desire. At the same time I do not see at present any means of accomplishing what is thus desired. I very much doubt whether any action taken by the Church of England Synod would produce any beneficial effect, and therefore cannot advise that you renew your efforts in the Synod. I could give several reasons for writing as I do, but do not think it necessary to place those reasons before you now.

Of course if any resolution of your Synod should be addressed to our Conference I can assure you that it will have respectful and earnest consideration.

Yours faithfully,

T. PIPER.

———

To the Editor of the *Register*.

Sir—As Mr. Miller says he sent me as Chairman of Congregational Union a letter, the copy of which appears in your issue of to-day. I passed it on to the "executive" of our Union, where it was read and considered. My term of office expiring in October, I thought no more about it. I ought to have acknowledged the receipt of the letter. I am sorry I neglected to do so. So far as I can estimate opinion concerning Mr. Miller's action, he is credited with good

intention, but as representing a very small section of his own Church.
His letter is without anybody's sanction but his own. He has
a perfect right to do what he has done, but he can hardly expect the
various denominations to give the serious attention such a communication requires when the leaders of his own Church treat it with indifference. In the matter of the multiplication of Churches in
the colony, the Episcopal Church is the chief sinner. 1 believe I am
right in saying that wherever fifteen persons, or some such small
number, requisition the Bishop to form a Church he is happy to do so.
This is done on principle, for the Episcopalian Church regards
all "orders" and Christian work outside its borders as "schis-
matical," or to put it mildly "irregular." We all desire greater unity,
and among so-called "Nonconformist" denominations an earnest
purpose to accomplish it is growing. At the same time it is felt by
many of us that the attitude of the Episcopal Church is very much
in antagonism to anything like real unity. Even Mr. Miller shows
the spirit of his Church towards "Nonconformists" by describing
them "as important factors in carrying out the work of Christ."
Our buildings for worship are called "chapels," whereas those
belonging to Roman Catholics and Episcopalians are called
"Churches." From Mr. Miller's point of view there are reasons for
using such language. Yet I venture to think that it indicates
a feeble understanding as to the meaning of "unity." Before Mr.
Miller's Church can intervene as a peacemaker among denominations
it will have to show a more generous and Christian spirit than it is
doing at the present. Let the Cathedral pulpit be open occasionally
to such men as Mr. Hastings, Mr. Mead, and Mr. Gilmore, then we
shall think that Mr. Miller and his Church has a right to talk to us
on Church unity. Till then it will only retard unity for Episcopalians
to interfere.

I am, Sir, &c.,

WALTER JONES,

Late Chairman of Congregational Union.

P.S.—The Rev. J. R. Glasson, College Park, is the present head
of our denomination.

Gawler, December 29th.　　　———

To the Editor.

Sir—Allow me to correct an error in the letter of the Rev. W.
Jones, which appeared in your issue of Tuesday, dealing with

the correspondence on above subject. Mr. Jones states that he "passed Mr. Miller's letter on to the executive of our Congregational Union, where it was read and considered." Mr. Jones has been labouring under a mistake, as Mr. Miller's communication has never been before our executive, nor has it been forwarded for this purpose.

I am, Sir, &c.,

W. PENRY JONES,

December 31st.   Secretary Congregational Union.

To the Editor.

Sir—Since you kindly published the correspondence on this subject I forwarded a month ago, a few criticisms have appeared, to which I beg space for reply. The Rev. Walter Jones, on December 29, wrote intimating that since the letter I sent him as Chairman of the Congregational Union was not sanctioned by Synod, I could not expect any reply; possibly a similar feeling caused others not to reply. Having failed to obtain action by Synod I was merely anxious to ascertain whether such action, if hereafter obtainable, would be agreeable to other religious bodies. It is not necessary to reply to some points mooted by Mr. Jones that are not relevant to the matter in hand. His statement, however, that "in the multiplication of churches the Episcopal Church is the chief sinner" is certainly not borne out by the statistics my letter contained, which show one Roman and three English churches as against eighteen chapels erected in this district, which is but a sample of others. Then it is not easy to see how inviting Nonconformist ministers to preach in the Cathedral would conduce to the union of Nonconformists among themselves. In 1858, when the Rev. Thomas Binney visited Adelaide, Bishop Short, in a letter to that gentleman, expressed his deep regret that he was not able to invite him to preach in some of the churches, and the whole matter was then thoroughly discussed. The like inability still exists, for which our present Bishop is in no way responsible. It is news to me that "whenever fifteen persons or some such small number requisition the Bishop to form a church he is happy to do so;" one sometimes does, from home, hear strange news of home. Mr. Jones thinks the term "chapel" as applied to buildings used for worship by Nonconformist bodies somewhat derogatory, and that they should be called "churches." The term is not of my choosing. In Willunga one such building has engraved on its front "Wesleyan Methodist Chapel," another "Primitive Methodist Chapel," others in the district being similarly labelled. Mr. Jones seems unaware that "chapel" is a very ancient term, originally applied to buildings erected in connection with parish churches when they become too full, or were too distant from some of the parishioners, while episcopal chapels often formed part of castles and mansions; many parishes in England have several "chapels of ease." Because of this, some dissenters objected to the term as too ecclesiastical, and called their places of worship "meeting-houses." I am glad to find Mr. Jones more "churchy." I now come to a part of Mr. Jones's letter which is somewhat puzzling. After acknowledging receipt of mine of September 14, he says—"I passed it on to the 'Executive' of our Union, where it was read and considered." The Secretary of the Union, however (the Rev. W. Penry Jones), on December 31 wrote—"Mr. Jones, has been labouring under a mistake, as Mr. Miller's communication has never been before our Executive, nor has it been forwarded for this purpose." Nothing explanatory having since appeared, it is matter of surmise as to where the said letter got to, as Mr. Walter Jones doubtless sent it somewhere. By a remarkable coincidence the Rev. F. Hastings on October 16 read a paper at the meeting of the Congregational Union, also on December 1 at the meeting of the Ministerial Association on the "Union of the Evangelical Churches," which, so far as reported, seems to have been nearly identical with my lost letter—certainly advocating the same leading ideas. Perhaps this was what Mr. Walter Jones took to be the reading and considering of my letter. The circumstance of Mr. Hastings taking the matter up I regard as particularly fortunate, for doubtless his paper had more effect than my letter would have had, both meetings he addressed coinciding in the views advanced. The Rev. J. W. Owen says—"Doing God's will—not economics or anything else—is the ground reason for unity." The Rev. S. Mead thinks—"There must be great spiritual forces in the hearts of Christ's disciples, constraining to a real fellowship of saints, ere anything satisfactory can result," while the Hon. Dr. Campbell urges a spiritual fellowship embracing various agencies as the true basis of unity. Agreeing that the spiritual aspect of the matter is infinitely the more important, I nevertheless feel that attention to temporalities is also needful, and that the wild waste of these, with other ills that divisions bring, will in nowise aid in realising greater spiritual unity. The general issue of attempting to elicit the views of the different religious bodies on the question I proposed may be thus summarised: The Rev. H. T. Burgess considers that in any attempt to promote unity " the Church of England may appropriately lead the way," and says—" I hope you will persevere along the line your letter indicates. I am thoroughly of opinion that were such a motion as you quote to be adopted by your Synod it would have great possibilities of usefulness." The Rev. T. Piper writes—" I very much doubt whether any action taken by the Church of England Synod would produce any beneficial effect, and therefore cannot advise that you renew your efforts in the Synod." The Primitive Methodists, Presbyterians, and Baptists have vouchsafed no answer, except that the Rev. S. Mead says he sent my letter to the Chairman of his Union, and personally doubts the likelihood of denominations uniting. The Rev. Walter Jones, as ex-Chairman of the Congregational Union, thinks that till " the Cathedral pulpit shall be open occasionally to such men as the Revs. Hastings, Mead, and Gilmore . . . it will only retard unity for Episcopalians to interfere." But this can hardly be regarded as representing the views of the Congregationalists, who have taken action at the instance of Mr. Hastings in the direction my letter indicated. When conversing with Nonconformist ministers on this topic, the opinion has almost always been expressed by them, that financial difficulties, and providing for ministers whose services might become dispensed with, would prove the chief obstacles to a union, of some at least, of the different bodies. If I judge South Australians rightly, any financial difficulties that might arise to hinder unity would soon be arranged for ; while superfluous ministers, instead of, as now, treading on each other's heels and hindering each other's work, could be transferred to where their labours would be more beneficial, being supported by funds of the united body till the localities served could maintain them, which, if opposition ceases, would not be very long. Hoping that the action taken by the Congregationalists will be persevered in, and that other bodies will cordially co-operate,

I am, Sir, &c.,

January 23rd.   E. K. MILLER.

To the Editor.

Sir—Mr. Miller's letter to me when Chairman of the Congregational Union I suppose did not reach its destination. I quite thought it had been sent on to the Executive, and from several utterances at the last Union meeting, as well as others, I gathered the letter had been read and laid on one side as impracticable. I was unaware of Mr. Henry Jones's letter of denial till Wednesday last, when it was brought under my notice by a friend. I am fully aware of the use of the word "chapel," though Mr. Miller seems to think I need a little enlightenment on its "ancient" significance. Some fifteen years ago a long discussion took place in the English papers as to the appropriateness of the term. I held a pastorate in England at the time, and well remember the scornful way in which some clergymen applied the word to Nonconformist places of worship. I had this in my mind when I wrote objecting to the term. Evidently Mr. Miller has no sympathy with that spirit. Mr. Miller says—"It is news to me that whenever fifteen persons or some such small number requisition the Bishop to form a Church he is happy to do so; one sometimes does, from home, hear strange news of home." I know for a fact this was said to people in a district where there is no Episcopal Church. If I remember correctly the number was "small" when the Episcopal Church was started at Hamley Bridge, not many more than fifteen. I mention this as an instance. The Episcopalians have a perfect right to try and enlarge their borders and their influence; but I don't think it wise to gird at the multiplication of Churches by other denominations when they are not without sin in the matter, if it be sin.

I am, Sir, &c.,

WALTER JONES.

To the Editor.

Sir—I cannot but be thankful that Mr. Miller keeps up the discussion on the question of Christian unity. I wish I had known of his letter when I read my paper before the Congregational Union. It would have strengthened my position. It seems, however, somehow to have gone astray, but by whose oversight I know not. I don't remember hearing even a reference to it when on the executive.* The tone of some of the letters is to be regretted. None of the

---

* The said letter seems never afterwards to have been discovered.

sects "live in glass houses." All have dissented one from the other, and been more eager to advance the individual sect rather than the cause of Christ. They will have to drop it, and consider each other more. There must be a cessation of this rivalry, and especially of over-churching in sparsely populated neighbourhoods. Our sectarianism has weakened our hold of the mass of men. The Christian Church must combine if it is to resist atheism and agnosticism. Therefore I earnestly hope that we shall see not only a deeper spirit of charity, but a more definite attempt at organic unity. Several years ago I conducted in the *Homiletical Magazine* a symposium on the reunion of Christendom. H.E. Cardinal Manning, the Ven. Archdeacon Farrar, the Rev. Hugh Price-Hughes, and others from different communions wrote letters and articles that revealed not only the widespread desire for reunion, but a readiness on the part of each to give up as much of the non-essential as possible. In the controversy here it is to be hoped that the same plan will be pursued. I was glad to see that that was the spirit and plan of articles in the religious papers of Adelaide, and notably of an article in the Australian *Christian World*. The maintenance of this aim and spirit will make the future of a united Australian Evangelical Church, gathered by mutual consent from all sects, not a dream, but a possibility.

I am, Sir, &c.,

North Adelaide, January 31st.   FREDK. HASTINGS.

North-terrace, Adelaide, December 29th, 1890.

Rev. E. K. Miller.

My dear Sir—I have read your communication to the *Register* re "Religious Unity," and regret you did not receive a more hearty response from the representative men of the various denominations to whom you addressed yourself. After a careful perusal of your letter, my first thought was—has Mr. Miller not missed the key to the final unity of Christendom? While I keenly appreciated your object, I felt that no unity, even of a formal kind, was possible on a mere "business" basis. I agree with you entirely that it is a reflection on all Christian Churches that their disunion involves so serious a waste of God's gifts. Human labour, human intelligence, and human means, or wealth, are assuredly God's gifts, and it is a saddening spectacle to see in front of us every day the utter waste of all these by those who seek to be His children. Of course there are even greater losses than arise from the waste of human effort and substance. In its disunited state our common Christian faith, embodied in all who profess to be Christ's followers, cannot command the supreme position as the director of the public conscience or great moral teacher of men. It seems to me in its present state the Church, as it is called, cannot go to the root of society and lift both body and soul the masses of men. It, therefore, fails in its mission as the great regenerator of the race. I fear we shall even have to part with the very name of Church, and take the gospel of Christ by another name, first to our own hearts, and second to the hearts of the men and women of this world. My humble view is, no business agreement will bring about even an external phase of unity, and the issue of your correspondence seems to support my contention. So far as I can see, there must be a spiritual basis of unity. And this unity must have this important characteristic, viz., that it includes a large diversity within it. Both our experience and our philosophy tell us, that vitality depends on this diversity. The spiritual basis of unity then, the unity which includes diversity, is found in the "Kingdom of God" as an embodied condition among men. I know quite well how the thought or idea of which the words "the Kingdom of God" is but the verbal expression, is a thought which is acknowledged by Christians, but only with a sort of theoretical significance. It has not the living power which the numerous allusions to it in Scripture would lead us to expect, or from the fact that is so self-evident in the Gospels, that "the Kingdom of God" was the burden of our Lord's teaching from beginning to end of His earthly career. How much then should this vital truth be revived in these days when the hearts of so many yearn for a closer fellowship, and when the faith of many is wounded by Christian dissensions? This kingdom is clearly the only basis offered to us for unity, and we are not left, God be praised, to devise any scheme of our own if we once grasp the thought in its sublime significance. Our first purpose must be to see the kingdom, and next, realise our citizenship. Our perception of its duties and its privileges, its responsibilities and its joys, as we dwell upon the thought, will widen and grow upon us, and as the perception grows and intensifies, there will come by increments also an embodiment in externals of the unity we seek. One

Lord, one spirit, one kingdom, one citizenship, and what more is needful as a basis of practical unity? Would it not seem strange if after all we should find that, outside the nominal Christian Church, this thought of "the Kingdom of God" is taking deep hold of the minds of earnest and noble men? It would indeed show how far the Church has missed her way to-day, if the great spiritual *cum*-temporal conception of Christ, while only perceived in a dim, attenuated, spiritual sense by His nominal followers, found a living response in its full significance in the thoughts and hearts of men beyond the pale of the Church. I am bound to confess that it seems so to me. May I ask that you and your brethren, whose privilege it is to reach the ear of men, will once more raise the cry of "the Kingdom of God?" Will you preach it as a veritable power to-day? Will you proclaim to all who are members of the Church that they are in a living sense either inside or outside of that Kingdom? And if they are inside, then every thought, every aspiration, every act, great or small, is within its jurisdiction. As the life principle of our bodies is present in every cell of every organ, so does the life principle of the Kingdom traverse every element of our complex nature and condition. There must, too, be a motive to bring about unity. It must be powerful, and come home with equal force to all men in all sections of the Lord's vineyard. This idea of "the Kingdom of God" finding embodiment on earth, presents this motive. No other thought does. Not even the great thought of the existence of God itself. Organisation, human co-operation, living activities of the highest order are all present in the conception, and further, it comes with the same force to all. There is in it no question raised as to Church polity, government, or formularies. For the sake of order in public worship, and for the satisfaction of the various modes of human thought, all these are necessary, I presume. That progress may characterise Christian life diversity in many things is needful, and while none of us are called upon to throw away our own methods, "the Kingdom of God" does not speak of any. The one thing needful is that the spirit of unity, which the vital perception of citizenship of the Kingdom brings, should possess the heart. And not merely the heart in some abstract sense, but the heart of everyday life of every Christian, no matter whether he be priest or prelate, the humble listener in the pe, or the distinguished occupant of a pulpit. Upon this basis, and this alone, do I see the possibility of " religious unity." What a glorious power would once more be exercised by our common Christian faith if the conviction of " citizenship" fell upon every heart within the visible walls of our churches; if from the " cup of cold water" to the ruling of a nation, every act was seen to be within the Kingdom of God. Surely this thought, then, solves the problem of unity. If each be filled with the perception of citizenship, where, I ask, is the barrier to cooperation for the extension of the Kingdom? Is unity of object, unity of labour, unity of co-operation not at the very bottom of a kingdom? If the Kingdom is to be realised, there cannot be, there must not be, allowed to be any barriers. Self-created distinctions must stand aside as secondary. Differences of belief and differences of mental attitude towards the Lord are all permissible, but citizenship seen and felt can alone give the bond of unity. Does not this then solve the problem you have raised? And is it not a solemn and true answer to the question proposed to the representatives of the various Christian denominations of this colony? Is there not here that spiritual power which once sought after and finally realised, would bring about that visible unity which you so earnestly ask for, but the embodiment of which at this moment seems encompassed with so many difficulties?

Believe me, my dear Sir,
Yours very faithfully,
ALLAN CAMPBELL.

To the Editor.

Sir—In my last communication on this subject I said the "Primitive Methodists, Presbyterians, and Baptists had vouchsafed no answer " to my letter of September 14th last, enquiring whether, in their opinion, any action on the part of Synod would tend to promote unity among nonconforming Christian bodies in this colony. I have since had the pleasure of receiving the subjoined letter from the President of the Baptist Association (Mr. A. S. Neill), in which, though it contains no answer to my letter—which he had not seen when penning his address—yet expressed in the address referred to the opinion that "there are too many sects," and hopes a "closer union is possible between Churches in this colony." I thought it needful to reply to Mr. Neill, and append that reply to prevent a possible misconception as to my views and objects in moot-

ing this, as I regard it, highly important matter. I was also glad to
see the letter from the Rev. F. Hastings, of January 31st, in your
journal, and hope his efforts, with those of the Rev. H. T. Burgess,
Mr. A. S. Neill, and others occupying similar positions, will result in
some basis for an organised union of Christian bodies being devised.

I am, Sir, &c.,

Willunga, February 27th.   E. K. MILLER.

North Adelaide, February 13th, 1891.

Rev. E. K. Miller, Willunga.

Dear Sir Responding to your published invitation for laymen
to express to yourself their views on "Christian Union," I send by
post the November issue of *Truth and Progress*, on page 198 of which
you will find my "cursory comments" on the subject. A condensed
report was published in the dailies, but I have no desire that the
importance of the remarks should be unduly magnified, as a Chairman's personal utterances do not bind the Baptist Association over
which he presides. My opinions may to some extent appear strange
to an Anglican clergyman, but my sincerity may be conceded, I
trust, having urged the cultivation of a spirit of union in private
devotion rather than the public assurance of union. I may explain,
that I knew nothing at the time of the communication you had
sent to the Association Secretary regarding the subject of Christian
union. In this same connection I enclose a note from Rev. T. V.
Tymms, author of the "Mystery of God," to his article on "Home
Reunion," in the *Baptist Magazine* for January. Availing myself of
the opportunity of greeting you in the assurance of vital convictions,
cherished in common,

I am, yours respectfully,

ANDREW S. NEILL.

February 20th, 1891.

My dear Sir—I thankfully acknowledge your kind letter of 13th
inst. with accompaniments, which, having been from home, I have
only just found time to carefully peruse. As you say, I was desirous if
possible of inducing intelligent Christian laymen to state their views
on the subject mooted in my letter to ministers of six leading denominations in September last, since those ministers seem very chary

of expressing their views thereon.   Your own and Dr. Campbell's are the only communications that have reached me save the few from ministers, which were duly published.   In your remarks as reported in *Truth and Progress* you say—" Some long for the time when Australians shall give up all the divisions of the old world, and one National Australian Church cement all who dwell beneath the Southern Cross. Personally, I see nothing in this but a beautiful dream." This certainly is not what I aimed at or dreamed of, for, in my estimation, it would be neither possible nor desirable. I quite agree with you that concentration of power in any single organisation would be very apt to issue in domination. My object simply was, through the instrumentality of Synod, or otherwise, to obtain an amalgamation of some of the nonconforming bodies, and so diminish the friction and waste both of effort and of means that now goes on. Taking these bodies as a whole, I think it may be said that Presbyterianism, more or less modified, is their prevailing form of Church government.   If they could only be brought to sink what appear to be minor differences, and combine for accomplishing the great work all are professedly engaged in, viz., the evangelisation of our race, far more potent for good their labours would become.   But in order to do this each body must be prepared to concede somewhat, to sacrifice if needful their predilections for the general good, and become generous enough to regard as fellow-Christians others who may happen to differ in opinion from them.   Page 177 of *Truth and Progress* you kindly sent me, under the heading " Methodist Immersion," affords an illustration of what I mean.   It is there seemingly set forth as a dogma, that if a person be immersed by a minister who had not been himself immersed, such person could only be regarded by the Baptist Church as an unbaptised Christian.   Now evidently were such a dogma made a *sine quâ non* to an individual's being recognised as a member of an amalgamated nonconforming body, it would prove a great bar to anything like organised union.   It certainly seems to me, that by very slight concessions some bodies might at once become united, notably the Methodists ; nor can I see any insuperable difficulty in the union of Presbyterians, Congregationalists, and Baptists, if it be only admitted that all have been, in one form or other, baptised.   This would result in two great Nonconformist bodies, who would probably soon absorb the remaining smaller bodies.   Your friend, Mr. Webb, spoke of the fact that in

Melbourne Presbyterian, Methodist, and Baptist ministers held a united prayer meeting. It is difficult to understand why they should not unite also in praise, and other acts of worship. To make something like a parade of desire for unity by uniting in prayer, while acting adversely to each other, as all sects must more or less do, seems scarcely consistent with that sincerity which should ever mark the Christian's course. I see by the newspapers, that the Ministerial Association propose to form a Council to promote a closer union of the Churches, and prevent overlapping in sparsely peopled localities. I do not know on what basis this Association has been formed, but feel certain that unless some definite principles are first adopted on which an organised union can be based, the effort will have no more of potency than an attempt to bind the Churches by a rope of sand. Trusting that in the position you are called to occupy your sympathy and efforts may be directed to the promotion of greater unity among the Churches than now obtains,

Believe me,
Yours faithfully,
E. K. MILLER.

A. S. Neill, Esq.,
   President of the Baptist Association.

Not long after this correspondence had appeared in the *Register*, a movement of a definite kind towards unity was commenced by the Methodist bodies. At sundry meetings and conferences the propriety and possibility of effecting an amalgamation have been almost unanimously affirmed. Indeed, so earnest are the majority of their leading ministers and laymen, that it promises to be but a short time before, under God's blessing, a basis for union will be devised and accepted by all those bodies.

Then, too, the different bodies of Presbyterians have become so far united as not to clash with each other, and are yearning for union with other bodies. The Independents also, who, as Dr. Jefferis once said, " with a tardy repentance now call themselves Congregationalists," are fast realising that the isolation of congregations is not the most effective way of disseminating Christian truth; the fact of a Congregational Union being established is an admission, to some extent, of the advisability of organised action. The Baptists, too, and sundry others, seem to be getting weary of separations, and the evils they entail. These things, then, being so, the question arises as to whether the evils all profess to deplore, cannot in some way be diminished. It seems to me that they may. Let us take a bird's eye view of the situation.

Taking the last census returns, for 1891, as the basis of calculation, we find it therein stated that there are in all fifteen bodies of persons professing to hold some form of Protestantism. Of these the members of the Church of England take the first place, numbering 89,271, or a percentage on the entire population of 27·86. This Church having been adopted as the National Church of England, and possessing a definite constitution, may be regarded as that from which all others have diverged. Next in numerical importance are the

Wesleyans, numbering ...	49,159 or	15·34	per cent. of the population
Bible Christians	15,762 ,,	4·92	,,	,,
Primitive Methodists ...	11,654 ,,	3·64	,,	,,
Methodist New Connexion	39 ,,	·01	,,	,,
Showing a total of Methodists ...	76,614 ,,	23·01	,,	,,

These figures show that were it possible for the Church of England and the Methodists—who are likely to become amalgamated—to co-operate, by which I mean, to arrive at some understanding which would enable them, *as bodies independent of each other*, yet each aiming at the common good, to *aid* each other, instead of *competing*, as is now the case, we should have a combined agency infinitely more potent for good than in their separated condition they can possibly become.

The like may be said of others. Thus the

Presbyterians number...	18,206 or	5·68 per cent. of the population
Baptists	17,547 ,,	5·50 ,, ,,
Congregationalists ...	11,882 ,,	3·71 ., ,,
Unitedly	47,635 ,,	14·89 ,, .,

These certainly might, with but slight concessions, become amalgamated, and agree to co-operate with the Church and Methodists. Neither body need speak of, or act adversely to, the other, but confine themselves to simply setting forth what they conceive to be the truth, leaving their hearers to decide as to which body they think it right to join. The only two other considerable bodies, the Roman Catholics, numbering 47,179, and the Lutherans, numbering 23,328, would probably have to continue as separate organisations.

The bodies mentioned assuredly might, if they could but bring themselves to lay aside the pride and prejudice so often mis-called principle, do away with very much of the schism, waste of effort and of means that now so seriously impede the work Christ would have accomplished—viz., the winning of the world unto Himself. My own view is, that the laity should bestir themselves in these matters, and *demand* that some arrangement be made to bring about greater unanimity, for it is the laity who are unduly taxed to maintain these often absurd divisions, and who are in every sense the sufferers thereby.

In the foregoing, I have merely spoken of dissent in regard to the practical results it has brought about, not adverting to the abstract principles on which it is based— viz., that every individual should choose for himself the form of church government and manner of worship he prefers. also selecting his own minister. Discussion on these matters would be out of place in these " Reminiscences," and require more space than can be afforded. My object has been the rather to cite a series of facts, in order that the tree may be judged by its fruit, and suggest what 1 think would prove at all events a partial remedy or diminution of the evils that exist.

CHAPTER XVII.

VOLUNTARYISM.

AMONG the difficulties that had to be encountered after the withdrawal of Government aid to religion, were of course those of providing for the maintenance of ministers, cleaning, lighting, and repair of churches and parsonages, with salaries of organists, and pew-openers, for the earliest churches had closed pews. In England the members of the Established Church had mostly been accustomed to have all these matters provided for by church rates, and the clergy were often sustained by endowments, or other funds not directly derived from their congregations; wherefore, it proved by no means easy for those brought up under such circumstances to realise that here they had to provide everything for themselves. Not very long since, one of my parishioners told me—when speaking of the difficulty of maintaining public worship—that she knew dissenters always had to support their own ministers, but thought the clergy of the National Church were supported by the Queen.

In the first instance, it was arranged for the clergy to be supported by seat-rents, and all other expenses were sought to be provided for by monthly collections. These, however, soon proved inadequate. It was, therefore, suggested that a stipend fund should be established at each church to supplement seat-rents, and an offertory taken at every service. The latter suggestion met with very general and strong opposition. Some said it was making the house of God a mere place for money-getting; others that they would rather leave the Church than have a plate thrust before them every time they attended worship, and such like. It was a long time before the vestries could be got to agree to this alteration; many of the Church's best friends fearing it would have the effect of diminishing attendance. The idea very largely entertained, that it was proposed that every one should contribute to the offertory at every service, was a great stumbling-block. Many-a-time and oft it had to be explained, at meetings and from the pulpit, that it was merely intended to afford every one an *opportunity* to contribute whenever convenient, whereas by a collection only on one fixed Sunday in each month many, through absence, would be precluded contributing. Then, too, the principle had to be continually urged, that it was every one's duty to tender a thank-offering to God from time to time, and that public worship afforded the most fitting opportunity for so doing; that the rendering of something to God, or for the service of God, ought to form a part of the worship of God. The opposition, which had been keen and general was long in dying away. Ultimately the taking of the offertory became a part of worship in all the churches, and not very many now would care to see it abolished. By this means the incidental expenses of most churches are met.

In regard to the support of clergy. As before stated, it was originally made to depend on seat-rents (there being no endowments) with, in some places, a stipend-fund. This was, and is, objected to by many, on the ground that it is not right to make anything like a *charge* on persons who wish to attend the worship of God; and, that as all are equal in the sight of God, there should be no distinc-

tion made in the house of God between those who are able
to contribute much, and those who are able to contribute little, perhaps nothing. Hence the establishment
of some free and open churches, where, as no seats are
let or appropriated, the clergyman's income is made to
depend entirely on the offertory, unless there be endowment. But in most churches seats were let, with the exception of a few reserved for the poor and visitors.
In some churches, seats were let at different rates,
those in the most favourable positions being charged
for higher than others; while in others, all were let at
equal rates. In the former case, where payments were
made to depend on the favourable or unfavourable
position of the seats assigned, it would manifestly come
under the rebuke of St. James, for it is neither more nor
less than saying to the "rich man, sit thou here in a
good place, and to the poor, stand thou there, or sit here
under my footstool," creating a distinction in the house of
God based on the monetary position, or disposition, of the
worshippers. Then, too, where equal rates are charged,
for instance, the very general rate of a pound per annum
per sitting, a poor man with a family can hardly be expected to afford it, such often quitting the church for
the chapel in consequence. On the other hand the well-to-
do are apt to think that when they have paid the amount
demanded they have done all that ought to be expected of
them; while there are not wanting those who will evade all
payment if possible. A well-to-do individual had occupied
sittings in one of my churches for three or four years without contributing anything. At length, a churchwarden resolved to do a little "dunning," on which the party ceased
attending, virtuously indignant. In the demanding seat-
rents, whether equal or unequal, there can manifestly be no

true voluntaryism : they cannot be regarded as in any sense
a *free-will offering* to God, or toward maintaining the
worship of God.

Two leading considerations are in this matter involved.
In the first place, it is admitted on all hands as desirable,
that opportunity for attending the worship of God should
be denied to none. In the second place, it is obviously
necessary to provide for the maintenance of that worship,
and those who conduct it. The principle of free and open
churches, for which many contend, is liable to at least two
important objections. Where no seats are assigned, a
person may have to sit at one time in one place, at another
in a different, there being no special seat he can go to, or
have a right to occupy. In the case of families, parents
and children will consequently often become separated,
especially where the attendance is large; and that children
should be with, and under control of, their parents during
divine worship is of course highly desirable. In short, the
worshipping of *families* together under this system cannot
possibly be guaranteed. In the next place, as the offertory
would be the principal, or only, source of income, there
could be no reliable basis on which to reckon for the maintenance of worship or support of ministers, who must consequently undertake their duties without knowing certainly
what they will receive, or probably when they will receive
it, of which unpleasantness I have had considerable experience—though not under this particular system.

In order to meet, so far as possible, the difficulties
connected with this matter, and that as little distinction as
possible should exist in the house of God, combining the
fullest freedom with provision for families to worship together—at the same time providing a financial basis—I for
many years adopted the following plan. On a person

wishing to obtain sittings, he would be shown all that
were unoccupied, and he chose such as would meet his requirements, which were assigned to him. He would then
be asked, what he proposed to contribute toward maintaining the worship in which he wished to join, being left perfectly free to name any amount his circumstances might
warrant or inclination dictate. Not a few, but mostly widows
with families—(I remember some in receipt of rations from
the Government)—have frankly said they could not specify
any regular payment, but would contribute through the
offertory from time to time as much as they could afford.
Working men with families hardly ever undertook to pay
as much as a pound a year per sitting. Tradespeople and
others with larger means were of course expected to contribute according to their ability. Under this system, it
often happened that the poorer members of the congregation occupied the more favourable positions, the employé
sitting beside or before his employer. The general issue I
found to be, that many in the humbler walks of life became
seatholders at low rates of payment who certainly would
not otherwise have so become, if they had attended worship
at all. I have met with not a few whose plea for non-attend-
ance at church has been, that they could not afford it.
Very few, however, of those apparently the more affluent,
felt it their duty to contribute in accordance with what one
would suppose to have been their means. Taking the
traditional pound per annum per sitting as their standard
they managed to get so far, but no farther. Out of my
last three congregations there was but one who contributed
above that rate, paying five pounds per annum for two
sittings, while others who, I should assume, could equally
well afford to do likewise, were content to pay as little as
ten shillings per annum for two sittings. What may be

called the commercial principle obtains with not a few—
viz., if we can get such accommodation as we require, and
a clergyman's services, for little, why should we pay more ?
Hence this experiment, in my case, was certainly not a
financial success, though it had the effect of bringing many
to worship in the church who would have otherwise gone
to chapels, at one shilling, or one shilling and sixpence per
quarter, or nowhere at all.

At the Synod meeting on May 15th, 1873, I moved—
" That this Synod recommend the vestries of the various
churches in this diocese to consider the advisability of
abolishing fixed seat-rents, and leaving every seatholder to
contribute whatever he may think fit toward the maintenance of public worship." After a long discussion this
was negatived by a small majority, I think four or five, in
a very full meeting, the Bishop voting against it. Since
then I am not aware of any definite movement having been
made in this matter by Synod.

Sometimes a guaranteed income is arranged for. When
taking charge of the Willunga cure, I was asked if I wished
a guarantee as to income. I declined, on the ground that
the guarantors must of course depend on the amount
specified being made up from seat-rents or other sources, in
which possibly they might be disappointed. As the guarantors would be among the best friends of the church, should
the amount specified not be forthcoming from the congregation, and they be called on to make good any material de-
ficency, they might become annoyed, and cease their efforts
for the church. Then, too, it would put the clergyman in an
unpleasant position to have to demand the amount guaranteed, probably at the same time knowing it had not been
received. Cases have occurred in which considerable annoyance has resulted from this system being acted on, loss

of very earnest church members resulting. In my own case, when establishing churches, to have commenced by demanding a guaranteed income would probably have proved a hindrance to the work being undertaken.

But in whatsoever manner the voluntary system may be carried out, it must of necessity be attended with difficulties, occasionally of a very serious nature. A minister can hardly fail to know some, at all events, of those who contribute the more largely toward the maintenance of his church, and might be tempted to treat such with greater deference or pay them more attention than others who, from their humbler position, and perhaps greater share of trouble or difficulty, especially need his counsel and aid. Or, what is even more dangerous, he might be led to gloss over or palliate the wrong doings of the more prosperous of his flock, instead of pleading with or reproving the inconsistent ones. A young clergyman, with a wife and children, once applied to me for advice under a difficulty of this nature. A member of one of his three or four small congregations, who was possessed of considerable means, was reputed to be living in adultery; his wife having been driven from her home in consequence, the matter became notorious. "What," said he, "am I to do? If I speak to him on the subject he will certainly be offended, and perhaps leave the church, and if he withdraws his subscription the church might as well be shut up, for he contributes more than all the rest put together." It was a painful position for a young man to be placed in, to feel that by attempting to do his duty he might probably have to forfeit his position; he shortly after left the cure. I have often been told by dissenting ministers that the like difficulties occur with them. Thus, some Independent ministers have said they feel themselves entirely *dependent* on the good-will of their deacons or others. I have known several dissenting ministers forced from their positions by cliques of the self-sufficient or well-to-do members of their flocks simply as the issue of prejudice, begotten, to my own certain knowledge in some instances, by the very faithfulness with which the ministers sought to do their duty. In fact, the overbearing spirit not unfrequently displayed by some laymen when they know a minister is dependent on them for the means of subsistence, often renders it exceedingly difficult for him to faithfully discharge his duty, and this is particularly the case in small populations.

Then, too, the element of self-interest occasionally crops up. I have known tradesmen influenced as to whether they would attend church or chapel by the consideration as to which was likely to bring them the more custom. A storekeeper having been elected warden by the seatholders of one of my churches, and in consequence collector of seat-rents, so managed that they were always in arrear, but willingly supplied me with goods on account thereof. Of course I saw the drift, but for peace sake yielded, never receiving cash while he held office. At length, my wife having purchased an article at another shop, he thought fit to become abusive, whereon I told him all business relations between us must cease. On this he left the church, becoming as vindictive as possible. This illustrates the class of people with whom ministers sometimes have to do. Then, too, the people squabble among themselves, and one will not continue attending church if another does. I remember a ridiculous instance of this. Two ladies belonging to one of my churches happened to attend a sale, and both began bidding for a bedstead. On its being knocked down, the unsuccessful bidder, somewhat nettled, asked of the other—" What does a widow like you want with another bedstead ? I'm sure you've got enough already." To which the reply in shrillest tones was—" What business is that of yours ? If I like to buy a dozen bedsteads you've no right to interfere. You call yourself a churchwoman and speak to me like that ! I shan't go to church again if you do; I wouldn't demean myself by sitting near you, so I tell you;"—and she kept her word. In sundry cases parties have left the churches because not chosen for the choirs, or because, having been chosen, they disagreed with the organist, or others in the choir. In one instance, a whole family permanently withdrew from the church and went to a chapel because a young daughter having offered to sing at a soirée, and her mother wishing it, she was not put on the programme, those conducting feeling she was scarcely equal to the occasion.

Such things as these, in themselves in the highest degree, absurd, are apt to become very real sources of annoyance and vexation to ministers labouring in small neighbourhoods; for those concerned always seek to justify themselves to others, and versions of the circumstances, more or less garbled, get into circulation. Should a minister try to heal some such breach, and especially should he advise that it ought not to interfere with the parties' attendance at church, he is at once set down as studying principally his own interest, for some persons conceive all effort, no matter how benevolent, must spring from self-interest in some shape or other. Acting out St. Paul's precept to those who minister the Word of Life, " Reprove, rebuke, exhort," is not easy under the voluntary system, especially where there are several places of worship in a small village or township, the adherents of each of which eagerly watch for differ-

ences in other congregations in the hope of attracting
fragments that become scattered. Indeed, so zealous are
some to win members to their own from other congregations, that they regard "sheep-stealing" as not only
justifiable, but meritorious. In one instance, I know that
a dissenting pastor, who had lost three sheep, waited on
them and almost with tears in his eyes begged them to
return, lest their example should be followed by others of
his diminutive flock. The senseless multiplication of
places of worship, in fact, often causes those placed in
charge of them to be driven to their wit's end to make
them pay: those who teach having almost to grovel to
the purse-proud vulgarity that in many an instance seeks
to lord it over a sensitive minded minister.

This miserable condition of things, the natural result of
uncontrolled voluntaryism, and the spirit of contention,
will never be remedied till nonconforming bodies resolve
to exercise so much common sense and Christian principle
as to agree not to build against each other, and compete for
custom, for it is nothing else. I am well aware that the
plea in all cases is, a desire on the part of a denomination,
or their leaders, to look after the spiritual well-being of
their members. But when it is known that those members
are but few, perhaps three or four families, erecting a
building for their accommodation and in the hope of a
few others being induced to join, is utterly unjustifiable
when there are other buildings, perhaps immediately
adjacent, in which the same essential truths are taught,
and this applies alike to churches and chapels. The only
remedy, it seems to me, is, for the at present divided
bodies to forthwith coalesce, so far as possible, sustaining
all ministers from central funds, and so relieving them
from direct monetary connection with their people.

Voluntaryism, however pleasant it may sound in theory, I have found oftentimes exceedingly unpleasant and un-satisfactory in practice; and while things continue as they are there can be no amelioration.

CHAPTER XVIII.

EXCHANGE OF PULPITS.

THIS subject has every now and then been brought prominently before the public, usually with special reference to dissenting ministers officiating in the Church of England. From what has appeared at various times, it is evident want of knowledge and confusion of thought in regard to the matter are prevalent in many quarters. A noteworthy instance of this occurred during the visit of the Rev. T. Binney to Adelaide in 1858, when public excitement was wrought almost to fever heat by newspaper writers and others. The wish was entertained by many members of the Church, as well as others, that that distinguished Congregational minister should be asked to preach in some of the city churches. The Bishop, to show that so far as he was *personally* concerned he was desirous to promote concord between the different Protestant bodies, forwarded to Mr. Binney a letter raising the whole question of the relationship existing between Churchmen and Dissenters. Since it affords a fair illustration of the feelings entertained on this subject by Churchmen generally, and is calculated to supply definite information on some points of importance, I have thought well to quote it at length. As Christian Unity is becoming one of the great questions of the day, the ideas of such men as Bishop Short and the Rev. T. Binney thereon, can scarcely fail to be of interest.

Bishop's Court, September 23rd, 1858.

Rev. Sir—1. During our social intercourse yesterday at the house of a common friend, you were pleased to take notice of a remark which fell from me to this effect—that we in this colony had the advantage of occupying " an historic stand-point," so to speak, from which we might look back upon our past social, political, and Church life in England ; and, removed from the smoke and noise of the great mother-city, might discern through all its greatness somewhat of folly and meanness, of defect and vice, in its habits and institutions.   The survey would not be unprofitable if it should lead us to perceive how we had been blinded by its attractions, so as to become unconscious of its faults ; and so hurried away by its feelings and associations as to be insensible of the conventional bondage in which we then lived and moved.

2. It must, I think, be admitted, that the clerical mind is peculiarly swayed by party principles and sectarian prejudices. Withdrawn very much from practical into contemplative life, and valuing abstract truth as the basis of all moral obligation and excellence, clergymen are too apt to exaggerate the importance of certain truths which they conscientiously hold, and to treat as essential principles of the doctrines of Christ, matters of inferential or traditional authority.   I do not suppose that Nonconformist ministers are exempt from this failing, though it may be fostered in the Establishment at home by the alliance of Church and State.

3. Be this, however, as it may, both clergymen and ministers may look back with some degree of regret that a mid-wall of partition should so have separated kindred souls ; pledged to the same cause, rejoicing in the same hope, and devoted to the same duty of preaching Christ and Him crucified to a dark and fallen world. By the very discomfort, however, of thus " standing apart " we are thrust rudely back upon the principles in which we have been brought up, and are constrained to put the question to our consciences—" Are you as sure of your ground as true to your convictions ? Are your views so authoritatively scriptural as to put you exclusively in the right?" And if, after careful review and earnest prayer, we still feel unable to quit the " old paths," yet does not this very enquiry dispose us to place a more liberal construction on the conduct of others, and to respect their equally stiff adherence to their conscientious convictions ? A candid mind will not fail to see

that much is to be urged on the other side of the question; and if with our present lights we had lived in the time of our fathers, we should not perhaps have been disposed to break up the fellowship of the Reformed Evangelical Catholic Church for non-essential points, or narrow its communion on matters of Christian expediency rather than Christian obligation.

4. I have thrown these remarks together by way of preface in order to show the course of thought into which an Episcopate of ten years in this colony has gradually led me. You yourself have given a fresh impetus to such reflections. Your fame as a preacher had preceded you. I knew that you would be welcomed by all who in your own immediate section of the Evangelical Church take an interest in religion, and by all in our own who are admirers of genius and piety, even though the echoes of your King's Weighhouse sermon had not quite died away. Hundreds I knew would ask themselves—"Why should I not go and listen to the powerful preaching of Mr. Binney?" And when they had heard you reason of righteousness, temperance, and judgment to come; of Christ, who He was and what he did; how he died for our sins and rose again for our justification, I felt assured that they would ask again—"Why is he not invited to preach to us in our churches? What is the barrier which prevents him and other ministers from joining with our clergy at the Lord's table, and interchanging the ministry of the Word in their respective pulpits? Was it any real difference with respect to the person, office, and work of the Redeemer, the power of the Spirit of God, or the lost condition of man without Christ and the Comforter?"

5. I am truly glad that so considerable a person as yourself should by your presence in this colony have forced me to consider again the question—"Why I could not invite you to preach to our congregations; to review my position, principles, beliefs, and prepossessions; more especially as the absence of sectarian prejudice on your part, and the presence of all that in social life can conciliate esteem and admiration, reduced the question to its simple ecclesiastical dimensions.

6. Again and again the thought recurred to me—*Talis cum sis, utinam noster esses!* Still I felt that neither the power of your intellect, nor vigour of your reasoning, nor mighty eloquence, nor purity of life, nor suavity of manners, nor soundness in the faith,

would justify me in departing from the rule of the Church of England; a tradition of eighteen centuries which declares your orders irregular, your mission the offspring of division, and your Church system—I will not say schism—but *dichostasy.**

7. But, while adhering to this conclusion, I am free to confess that my feelings kick against my judgment ; and I am compelled to ask myself is this "standing apart" to continue for ever ? Is division to pass from functional disease into the structural type of Church organisation ? Are the Lutheran and Reformed, the Presbyterian and Congregationalist, the Baptist and Wesleyan bodies to continue separate from the Episcopal communion so long as the world endureth ? Is there no possibility of accommodation, no hope of sympathy, no yearning for union ? Will no one even ask the question ? None make the first move ? Must we be content with that poor substitute for apostolic fellowship in the Gospel—" Let us agree to differ ;" or an evangelical alliance, which, transient and incomplete, betrays a sense of want without satisfying the craving ? Or, are we reduced to the sad conclusion, that as there can be no peace with Rome so long as she obscures the truth of Jesus, and lords it over God's heritage, so there are no common terms on which the Evangelical Protestant Churches can agree, after eliminating errors and evils against which each has felt itself constrained to pro-test ? Are not Churchmen, for example, at this day just as ready as you, Rev. Sir, can be, to condemn the treatment of Baxter, Bunyan, and Defoe by a High Church Government ? And do not Independents and Presbyterians readily allow that a Leighton or Ken relieve Episcopacy from the odium brought upon it by the severities of a Laud or a Sharp ?

8. It appears to me, that in this colony we are placed in a peculiarly favourable position for considering our Church relations, because one great rock of offence has been taken out of the way—I mean the connection between Church and State. We can approach the matters in dispute simply as questions of evangelical truth and Christian expediency. Neither social, nor civil, nor ecclesiastical distinctions interfere to distract our view or irritate our feelings. There is no Church-rate conflict here. I have accordingly seized the opportunity of laying before you a few thoughts on the possibility of

---

*Gal. v. 20, " seditious ;" literally " standing apart."

an outward fellowship, as well as inward union, of the Evangelical Churches, with the hope that they may suggest enquiry if they lead to no immediate practical results.

9. The questions I would propose for consideration are—

    1st. Whether an outward union, supposing no essential truth of the Gospel to be compromised, is desirable amongst the Protestant Evangelical Churches ?

    2nd. What are the principles and conditions on which such union should be effected ?

I submit my ideas to you with great diffidence, but from the desire to show that there is no unwillingness on my part to consider how we might possibly serve at one and the same altar, walk by the same rule, and preach from the same pulpits the words of this salvation.

10. With regard to the first point, I conceive outward union to be desirable, because it appears to me to be scriptural and apostolic. That all the congregations of the Universal Church were subject, under Christ, to the Twelve Apostles, and that the decree directed by the Holy Ghost, but framed by James with Simon Peter, Paul, and Barnabas, and assented to by the elders and brethren, was delivered to the Churches to keep, is recorded in the Acts of the Apostles. That the whole Church was viewed as one visible body by St. Paul is evident when he bids the Corinthians give offence to neither Jews nor Gentiles, nor the Church of God ; and whatever be the figure under which the Holy Spirit characterises the body of true believers in Christ, unity of organised life is the substratum of the idea ; be it in vine or olive-tree, family or household, city or kingdom, the body or spouse of Christ, the thought is still the same.

What, then, should we think of a family whose several members, inhabiting the same house, kept each to his own chamber, and though continually jostling on the common stairs, rarely exchanged a friendly salute, and never a visit ? Is this family life ?

And is it true Church life to say, I am of Peter, and I am of Paul, and I of Luther, and I of Knox, and I of Wesley, and I of Whitfield, and I of the Fathers? Are we not carnal, and speak as men ? In the apostolic age there must have been outward union of the Churches, so far at least as the general order of a common worship, the celebration of common sacraments, the profession of a common creed, and preaching in common the Word of Life. The spirit of Diotrephes we may hope was rare.

11. If the *odium theologicum* be indeed the worst type of that disease, it might be expected that a real union of the Churches and their publicly acknowledged fellowship in the Gospel might arrest the progress of that malady. It is the effect of party feeling, jealousy, and suspicion, fostered by rivalry and contention. Thus Christian sympathy, which is meant for mankind, is too often restricted to a system or a sect. On the other hand :

12. In what an attitude of strength would such union place the Gospel of Christ before Jew and Gentile ; before Brahmin and Mohammedan. No subtle Pundit would then point to the differences of Christian teachers as indicating error, at least in some, and uncertainty in all. No Bossuet could enumerate, and perhaps exaggerate, the variations of Protestants, and, unmindful of the like in his own communion, claim for the Church of Rome the symbol of Unity, as the mark of its being the True Church. But now, instead of fighting the Lord's battle as one great army, our resistance to the Powers of Evil is like the death struggle at Inkerman : a series of hand-to-hand combats, broken regiments fighting in detached parties, never receding indeed, but incapable of combined effort or mutual support.

13. It may, however, be urged, on the other side, that the divisions of the Church are helps to its vitality, even as the troubled sea which cannot rest is thereby preserved from stagnancy and corruption ; that rivalry promotes exertion, and exertion results in expansion. Yet has not the Bible Society attained its present strength by acting on the opposite principle ? Is it not because all Protestants can unite in furthering its object, truly catholic, and, because catholic, triumphant ?

14. The union I contemplate is not a yoke of subjection—an iron rule suppressive of individual or sectional thought, aspiration, energy, and action ; far otherwise. If the Great Apostle of the Gentiles would provoke his brethren after the flesh to jealousy in order to save some—if he stirred up the Churches of Macedonia by the forwardness of Achaia, and reciprocally urged the Achaian Churches to be ready with their contributions lest he should be ashamed of his boasting concerning them—certainly a loving zeal striving for the mastery is not to be cast out as unmeet for the

Christian commonwealth. Unity is compatible with variety, and variety is pregnant of competition. God has created but one vertebrate type of animal organisms ; but how infinitely diversified are the specific forms ? I know no reason why in our reformed branch of the Catholic Church there might not be particular congregations of the Wesleyan rule, or some other method of internal discipline, or usage, or form of worship, even as the Society of Ignatius Loyola, or Dominic, or Francis exists in the bosom of the Roman obedience. The seamless coat of the Redeemer was woven from the top throughout. The Roman soldiers said "Let us not rend it." Why should chronic disunion be the symbol of Evangelical Christianity ? I cannot call alliance union ; nay, it is founded on stereotyped separations. I pass to the second question—

> 2. What are the principles and conditions on which a union of the Protestant Evangelical Churches should be effected ?

15. It must be evident, I should suppose, after an experience of three hundred years, that neither the Episcopalian, nor Presbyterian, nor Congregationalist can reasonably hope to force upon the Christian world his own particular system. Is either one or the other entitled by the Word of God to exclude from salvation those believers who do not follow the same rule of church government? If, however, submission may not be demanded on the ground of its necessity to salvation, then any negotiation for outward union may and must proceed on grounds of what is best and wisest, most likely to unite, as being most in accordance with Scripture and apostolic tradition ! We must lay aside hard words — schism, Church authority, sectarianism. In the comity of nations *de facto* governments are recognised and treated with ; the question whether they are *de jure* is left in abeyance. So must it be in respect to any union of the Churches. They must meet together like brethren who have been long estranged, yet retaining the strong affection of early youth ; resolve to forget the subject of their dispute, and walk together in the house of God as friends. It will be unnecessary to ask—" Which man did sin—this man or his parents ?" or to say—"Thou wast altogether born in sin, and thus thou teach us," or—"We forbade him, because he followeth not us." No ; we must meet in the spirit of godly fear, of mutual respect, with the earnest desire by all right concession to promote God's truth, and advance Christ's kingdom. We must receive one another, but not to doubtful disputations.

A second principle is—" Whereto we have attained," or shall attain ; that some rule must be publicly acknowledged, in that rule we must walk and by it steadfastly abide.

I firmly believe with Mr. Maurice, in his " Kingdom of Christ," that the Church of the apostolic age embraced every principle for which in later times each section of the Christian world has felt it necessary to contend, even to separation from the main body of the brethren. But the Church of the apostolic age, the true visible model Church, does more. It harmonises them all ; giving to each its due place, its real proportion. Each portion of the truth, obscured, distorted, or denied in the mediæval Church, each detail of the outward building of God, has been jealously rescued from corruption or decay by sects or individuals. It remains, perhaps, for this or the coming generation to restore the original fabric, and take away whatever is inappropriate, unsightly, or inconvenient. But is the spirit as yet willing ? Alas, I know not. It is certain that the flesh is weak.

17. Let me endeavour to state, as accurately as I can, what seems to be the leading idea, the characteristic principle, of each section of the Christian Church :—

The Church of Rome, then, contends for external unity, founded on one objective creed, in subjection to one visible head of the Church on earth.

The Lutheran for justification by faith, antecedent to and irrespective of works.

The Reformed Calvinistic Church upholds the free and sovereign grace of God.

The Anglican witnesses for a scriptural creed, apostolic orders, and a settled liturgy.

The Presbyterian asserts the authority of the Presbytery, as derived immediately from the Holy Ghost.

The Congregationalist claims unlimited right of private judgment, and the independent authority of each congregation, as a perfect Church, over its own members.

The Wesleyan preaches spiritual awakening, sensible conversion, and social religious exercises.

The Baptist contends for personal religious experience previous to admission to the Church.

Every one of these principles is substantially, though not exclusively, true. When their mutual relations are forgotten, each becomes exaggerated ; the beauty of proportion is lost, and a faulty extreme is made the Shibboleth of schism.

Is there no analytical process possible, no law of affinity, by which the spiritual mind could precipitate the error, and leave pure and limpid the Gospel stream ? or remove from the much fine gold of the Temple the dross with which it is alloyed ? Would there not still remain a Scriptural truth, a godly discipline, a settled order, a common altar, a united ministry, a visible union as well as fellowship in the Spirit ? Might there not still be variety in unity, partial diversity of usage, and a regulated latitude of divine worship? The Episcopalian, the Presbyterian, and Congregationalist, might consent to harmonise what they cannot exclusively enforce ; they might surely "in understanding be men," and exercise the great privilege of spiritual men — that is, combine freedom with submission to law, and general order with specific distinctions.

18. But it is time to draw these general remarks to a close, and define with somewhat more precision, that Church of the future which is to conciliate all affections and unite all diversities. I scarcely know which to admire most, the pleasantness of the dream, or the fond imagination of the dreamer. Still, let me speak, though it be "as a fool." My object is not to dictate proceedings, but to suggest consideration ; to provoke inquiry, but not force conclusions. And since concession in matters not absolutely essential to salvation, or positively enjoined, must be the basis of the system adopted by the various Evangelical Churches, it may be fairly put to me in the language of the proverb—"Physician, heal thyself." I will begin, then, with the Church of England, and will state what it appears to me can be given up for the sake of union. 1. A State nominated Episcopate. 2. Compulsory uniformity of divine worship.

Already the former has given place in Canada and New Zealand to an Episcopate freely elected by the Church itself.

The latter, it appears, even in England, is only required from the clergy in parish churches, but not when preaching in the fields, or streets and lanes of the city.

In addition, then, to the separation of Church and State in this colony, and the absence of the legal machinery connected with that union, greater freedom and diversity of the modes of worship seem attainable ; and an Episcopate, moderate in its pretensions as well as constitutional in its proceedings, associated with, and not lording it over, the Presbyters ; above all, chosen by the free suffrages of the united clergy and laity.

I believe the doctrinal articles of the Church of England, and many others among the Thirty-nine, are allowed on all sides to be Scriptural. I conceive, then, that a settled form of sound words, a deposit of objective faith, would not be deemed a yoke of bondage, but a guide to truth.

I conceive, also, in order that all might worship with the understanding as well as the spirit, that certain liturgical offices, such for instance as the litany, might form part of the stated services, but not to the exclusion of extempore prayer in connection with the sermon, at the discretion of the preacher. So also in the administration of the Sacraments and conferring Holy Orders, a portion of the office might be fixed and invariable, and a portion left to ministering pastors.

These points being settled, the trial, nomination, institution, or designation of pastors, the dissolution of their connection with their flock, or removal, their mode of payment, the internal discipline of the congregation over their members and officers, are details which may well be left for after regulation; if, indeed, there is really much, or any, injurious difference at present existing in these matters.

A spirit of mutual forbearance and real affection must be largely shed abroad before such a system as here spoken of can possibly be inaugurated. Even if thought feasible for the future, how can it be made to take retrospective effect ? How can we, who are *de facto* ministers, and think ourselves to be *de jure* so, besides being pledged to our respective systems, throw ourselves out of the one to enter upon the other ?

Let us search the Scripture for guidance. The beloved disciple was instructed to write by the Holy Spirit to the seven angels of the seven churches of Asia, and Titus was left by St. Paul in Crete to ordain elders in every city as he had appointed him. But besides these later exertions of apostolic authority, we find Barnabas and Saul separated by the Holy Ghost to a special mission through the laying on of hands, and prayers, of the prophets and teachers of the Church at Antioch, Simon, Niger, Lucius of Cyrene, and Manarn.

Assuming the existing ministers of the several denominations to be recognised *de jure* by their congregations, and *de facto* as such by the Anglican Church, might not the Bishops of the latter, supposing the before-mentioned terms of union were agreed upon, to take effect prospectively, give the right hand of fellowship to them, that they should go to their own flocks and mission, also as preachers to the Anglican congregations, when invited by the pastors of the several Churches? If the licence of the Bishop can authorise even lay readers and preachers, how much more men like yourself separated to the work of God, eloquent and mighty in the Scriptures ! Indeed, I do not feel sure that I should have violated any ecclesiastical law in force in this diocese or province, by inviting you to give a word of exhortation to each of our congregations.[*]

In this way, then, of union without compromise, but on declared assent to certain fixed principles and truths, existing ministers might co-operate with us in the preaching of the Gospel, and under the benign influence of this brotherly love, a Reformed Catholic Church might grow up, and, like the rod of Aaron, swallow up our sectarian differences.

20. I have said nothing about hypothetical ordination, which has been suggested (like conditional baptism where irregularity in the administration may be suspected), because it savours of evasion or collusion, neither of which is agreeable to Christian simplicity and due reverence for God's ordinances. Neither have I suggested the consecration as Bishops of existing Wesleyan Superintendents and Presbyterian Moderators, or those who, like yourself, seem sealed alike by nature and the Spirit to be special overseers in the Church of God. Missions, as preachers to our congregations, without imposing the obligations incident to the incumbents and curates of churches, but not until full evidence had been given before licence of soundness in the faith, would seem to meet the exigencies of the case so far as regards the present generation of ministers who have received Presbyterian orders.

Having attained to this step, perhaps God would reveal to us a yet more excellent way. Old systems have, in fact, been found wanting.

---

[*] Canon 51 of the Province of Canterbury, A.D. 1603-4, requires "conformity as a *sine quâ non* to preaching in the parish churches of England." I do not know that it is binding in colonial dioceses. It shows that persons were licensed to preach who were not disposed to take upon themselves all the obligations of the parish priest under the Establishment.

Which of the Churches now existing is so perfect, so Scriptural, so apostolic, as to insure instant acquiescence from the inquirer to the exclusion and condemnation of all others? If there be none, will all the learning, and eloquence, and traditional authority devoted to the support of each persuade the present or future generations to substitute another for that in which they have been brought up? A few may perhaps be convinced or converted, but the masses never. A fresh combination must, therefore, be sought; traditional prejudices must be set aside; cherished associations laid upon the altar of love, to rise, like angel messengers, in the flame of sacrifice, to purer and loftier spirituality! Oh, for that millennial reign of peace when a Chalmers or a Cumming, a Binney or a Watson, might serve at one altar and plead from one pulpit with the Bishops and the clergy of the Church of England! It is the cause of God and Christ, of truth and holiness, of righteousness and peace, of faith and duty, of grace and salvation, of man delivered and Satan bound, of God alone exalted on that day, and reigning on Mount Sion gloriously. Then might the fulness of the Gentiles come in, then Israel be restored, then Babylon overthrown, and that regenerated state of this fallen world be made manifest for which Jehovah reserved the last great display of His providential love—the union in the God-man of the Manhood with Himself.

I remain, dear Sir, respectfully yours,
AUGUSTUS ADELAIDE.

The publication of this letter evoked considerable discussion, and it was regarded as a very important step towards the attainment of Christian union. The conclusion was by many jumped at, that the Bishop merely wanted a formal request from the members of the Church to induce him to invite Mr. Binney to preach in the churches. The fact that his Lordship had distinctly said, in the sixth paragraph, that neither Mr. Binney's intellect, or other talents, would "justify him in departing from the rule of the Church of England," was overlooked, and a Memorial was drawn up and signed by Sir Richard Mac-Donnell (the Governor), and sixty other leading church-

men, asking the Bishop to invite Mr. Binney, " previous to
his departure from Adelaide, to fill one of our pulpits in
this city ; in the belief that Christian union and Christian
love will be thereby promoted and diffused in the hearts of
those who, holding the like faith in the great saving
doctrines of our common religion, have hitherto been
kept asunder by differences in matters of form and discipline."

Directly after writing Mr. Binney, the Bishop had
started for several weeks' tour in the north, and it was not
possible to forward this memorial to him, while he could
scarcely have anticipated the course that was adopted.
Under these circumstances, the Memorialists applied to the
Dean and Chapter, inquiring whether, in the Bishop's
absence, they could give authority for Mr. Binney to preach
in the churches. That body having met to consider the
matter, forwarded the following :—

It was resolved unanimously that it is not within the province of
the Dean and Chapter to comply with the above request.

JAMES FARRELL,
October 19th, 1858.   Chairman.

On October 20th, at a public breakfast to Mr. Binney,
this subject formed the chief topic spoken to, when Sir
Chas. Cooper, the Chief Justice, said he had not signed the
Memorial to the Bishop because he thought it not right to
ask his Lordship to do what the constitution of the
Church forbade his doing. The next day, October 21st,
Mr. Binney wrote the Bishop as follows :—

My Lord Bishop—The letter which your Lordship addressed to me
"on the Union of Protestant Evangelical Churches," reached me on
the evening of the 5th instant, the day on which you were to leave

Adelaide on a five weeks' tour. . . . I was at the time and
have been ever since quite unable to give it that attention which
its importance demanded, at least so far as writing for your Lordship's eye, or with a view to publication, what might occur to me
on carefully weighing its principles and suggestions. . . . A
very few words must suffice for the present. I beg then to assure
your Lordship that while I highly admire the kind and Christian
feeling that prompted your communication, and cordially sympathise
in the desires and the aspirations after more visible union to which
you have given utterance, I greatly fear that the " idea " you
entertain and would seek to realise includes too much, and not only
too much, but that it has that in its elements which must be
softened or lost sight of before it can find acceptance with others. It
sometimes has the appearance of the old attempts at " comprehension," by which the early Nonconformist used to be solicited back
again to the Episcopal Church ; at others it looks like a wish to form
a "Church of the Future" out of a fusion of the different bodies at
present existing, all altering something, the result being a new order
of things, in which, however, your ecclesiastical peculiarities shall
predominate. Now, without entering into the question as to the
likelihood of this being the case (which, however, I think unlikely),
supposing amalgamation and fusion to occur, I content myself with
saying that it is premature to indulge in visions of the ultimate
before we have taken such steps as are possible to us—the only steps,
perhaps, that may be possible for years to come. What we need
first, before anything else can be thought or hoped, is, *not* the
absorption by one church of others—not the conformity of others to
it, of the toleration by it of the peculiarities of others, nor yet an
attempt to constitute a platform of discipline or service in which all
may give up a little (or *much*, perhaps, in some cases), and unite.
No, it is not this. First and foremost, and *alone*, must come the
honest and hearty recognition of each other, as churches and
ministers (*de facto* only, if you like) by the different Protestant
Evangelical denominations, their members and clergy. Let such
recognition be shown by the occasional interchange of pulpits, and
let *this* again be understood to involve nothing, and simply nothing,
but their substantial oneness in faith, as holding in common the
essential truths of the common salvation. The *liberty* thus to invite
service would compel no one to invite it, nor any to open their

pulpits to persons—good men in their way—whom for many reasons
it might be inexpedient to receive. Then, again, the *rendering* of
service, so far simply as preaching is concerned, should be held to
imply nothing on either side beyond the oneness of faith just referred
to. Had your Lordship, for instance, invited me to preach in the
pulpit of your Church, you ought to have been considered as
committing yourself to nothing but to the recognition in me of
a preacher of that Gospel which we hold in common, and of a
minister of Christ according to the constitution of that portion of
the church to which I belong. It is obvious, also, that I could not
have been required to receive any *licence* from your Lordship; you
would not have become my bishop, though you are one in your own
communion, and I respect you as such. Those who would have
needed your licence would have been your own clergy ; *they* might
have wanted your permission to act. In the same way, neither you
nor they would have been so far compromised as justly to be regarded as giving your sanction to notions or customs among the
Congregationalists of which you may disapprove, anymore than I, by
consenting to preach the Gospel to your flocks, should have been
justly supposed by that to profess *anything else*—to accept for
instance that interpretation of your "*offices*" (I distinguish them from
the Liturgy) which involves sentiments which I do not hold; which
sentiments if required to be held and professed, are, in my view, an
adequate ground of clerical nonconformity. No church, either,
whatever, should suppose that it confers a favour on the minister of
another by receiving him to its pulpits, but rather that it does what
is proper and seemly for itself. When something of this sort is understood, and the first step taken in harmony with it, other things will
follow. All other things and theories, however, must, I fear, be postponed till this be done. I believe it might be done by very many of the
Protestant churches in relation to each other—done without compromise and without dishonour ; and that great and blessed results
would soon follow from it. That your Lordship may have the
happiness of helping in so desirable a consummation, and may thus
realise that after which your spiritual nature seems to yearn and
pant, is the sincere prayer of,

My Lord,

Your friend and servant in common faith,

T. Binney.

This letter, with copies of other correspondence, reached the Bishop while on his return journey, and must have occasioned him no little surprise. He replied as follows:

Anama, November 5th, 1858.

Dear and Reverend Sir—On my arrival yesterday at this place, I received your note accompanied by a printed copy of our correspondence. . . . I should have preferred to receive from you, at your leisure, the matured conclusions of your judgment on the interesting topic to which I have drawn attention. . . . If I have doubts how far the Ecclesiastical Statute Law of the Established Church of England is applicable to this or other Colonial Dioceses, I have none as respects its spirit, nor of the inspired authority of the apostolic "tradition of eighteen centuries" on which that law is founded. . . . I could not, therefore, nor can I, feel justified in departing from that traditionary rule, even in your case. Had I felt sure that no Statute Law would have been violated, I should not have transgressed the "custom" of our Church without first consulting the Metropolitan and other Bishops of Australasia, as well as the Archbishop of Canterbury; consequently I think I ought not to have been invited by those high in authority in this colony to take a step on my own responsibilty which, though possibly not an actual, would at least have been a virtual, transgression of the law of our Church. . . . Having stated why I was unable to invite you to preach to our congregations, I took occasion from thence to urge a consideration of the terms on which at some future time, possibly, that inability might be removed. The indispensable conditions appeared to me to be three—

    (a) The acceptance in common by the Evangelical Churches of the orthodox creed.

    (b) The use, in common, of a settled liturgy, though not to the exclusion of free prayer, as provided for in the Directory of the Assembly of Divines at Westminster.

    (c) An Episcopate freely elected by the United Evangelical Churches, not (as I have been misapprehended) exclusively by our own.

No notice, however, was taken of these preliminary conditions in the Memorial addressed to me. Without them, there would be no security against the intrusion even of heretical preachers in our pulpits.

I am, dear Sir,

Truly and respectfully yours,

AUGUSTUS ADELAIDE.

This, of course, settled the question asked by the Memorial, the original of which the Bishop did not receive till some time afterwards. A Counter-Memorial was also handed to his Lordship, signed by one hundred and sixty-two members of the Church, designed to strengthen his hands under the difficulty which had arisen.

On this subject, my view has always been, that the numerous dissenting bodies should first amalgamate, and become reduced to two, or perhaps three, bodies. When this shall have been accomplished, it will be time enough for the Church to consider her relation to those bodies, or any of them. She could hardly be expected to acknowledge and confer with each and every of the numerous sects now existing. Then, too, as to the vague idea respecting the admission of dissenting ministers to officiate in the churches, which is by many clamoured for—I fail to see that its being acceded to would be in any way a guarantee for, or tend to promote, unity among the different religious bodies. The reverend gentlemen composing the Ministerial Association, I believe, frequently exchange pulpits; but I am not aware that their so doing has brought about anything like organic unity between the various bodies they represent What ground, therefore, is there for the idea so often urged that the occupancy of the Church of England pulpits by those gentlemen, or any of them, would be attended with a different result ? If pulpit interchange

among themselves be a failure in respect to union of the
sects, why should interchange with the Church be expected
to be anything else ? The allegation so often made, that
the position occupied by the National Church, and
especially her not admitting ministers of other bodies to
occupy her pulpits, constitutes the great bar to Christian
union is, to my mind, a mere bald assertion, without
a scintilla of fact or reason to support it. Akin to such
random assertion is an illustration I have more than
once heard on the Bible Society's platforms to the effect
that the different religious bodies may be compared to the
regiments of an army, diverse in uniforms and equipments,
using different weapons, but all working to one end, the
salvation of souls, and under one head, even Christ Jesus.
But they who use this *simile* omit to say that the regiments of an army never intentionally fire into each other's
ranks, denounce each other's principles of action, cross each
other's tracks, or seek to cajole members from one
regiment to another. In fact, the *simile*, as generally used,
is but a piece of claptrap, though I quite believe some who
use it do not see it in that light. While, therefore, exceedingly anxious to see less division among religious bodies, I
fail to see how throwing open the pulpits of the Church to
the ministers of other bodies indiscriminately, could in any
way conduce to that end ; I say indiscriminately, because I
do not see how. were the ministers of one body admitted,
others could be excluded, whether presumably orthodox, or,
as some are alleged to be, absolutely heterodox.

CHAPTER XIX.

ALTERATIONS IN THE MANNER OF CONDUCTING DIVINE SERVICE.

WHEN Bishop Short arrived, and for some time after, it was the custom for clergymen, after reading the liturgy, to change the surplice for a black gown in which to preach. This had been the universal custom in England till, as a result of the movement commenced by Messrs. Newman, Froude, Pusey, and others, preaching in the surplice began to be practised by those accepting their views, it being regarded as a party badge. I well remember the late Lord Brougham saying in regard to the disputation that arose on this matter, that " if the only difference of opinion were, as to the propriety of a clergyman preaching in a black gown or a white one, it augured well for the soundness of the Church's teaching and doctrine," or words to that effect. While this custom of changing the surplice for the gown before sermon was practicable, and long continued in the Adelaide and other town churches, it was soon found impracticable in country places. A clergyman having to officiate at perhaps two or three churches—in a barn, court-house, or other temporary place of worship—and often riding twenty or thirty miles, found it very inconvenient to carry a gown strapped on his saddle in addition to other requirements, while few outlying places had vestries, or other convenience for changing ; I soon left off carrying mine. From its simply being more convenient, therefore, and not at all as a badge of party, the surplice became generally used in country places for the entire service; the town churches ultimately adopted the same custom. Bands, however, continued to be worn by all the clergy during Bishop Short's episcopate, the admirable portrait of his Lordship in the Church Office showing what his " use " was. His successor, Bishop Kennion, however, not using them, the clergy gradually followed his example, so that the old custom of a clergyman preaching in gown and bands, so far as the Diocese of Adelaide is concerned, has wholly passed away. The morning service, too, at first followed that of England, viz., morning prayer, litany, ante-communion, and sermon, and monthly administration of communion afterwards. This being found too long, it became customary to alternate the litany and ante-communion, omitting one or the other.

In a few years, the accession of clergy brought in some who introduced changes in the manner of conducting service which were watched by the laity with a jealous eye. These changes now and then generated much ill-feeling, sometimes resulting in actual conflict. The trustees and wardens of one church went so far as to padlock the church door against the clergyman, refusing to let him continue officiating. During this collision, the Bishop requested me to go to that church to marry a couple whose banns had been published there. On reaching it, I found the box containing the registers and service-books had been removed to the adjacent school-room, I believe by the clergyman, who had held a service or two there, when unable to gain admission to the church. Going to the school, I found the box, and requested the teacher, whom I had trained and placed there, to lend me a couple of boys to carry it to the church, which he readily did. On the way, we were met by a fussy individual, who demanded—" Pray, sir, by what authority are you removing that box ? " My reply naturally was—" Pray, sir, by what authority do you inquire ? " Somewhat non-plussed, he said he was a warden, or trustee, I forget which, and that it was his duty to look after the property of the church. I told him the Bishop had sent me to marry a couple, that the books were needed, and that I would leave the box, &c., in the vestry, then walked in and left him, evidently much chagrined, for my action, as a legal friend afterwards told me, and as indeed I intended, had spoiled a pretty little law-suit. On reporting the incident to the Bishop he was pleased and amused.

In another instance, so strong ran the strife, that a leading layman at a vestry meeting declared, that were it not for the clergyman's cloth, he would give him a sound thrashing ; to which the not very clerical reply was—" If you like to step outside, my cloth shall not be in the way, for I will pull my coat off." The matter ended without blows through the intervention of others, but the clergyman had to vacate the cure. In another instance, contention arose, issuing in protracted litigation, whereby a considerable part of an endowment bequeathed to a church became sacrificed to defray law costs; the clergyman ultimately leaving the diocese. These, of course, were somewhat extreme cases. But when such results, differing only in degree, follow from a clergyman's introducing novelties, reviving obsolete customs, or diverging in any material degree from the ordinary routine of service, it is hard to conceive that any benefit supposed to follow such divergence can outweigh the positive injury done, advance the interests of the Church, or contribute to the spiritual well-being of its members.

The Bishop, in 1869, gave some formal decisions and directions in regard to certain changes that had been introduced, printed copies of which were forwarded to all the clergy. Complaint had been made that the usual collect or short prayer before sermon had been omitted; that when saying the creed, the clergyman turned to the communion-table, having his back to the congregation; that he bowed every time the name of Jesus occurred during the service; that when administering holy communion he stood and knelt at the middle of the table, with his back to the people; and that the "Grace of our Lord Jesus Christ," &c., was omitted after sermon when communion was to be administered, before non-communicants left the church. Of these several complaints the Bishop dealt first with "kneeling at the middle of the table to receive the communion, with back to the people."

Two pleas were advanced to justify reception of the communion in this particular manner—viz., that it was *more convenient* for the minister to so receive, and that the rubric directing the minister to "stand at the north-side of the table" might be held to mean at the northern part of the front of the table. Respecting these pleas, the Bishop decided as follows, "in order to appease diversity and resolve doubts":—

Kneeling at the Table after consecration of the elements in order "to receive the communion, *with back to the people*," . . . appears to me to be *prohibited by implication*. It is most liable to misconstruction, and has given offence. . . . At the beginning of the Order for Holy Communion, the Rubric directs the priest to "stand at the North-side of the table." Two explanations are given of this *North-side*. The *customary position* during the *whole* of my *life and experience* as a clergyman, fixes the meaning to the North *end* of the Table. . . . It is not necessary to enter into an antiquarian research as to whether the " North-side " means the North-side of the Table's front, . . . or centre part of that front. It is enough that the " North-side " was understood to mean the North *end* so long ago as 1637, both in the English and Scotch Prayer-books. The custom, therefore, of more than one hundred and fifty years leads me to accept the North-side of the table at which the Rubric directs the priest to stand, as the North *end* of it. *There* he is to " stand or kneel " at different parts of the office up to the Prayer of Consecration ; when the Rubric directs that " standing before the Table" he is so to order the bread and wine that he may with the more readiness and decency " break the bread *before the people*," and "take the cup into his hands." To comply with these directions, he *must* go from the North end to " before the Table." He is then to " order the bread and wine " so that he may the more readily " break the bread before the people," and " take the cup into his hands," and " also lay his hand upon every vessel in which there is any wine to be consecrated." What is the meaning of breaking the bread " *before the people* " but that he may " be seen of the people ?"

Bearing in mind that our Order for Holy Communion and its Rules were *reformed* from the " Canon of the Mass and the Rites of celebrating it," our Rubrics, both in what *they direct* and in what *they omit*, have a special meaning. Being also *legal* enactments, they cannot be broken with impunity, as matters indifferent.

In celebrating Mass, the Priest is directed to stand *before the middle of the Altar*, and there to say the prayer and do the acts of consecration " *secrete*," secretly, *i.e.*, either *unseen or unheard* of the people. He then rises and shows the consecrated host to the people. In like manner he consecrates and shows the cup. Can there be any reasonable doubt that " before the people " in *our* Rubric was intended to supersede the " *secrete* " of the Roman service? Having so ordered the bread on the paten and the wine in the chalice and other vessels, the officiating minister is to lay his hands on the bread and on every vessel " before the people," *i.e.*, *in their sight ;* and say the prayer of consecration *audibly*, *i.e.*, in their hearing. For this purpose he must return to the North end of the Table, *where* from the beginning of the office he was directed to stand. He is forbidden by the 20th Article to " lift up " the Sacrament, which he must do if, standing with *his back* to the people, he is yet to consecrate " so as to be seen by them ;" or, he must turn himself toward them when consecrating. Standing at the North end of the Table, he avoids both lifting up and *secret* consecration with back to the communicants. *There*, then, he should himself receive the elements, and so distribute them to the clergy and people.

The plea of *convenience*, therefore, as the reason for *kneeling* down in *front* of the Table, and then receiving with *back* to the people, is groundless. It is an alteration "contrary," apparently, to the meaning of the Rubric, and so to the law; contrary to the accustomed practice. It is open to reasonable suspicion, as compatible with "adoration of the elements." Therefore, to "appease" the "diversity" of practice, which has caused doubts and variance, I direct the minister to discontinue his practice of receiving the elements after consecration kneeling in front of the Communion Table with his back to the people, and of saying all the prayers of the Communion Service in that position. I direct him, "standing before the Table," so to order the bread and wine that he may with more readiness and decency break the bread *before the people, i.e.*, the better to be seen of them, and take the cup into his hands, then to return to the end of the Table commonly known as the North-side, where the priest at the beginning of the Order for Holy Communion is directed to stand, and where the Gospel is accustomed to be read, and *there* say the prayer of consecration.

I proceed to the other alterations complained of, and in connection with the preceding subject will consider "turning to the Communion Table at the time of saying the Belief." This practice is defended on the ground that it is "customary to turn towards the *East*" when we repeat the Creed; and that churches in England are generally built East and West. . . . The rule of "orientation" in building churches, though usual in England, is not universal in the Eastern Church. It is not the rule of the Latin or Western Church. It is not the rule of this Diocese. To turn towards the Communion Table in the churches here is not identical with "turning to the East."

Turning, then, towards the Communion Table in this Diocese while repeating the Creed is not to preserve what is Anglican or Catholic. It is liable to be confounded with the practice of the Roman Church, which directs lowly reverence to be made to the altar, as the throne of the Redeemer corporeally present on it in transubstantiated bread. Misprision, therefore, of false doctrine may be fastened on this turning to the Communion Table, which it is well to avoid. The truer notion of the sanctity of holy places is well stated by a learned monk and ecclesiastic, Walafrid Strabo, writing in the ninth century—" *Non est ubi non sit Deus* " (there is no place where God may not be) : some, perhaps, limiting His presence to the altar. A devout saying of the Creed is possible, no matter in what direction the officiating minister faces. Turning to the Communion Table is not " ordered." It is not " prohibited." It is in the category of those things in which, if doubt arises how to execute the Book of Common Prayer, the Bishop is by his " discretion" to take order for their resolution, and to " appease diversity."

In a matter like this, indifferent in its nature, the rule of St. Paul surely applies, . . . " let us follow the things which make for peace, and things wherewith one may edify another." I do *not* know that turning to the Communion Table is edifying. I *do* know that it *does not* " make for peace." Although " turning to the East while the Creeds are read," Sir R. Phillimore says, has been " allowed," yet " turning to the Communion Table" whenever it does not stand *towards* the East, *may* have an entirely different interpretation. I therefore " direct " the minister for " peace " sake to discontinue the practice of turning to the Communion Table when saying the Creeds : inasmuch as in his church, as well as many of the churches of the Diocese, to do *so* is *not* to turn toward the East.

Under the like rule of St. Paul appears to me to fall another " alteration " and practice complained of, namely " bowing the head on every occasion of the name of Jesus." In defence of this custom is pleaded the direction contained in the 18th Canon, " that lowly reverence shall be done by all persons present, as it hath been accustomed ; testifying by these outward ceremonies and gestures their inward humility and due acknowledgment that the Lord Jesus Christ, the true and eternal Son of God, is the only Saviour of the World." This usage, however, is neither " ordered " nor " prohibited " by the Book or its Rules. The Canons of the Province of Canterbury have no legally binding force either in England or in the Diocese of Adelaide. The Canon of 1604 states that such reverence at the name of Jesus " hath been accustomed." According to my experience it has been *restricted* (till of late years) to bowing the head when the name of Jesus Christ is mentioned in the

Creed. *There* it is a recognition by the congregation of our Lord's *divine* nature, and of our immediate relation to him as his redeemed servants. I am inclined to think that the oft-repeated reverence in other parts of the service savours of a "voluntary humility"—and detracts from the solemnity and force of that special act of devotion in the Creeds. The latter I would in nowise give up; the former, having never been accustomed to notice till of late in any church or cathedral at home, I think may be discontinued without loss of edification. An inward reverence may still be maintained by the priest and the people, without danger of falling into formality, or the parade of humility. I advise, therefore, in the interest of peace and to "avoid giving offence," to make due and lowly reverence at the name of Jesus Christ when saying the Creeds, and do not think it obligatory at *every* mention of the name in the service.

Respecting the "omission of prayer before sermon." There is no Rubric which "directs" such prayer to be offered. It is not, therefore, "ordered;" neither is it "prohibited;" but may be regarded as "subsidiary" (to use the language of Sir R. Phillimore) to what is "ordered;" for if "to preach the word" is the bounden duty of every Minister who has the care of souls, to pray for grace to preach the word faithfully, and that the people may hear and receive it to their edification, can *never be out of place* when the preacher is about to enter on that duty. Moreover, it has the sanction of the 55th Canon. But, "doubt having arisen in the use and practice of this matter," and such doubt having been brought under my notice, I, in the exercise of my "discretion" direct that "preachers and ministers shall, before all sermons, lectures and homilies, move their people to join with them in prayer," after the accustomed manner. (55th Canon.)

As to "omission" of "blessing at the end of the prayer for the Church militant" when the Holy Communion is administered. No such grace or blessing is "ordered" at the conclusion of the sermon nor at the end of the prayer for the Church militant, when the non-communicants (if there be a Communion) leave the church: And if there be no communion, one or more of the Collects shall be read "*concluding*" with the blessing." When there is a Communion, the introduction of "The grace of our Lord Jesus Christ, &c.," breaks the continuity of the office for Holy Communion.

.　　.　　.　　It is not " subsidiary to anything ordered, but rather contrary to the Order and Rules of the Book. It is not " in accordance with primitive and Catholic use," even if it were itself proper ; for in Apostolic times, when the disciples came together on the first day of the week to break bread (as at Troas, when Paul preached to them) it is not to be imagined that any left the assembly, or continually absented themselves from the Lord's Table. It appears to me, therefore, that it would be beyond the limits of that " discretion " which the Ecclesiastical Law of the Church of England assigns to the Bishop, if I were to " direct " a minister to introduce such a " benediction." Such direction could not be *enforced*, nor could neglect to obey the monition, if issued, be such " contumacy " as the Law would visit with Ecclesiastical penalties. . . . I may add, that it is not the custom in the Diocese of Melbourne to introduce the " grace " at the end of the prayer for the Church militant.

Subsequently, after a visit to England, in his Pastoral Address in April 1869, his Lordship said—

I shall confine my address to subjects which touch upon the spiritual well-being of our Church. 　.　　.　　. 　Among those subjects Ritualism at this time occupies a most prominent place, although it is difficult concisely to define what is meant by that comprehensive term. It is impossible, however, to be ignorant of the alarm which innovations in church vestments and ceremonial acts—and much more in certain teaching concerning the Sacrament of the Lord's Supper—have aroused at home, and which, like a tidal wave, has burst upon every shore on which the Church of England has planted itself.

After speaking of the greater attention given to daily prayers, more frequent celebrations of Holy Communion, and other beneficial effects of what is sometimes called the " Oxford Movement," his Lordship said—

New-born zeal is not always wise. Then followed the adoption of forms, rules, and manuals of devotion borrowed from Romish sources, and not always free from Roman error. But it was not until the open adoption of corresponding rites and vestments that the great body of churchmen became aware of the Romanising tendencies of a small but active party in the Church.

Proceeding to give an elaborate explanation of the Holy Eucharist, his Lordship concluded thus—

I have entered more fully into these particulars respecting the doctrine of the Church of England because of the great confusion of thought and misunderstanding of terms prevalent concerning it. Our Articles neither reduce the ordinance to a mere memorial form, nor admit a *bodily* presence or atoning sacrifice therein. Rather, we "keep a feast" upon the sacrifice once offered for the "strengthening and refreshing of our souls by the spiritual body and blood of Christ," . . . "feeding on him by faith with thanksgiving." Such being, to the best of my judgment, the teaching set forth in the Articles and Prayer-book, I am clearly of opinion that all ceremonial acts, ornaments of the Church, or minister, at the time of celebration designed to teach or imply a different doctrine, are illegal, unfaithful, and disloyal to our Church. May the Holy Spirit keep us from such error, which is the certain source of division and weakness, and falling away.

On the matters referred to, Bishop Short's opinions, decisions, and directions were clear and unmistakable, and it would have been for the best interests of the Church here had they been universally acted on. Since my retirement, having had opportunity of worshipping at different churches, I observe that instead of compliance therewith, there has arisen in many places a spirit of unrest and anxiety for change, leading to the introduction, often very insidiously, of most of the things his Lordship condemned, and others in addition. Many of such alterations can hardly be regarded otherwise than as frivolous, unless indeed they are intended to be, as many suppose them to be, indicative of a desire to assimilate the services and teachings of the Church of England, so far as possible, to the services and teachings of the Church of Rome. A few illustrations will show what I mean. The ordinary full-length surplice has become superseded by a very short and scanty one, necessitating the wearing of a cassock; the plain black stole is discarded in many instances for coloured ones, varied according to the Church's seasons, often elaborately ornamented with crosses and fringes; a few clergy adopt the biretta. I saw no coloured or ornamented stoles in Melbourne, or elsewhere in Victoria, nor the biretta.

The chancel and communion-table have undergone considerable change, the Commandments, Creed, and Lord's Prayer being often discarded. In place of the original plain table, a so-called "altar" is constructed, at the back of which is a shelf or "reredos," bearing a cross and vases of flowers, often backed by some work of art, with curtains on each side. The former plain cloth or velvet covering for the table and cushions for the books have given place to richly ornamented coverings and frontals, changed according to the seasons. Such elaborate ornamentation being bestowed upon the "altar" naturally tends to beget in many minds, and presumably is intended to beget, a greater degree of reverence for the thing itself than was originally sought to be engendered in respect to the communion-table. This is exemplified by some clergymen whenever approaching or passing the "altar," making a devout obeisance thereto, and crossing themselves, while some members of the congregation do likewise on entering and leaving the church. In what sense the "altar" is by such regarded, appears to be at least doubtful. Of course the word itself, strictly interpreted means, that whereon a *sacrifice* is offered. But the Church of England ignores the doctrine of a *sacrifice* being offered in the celebration of holy communion. The word "altar" is not to be found in her liturgy, and its use, therefore, cannot in its *strict sense* be regarded as consistent with her teaching. The term is consistently used by the Roman Church, which teaches that her priests do continually *offer sacrifice* in the mass. To whom, therefore, or to what, acts of homage are tendered by our clergy and others in bowing to the "altar" is by no means clear; indeed I doubt if some who make a point of so doing have any distinct idea on the matter. It might be well if those who apparently deem this a duty, or indication of deep piety, were to put to themselves the question: "To whom or to what is my obeisance rendered?" The Romanist, believing that in the transubstantiated bread the Saviour is corporeally present on the altar, has a definite object that he deems worthy of homage. But the declaration at the close of our communion service explicitly states that "no adoration is intended or ought to be done either to the sacramental bread or wine there bodily received, or unto any corporeal presence of Christ's natural flesh and blood. For the sacramental bread and wine remain still in their very natural substances, and therefore may not be adored, for that were idolatry to be abhorred of all faithful Christians." Then, as the bread and wine are on the communion-table only during celebration of the sacrament, it cannot be always to them that obeisance is tendered.

As the communion-table has become an "altar," so the term "clergyman" or "minister" of the church or district is becoming changed to "priest-in-charge." This, I take it, is intended to convey something more than our common phraseology attributes to the term "priest" as distinguished from "deacon," especially as the doctrine of sacrifice in connection with holy communion is by some advocated. How far it is justifiable to apply the term "priest" in its *strict* sense to ministers of the Gospel may perhaps be best stated in the words of the "judicious Hooker." In his Ecclesiastical Poetry, book v., ch. lxxviii., § 2 and 3, he says—

Touching the ministry of the Gospel of Jesus Christ ; the whole body of the Church being divided into laity and clergy, the clergy are either presbyters or deacons. I rather term the one sort Presbyters than Priests because in a matter of so small moment I would not willingly offend their ears to whom the name of Priesthood is odious, though without cause.   .   .   .   When learned men declare what the word *Priest* doth *properly* signify, *according to the mind of the first imposer of that name*, their ordinary scholies do well expound it to imply sacrifice. Seeing then that sacrifice is now no part of the Church ministry, how should the name of Priesthood be thereunto rightly applied ? To this a footnote is appended—"For so much as the common and usual speech of England is to note by the word *Priest* not a minister of the Gospel but a sacrificer, which the minister of the Gospel is not, therefore we ought not to call the ministers of the Gospel Priests. And that this is the English speech it appeareth by all the English translations, always *hiereis*, which were sacrificers, Priests, and do not on the other side translate *presbuteros* a *priest*." (P.C. lib. i., p. 198.)

The word priest is but a contraction of "presbyter," perhaps through the French "prestre ;" the translation of *presbuteros* throughout the New Testament being "elder," and never corresponding to *hiereis*, a "sacrificer." When, therefore, the designation "priest" is so strongly insisted on in connection with "altar," the suspicion is not altogether unjustifiable that the Romanist idea of a sacrifice is sought to be re-introduced and foisted upon our communion service. This suspicion is not diminished when lighted candles are used at the administration of the sacrament, and sometimes incense, with, apparently, a worshipping of the elements.

In many cases water is mixed with the wine in the sacrament, for which I find no authority in either the Scripture or Prayer-book. This mixing has been declared not to be *illegal* if it take place *before the service*. Ordinary minds will be able to discern little difference as to the thing itself, whether it be done *before* the service, or, as by some, *during* the service. The argument as to its legality, and therefore justifiability, in the one case and not in the other, smacks of the Jesuitical. Its being in accordance with the Scripture or the Prayer-book ought to decide the question. As a matter of fact, I know many persons have ceased to communicate where this is done. Then, too, it has become customary with some to carefully cleanse the cup and chalice at the table after celebration, with a great deal of formality, the celebrant solemnly drinking the rinsings; the people not rising from their knees till all this is done and the clergyman retires.

The administration of holy communion in the early morning, which of late years has been introduced, as a mere matter of preference is availed of by many; and where the number of communicants is large is an un-doubted convenience. But when urged as *imperative* or highly desirable in order that the ordinance may be received *fasting*, in accordance with the custom of the Roman Church, it is very apt, taken in connection with other things, to become a means of preparing the worshippers, especially the young, for accepting in full the doctrine of transubstantiation.

Then, too, it is often enjoined that the bread, for which

some substitute a wafer, should be received in the palm of
the left hand, and the right hand placed under it so as to
make the form of a cross. Nearly throughout the communion service many clergy scrupulously maintain what
is called the " eastward " position, *i.e.*, with back to the
people, no matter in what direction the table stands. This
sometimes involves an absurdity. For instance, a brother
clergyman assisting me at a church, the chancel of which
was at the western end, at the reading of the Creed turned
his *back* to the east, reverently bowing toward the west, or
the communion-table; I maintaining the opposite position.
The Adelaide Cathedral standing north-west, bowing
toward or standing before the holy table therein can only
be deemed " eastward " by a figure of speech. Only once
in Melbourne did I observe the so-called eastward position
adopted. When Dr. Torance was inducted by Archdeacon
Langley to the cure of St. John's Church, Latrobe-street—
at a choral evening service by apparently combined choirs
—a very large number of clergy were present, but none
turned toward the table at the reciting of the Creed; at
Elsternwick church, where I several times officiated, it
was never done.

The position of the reading-desk, too, in many churches
has been changed. Instead of facing the congregation
when reading the Liturgy, the minister stands *sidewise* to
them, so that in a large church it is difficult for him to be
heard at the further end. In reading the Lessons, however,
with the Commandments, Epistle. and Gospel, he faces the
people. Hence we have three positions adopted: the
minister standing sidewise to the people when reading the
Liturgy; facing them when reading the Scripture, and
preaching; and turning his back to them during the Communion Service. The special advantage of these altera-

tions of position I leave those who adopt them to explain.

Where the "eastward" position is strictly observed during the administration of holy communion, the bread is not broken "before the people" according to the rubric, it being impossible for the communicants to see either paten or bread till the priest, after consecration, holds them up as high as he can. I have often seen this done, both with the bread and the wine, although the twenty-eighth Article expressly forbids the elements being "lifted up."

The most marked illustration that I have witnessed of the alterations that are made in administering holy communion was at St. Oswald's Church, Parkside. My attention was called to an advertisement in the *Register* of May 30th, 1893, which read as follows :—"Confraternity of the Blessed Sacrament. — Annual Festival. — Corpus Christi (June 1). High Celebration at St. Oswald's, Parkside, 10 a.m." Desirous of learning why this festival of the Roman Church was being introduced into the Church of England, and witnessing a "high" celebration, I attended the service.

On entering the church, I observed the "altar" and "reredos" profusely decorated with flowers; in the centre a large cross; with four candles on each side of the sacramental vessels. A large wooden cross stood at one side of the table and a banner at the other. Leaflets were distributed containing the Agnus Dei, and versicles, to be sung during the service. An acolyte in red proceeded to the chancel, lit the candles, and brought the cross and banner from beside the table to the vestry, near the front door. A procession of surpliced choristers and clergy entered, singing, the cross being borne in front by the acolyte, and the banner bringing up the rear. On reaching the chancel, all devoutly crossed themselves and filed off to their respective places. The celebrant wore a biretta, and richly ornamented chasuble, precisely like a Roman priest. Handing his biretta to the acolyte, who kept at his elbow throughout, the celebrant took the so-called "eastward" position, but facing north. At the prayer of consecration it was simply impossible to see him break the bread; but when he had, as I suppose, so done, still keeping his back to the people, he lifted the paten as high as possible, paused, replaced it on the table, stepped back, and fell on his knees, so completely prostrating that his forehead almost touched the floor, continuing in that position for two or three minutes. Rising, he proceeded to consecrate the wine, which I think he mixed with water, elevating the cup as he did the paten, but not prostrating. After he had partaken, another clergyman from the choir, a deacon, proceeded to the table, and having communicated, was given the cup. The two then, elevating cup and paten as high as possible, turned to the congregation. One lady advanced to the chancel steps and received the elements in both kinds; on which the clergymen returned to the table and proceeded with the service, though another lady had left her seat and advanced into the aisle, evidently with the view of communicating also, but was disappointed. Out of a congregation of quite thirty adults, beside those officiating, there was but *one* communicant, though the rubric distinctly says that "there shall be no communion except *four, or three at the least,* communicate with the priest." The service closed with a very elaborate ceremony of "ablution," as the leaflet expressed it—quite a distinct service, lasting about ten minutes—while verses were being sung. The sermon did

not explain why this particular festival of the Roman
Church was being celebrated in an English Church, though
it was emphatically declared that Christ would be then
and there " miraculously " present on the "altar." Those
officiating retired as they had entered—singing in procession, with cross and banner. The whole thing seemed
to be an imitation of the Roman mass, minus the Latin.
I have since been informed that such services have been
held in other churches, and that censers and incense from
the Roman Church have been borrowed to make them the
more complete. One clergyman applied to a dignitary of
the Roman Church for a supply of wafers for sacramental
purposes; he was promptly refused, and very properly
told that if he held the views expressed, he ought to join
that Church. He, however, attained his end surreptitiously,
by writing to some nuns, requesting them to forward a
supply of wafers, signing himself " priest," and they,
little dreaming that any one not a priest of their own
Church would make such request, complied, to their
after intense mortification. These things serve to show to
what lengths those will go who become subjects of this
strange infatuation, if I may so call it.   •

Another step towards Romanising the Church has been
the recent placing of a large crucifix in the Cathedral.
Quite lately, too, I discovered that what I had supposed
to be a simple cross on the communion-table of a church,
has on it an image of the Saviour, so small as not to be
observable at a little distance. This introduction of images
for the people to bow to in direct violation of the second
commandment should certainly be stopped. It would seem
that the object really aimed at by these things is the
attainment of power and influence akin to those claimed
by the Roman priesthood over their people without incur-

ring sundry disabilities — as celibacy, submission to despotic authority, &c.—to establish in fact an Anglo-Roman Church.

Prayer before sermon has become very generally superseded by the Invocation used in the Roman Church—" In the name of the Father and of the Son and of the Holy Ghost." Why this should be, or upon what authority it has been introduced, I have not been able to ascertain. The 55th Canon distinctly says that " all ministers shall move the people to prayer before sermon and lectures," and Bishop Short expressly enjoined obedience to that Canon. During two visits to Melbourne, I heard the Bishop and Dean of Melbourne in the cathedral each offer prayer before sermon, and the same was done in other churches I visited; the Invocation I heard nowhere. At one church designated " high," there was neither prayer nor invocation, but as the last notes of the hymn died away the clergyman announced his text. That church was three-parts empty.

At one time it became customary with many clergy to close morning service when there was no communion with the prayer for the Church militant, so doing being deemed a sign of " high churchism." This, however, has fallen into disuse; many omitting *all* prayer after sermon, and pronouncing only the latter part of the benediction. Whether this omission of prayer before and after sermon and the first half of the benediction is of any special advantage to the worshippers is matter of opinion; I cannot see that it is.

The manner of commencing service, too, has become materially changed. Formerly, the clergyman unostentatiously entered the church from a vestry adjacent to the chancel, proceeding unattended to the reading-desk or chancel. Now, there is often a procession of surpliced choristers, singing, sometimes marching from the front entrance up the length of the church, followed by the clergyman. One such procession I saw headed by two red-robed acolytes bearing a cross; on reaching the chancel all bowed reverently to the " altar " and crossed themselves before filing off to their places. In that church bowing took place at every mention of the name of Jesus, and during the singing of the first verse of the Gloria Patri between the Psalms.

The ordinary reading of the Liturgy is now frequently altered to the monotone, everything in the service, as far as possible, being musically rendered ; the celebration of the Eucharist, too, is often choral. When, as sometimes happens, the clergyman has not a suitable voice, or the choir is inefficient, the effect is unfortunate, and feelings the reverse of reverential are liable to be engendered. The idea that every small church should imitate the cathedral service, I regard as a very mistaken one. So far as my experience enables me to give an opinion, I feel sure that the great majority of worshippers much prefer what is called the plain or ordinary parochial service to an entirely musical one. Some have told me they have ceased attending churches where such services are conducted, because they could not join therein, and that they regarded the musical service as little else than a duet between the clergyman and choir. Then, too, organists and choirs are apt to so arrange that members of the congregation should not join in the singing. An organist of mine complained that persons in the congregation annoyed him and his choir by attempting to sing, and that he wished it could be prevented.

The tendency to convert what was designed to be the

" house of prayer" into a house of singing, not unnaturally
leads those who conduct the music sometimes to regard
themselves as chiefly responsible for the services of the
church, and the clergyman as quite a secondary individual.
Illustrative of this, on an Easter Sunday morning, the
organist of one of my churches on coming into the vestry
to give me the list of hymns, handed me also a sheet of
music for the Litany, saying the choir purposed singing
it that morning, and wished me to do so likewise. I
declined, not being used to it, and not having practised
with the choir. My friend, however — a very efficient
volunteer, to whom we were much indebted for long
and gratuitous service—proved pertinacious, and declared
that unless I complied he would then and there resign,
and leave the church. It was time for service, the church
was full, and many expecting a little special music; so,
for peace sake, I ceded the point, and the service was
carried out as arranged by the organist and choir. I need
hardly say the like did not occur again. Recently, a
young organist commenced drilling his choir into sundry
alterations in the service. Every time the Gloria Patri
occurred between the Psalms they would wheel round and
bow towards the communion-table, at the southern end of
the church; there were also other matters many members
of the congregation objected to the introduction of; consequently some purposed leaving the church. The clergyman having declared the changes had been introduced
without his sanction, the organist was dismissed.

I never adopted the singing of prayers from feeling
that attention to the accurate rendering of the music must
needs interfere with that deep humility of heart and con-
trition of soul which befit those approaching the footstool
of the Almighty. We read of music being employed in the

service of praise in God's earthly courts and by the hosts
of heaven, but not in the offering of prayer, of which the
latter have no need.   On the contrary, penitential periods
among the Jews were always marked by fasting and weep-
ing; clothed sometimes in sackcloth and ashes, and with
downcast countenance, the people were exhorted to appear
before God.   Neither the Pharisee nor the Publican
Christ spoke of in the parable are represented as *singing*
their petitions.

Besides changes in the manner of conducting public
service, doctrinal teaching of an unusual character has
been introduced by some.   Auricular confession is openly
advocated, and I have been told in some cases practised.
I have myself heard praying for the dead preached, as
also that Christ is always mysteriously present in the
ordinance of the Lord's Supper, which was likewise said
to have the character of a sacrifice; ideas pretty well, if
not quite, parallel with the teaching of Rome.

In connection with these alterations, it may be asked,
What course has the Bishop taken in regard to them?   In
considering this point, it has to be borne in mind that the
position of a Bishop under the voluntary system is an exceedingly difficult one.   The theory of the Church of
course is, that a Bishop is responsible for providing for all
in his diocese instruction in the Christian faith, and this
he can only accomplish through the instrumentality of his
clergy.   But there are large numbers who reject his
authority and decline his help—belonging to other religious organisations, or ignoring religion altogether.   Yet,
with his jurisdiction thus reduced, a Bishop must needs
have many and great difficulties to contend with in discharging the duties of his high office.

In the first place, though no clergyman can officiate in

a diocese without a licence from the Bishop of that diocese, in comparatively few instances has the Bishop the power of appointing clergy to cures, the power of appointment generally resting with the trustees or vestries of the churches. Hence, though the Bishop may procure clergy from England or elsewhere, he cannot guarantee their acceptance by congregations; and they, again, naturally hesitate at appointing as permanent pastors those of whom they know nothing. Of late it has been customary for new clergymen to act as chaplains to the Bishop, who appoints them temporarily to mission churches or vacant cures; but many who take such positions fail to become settled in the diocese. Then, in obtaining clergy from home, the Bishop has to depend on others to select for him, and such selections may not always be successful, or there may arise difficulties in inducing suitable candidates to present themselves for employment where so much is necessarily uncertain.

Wherefore, from causes over which he has absolutely no control, a Bishop here must often find himself very awkwardly placed. On the one hand, the various congregations look to him, as having the sole power to licence ministers, to supply them; while on the other, the Bishop must often find it difficult to procure ministers he deems suitable, and cannot rely on such as he may obtain being accepted or retained by the congregations. Naturally anxious, as every Bishop must be, to keep his cures supplied, he may judge it better to occasionally yield to clergymen's proclivities, provided extremes be avoided, rather than interfere where, perhaps, some might think he ought—unless, indeed, a definite complaint or charge is made, as was the case when Bishop Short issued the decisions and directions before quoted.

As to most of the alterations in the manner of conducting service in what are sometimes called *advanced* churches
I have not yet heard anything like a definite statement as
to the actual good likely to be accomplished by those
alterations, or any precise point at which *advancement* is
intended to stop. The mixing of water with the sacramental wine, the substitution of a wafer for the "best
and purest wheat bread that conveniently may be gotten,"
as specified in the rubric, the minister's standing sidewise
or with his back to the people, lifting up the consecrated
elements, and bowing or prostrating to them, with the
cleansing of the vessels and drinking the rinsings after communion, are, to my mind, in no way calculated to engender
increased reverence on the part of the laity, nor is the
adoption of the biretta and chasuble.

Many plead these alterations as justifying their ceasing
to communicate, or to attend church regularly; while not
a few, to my knowledge, have altogether withdrawn themselves, some to attend other places of worship, while more
abstain from worship altogether. For myself, I confess
to having experienced feelings of annoyance at witnessing
some such innovations, and have declined taking part
in conducting services where they are introduced. I
believe that at a few churches where such alterations have
been made, attendances have increased, and the number of
communicants also. But this only occurs in large centres
of population, and when the preacher happens to be popular. I know of no such instances in country districts,
and believe them to be extremely rare. I have heard
persons remark—"Mr. So-and-so is such an excellent
preacher, that we put up with his peculiarities as to
ritual; besides, we are not bound to agree with everything
he says or does." Others have said—"We like to go

where we can hear good music, and don't care for much
else." Hence, through dogmatic perseverance on the part
of some of the clergy, and indifference, or " itching ears,"
on the part of the laity, the young are becoming indoc-
trinated with ideas widely different from the teachings of
Scripture and the Church of England.

Then, too, the prospect of this condition of things becoming altered is not very promising, as many of the
clergy imported display ritualistic tendencies. I remember
a remark of the Rev. J. H. Newman respecting certain
distinguished clergy who opposed the Tractarian movement at its initiation on account of its Romanising character. " We do not expect to convert such men to our
views," said he, " but we intend that they shall become
as extinct as the dodo ; " indicating, of course, what has
since happened—viz., that the clergy of the then future
would be, so far as possible, trained to ritualistic or, as I
think they might be more correctly designated, Romanistic
doctrines and practices.

The late judgment of the Archbishop of Canterbury in
the case of Read v. the Bishop of Lincoln decided that some
things Bishop Short prohibited, and certain other things
that at the said trial were complained of, and which have
of late been practised here, are not *absolutely prohibited*
by the ecclesiastical laws of England, and therefore could
not be declared illegal. His Grace, however, concluded
with these weighty words:—

Public worship is one of the divine institutions which are the
heritage of the Church for the fraternal union of mankind. . . .
The Church, therefore, has a right to ask, that her congregations
may not be divided, either by needless pursuance or exaggerated
suspicion of practices not in themselves illegal. Either spirit is in

painful contrast to the deep and wide desire which prevails for mutual understanding.

It is by "needless pursuance" of sundry of the things before mentioned by some of the clergy that "exaggerated suspicion" becomes engendered, and people are led to withdraw themselves from Church services. What we have to consider, therefore, is, whether certain teachings and practices which the English ecclesiastical laws, as interpreted by lawyers, do not expressly prohibit, but which are commonly understood to be of a more or less Romanistic character or tendency, should be introduced into and made part of the work of our churches? But those laws do not bind the Church in the colonies. Though the Church in England is controlled, and the efforts of the bishops to check innovations are often hampered, by those laws, the Church here is, I conceive, fully at liberty to accept or reject them, or any part of them : also any decisions based on what may be called hair-splitting interpretations of them. The Church here is represented by its Synod ; *it therefore becomes the duty of Synodsmen* to recognise their obligations and responsibilities in regard to these things, and to act accordingly ; to strengthen their Bishop's hands, and prevent the Church being further diminished. Though it is laid down that the clergy have the primary claim to decide upon questions of *doctrine*, I apprehend the laity have an equal claim, and that it is their *imperative duty*, to consider and decide upon the introduction of rites and ceremonies, especially such as are calculated to make our churches little else than chapels-of-ease to Rome.

CHAPTER XX.

THE ABORIGINES.

ON the arrival of the Bishop and his party, it was found that the South Australian Government had by no means neglected its duty in regard to the natives, having appointed Mr. Moorhouse, a duly qualified medical gentleman, as Protector, and a most kind and efficient Protector he proved to be. A number of huts had been erected on the Park Lands for the use of such of the natives as chose to use them, while blankets, &c., were freely supplied. Schools for boys and girls were also established near Government House, and under the able and devoted superintendence of Mr. Ross, were successful in imparting the rudiments of education and of Christianity to large numbers. As a rule, the children learned quickly, but the older ones were frequently induced by adult natives to quit the school and go into the bush, returning after awhile. They were carefully trained in Scripture truth, and there were certainly not wanting instances in which such training produced good results. Some of the girls became domestic servants, usually giving satisfaction until enticed away, resuming their wandering life and native habits; some would cast aside their ordinary clothing, wrap a blanket round them, and stay for a few days or weeks with their tribe in the bush, and returning, adopt again the dress and customs of civilisation.

There were many of the Adelaide tribe about the city and suburbs when we landed, but the earlier settlers spoke

of their having been much more numerous. Naturally one
felt disposed to show every kindness to those whose hunting grounds we had usurped, and they were not slow to
take advantage of this, becoming most persevering mendi-
cants. We often employed them to cut up firewood,
and do other odd jobs, but love of work was certainly not
their forte ; the gentleman usually preferred basking in the
sun, or smoking, while his lubra, or wife, went begging.
With one man my wife had an unpleasant experience. He
had often been employed by us, and at other times had
food given him ; but becoming troublesome, I hoped
on changing residence to be quit of him. But, no ! he
readily tracked the vehicle that conveyed our goods, and
one morning, when I was from home, put in an appearance.
Entering the kitchen where my wife and the servant were
preparing dinner, he stationed himself with his back to the
fire, watching them dress a fowl. Having broken an egg my
wife attempted to throw the shell into the fire-place, but it
unluckily struck the visitor. Instantly he was in a rage,
becoming as pale as a blackfellow well could ; and seizing
a carving-knife made as though he would commence an
attack. Possibly, however, he thought the odds might
prove against him—the servant being present, a tall strong
young woman—so he turned his wrath upon the fowl, and
began sawing away at its leg. On this my wife quietly laid
hold of his wrist, and took the knife away, he offering no
resistance. Had anything like fear been exhibited the result might have been different. A tradesman's cart
arriving just then, the driver was informed of what had
occurred, and requested to get the blackfellow away, which
he did. Asking him why he took the knife, he replied—
" What for lubra throw that at me ? Me plenty kill her."
Of course we took care he did not trouble us again.

The same difficulty existed in respect to the children of the natives when they had completed their school curriculum as occurs with the children of whites—viz., continuing the training begun in school. Just at the age when maintaining a salutary influence over them was most important, they were cast adrift to return to their tribes and habits, or associate with the lower class of whites, often yielding to vice. To remedy this, Archdeacon Hale (afterwards Bishop of Perth, and then of Brisbane) devised a plan for establishing a native missionary station, which with Government assistance he succeeded in carrying out. A suitable block of land being required, thirty-three sections near Port Lincoln were selected, and proclaimed a reserve for the use of the natives, and two other sections bought. On these the Archdeacon, who had undertaken the entire management, with two white assistants, and five young couples of natives from the school in Adelaide, pitched their tents in October 1850. A month previously they had attempted to settle on Boston island, but the absence of fresh water compelled them to leave it. Till they could build huts, the whites had to live in tents, and the natives in wurleys. In due time cottages were erected, fences put up, crops got in, and the usual stock for a small run obtained.

In giving an account of this undertaking in "The Aborigines of Australia," published by the S.P.C.K., Bishop Hale says—

I identified myself with all the pursuits and proceedings of our inmates ; and I did this not only as a policy—it was quite in accordance with my own inclination. I liked to be associated with the men in their work as well as in their recreation. I stood aloof from nothing. I took to bullock-driving as well as ploughing. We were nothing without our bullocks. The manner of our drivers was all kindness and good temper, and the result was, that our bullocks were quiet, obedient, and handy in the extreme. I confess I took the greatest interest in them, and I was soon able to handle them. . . . In my journal, under date April 28th, 1852, I find this entry—"This morning, while Jack was absent looking for some bullocks, and Charley in a different direction, I yoked up a team of six bullocks, and put them into the dray, the first time I have accomplished this feat myself. . . . I was anxious to get the dray ready, that the absent drivers might start for their work at once when they returned."

In 1856, Archdeacon Hale, having practically demonstrated the possibility of christianising the aborigines of this land, surrendered charge of the Institution on which he had expended so much labour, and no little of his personal means, having been called to the Bishopric of Perth. The charge of the Institution then became transferred to the Rev. O. Hammond, who, having been an experienced surgeon, had been ordained with the view of placing the natives in it under combined clerical and medical care. This course was deemed advisable owing to the prevalence of lung disease among them.

In 1858, I made a vacation trip to the settlement, which was called Poonindie, and the impressions derived were embodied in a letter to an Adelaide newspaper, which I append :—

To the Editor of the *Times.*

Sir—Public attention having been frequently drawn to the attempts made to ameliorate the condition of our aboriginal population, and to the Poonindie Native Training Institution in particular, you will perhaps oblige by allowing me to state the result of observations and inquiries made during a recent visit to that Institution.

To prevent misapprehension, I would observe that my visit was strictly of a private character, undertaken partly as a means of relaxation from other duties, and partly with the view of acquiring correct ideas as to the actual condition of the Institution. I was anxious for certain information, from having been asked to preach on its behalf, and from being afterwards applied to for details concerning it, which I was quite unable to furnish.

The depreciatory tone of remark occasionally adopted by the public journals, coupled with statements from parties I thought likely to be well-informed, led me to anticipate finding at Poonindie little more than the remains of a well-intentioned, but almost abortive attempt to improve the social, moral, and religious condition of the natives. The following facts, noted during an eight days' residence there, will show how far such anticipation was justifiable.

On the 28th last December, I first sighted Poonindie, at the distance of about three miles. The impression derived from a distant view of the settlement, prettily situated on a well wooded plain, midway between a range of high hills and the sea, was decidedly pleasing. A cluster of some thirty white cottages glistening in the rays of the setting sun, with what appeared to be a very pretty little church in their midst, brought vividly to mind the village homes of England.

On entering the settlement there was nothing to dispel the pleasurable feelings the distant view called forth. The church, cemetery, Superintendent's residence, cottages of the natives, mill, general kitchen, workshops, stockyards, slaughterhouse, and various other appendages to a combined farming and pastoral establishment, exhibited a general neatness and order which were most gratifying.

At the time of my visit forty-eight natives were residing at Poonindie—viz., twelve married couples, one widower, six young unmarried men, eight lads from ten to fifteen years of age, and nine children from two to nine years of age (six boys and three girls). Considering that there have always been a number of married couples at the settlement, the paucity of young children is very remarkable. I was informed that during seven years but three births had occurred, and that two of these were premature, there now remaining but one child born at Poonindie. Of course this unlooked for state of things tells most seriously against the prospective usefulness of the Institution as a place where a band of natives might, from earliest infancy, have been trained up and made instrumental in bringing others of their race under the influence of civilisation and Christianity. It also causes the Institution to be wholly dependent for the maintenance of its numbers on the voluntary additions it may receive from the rapidly decreasing native tribes.

The dwellings assigned to the natives mostly consist of whitewashed log huts, erected on the first establishment of the Institution by Archdeacon Hale. Some of these are very small and low, the ridge of the roof being but about six feet from the ground, and all are much dilapidated from the sheaoak logs rotting in the ground. The floors of these huts—bare earth—having worn lower than the surface of the exterior ground, their occupants must in winter often sit or sleep over a pool of water or mud. Under such circumstances colds, and with the natives their so often fatal consequences, cannot be wondered at, nor can the people be blamed for often making their fires and sleeping outside the huts.

An effort is now being made to remedy this state of things by building brick cottages, well thatched with long grass, the bricks being made on the ground. These cottages are put up in pairs, each having a sitting and a sleeping apartment, measuring together eighteen feet by nine feet, with a raised brick floor and fireplace. Only one pair is as yet occupied, and look very neat and comfortable. The natives living in the new cottages have not been known to sleep out since entering them.

Formerly, the people were allowed to take the rations to their huts and cook and eat them as and when they pleased, but a better arrangement now obtains. Near the centre of the village is a large stone kitchen, where, at the ringing of a bell, all assemble for meals, one or two being constantly employed in cooking for the establishment. A material saving is thereby effected, while comfort and order are decidedly promoted.

Other improvements are being steadily effected as time and means admit. About five hundred rods of fencing (three wires and a toprail) have just been completed, whereby a large additional portion of land along the banks of the Tod will be brought under cultivation. This season about twenty-four acres of wheat and six acres of hay have been sown and gathered by native labour. Judging from the appearance of the wheat crop, I should say that the land at Poonindie is well adapted for agriculture, notwithstanding a general impression to the contrary. A garden lately commenced seems also likely to flourish well.

There are three or four out-stations, in charge of the natives, with six thousand sheep and two hundred and fifty cattle and horses. Since about one thousand sheep, besides cattle, are yearly consumed by the establishment, the increase of stock will, of course, be proportionately less than on other runs.

There would seem to be less difficulty in getting the natives to work than I had imagined. The major part I found engaged in the wheat-field, one white man being engaged to manage the reaping, or rather mowing machine, and some twenty-five blacks making bands, tying up sheaves, &c. The machine being drawn by bullocks, a poor fellow who lately lost a hand by the bursting of a gun, unwilling to be idle, assisted as driver. While most were thus occupied, others were breaking-in colts, tending the milch cows, or the butcher's sheep—in short, all seemed actively and cheerfully employed. Illustrative of the proportion of work the natives can perform, I was told that at the last shearing, when four white men and four native shearers were engaged, the four natives sheared six hundred and seven sheep while the whites sheared eight hundred and seventy-two.

With a view to encourage habits of industry, each man is paid according to what he is able to do, from two shillings and sixpence to five shillings weekly, besides being provided with clothes, rations, and tobacco. In the matter of clothing considerable expense is incurred, the natives being in general careless and destructive of clothes. A laughable instance of this occurred while I was there. A native woman had obtained permission to visit Adelaide. As she was absent rather longer than her husband expected, he became uneasy; his companions jestingly told him they had no doubt his wife had run away and rejoined her tribe. This so excited him, that, in a fit of jealousy, he tore to pieces all the dresses she had left behind. On the wife's return, a few days after, the husband with a rueful countenance assured her he was " very sorry, indeed, that he did tear her puttas (frocks)."

Knowing that many deaths had lately occurred at Poonindie, and having been often told that the natives there were specially subject to pulmonary, syphilitic, and cutaneous diseases, I inquired par-

ticularly respecting their general health. With respect to deaths,
I found that there were in the quarter ending—

September 30th, 1856	...	...	...	5	deaths
December 31st, 1856	...	...	...	8	,,
March 31st, 1857 ...	...	...	...	0	,,
June 30th, 1857	...	...	...	5	,,
September 30th, 1857	...	...	...	2	,,
December 31st, 1857	...	...	...	1	,,

These include two infants prematurely born, and one accidental
death. The average of one death monthly, from disease, in a community of, say, sixty persons is undoubtedly high ; but since eleven
out of eighteen such deaths occurred in the last two quarters of
1856, we may, perhaps, be justified in assuming that some special
unhealthiness of the season had much to do with the matter. Among
those who then died, were some who were out of health on entering
the Institution, and did not recover. I found but two ill from
pulmonary affections, one of whom was not expected to continue
long.

On the subject of deaths among the natives generally, I was informed by Mr. Hawson, superintendent of stock at Poonindie, and
for many years resident in that neighbourhood, that there had been
a very great mortality among the blacks in the bush during the last
three or four years ; where formerly he had been wont to see one or
two hundred together, he now rarely found thirty or forty, while
their graves were to be met with in all directions, and were very
numerous near Poonindie. I found this statement fully borne out
on questioning some of the more intelligent natives in the Institution ; from this it seems clear that whatever may be the primary
causes of such mortality, it is not restricted to Poonindie.

As to the alleged prevalence of syphilitic affections, Mr. Hammond, whose medical knowledge enables him to give decided opinions
on these subjects, assured me he had never discovered the slightest
indication of syphilis, or the kindred diseases, among the natives.

On taking charge of Poonindie, Mr. Hammond found many cases
of cutaneous disease ; he also states that on natives from the bush
being admitted they are usually found suffering from such disease,
generally the itch, and much care and attention is required to
subdue it. The natives living in the bush frequently apply for
medicines for these complaints, and are of course cheerfully supplied.

I found but two cases of this kind at Poonindie, and those nearly cured.   Regular habits and cleanliness are fast improving the condition of the natives in these respects.

It does not appear that the natives who once settle at Poonindie ever desert it. Mr. Hammond assured me he had not known a single instance of desertion.   Some have been expelled for misconduct, and others, chiefly those from the Port Lincoln tribes, will occasionally absent themselves for a few weeks—as they allege—to visit their relatives, but invariably return. Those from Adelaide and the Murray are sometimes allowed to visit their friends also, but so far from taking advantage of these opportunities to desert, they always come back, often bringing others with them to join the Institution. There is one circumstance connected with this which a little surprised me—viz., if any of them become ill while absent they immediatley hasten back to Poonindie, the desire to die and be buried there being apparently very strong in all. I should have thought they would have preferred being buried with their tribes; but it is not so. Several instances have occurred of a return under such circumstances being almost immediately followed by death.

My attention was specially directed to the means adopted for religious and general instruction.   This is chiefly carried on in what I at first took for a church, but which was really a schoolroom—used also for public worship—having an upper story in use as a store-room.

At seven o'clock every morning, the schoolroom bell summonses the villagers to morning prayer. No sort of compulsion is used to secure attendance at this or other services, though care is taken to impress all with the importance of regular devotional habits. During my visit the general attendance at morning prayer was from twenty to twenty-five. From nine to twelve, and from two to four o'clock each day, the females and such of the men and boys as are not at work, meet in the school to receive instruction from Mrs. or Miss Hammond—Mr. Hammond assisting when his many other duties will allow ; and in the evening, from seven to nine o'clock, those who have been engaged during the day form a class under Mr. Hammond.   At nine o'clock the bell rings for evening prayer, when the attendance is rather greater than in the morning.

The general instruction seems confined to reading, writing, and a little arithmetic ; great care being taken to make them understand what is read. Being anxious to ascertaim for myself the capacity of the natives to receive instruction and their aptness in learning, I requested Mr. Hammond to allow me to conduct the classes in his absence. Several of the newly-admitted natives were scarcely able to read a word of English, while others could read and write readily. Being a stranger, I had to exercise no little ingenuity to overcome the reserve and timidity common to the native character. On failing— which I often did—to obtain an answer to a direct question, and subsequently approaching the point in a different manner, I found them not only able to answer, but some of the senior residents well informed. With blacks, as with whites, knowledge seems more readily acquired in youth than in more advanced life ; and some of the lads, considering their opportunities, are very intelligent, displaying an aptitude in learning quite equal to the average of English boys of the same age. The proficiency of some of the elder natives in music much surprised me. It is usual to commence morning and evening prayer with a hymn, and this is generally led by two or three flutes, very well played, the time being accurately kept. To test their knowledge, I asked them to play sundry pieces they had not before seen, some of them not very easy ; in every instance the music was correctly played, the only errors being the overlooking a dot after a note, or some such small matter, which on being pointed out was at once corrected.

As I proposed administering the Lord's Supper on the Sunday after my arrival, and was told that some of the natives would probably present themselves as communicants, I was careful to enquire very closely, and on several occasions, as to their knowledge and appreciation of the leading doctrines of Christianity. While catechising on these subjects, I was much pleased with the serious-ness of demeanour the seniors exhibited. When the conversation turned on the solemn truths declared concerning man's redemption, there was an earnestness in listening and an expressiveness in the hesitating whispered answers, which went far to assure me that some at least of these sable converts had not received the grace of God in vain. Among the eighteen men and women composing the Bible classes, I may safely affirm there are several possessing con-siderable knowledge of the principles of Christianity, and exhibiting many marks of true piety.

On the evening of Sunday, the 3rd of January, after returning from Port Lincoln, I took part in the public service at Poonindie. The schoolroom, lighted with four moderator lamps, and fitted with a neat reading desk, serves as a very commodious little chapel ; and when nearly filled with comfortably attired native worshippers—a few white faces interspersed heightening the effect—presented a novel and deeply interesting picture. Mr. Hammond having read prayers, I addressed them in the simplest language I could command from Isaiah, c. lv., v. 1—"Ho ! everyone that thirsteth, come ye to the waters." Greater decorum, or a more devout attention to, and participation in, the service of our Church than was displayed by these poor aborigines, it was never my lot to witness. Twelve native men and three women, with four whites, remained to partake of the sacrament, and few I think quitted the chapel on that occasion, without being deeply impressed with gratitude to God, whose will is that all might be brought to the knowledge of the truth. Widely different was the scene thus imperfectly described from one I witnessed on the afternoon of the same day. During the ride from Port Lincoln, I fell in with a policeman and two settlers, bringing in a couple of natives for sheep-stealing. These unfortunates were chained together by the neck, like a brace of hounds, and had been driven on foot one hundred miles in three days, a thing I should have deemed impossible. I need scarcely say they looked the personification of misery and exhaustion.

I have cited the observations I made at Poonindie thus at length, from a desire that others who entertain erroneous ideas—and I know that many do—as to the condition and working of that Institution may learn, as I did from personal investigation, that it is not in so low and hopeless a state as has been represented. Many and great difficulties have had to be encountered, and others will doubtless arise ; but still there is so much of success attained as may well cause these to be forgotten, and call forth much thankfulness.

The natives of this land can, to a great extent, be civilised ; they may be brought under the influence of the Gospel ; in saying which I merely speak that I do know, and testify to that I have seen.

Yours faithfully,
E. K. MILLER,
Incumbent of St. George's, Woodforde, and
St. Martin's, Campbelltown.

February 17th, 1858.

Not long after, Bishop Short paid one of his accustomed visits to Poonindie. The steamer by which he travelled reached Port Lincoln about 11 a.m. on Sunday; therefore, his Lordship, on landing, proceeded direct to the church, where service was going on. In due course the clergyman officiating, the Rev. O. Hammond, gave out his text— "What doest thou here, Elijah?" Very appropriate, as his Lordship's visit had not been expected.

In dealing with the natives, it was found expedient to pay them regular wages, which they were at liberty to spend, or place in the Savings Bank. Many of them became very efficient ploughmen, shearers, &c., though their want of stamina renders them unable to work so long or so hard as whites. During above forty years the Institution has not only held its ground, but advanced considerably. Its recent position is concisely stated in the Diocesan Year-Book for 1892, as follows:—

The Poonindie Institution is self-supporting, receiving no grant-in-aid from Government or any other source. Its revenue, therefore, wholly depends on what is raised on the land from year to year. The entire operations of the farm and station are carried on by native labour under an European superintendent, the only white labour at present employed being that of a baker, who bakes for the whole institution—between eighty and ninety inmates—and another white man who attends to the feeding of the horses, &c. Out of the revenue raised the Institution has to meet all demands. These include payment of superintendent, schoolmaster, visiting medical officer, stipend to the incumbent of St. Thomas, Port Lincoln, for periodical services, wages to every person employed, board of every resident, and in addition, clothing of orphan boys and girls and neglected children, and all expenditure incidental to the working of a farm and sheep-station. It will thus be seen that the demands on the income of the Institution are very heavy, and that a bad season or a fall in prices are matters of serious moment.

The dying out of the native races as European settlement advances is one of those problems that furnish much food for speculation. That so it is, is undeniable, and also that pulmonary disease is the chief cause. On this the official report of Dr. Lawson, of Port Lincoln, is conclusive. He says—

I have had some thirteen years' professional experience amongst the aborigines of this colony. Having acted as medical attendant to the [Poonindie] Native Training Institution since its commencement in 1850, and having visited and prescribed for, I believe, every case which has proved fatal, I can with confidence state that the principal cause of death was of a pulmonary character, in one form or other. . . . The disease is very common with natives [in the bush], only their deaths are not particularly taken notice of or inquired into. Let the cause be as it may, once they are attacked, there is little or no hope of their recovery. This has been proved at the Poonindie Institution, where they have had all the comfort and attention that could be given in such cases. They are by nature too weak, I may say, to stand any disease.

But the establishment of the Poonindie Institution was not the first effort that had been made to benefit the aborigines in the Port Lincoln district. In 1849 some Lutheran missionaries arrived from Germany to labour among the natives, and one of them, Mr. Schurmann, started a school for natives not far from Poonindie, being allowed a small salary by the Government as schoolmaster and interpreter. After awhile, however, this salary was discontinued, and the school closed, most of those under Mr. Schurmann's instruction—which had been successful in many instances—being admitted to Poonindie.

Members of several bodies of dissenters also united, under the title of the "Aborigines' Friends' Association," in the establishment of Institutions at Point Macleay and Point

Pearce, where a considerable number of natives have been educated and christianised. Indeed, I believe in nearly every instance where an attempt has been made to educate and train the *young* among the natives, a fair measure of success has resulted, though the older ones seem impervious to teaching, and too strongly attached to their native customs to adopt a settled mode of life. Not a few half-caste children have been educated in the different native institutions, and these often become domestic servants and labourers of a very useful type.

CHAPTER XXI.

MATRIMONIAL INCIDENTS.

THERE being no marriage law specially adapted to the requirements of the colony at its founding, an Act of the Legislative Council was passed in 1842 validating all marriages previously contracted in it, and enacting that marriages thereafter celebrated "according to the ecclesiastical laws of the United Church of England and Ireland—by clergymen of the Church of Scotland"—according to the "usages" of Quakers and Jews — or by duly authorised Registrars — should be deemed to have been legally contracted. This was followed by several amending Acts; so that now, all registered Officiating Ministers, and Registrars, are authorised to marry after issue of licence based on Declarations made by both parties to the marriage, at any hour, and in any place specified in the licence; the publication of banns being reduced to a purely ecclesiastical matter, and quite optional.

On Bishop Short's arrival, the question of the clergy celebrating marriage anywhere but in the churches naturally arose. Scattered as the people were, with churches few and far between, it was simply impossible to enforce the rules of the Church as to marrying in a church. Hence the Bishop issued a circular authorising the clergy to marry in private houses when the nearest church was above ten miles distant. This rule, however,

was soon found unworkable; it often happening that parties
at a less distance than ten miles were without means
of conveyance, and to insist on their walking several miles
to and from a church in summer heat or winter rain was
simply to drive them to the nearest dissenting minister
or district registrar, and so, from the ministrations they
would prefer. Then, too, the matter of competition could
not be wholly lost sight of. The Marriage Act fixed the
fees for a licence at three pounds, and for the marriage ten
shillings; but some dissenting ministers charged less, it
being often remarked that they would marry for what
they could get. With a view to encourage marrying in the
churches, the Bishop's table of fees fixed one pound as the
total cost of marriage by licence in a church after publication of banns. Notwithstanding this, the tendency is,
especially in country places, to marry in private houses;
and though the clergy may, and very often do, object, they
are quickly told that if they cannot oblige, someone else
can be found who will, and their declining is liable to be
followed by the parties withdrawing from the Church
altogether.

In the earlier years there were fewer females than males,
as was to be expected in a new settlement, and in the bush,
a woman was for some time a rarity. Consequently, when
an emigrant ship came in known to have a proportion of
single women on board, the bachelors were usually advised
to be on the *qui vive*, often getting recommendations to
rush the ship and secure first choice. By way of jest, a
party would sometimes scan a vessel with glasses as she
was working up to the anchorage, one exclaiming—" I
bespeak the blue dress," another—" I go for the pink
bonnet," another—" I'm for the plaid shawl," and so on.

Illustrative of this position of things the following incident occurred to myself. About a year after my arrival, a lady called with a letter of introduction from a cousin of mine, a surgeon in London, of whom she had been a patient. She had just landed—her luggage being still on board—and wished information as to lodgings, &c. She was invited to come to us for a few days till suitable accommodation should be found. The days, however, became weeks, and the weeks months; at length relief came; "suitable accommodation" turned up in an unexpected fashion.

One Sunday afternoon, as I was busily preparing my sermon for evening service, I was told a gentleman wished to see me. After some demur—anxious not to be interrupted—I consented to see him. Inquiring the object of his visit, and requesting him to be brief, the following conversation took place :—

"I believe, sir, you are guardian to a young lady ?"

"No, I am not; there is another Rev. Mr. Miller of the Scotch Church residing near, doubtless it is he you wish to see."

"Oh ! no, sir, I am certain this is the house."

"Well, there must be some mistake, for I am not guardian to any young lady."

"But is there not a young lady staying with you ?"

"There is a lady staying here, but I am not her guardian." The fact being, she was taking too much care of me, and could scarcely be called young, having passed the age spinsters are never supposed to attain.

"Well, sir, it is respecting that lady I wish to speak with you."

"Be as brief then as you can, for my time just now is of importance. May I ask your name ?"

"My name is ———, and I am in business in Hindley-street; being alone, I much feel the want of assistance, or a partner, in the business—and I thought—that—perhaps—if you have no objection——" He couldn't get any further.

" Oh! I see; being in business, and needing an assistant or partner—maybe a partner for life—and supposing me to be guardian to a certain lady, you come to ask my sanction for your paying your addresses to her; is that it ?"

" Yes, sir," with a sigh of relief.

Matters became interesting.

" Well, the lady referred to is not in at present, but as she is quite competent to judge and act for herself in so important a matter, I can only refer you to her. May I ask if you have met her often, and where ?"

" I have not had the pleasure of meeting her."

" But I suppose you have seen her somewhere ?"

" No, sir."

" You know her name, or have some other knowledge of her ?"

" No, sir, I can't say I have."

I looked at my visitor to see if he exhibited any signs of lunacy, or was jesting; but no; he was perfectly serious and self-possessed. The idea of a man coming to ask permission to pay his addresses to a person he had never seen, and whose name he did not know, was almost too much for my risibilities. Controlling myself, however, as well as I could, I told my visitor that his calling and its object should be mentioned to the lady concerned, and it was arranged that he should call the following evening to know if she would grant an interview. Bowing my visitor out with as much gravity as I could command, I related to my wife what had occurred, to her intense amusement, leaving her to communicate the matter to the party more immediately concerned as soon as she should appear. I returned to my sermon ; but have always been doubtful as to whether the fifthly, sixthly, and seventhly of that particular sermon bore the proper relation to the thirdly and fourthly.

On reaching home after service I found the lady had returned, and been informed of the important business on *tapis.* Immediately, questions came thick and fast. "What *did* I think ? Was not the idea *preposterous ?* Could not think of such a thing for a moment ; the man couldn't be in his right mind. What did he look like ? " &c., &c. As soon as the rapid catechising permitted, I replied that he looked like a respectable tradesman ; that I knew the shop he said was his ; that he acted and spoke in a very rational and business-like manner ; that he seemed to be about her own age ; that he evidently meant business ; that the proposal of a gentleman engaged in probably a good business should not be lightly regarded by any lady arrived at years of discretion ; that the matter was far too important to be hurriedly decided on ; that it should be seriously considered—slept upon—perhaps dream't about, &c. ; at all events no conclusion need be, or should be, arrived at till the morrow.

Next day, the burning question in the lady's mind of course was: Should she see the gentleman who was to call in the evening or not ? sometimes one decision sometimes another being arrived at ; meanwhile, however, my wife informed me the toilet received very considerable attention. True to time, evening brought the visitor—no doubt somewhat anxious as to what his reception, if any, might be, and as to what sort of a lady he was going to see for the first time with the view of making her his wife. I duly ushered him in, informing him that the lady had decided to grant an interview ; chatted a few moments, and called my wife, who entered accompanied by our lady friend. A brief introduction, a little chat on matters indifferent—I of course had another engagement, and my wife presently withdrew. What transpired on that, as on other similar occasions, was never precisely known; but this much *was* known, that six weeks afterwards the wedding took place.

It has been said that great events sometimes from little matters rise; it was so in this case. Just previously to my visitor's calling, two men had been occupied in painting and papering the house. In one room they had to move a great many trunks, &c., all bearing the name of our lady visitor. My wife happening to be near, one of the men said—" Who is this Miss ——— ? She has got a lot of luggage; does she want a husband?" My wife replied—" I don't know ; very likely she would not object to a suitable offer." One of these men was brother to the courageous bridegroom.

Shortly after the discovery of gold in Victoria, a number of diggers returned to Adelaide with more money than they had ever dreamed of possessing, which many proceeded to waste in every imaginable way. A man would take a fancy to a girl, show her a lot of money, ask her if she would marry him, and if consenting, take her forthwith to a draper's and have her dressed out in the most extravagant fashion ; get married, hire some vehicles, and a band, invite a batch of boon companions, have a procession through the streets, with as much noise and display as they could make, winding up with a public-house jollification. This sort of thing, in varying degree, continually took place. One of the principal drapers told me that a man ordered a bonnet for his wife that should cost ten pounds; but that after putting on the most expensive trimming, they only brought the cost up to five pounds. On his being informed of this, he threw the bonnet on the floor, stamped it to pieces, and then ordered another like it, so as to make up the ten pounds. Another would order that his wife's dress should not cost less than fifty pounds; " consequently," said he, " we are not doing business in the ordinary sense, we are coining money."

At that time, the first Marriage Act, passed in 1842, was in operation, requiring marriages, unless in the case of Jews and Quakers, to be celebrated by the clergymen of the Churches of England or Scotland, and authorising the issue of licences "according to the ecclesiastical laws of the United Church of England and Ireland," or by the Registrars of districts. Consequently, the Rev. James Farrell, as Bishop's surrogate, was the only clergyman in Adelaide authorised to issue marriage licences, making a rich harvest of fees during this era of reckless marriages. This had something to do with the marriage laws being altered by the Amending Act of 1852 so as to admit of other ministers having the like privilege. Dean Farrell told me of sundry instances in which a man having obtained a marriage licence one day would come the next to say he had changed his mind, and inquire whether, as he was not going to marry, the licence fee would be returned. Often, shortly after marriage, a man would disappear, going again to the diggings, or elsewhere, when his suddenly acquired wealth had become exhausted, and be no more heard of.

It was pleasant in the early days to celebrate marriage in the country, when a genuine rustic party assembled, many coming from a distance on horseback. Sometimes six or eight couple would ride up to the church, forming quite a cavalcade. At other times, when very far from a church, the marriage would be celebrated in a hut, which being too small for the wedding "breakfast," it would be spread out under the shade of the trees. On one such occasion the rubric which prescribes that the ring should be placed on "the fourth finger of the woman's left hand" had to be departed from, as the fourth and another finger had been lost.

The oddest difficulties were sometimes experienced in connection with matters matrimonial. An individual, whom I knew to be a grandfather, one morning called at the Parsonage to inquire whether I could marry him that day. Of course I could, on the necessary declarations being made and licence issued. The forms were accordingly filled up, but he absolutely refused to go to the church, above a mile away, insisting on being married at the Parsonage. At length consenting, I inquired when he would bring the lady. "Oh!" said he, "she is in the trap at the gate." Horrified at the idea of the lady having been sitting in the sun for an hour or more, I requested him to at once bring her in. She proved to be a young person I knew slightly, but *quite alone.* "Have you brought no friends or witnesses?" said I. "No," he replied, "we just came by ourselves; but I suppose you have some folks here who can act as witnesses." My wife and son were brought in. All went well till the ring was wanted, but he had not provided one. My wife slipped hers off, and lent it for the occasion, so the marriage was celebrated and documents duly signed.

I afterwards learned that the gentleman had on sundry occasions rallied the young woman about becoming his wife; but from disparity of age, &c., she thought he was only joking. The evening previous he had seen her, and demanded an answer. Finding him serious, she said she would take a week to consider. Next morning, however, early, while she was busy, he again called, requiring an immediate answer, saying—" Now or never; now or never." Work was therefore suspended, and her aunt with whom she was living consulted, with the result that " Now " was thought better than " Never." Accordingly she was taken to an adjacent store, fitted out, handed into a vehicle, and driven to the Parsonage. On another occasion also, my wife's ring was brought into requisition, and then too in the case of a grandfather re-marrying.

The oldest couple I had the privilege of uniting in holy wedlock was a gentleman within a month or two of eighty to a lady about sixty-four. This match was somewhat oddly made up. Having lost two wives, and needing some one to take charge of himself and house, the old gentleman had proposed to more than one eligible widow, but without success. Lamenting his hard fate to a certain storekeeper, the latter said he thought he knew one or two ladies who would be glad of a home, and who he thought would be suitable. The question of introduction, &c., being discussed, it was arranged that the storekeeper should manage to have the ladies he thought eligible at his store on a certain date, and the widower was to drive over to view. The idea was carried out, two or three dames were ready for inspection on the day named, but the gentleman failed to arrive. Being of a jovial temperament, he had managed to capsize his gig on the way, and his appearance being somewhat marred, he resolved to defer the important interview till he should become more presentable. Another appointment was made, the ladies were on view, one was selected, and having consented, banns were published, and the wedding took place.

The greatest difficulty I ever experienced in matrimonial matters occurred when marrying a man who in colonial parlance had a "shingle loose" to a little gipsy-looking body who had previously got rid of two husbands, I cannot say *buried*, because she was not at all sure the first husband was dead when she married the second, who certainly did die. On the wedding party arriving at the church, I noticed the bride leaning on the arm of an elderly individual not noted for sobriety, while the bridegroom escorted the bridesmaid, a widow of some fifty summers; these were followed by a score or more of on-lookers, not of the party, but who had evidently come with the idea of being in some way amused.

Having duly placed the bridal party, I proceeded with the service till the question came—"Wilt thou have this woman to be thy wedded wife?" when, without allowing me to go further, the bridegroom exclaimed, with a rubicund and smiling face—"I manes to." "You must not interrupt me," said I, "but when I have read the whole of the question, reply *I will*." "All right, sir!" I recommenced the question—and having allowed me to read it through, he remained silent. "You must reply *I will*," said I. "Well, I will," he answered. The individual who led in the bride duly gave her to be married. Then I told the bridegroom—"Take the lady's hand in yours, and repeat after me—"I, Elijah ————" "That's my name, sir," said he. "I know it is your name, but you must repeat it and what else I may read. Now—I, Elijah ————" "That's me," he exclaimed. "I know it is you, but I want you to say your own name and the rest just as I say it." Thinking to stop his telling me it was his name, I read the two names together somewhat quickly. "I, Elijah ———, take thee, M. A.————, to be my wedded wife." A pause. I

repeated the formula. At length he burst out with—" I'll
take this good old widder." This was altogether too much
for the on-lookers, most of whom had been on the titter, and
some now laughed outright. Looking gravely down the
church, I said I could not permit a service to be interrupted, and must request any who could not be quiet
to leave, when several rushed out holding their sides. I
was about to make another effort, when the bridesmaid
struck in, admonishing the bridegroom in tones at once
emphatic and shrill—"You should say what Mr. Miller tells
you; why can't you say your name, and all the rest?"
" Pray don't interrupt, Mrs. ————," said I, "it is a new
situation for Mr. ————. No doubt he will be able to
understand me presently." Again I commenced the
formidable question, and managed to get him to say his
own name and what followed till it came to "love and
cherish till death do us part, according to God's holy
ordinance," when he came to a full stop. "You must say
these words after me." "Please, sir, I can't think on
'em." "If you can't repeat these words after me I can't
marry you." "Oh, well, come on, sir, I'll try again." By
dint of patience, and giving him two words at a time the
ceremony was at last got through, to my no small relief, for
maintaining a calm countenance was by no means easy,
especially with his self-satisfied grin to encounter. As for
the bride, there was no difficulty with her.

Some hours after, while lunching with another of my
parishioners, his children came running in, exclaiming—
" Here comes the wedding party with a flag flying!" After
the marriage, they had driven to a public-house, where the
bridegroom had been employed as ostler, and been profusely
treated. After making them both tipsy, their "friends"
got them again into the cart, tied a long stick with a red

handkerchief to the back of the cart and started them off.
As they passed where I was, the bridegroom, being with the
bride at the back, was so vigorously engaged in kissing
her, that he lost his balance, falling backwards over the
tail-board into the road. The bride's "father," who was
driving as well as he could, was with difficulty made
to understand that the bridegroom was overboard, and that
he must pull up, which at last he did.

Some six weeks afterwards, on a Sunday afternoon, after
service, as I was taking refreshment at "mine inn" before
starting for my next service ten miles off, I was told
Mr. Elijah —————— wished to see me. He was shown in.
"Well, Elijah, what is it?" "Did you see my missus
to-day, sir?" "No, Elijah, I did not; but she might have
been in the church without my noticing her; why?" "She
said she was a-coming to see you to-day, sir!"   "Well,
perhaps she did see me, but I did not see her. If she wishes
to see me you had better fetch her at once, for I cannot
stay long." He sat twisting his hat about nervously without offering to move. "What does she want to see me for,
is it anything particular?" "Yes, it is a bit partickler."
"If she is not here very quickly, I must leave the matter
till Thursday, when I shall be here again." As he made
no movement, and was evidently anxious about something,
I asked—"Do you know what it is she wants to see me
for? Can you not tell me?" "Well, sir, she wants to ask
you summut." "Very good; what is it, what is it like? If
I can give you any information I will gladly do so." "Well,
sir, she wanted to ask you whether—if——" Here he
stopped. "She wants to ask me if—what?" She wants
to know," he stammered out, "as how if you couldn't unmarry us?" "What's that, Elijah?" hardly believing my
ears. "She wants to know if you would please unmarry

us?" "I suppose it is really *you*, who wants to know that? Why, man-alive! it's not six weeks since I married you, and trouble enough I had to do it; what's the matter, that you so soon want to get unmarried?" "I didn't think she was such a queer sort of a woman, sir." "You knew her long before marrying; but what have you been quarrelling about?" "She says I spend all my money at the public-house, and I don't." "Well, I would advise you to keep away from the public-house, and whatever you have, have it at home, and share it with your wife, and talk to her like you used to do before marriage, and no doubt all will come right again." "I wish you would come and talk to her a bit, sir." I was obliged to excuse myself from this, telling him I could only unmarry him in the churchyard, which I a few years after had to do.

A mother once applied to me for advice concerning the illegal marriage of her daughter, aged sixteen. The young lady was accustomed to ride some ten miles for music lessons. On the last occasion of her taking the journey, a youth of some eighteen summers became her escort. Whether the usual music lesson was taken did not transpire. The two, however, called on a dissenting minister, with the result that they became united in the holy bonds of matrimony. The girl's mother, on learning what had occurred, was naturally indignant, and anxious to punish someone. Of course, examination of the declarations was the first thing to be done, and I took the mother to the Registry Office in order thereto. We found, as I expected, that false declarations had been made by both, rendering them liable to imprisonment; the youth had stated himself as twenty-one years of age, and the girl as having no one in the colony competent to give consent — the consent of parent or

guardian being needful in the case of all minors   Then
the question arose as to the minister who officiated.   According to the Marriage Act, any one marrying a minor
without consent of parent or guardian is liable to a fine of
from fifty to five hundred pounds; and in this case the
manifest youth of the parties ought to have prompted inquiry before acting.   It turned out, however, that the
officiating minister was but nineteen years of age!   Any
penalty, therefore, must have fallen practically on his
father, who was a shoemaker, and quite unable to pay, and
imprisoning the youthful trio was not to be thought of.   I
therefore persuaded the girl's mother not to prosecute, and
she let the matter drop.   It may be asked: How came such
a youth to be in a position to celebrate marriage?   Clause
IX. of the Marriage Act says that a minister desiring to be
enrolled as authorised to marry, must forward an application to that effect to the Government, " with the testimony
of some person already on the roll . . . that he
is a minister and statedly acting as such   . or, a
certificate from twenty householders . . . that he
is officiating as minister of the congregation of which
they are members."   By which of these processes this
youthful minister's name got placed on the roll, I did
not take the trouble to ascertain.   Of course the framers
of the Act never contemplated the appointment of a minor
as officiating minister, and the incident only shows how
difficult it is to frame Acts of Parliament so as to preclude
all abuse.

CHAPTER XXII.

IN RETIREMENT.

FTER passing through the troublesome and some-what painful process of breaking up the home of so many years, and taking leave of many friends, my wife and I, not having previously been able to quit home for long, spent a few months in travelling, partly in the North, among my old parishioners, and partly in Victoria, where our second son was in business. When tired of travelling, we settled down near the sea, at Brighton, thinking to spend the remainder of our days in that quiet and pleasant locality. Having expressed a wish, when superannuated, not to be altogether idle, the Bishop granted me a general licence, whereby I was enabled to assist in church services as occasion might require, often helping Canon French—then in charge of the district, in connection with Glenelg — by conducting services, funerals, &c., at Brighton. Occasionally, also, I took services at other churches, during the absence of their ministers; but when invited to act where a highly ritualistic style of service had been introduced, I felt bound to decline.

About a year after my settling at Brighton, Canon French was appointed Archdeacon of Petersburg and the North, and left for his new sphere. Not long after, circumstances arose that caused me to decide on leaving Brighton also, and I had regretfully to give the necessary

three months' notice to quit the house I occupied. When
on the eve of moving, a serious ailment befel my wife.
Fortunately I was able to obtain the house adjoining that
of my daughter, Mrs. A. E Lucy, whose aid through the
ensuing illness was most valuable. From the first it was
seen that the attack would prove fatal; and on the 29th
of October last, after several months of suffering, death
terminated a life of incessant toil and endeavour to do
good.

On the family gathering being completed, two days previously, by the arrival of our second son from Melbourne,
I administered holy communion to all assembled, a most
solemn occasion, each knowing it would be the last with
the departing loved one. Shortly after she took an
affectionate leave of each one separately, and then lay
quietly down to die, saying—" I am going home." The
next day, Sunday, was the forty-seventh anniversary of
our marriage, and she seemed to be dying throughout
it, but lingered till the following day, when, in full
possession of her faculties, she, who had so long been my
faithful partner, breathed her last. All the consolation,
therefore, that a truly happy death-bed could afford we
were privileged with; but it was a great wrench.

My wife's decease, and my children being above age,
rendered it no longer necessary for me to continue sub-
scribing to the Clergy Widow and Orphan Fund, to which
I had belonged from its establishment. The regulations
of that Fund provide that—" If a clergyman remove
from the diocese, or cease to hold the Bishop's licence, he
shall cease to be a member of the Fund, but shall be
entitled to receive back one-half of the amount he has
subscribed." I therefore gave notice of withdrawal, and

applied for half the amount of premiums paid. This was objected to, on the ground that I held a general licence from the Bishop. Consequently I resigned that licence. Then I was told my resignation could not be considered complete till I also withdrew my name from the Government roll of ministers authorised to celebrate marriage. This requirement I also complied with, and then received the proportion of subscriptions applied for. It has thus, strangely enough, been brought about that, after having uninterruptedly held the Bishop's licence for well nigh forty-seven years, and labouring to establish a branch of the Church in the colony, I find myself no longer authorised to exercise the office of a minister therein, and what little duty I might be able to do, I am no longer authorised to do.

CHAPTER XXIII.

CONCLUSION.

IN concluding these Reminiscences, it will not be out of
place to inquire what has been the issue, so far, of
the endeavour to establish a branch of the Church of
England in this colony. The best, if not the only, way to
approximately ascertain this, I conceive, will be, to see what
proportion the professing members of the Church of
England bear, and have borne, to the general population,
and to the members of other denominations. This we find
officially stated in the Government Census Returns. The
earliest I have been able to find are for 1860, and the latest
for 1891, and they show as follow :—

	1860	1876	1881	1891		
Church of England	36·94	26·30	27·09	27·86	decrease	9·08
Roman Catholics	13·21	15·32	15·23	14·72	increase	1·51
Wesleyans	12·14	16·90	15·04	15·34	,,	3·20
Bible Christians	3·55	4·41	3·70	4·92	,,	1·37
Primitive Methodists	3·12	4·55	3·71	3·64	,,	·52
Presbyterians	4·08	6·87	6·40	5·68	,,	1·60
Baptists	2·90	4·90	4·09	5·50	,,	2·60
Lutherans	9·52	8·03	7·01	7·28	decrease	2·24
Congregationalists	5·31	4·09	3·54	3·71	,,	1·60
Christian Brethren	1·40	·65	·65	·14	,,	1·26
Unitarians	·41	·31	·27	·21	,,	·20

These figures furnish food for serious thought. The first
thing to be noted in them is, that of the various religious

bodies, the Church of England shows by far the greatest retrogression, while most of the others have advanced. This is humiliating, but so it is. Between 1860 and 1876, it would seem that no less than 10·64 per cent. of her members fell away. There has been a slight recovery since, but still the diminution of membership between 1860 and 1891 shows 9·08 per cent. In respect to this, the question naturally arises, was there any special cause for this so great, and seemingly somewhat sudden, recession ? I think there was.

The excitement caused by the action of the Australasian Bishops at their meeting in Sydney, as recorded in Chapter XIII. had scarcely died away, when among the clergy arriving were some who began to introduce alterations in the services, bowing towards the communion table every time they passed it, celebrating the eucharist with back to the people, advocating auricular confession, &c. " Needless pursuance " of such things naturally begat what doubtless was in many cases " exaggerated suspicion." A great amount of irritation became engendered, while disputations in Synod and otherwise continually occurred. At length complaints were formulated, and laid before the Bishop, who was thereby compelled to take action, issuing, in 1869, sundry formal decisions and directions, from which I have quoted in Chap. XIX., in order "to appease the diversity of practice which had caused doubts and variance." But, as was to be expected, these were inadequate to fully "appease" the minds of those who had adopted extreme views on either side; and as the controversy continued year after year, many who had taken a lead in Church affairs became alienated—being, as some expressed themselves to me, "driven from the Church by ritualism." Then, too, it is not to be wondered at that those inimical to the Church seized the opportunity to inveigh against her, representing her as the "hotbed of Popery," &c.—acting on the old adage, "throw plenty of mud, some is sure to stick." These things, I am fully convinced, caused, more than anything else, the remarkable recession recorded. Bishop Short in his Pastoral of 1869 spoke of "certain teachings concerning the Sacrament of the Lord's Supper" being strongly objected to, and of such objections as "bearing witness to the intense dislike of Papal domination and Roman Catholic doctrine, which, after three centuries, still animates the great body of Protestants." There was an increase of ·77 from 1881 to 1891, due to the remarkable energy of Bishop Kennion, with the addition of over twenty clergy and about fifty churches. Still, as the preceding figures show, there has been a net decrease of 9·08 out of 36·94, or say twenty-five per cent., during thirty years What has become of these? The increases of other religious bodies will not account for them; probably but a very small minority have joined those bodies. I quite believe ritualism has been mainly instrumental in driving one-fourth of the members of the Church from attending her services, most of whom it is to be feared attend no other services. As a rule, those who take offence make no complaint—but simply stay away.

A brother clergyman, in Victoria, has kindly furnished me with the following statistics, showing the position of the Church of England in that colony :—

In 1871, the proportion of church members to population was
36·01 ; in 1881, 36·74 ; in 1891, 37·33.

During twenty years, from 1871 to 1891, the alterations in proportion to population of the different religious bodies were as
follows :--

Church of England, increase	1·32		Roman Catholics, decrease		1·56
Methodists	,,	·98	Presbyterians	,,	·83
Baptists	,,	·21	Congregationalists	,,	·56
Other Protestants	,,	1·48			

The Church of England is the most progressive, Evangelicalism,
and not ritualism, being the usual tendency, almost throughout
the colony.

This shows a gradual but steady increase of membership, by adherence to the true principles and ordinary
services of the Church.

The principal advance here has been made by the Methodist bodies, the Wesleyans, Bible Christians, and Primitives
together aggregating 23·90 per cent. of the population, a
gross increase of 5·09. In event of these bodies becoming
amalgamated, as is likely to be the case ere long, they will
in all probability equal or exceed the Church in another
decade, and should they decide on adopting the Church
Liturgy, or part of it, as is the case in some places in
England, they will probably attract many more members,
and constitute the leading Church of South Australia.

Another matter that these figures show has been to me
quite a surprise, and that is, the smallness of the Congregational element in proportion to population, the percentage
for 1891 being stated at but 3·71. It seems almost incredible
that so comparatively small a body should have been able
by clamour and persistence not only to take the lead in
abolishing State aid to religion, but also in excluding
Scripture teaching from the public schools. Others of course

assisted in accomplishing these things, but the Congregationalists led the van, and the issue is highly creditable to
their tact and perseverance, however discreditable to a
community of Christians. Were it possible for the Church
of England, the Roman Catholics, Methodists, Presbyterians, and Lutherans—aggregating 79·44 per cent. of our
population—to combine, a different condition of things,
educationally, would be quickly brought about. As it is,
these large bodies have all beenover-ridden by the efforts,
mainly, of one of the smallest sects.

That the Church of England will continue to hold an
important position in the colony there cannot be the
slightest doubt; but that the premier position she has
hitherto held will be maintained, is highly problematical.

I would earnestly commend the foregoing facts and
figures to the serious consideration of all Churchmen, and
especially my brethren of the clergy, for on the course they
may see fit to pursue in the near future, will very largely
depend the well-being and advancement of the Church of
England in South Australia.

APPENDIX A.

AMOUNTS RAISED IN THE DISTRICTS OF MAGILL AND CAMPBELLTOWN FOR CHURCH PURPOSES FROM 1851 TO 1861.

—	Income from all sources including fees.		Total Income.	Maintenance and additions.		Total for General Purposes.	Gross Receipts.	Mems.
	St.George's	St.Martin's		St.George's	St.Martin's			
	£ s. d.	£ s. d.	£ s. d.	£ s. d.	£ s. d.	£ s. d	£ s. d.	
Jan.1, 1851, to Easter 1852	63 13 4	—	63 13 4	9 3 11	—	9 3 11	72 17 3	
,, 1853	85 19 6	—	85 19 6	31 17 5	—	31 17 5	117 16 11	Magill Churchyard laid out and planted.
,, 1854	105 4 0	—	105 4 0	50 16 1	—	50 16 1	156 0 1	Harmonium procured. Service at Paradise begun.
,, 1855	127 6 1	—	127 6 1	86 17 10	—	86 17 10	214 3 11	Five - acre glebe secured, Magill.
,, 1856	109 3 0	—	109 3 0	107 11 8	40 10 0	148 1 8	257 4 8	Two acres secured at Campbelltown.
,, 1857	137 15 0	—	137 15 0	147 6 2	9 8 0	156 14 2	294 9 2	Forty pounds endowment to Magill obtained.
,, 1858	173 7 6	11 17 6	185 5 0	120 2 2	83 13 9	203 15 11	389 0 11	Schoolroom erected, Campbelton.
,, 1859	172 6 8	17 19 0	190 5 8	61 6 10	22 9 6	83 16 4	274 2 0	Magill parsonage fund commenced.
,, 1860	191 5 6	18 17 0	210 2 6	370 16 7	104 13 6	475 10 1	685 12 7	Parsonage erected.
,, 1861	192 18 6	18 11 0	211 9 6	89 16 9	324 6 10	414 3 7	625 13 1	St. Martin's Church erected. Cottage service at Payneham begun.
	£1,358 19 1	£67 4 6*	£1,426 3 7	£1,075 15 5	£585 1 7	£1,660 17 0	£3,087 0 7	

* NOTE.—On leaving the district I was presented with an address and a purse of £25 by Mr. H. E. Downer on behalf of the congregation.

INCOME FROM ALL SOURCES, INCLUDI

Year.	Willunga.			Noarlunga.			Aldinga.		
To Easter,	£	s.	d.	£	s.	d.	£	s.	d.
1863-4 ...	178	6	4	90	14	0	—		
1864-5 ...	178	4	4	82	3	10	—		
1865-6 ...	117	4	4	79	12	6	—		
1866-7 ...	165	4	0	72	18	0	—		
1867-8 ...	149	8	0	79	15	0	45	17	1
1868-9 ...	118	17	9	61	17	6	62	0	1
1869-70 ...	102	17	6	62	17	6	50	19	1
1870-71 ..	93	1	0	54	11	6	42	4	0
1871-2 ...	88	3	0	66	13	6	68	7	10
1872-3 ...	83	15	0	71	0	0	63	4	11
1873-4 ...	65	18	0	61	8	0	50	16	11
1874-5 ...	61	10	6	65	6	0	40	0	9
1875-6 ...	79	15	0	64	0	0	41	19	6
1876-7 ...	98	15	0	52	12	0	32	6	0
1877-8 ...	101	5	0	64	2	6	45	17	6
1878-9 ...	92	2	6	52	15	0	37	6	3
1879-80 ...	94	2	0	54	2	6	47	8	0
1880-81 ...	121	4	6	40	5	0	31	6	6
1881-2 ...	82	0	0	54	16	8	33	2	6
1882-3 ..	82	0	0	40	14	6	60	1	9
1883-4 ...	85	1	0	53	18	6	72	18	9
1884-5 ...	81	13	0	51	1	0	40	17	10
1885-6 ...	93	0	3	47	0	0	40	13	9
1886-7 ...	92	19	6	46	4	0	53	4	1
1887-8 ...	91	3	0	44	3	0	47	16	11
1888-9 ...	86	12	10	51	10	0	39	14	6
1889-90 ...	88	19	6	48	1	6	42	14	0
1890-91 ...	91	15	11	44	12	4	60	1	7
1891 to Dec. 31	75	11	8	37	6	0	33	16	9
£	2,940	11	3	1,715	4	5	1,211	17	7

APPENDIX B.

AMOUNTS RAISED FOR CHURCH PURPOSES IN THE DISTRICTS OF WILLUNGA, NOARLUNGA, ALDINGA, AND MYPONGA FROM JANUARY 1, 1851, TO JANUARY 1, 1892.

Year.	Income from all Sources, including Fees.					Maintenance and Additions.					Grand Receipts.	Remarks.
	Willunga.	Noarlunga.	Aldinga.	Myponga.	Totals.	Willunga.	Noarlunga.	Aldinga.	Myponga.	Totals.		
To Easter,	[illegible]	[illegible]	[illegible]	[illegible]	[illegible]	[illegible]	[illegible]	[illegible]	[illegible]	[illegible]	[illegible]	Parsonage largely repaired and plate re-[illegible].
[illegible]	[illegible]	[illegible]	[illegible]		[illegible]	[illegible]	[illegible]			[illegible]	[illegible]	Three acres added to glebe to obtain road.
[illegible]	[illegible]	[illegible]	[illegible]		[illegible]	[illegible]	[illegible]			[illegible]	[illegible]	Willunga Church completed, and [illegible] harmonium purchased.
[illegible]	[illegible]	[illegible]	[illegible]		[illegible]	[illegible]	[illegible]			[illegible]	[illegible]	Aldinga Church built.
[illegible]	[illegible]	[illegible]	[illegible]		[illegible]	[illegible]	[illegible]	[illegible]		[illegible]	[illegible]	Noarlunga Church completed with chancel and vestry.
[illegible]	[illegible]	[illegible]	[illegible]		[illegible]	[illegible]	[illegible]			[illegible]	[illegible]	Harvest commenced at Myponga and Sellick's Meadows.
[illegible]	[illegible]	[illegible]	[illegible]	[illegible]	[illegible]	[illegible]	[illegible]		[illegible]	[illegible]	[illegible]	Acre site for Myponga Church secured.
[illegible]	[illegible]	[illegible]	[illegible]	[illegible]	[illegible]	[illegible]	[illegible]		[illegible]	[illegible]	[illegible]	Teacher's residence built, Myponga.
[illegible]	[illegible]	[illegible]	[illegible]	[illegible]	[illegible]	[illegible]	[illegible]		[illegible]	[illegible]	[illegible]	
[illegible]	[illegible]	[illegible]	[illegible]	[illegible]	[illegible]	[illegible]	[illegible]		[illegible]	[illegible]	[illegible]	Myponga Church built.
[illegible]	[illegible]	[illegible]	[illegible]	[illegible]	[illegible]	[illegible]	[illegible]		[illegible]	[illegible]	[illegible]	Coloured organ bought for Aldinga.
[illegible]	[illegible]	[illegible]	[illegible]	[illegible]	[illegible]	[illegible]	[illegible]		[illegible]	[illegible]	[illegible]	First bazaar for Willunga new Church.
[illegible]	[illegible]	[illegible]	[illegible]	[illegible]	[illegible]	[illegible]	[illegible]	[illegible]	[illegible]	[illegible]	[illegible]	Half-acre site for Willunga Church secured.
[illegible]	[illegible]	[illegible]	[illegible]	[illegible]	[illegible]	[illegible]	[illegible]	[illegible]	[illegible]	[illegible]	[illegible]	Aldinga Church endowment commenced.
[illegible]	[illegible]	[illegible]	[illegible]	[illegible]	[illegible]	[illegible]	[illegible]	[illegible]	[illegible]	[illegible]	[illegible]	Noarlunga Church renovated.
[illegible]	[illegible]	[illegible]	[illegible]	[illegible]	[illegible]	[illegible]	[illegible]	[illegible]	[illegible]	[illegible]	[illegible]	New Church built at Willunga. Parsonage re-roofed with slate.
[illegible]	[illegible]	[illegible]	[illegible]	[illegible]	[illegible]	[illegible]	[illegible]	[illegible]	[illegible]	[illegible]	[illegible]	Myponga resigned.
1891 to Dec. 31	[illegible]	[illegible]	[illegible]	[illegible]	[illegible]	[illegible]	[illegible]	[illegible]	[illegible]	[illegible]	[illegible]	Maintenance and Additions accounts omitted being copied. Curacy resigned.
	£ [illegible]	1,715 [illegible]	[illegible]	76 [illegible]	[illegible]	[illegible]	75 [illegible]	[illegible]	[illegible]	[illegible]	[illegible]	

Memo.—During [those years] I was establishing Myponga Church I was allowed £15 per annum for forage from Synodal funds.

ERRATA.

Page 40, line 15, for " 1851 " read " 1849."

Page 246, end of line 9, for " in " read " on."

Page 256, line 6, for " Poetry " read " Polity."

Page 256, at beginning of line 24 insert " which translate."

Page 269, line 12, for " work " read " worship."